Mollie, without you this book never would have got off the ground.
Thank you for always being the light when I find myself in darkness,
you have helped me to believe in myself.
Love you lots, enjoy your jaunt around the world.

BLACK SMOKE RISING

Book One
of The
Meohithra Chronicles

CAROLINE CUELL

For trigger warnings and a playlist head to carolinecuell.com

First published in the UK in 2025.

Copyright © Caroline Cuell, 2025.

The moral right of the author has been asserted.

No part of this publication may be reproduced, distributed, or transmitted in any form or by any means, including photocopying, recording, or other electronic or mechanical methods, without the prior written permission of the publisher, except in the use of brief quotations for book reviews. For permission requests, contact Caroline Cuell at carolinecuell.com

The stories, all names, characters, and incidents portrayed in this space are fictitious. No identification with actual persons (living or deceased), places, buildings, and products is intended or should be inferred.

Print ISBN: 978-1-0684272-0-6

Printed in the UK Kindle Direct Publishing

'Bad men need nothing more to compass their ends,
than that good men should look on and do nothing.'
– JOHN STUART MILL

Chapter One

Getting Away With Murder

The midday sun spilled across the courtyard, reflecting in everything with its golden rays. Bastian found his fingers restless; they took it in turns to press their nails into the pad of his thumb. A familiar feeling of dread washed over him, nausea building in the pit of his stomach as he listened to the head of the royal guard, Gerritsen, read out the crimes of the man stood before them. Two more members of his father's guard held the prisoner in chains.

The man's hair was long and starting to mat; his clothes were dirty, and there was grime marring his otherwise-unblemished skin. Bastian thought he could not have been too much older than himself. What crime could he have committed that was so heinous as to be brought before the king? Most of the charges against him were small: a few thefts, a public disturbance in the local tavern; it only added to Bastian's confusion as to why they were there. As he looked across the dais that had been erected in the courtyard, past his brother, Bastian's eyes were fixed upon his father, the king, who sat upon his golden throne. His father's thoughts, as always, remained impossible to fathom. Thin lips pressed into a grim line; icy eyes glared with no sign of empathy; he sat still, as if carved from stone. Golden crown clinging to his brow, the king wore black trousers with a golden tunic and a red cloak that clung tightly around his shoulders. The king's long platinum-blond hair, slowly, turning white with age, moved gently in the breeze. It was the only true indicator that he was a living, breathing person and not a statue.

"…and the final charge brought against Robert Houston is that of treason."

Bastian's gaze snapped back to the man brought before him as Gerritsen's monotonous voice continued booming for the court and crowd alike to hear.

"You are accused of taking a fae woman into your bed."

Hushed whispers broke out in the court, unlike the crowd that had gathered at the back, who now stood silently as the king's voice clapped like thunder across the scene.

"Silence."

Waiting for the king's subtle nod, Gerritsen resumed.

"Robert Houston, how do you plead?"

Bastian watched as Robert looked wildly along the line of people in front of him. It made him sick to his stomach to see the man look so afraid, his voice high pitched as he made his plea.

"I started a fight when I was in a drunken state and I stole the meat from the market to feed my family. But I ain't bedded no fae. I wouldn't sully our kind like that. I believe the same as the king, honest. I'd never risk my family line being ruined by dirty blood. Please sire, I have a wife and children, they'll starve if I'm not there to provide for them."

The king didn't miss a beat.

"Guilty."

Bastian had to look away as the man was dragged away, proclaiming his innocence with every ounce of air in his lungs. He couldn't bear it, any of it. The screams, the pained noises Robert made as he fell to his knees. Nausea coiled in the pit of his stomach as the guards continued to drag the prisoner by his restraints through the sandy gravel as if he was a wild animal. Looking to Nico, Bastian hoped to find some kind of reassurance from his brother, but he saw that, after one deep breath, Nico's eyes only closed for a moment. When they opened again, his gaze was steely, never leaving the scene that played out in front of them, refusing to acknowledge that Bastian had even looked in his direction. He should be used to it by now, this was how it had always been. The heir and the spare, especially after his mother's death. Bastian was sure the king had never truly recovered from it, and in his opinion, it was what had started his gradual descent into madness, although Nico would've begged to differ. These days his father's grief had been overridden by a lust for power and vengeance. He pitied anyone who dared openly question him. His brother brought Bastian some comfort, he was sympathetic to his weakness in private, but in public Nico's dutiful persona never wavered.

The guards dragged Robert up onto the small wooden platform that had been erected in the square not two days ago. Clothing now torn, arms and legs bleeding from where he had been dragged across the courtyard.

Bastian knew this outcome was a foregone conclusion. There was never going to be a fair trial. If accused of treason, the king would never truly hear your case. Dracul had told his children many times over the years, with an accusation like this, there was no way to prove that the accused was innocent. So in his eyes, the only thing that could be done was to treat them as if they were guilty, regardless of whether it was true or not. It avoided whispers in the realm that the king was going soft, and such talk would never do. Better to snuff out one life than risk loose lips that could lead to another civil war; or it would seem, the loss of the king's reputation in general. Bastian had never been able to embrace his father's teachings, not the way Nico had. He detested them with every fibre of his being, and it made him worry for his brother's soul. While Nico still remained a decent person underneath it all, Bastian was in no doubt at all, that his father was now a fully-fledged monster with no hope of redemption.

Most of the crowd whooped and cheered, clearly having come just to see an execution. Others watched silently. Bastian wondered if they were the ones who knew the man. Bastian could barely breathe as he tried to keep his face impartial to what was unfolding in front of him. His heart raced and his palms became clammy. Biting his cheek, he watched as Robert Houston was brought to a stop, his shackles secured to the platform, as the guards moved swiftly down the ramp into the crowd. Gerritsen stepped forward so that he was standing in front of the platform, slowly removing his armoured uniform until he stood in just braies. Silence fell as he called out in a mocking tone, "Any final words?"

Houston looked out into the crowd, his eyes sweeping across it until they came to rest on the king. Now resigned to his fate, the thick iron shackles stopping him from shifting and making his escape, Robert shouted loudly to make sure he was heard, as fire raged behind his eyes.

"You cannot rule like this forever. Your reign of terror will end. And when it does, there will be a special seat in the underworld saved just for you."

Gerritsen started to shift as Houston spoke his final words, his human skin quickly replaced by black scales which rippled their way along the surface of his body, shredding his remaining clothing as they fell into place like dominos. His eyes growing with his skull as it morphed, his pupils turning into reptilian slits. Spikes pushed up from his spine, large horns erupted from his head. Once the transformation was complete, the creature that now stood in the place of Gerritsen was a dragon the colour of obsidian, terrible and deadly. Arching his back the beast roared, and Bastian closed his eyes, muttering a silent prayer to the gods, hoping no one would notice. Hearing the fire escape Gerritsen and engulf poor Robert, Bastian was only thankful the screams of agony were short lived. That was the only saving grace of dragon fire, it was mercifully quick. Although, he thought, so was beheading, but that was too simple for their father's tastes: he liked to put on a bit of a show. After all, as Dracul always said, what was the point in their being able to shift into dragons if they didn't use it to their advantage from time to time?

Bastian's stomach turned over again as he watched the wooden platform and what was left of Robert Houston burn to ashes. When Gerritsen shifted back into his human form, the closest guards quickly shielded his naked body with a black cloak, allowing him privacy to reassemble his armour.

"Let that be a lesson to everyone. Now go," the king bellowed into the courtyard.

The crowd of commoners quickly dispersed, but the people of the court began to leave at a much slower pace. Chatting idly, as if what they had just witnessed had had no impact on their wellbeing whatsoever. Without a word, the king got up, heading briskly back towards the doors of the palace, his cloak billowing behind him, suspended by the light breeze. It was only then that Nico offered a glance in Bastian's direction. He knew his brother was aware that he was far from well, but it was not until they turned to re-join their father that Bastian felt Nico's hand pat him on the shoulder. His voice was low and gravelly as he whispered to avoid being overheard.

"It had to be done brother, otherwise the people will think they can get away with all sorts."

"As always, I think our father just got away with murder. But no one cares what I think, do they?"

Bastian snapped back, the contents of his stomach still threatening to reappear. Bastian longed for simpler times. He could still just about remember when he had been young and the fae still lived among them, before the elves had reclaimed Carpathia, and the remaining fae on their isle had moved to join the rest in Viriador. Two of his best friends had been fae. Once they moved across the sea, he had never heard anything of them again. To this day, he still wondered what had become of them. Bastian had never made such good friends since. While he did have many acquaintances, they weren't the same as the pure friendships of his childhood. Even though he and Nico didn't see eye to eye most of the time, and while it was questionable whether they had the same moral compass, for most of his life Nico had been all Bastian had, and for that he would always be thankful. Regardless of his brother's need to please their father and be the golden heir he desired, he could at least count on the knowledge that they would always have each other's backs.

Nico grumbled as they approached the huge golden doors, beautiful ornate carvings of flowers and flames etched across their surface.

"Well, just be glad, brother, that it's me and not you that will no doubt be instructed to go and inform some poor wailing woman that she is now a widow."

Chapter Two

A Perfect Show

The sun crept through the open window as Astraea watched the world below go by. High-born fae milled around the courtyard below the palace, dressed in all their finery. The traders that catered to those who were interested in purchasing the finer things that money could buy had just finished setting up their stalls, ready to sell their wares to those privy to the grounds of the Viriadorian Palace.

Tilting her face to the sky, Astraea let the sun's rays warm her for a while as she tried to ignore the tugging at her back. Listening while Melana chattered idly as she laced the back of her corset, Astraea murmured her agreement where needed. The garment itself was beautiful, that wasn't the problem. It was made of pale green linen, with pink ribbon running through the eyelets at the back. A cream block at the front had a large singular pink rose stitched into it, with several smaller pink flowers swirling around the outskirts. There was no denying that any lady would think her mad for not being thrilled at the prospect of wearing such finery, but Astraea couldn't help but sigh, letting her shoulders sag.

"Back straight, Princess."

A pinch to her sides made Astraea jump, consequently also making her straighten her back immediately. Exhaling loudly, she rolled her eyes, turning slightly to face Melana.

"Was that really necessary?"

"Yes. You haven't really been paying attention all morning. It's like you're in another world."

Astraea looked at her friend and smiled. Melana looked stunning as always. Today she wore a gold-coloured gown, tight fitting at the top, accentuating her ample breasts, but from there it flowed gracefully down to the floor. Melana's mother was her mother's – the queen's – lady in waiting, and now Melana was hers. It seemed fitting: they had been friends all their lives.

Their parents had grown close from the time they had come to this land, among the first to stake their claim upon it. Astraea's father especially. As their king, he had been instrumental in building their community up from the ground. She knew her mother and father had been childhood sweethearts, but before they came to Viriador they had shared the land of Predoran with the dragons who were still located across the Barren Sea. The family of Astraea's father, King Emil, had ruled the fae that resided in Predoran, the Castillo's claiming responsibility for their dragon kin. But when Carpathia fell to the dragons, many of the fae, feeling ill at ease with the invasion and growing unrest, had relocated to the Glowing Isle, claiming Viriador, their families included. When the elves eventually fought back, reclaiming Carpathia, Dracul Castillo decreed that he wanted dragons and dragons alone in his lands. New laws were made to suit the dragon king's change of heart. Hybrids were outlawed. Unions between their kinds made punishable by death.

Still, she supposed their new land was far more charming, judging from the tales that her mother and father had told her. It was incredibly pretty here, especially the flowers that bloomed wherever one could think to roam. Predoran sounded perfectly fine but rather barren in comparison to Viriador. Here plants and trees grew in abundance, flowers of every colour were everywhere you looked. There was little gold around here, not like in Predoran where almost everything had gold incorporated into it. The fae unlike the dragons, favoured silver or rose golds, and the kingdom they had built for themselves reflected this. The buildings were white and most of their decorative features if they weren't silver, were serene pastel colours. While the weather around the Palace was often cold, the closer to the east coast you went the warmer it got.

Astraea ran a hand down the soft, brown skin of Melana's arm. The contrast was stark; Astraea was as fair as Melana was dark, but their bond was that of sisters. There was nothing they couldn't face together – including an appearance at court today, where she was to hear the requests of the people.

"Forgive me. I just wonder what a simpler life would have been like at times. As you know, I've never been a huge fan of these dresses."

Melana let a soft chuckle escape her as she turned Astraea back around to continue lacing her corset.

"My friend, if it was up to you, we would be off with Wren, having adventures disguised as men."

Astraea smiled; it was true, of course. She would have traded her place for Wren's in a heartbeat, if she could have. The pair of them had found him as children, when they had strayed far further than they were allowed. They had found him washed up on a beach on the east coast, his ship having been wrecked, from what they could gather from his dehydrated ramblings. Melana's family had taken Wren into their care that day and had always treated him as one of their own. Once he was well enough, Wren was trained in the fae's army, learning to fight should there ever be a need. In the absence of war, he got to go and explore all the corners of their land, and Astraea supposed she was jealous. It was only recently that he had been promoted to one of her personal guards, and the three of them got to spend a lot more of their time together again. Just as they had in their childhood. Melana, on the other hand, would happily wear dresses for days. While she had loved all their games as a child – climbing about getting covered in muck as they explored all the places they shouldn't and driving their parents to distraction – now that her eighteenth year was upon her, Melana had turned into a fine woman. Astraea thought she would have made a much better princess than her, if she was being honest. Melana was kind, compassionate, and held so much empathy for others; it was what the Princess loved most about her oldest, dearest friend. Even that day down on the beach as children, it had been Melana who insisted they get help for Wren. Astraea had been far too frightened of her parents finding out where they had strayed to, even if she had wanted to help the boy.

"There, do you want to look in the mirror?"

Making her way over to the mirror that stood in its rose gold frame, Astraea noticed that Melana looked particularly pleased with today's selection of garment for her. As she looked into the reflective glass, she could see why Melana was so pleased with herself. She looked every inch the princess she was meant to be. Her cream gown started at her breasts and flowed to the floor; small ruffles of cream material sat at the tops of her arms, securing the dress in place. The patterned corset hugged her over the top, making Astraea look as if she were wearing a corset and skirt, but this way it was much more secure. After all, a princess wasn't allowed wardrobe malfunctions; that would be most unseemly. Melana had styled her hair perfectly, as usual. Her blonde hair was braided down her back, the tips of her dainty ears peeking through. The queen always remarked on how her ears were much more elven than fae, because of their size, but Astraea thought they were long enough. Small ringlet curls fell to the sides of her face, framing it beautifully. Astraea's icy blue eyes stared back at her as she watched Melana bring her tiara to rest, sliding it into her hair.

"There we go, now you look perfect. Shall we?"

Astraea gave herself one last look in the mirror, allowing her eyes to roam up and down. She wasn't so sure she felt like the perfect princess her parents would have liked, but as long as Astraea looked the part to the people, she doubted they would care too much. Looking up at the tiara that held her family crest – the sun, moon, and stars – Astraea forced her best smile onto her face, and turning to the door, she nodded.

"Ready."

* * * * *

The metal was cold against Wren's skin, as he ran his fingers over the hilt of the sword sheathed at his side. Running his thumb over the swirling ridges of its design, he let himself lean back against the wall while he waited for the princess and his sister Melana. He knew she was his sister in name only, but she was as close to a sibling as Wren was ever likely to get. His family had been lost to him the day that Melana and Astraea had found him, washed up on the sandy shoreline, drifting between this world and the next.

If he closed his eyes and concentrated hard enough, Wren could just about conjure the faces of his parents and his blood sister from the depths of his mind. Although they could never replace his parents, Wren couldn't have asked for better substitutes. Abraham was as good a father to him as his own had been. He taught him well, bringing him up to be hard working and honest. Abraham even had the same dark skin as his birth father, and when he was still a child, Wren would sit on his lap to hear stories of far-off lands. Looking at the hands that held him, he imagined what it would have been like to still have his father at his side. Ada, unlike Wren's birth mother, had the same dark skin as Abraham, the same skin that Melana too shared. Ada doted on Wren, teaching him to sew and bake, sneaking him extra portions of pudding when he came in tired from his training with the guard. Always the first to embrace him and make sure Wren felt that he belonged, and he did, he felt loved. But Wren wasn't dark skinned like his adoptive family, he wasn't fair skinned like Astraea either; it was a constant reminder of his past. The girls had been his friends and allies, his fiercest supporters since the day they had met. Wren was proud to consider the princess one of his closest friends, and as her personal guard, he had spent many hours in this hallway. Positioned there at the only entrance to Astraea's chamber, he could ensure she remained safe from harm. Leaning his head back on the cold stone wall, Wren looked up at the skylight above him. He watched small birds dance their way through the crisp blue sky, not a cloud in sight.

As the hefty oak door of her chamber opened, Wren smiled, standing to attention, making Astraea giggle.

"Oh, Wren, do behave."

"I like to take my job seriously, Princess," he said, winking. "It's what I've trained my whole life for, after all."

Wren bowed to Astraea as she stood in front of him, locking eyes with Melana as she pushed the heavy door closed behind them; he was only half joking, and she knew it. When Melana's family had taken him in, Wren had found himself in the king's guard so that they could pay for his keep. Despite the fact that he had lost his leg, having it amputated just above the knee, once he was able, he trained with the guard daily, and they trained him hard. It had been gruelling at first, not only the intensity of the sudden influx of physical activity for his body to handle; but also, the leg that had been built for him caused him all sorts of problems at the beginning. Now he was an adult, Wren had a much more practical prosthetic limb, which he had helped to craft himself. It was still made of wood and steel, but it fitted him so much better than any of the others ever had. It seemed to work well as an extension of himself, and above all else, he found it comfortable. Years of training meant that Wren could fight just as well as the next person; unless he was undressed, you would never have known the secret lying beneath his clothing. Having to fight to keep his place on the guard had helped shape Wren; he had put everything he had into it. He was stronger now, both physically and mentally, than he had ever thought possible, but as Wren looked at Melana, he could see from the familiar look in her eyes that she still worried for him.

After a moment, the ladies descended the grand marble staircase, gripping the wooden banister with all its intricate carvings, weaving along the structure as they went. Wren was not far behind them, dressed in black breeches that came to just past his knees, and a white shirt with ruffles at the neck and cuffs. His boots had a slight heel and laced up his calves, disappearing beneath the trousers. The sheathed sword at his side bounced against his good leg as he descended the staircase after them, watching Astraea and Melana chat as they walked along the hallway, the floor covered in red and cream patterns, the walls, more cold marble. They stopped, turning to him as they came to the two marble pillars outside the throne room.

"Whatever they send me off to do, this time you two are coming with me, right?"

"Of course."

They both responded as one, Wren giving Astraea his best lopsided grin. He watched Astraea turn to face the throne room, visibly stiffening her posture as she prepared to enter. Knocking on the door, Astraea waited, clasping her hands together in front of her patiently, until the doors were thrown open wide for them. When they began to enter, Astraea walking just ahead of them, Wren couldn't help but feel sorry for her as he observed the many people waiting on either side of the room. He could see her breathing had changed; it was shallow now. Astraea was doing her best to put on a show, just as she had done many times before. Gone was the happy carefree woman that he knew her to be, now her behaviour was stiff, the perfect dutiful princess that her parents expected her to be. Wren had to stop a smile spreading across his lips as he recalled all the times he had taught Astraea to shoot with a bow. Her parents would have aneurysms if they knew. As she took her place on a small silver throne to the right of her mother, Wren took his seat just to the side of the royals, next to Melana and their other close contact servants.

As the audience with King Emil and Queen Briana wore on, Wren listened, feigning interest as the same mundane requests from the people of the realm were discussed. His eyes wandered over to Astraea and he noted the same look of forced interest; her lips were white, pressed tightly together as she struggled to keep focus. Her hands were clasped tightly in her lap to stop her fidgeting fingers fighting against one another. At this moment Wren did not envy her one bit. All eyes in court were on them.

The plea being heard at the moment was a land dispute that had been left unresolved, despite intervention from the royal guard months ago.

The villager was explaining that their neighbour had simply ignored the visit and continued to act as they always had.

Silence descended as the Queen raised her hand. She stood, and Wren couldn't help but admire her beauty. Queen Briana had the same fair skin as Astraea, the same long blonde hair that fell in waves, and the brightest blue eyes. She wore a long blue dress that flowed to the floor, simple yet elegant. Leaf-inspired silver bangles trailed up her arms and the Thandal family tiara sat upon her head; it was the same as Astraea's but set slightly larger. As she moved gracefully towards her daughter, Wren watched as Astraea struggled to hide her emotions. The Queen came to stand just behind Astraea, placing a hand on her shoulder as she began to explain how perhaps someone else to moderate the situation would be the ideal solution, someone like the princess. Astraea's eyes had widened for a split second but quickly regained her composure. However, Wren thought he could see a flicker of sadness in her eyes. This was everything Astraea hated; they all knew it, even her parents, but as their only heir, this was what she was being raised for. Albeit small conflicts to begin with, the essence was still the same: how to resolve conflict and keep the peace; how to be a queen and rule their kingdom. The Queen moved back to her throne, and the next villager with problems they hoped the royals could help them resolve was presented.

Wren spent the rest of the audience contemplating how no one could help the family they were born into. He was always looking for ways to better himself, no, to prove himself; and he couldn't help but wonder what he would have accomplished if he had been born into a different life. Would privilege have bettered him or made him lazy and reluctant? Wren supposed he would never know, but that didn't stop his mind wandering while they were stuck in the throne room.

Chapter Three

Indecent Proposals

The throne room glittered; the gold embellishments lit up with the reflection of the many candelabras dotted around its wide-open space. The large stone pillars that lined the hall were adorned with golden dragons, flowers and foliage that wound their way around them as they travelled up to the ceiling. Sweeping stone arches, expertly carved and adorned with their own golden decoration towered above them. Most days, Nico found this room stunning. An architectural marvel that fascinated him and filled him with wonder. If he looked for long enough, he could always find some small detail that he had never noticed before. But not today. At this moment, Nico stood before his father as he gave his orders.

Sitting upon his throne, two solid-gold dragons flanked Dracul at his sides, their wings drawn back into large arm rests. The back of the throne was solid gold; like the seat, it was lined with red fabric held in place with little gold studs. Grinding his teeth, Nico watched him sneer with glee at his new proposal. King Dracul Castillo leant back, relaxed upon his golden throne. Happy to give out orders, but never getting his hands dirty. He had asked his father once why he was never involved directly in dishing out his version of justice. The answer had been that the job of the king was to rule, to delegate, to oversee. He had told Nico how, when he had been prince, his father had done the same to him. But what he was proposing now was not only insulting to Nico, it also had the potential to harm his brother. Another step in his father's downward spiral. Already the cogs in his mind were whirring, trying to think of a way around this new hurdle. When his father had finished, Nico nodded and brought his right arm up across his chest, and tapped his shoulder with his closed fist.

"As you wish, my King," he said.

With that, Nico immediately turned on his heels, making his way from the throne room.

* * * * *

When he shut the huge golden doors behind him, Nico wasted no time in heading straight to Cyrus's quarters. He did not knock, just threw the wooden door open wide before slamming it shut behind him. A man with ink-black hair and honey-coloured eyes was sitting at his desk, surrounded by books and papers. His skin was pale. Sharp but delicate features looked up at Nico, unfazed by the intrusion. Looking at Cyrus for a moment, Nico leaned against the closed door, pushing both palms into his eyes before sliding to the floor. Cyrus looked over the piles of books at Nico, who sat crumpled on the floor with his head in his hands, and simply raised an eyebrow.

"Bad day?"

Nico stayed quiet for a minute, struggling to regain his composure. He let his hands fall away from his face, revealing his slightly red eyes, leaving Cyrus to wonder if the pressure of his hands against his eye sockets was the cause, or rogue tears that had made their escape. When he finally stood again, Nico's mask was firmly back in place. He looked cold, irritated even, but the emotion he had expressed a few moments earlier was gone.

"You could say that," Nico said. "I need your help."

That got the man's attention. Cyrus stood, moving slowly round the desk, coming to rest just in front of it so that he could lean against it while Nico vented.

"I'm all ears."

As Cyrus had pre-empted, Nico paced and spoke in an animated fashion, clearly frustrated.

"My father wants me to train Bastian to be king."

"Bastian?"

Unable to believe what he was hearing, Cyrus couldn't help but raise both eyebrows to his hairline. Of all the words he thought might leave Nico's mouth, these had to be the furthest from anything he could have imagined.

"Yes, you heard me. In case I was to do something unfortunate, like die."

Nico glared, his gaze arctic, and tone sour, as Cyrus stifled a laugh.

"Sorry, carry on."

"I do not find this at all funny," Nico ground out.

"I mean, it is, but please do continue."

Cyrus laughed, unable to contain it a moment longer, and as much as it irked him, Nico could not blame him. The whole scenario was utterly ridiculous.

"I cannot quite fathom how it has taken father so long to acknowledge this possibility. How has this never crossed his mind before? Bastian's been overlooked his whole life, father has always treated him as an afterthought. Not even an option. He has spent the last twenty years behaving as if Bastian does not exist. I won't have him dragged into this now. He is not like me. Bastian hates the way father rules, and he definitely has no interest in claiming the throne."

"So, what exactly do you propose we do? Kill the king?"

Visibly deflating, Nico flopped into the window seat of Cyrus's room, after taking a moment to stare out at the courtyard below. He found it bare, apart from the makeshift dais and the pile of ash that sat where the platform had stood just an hour before. It was a sad sight. Devoid of life, a far cry from the memories of his childhood, where the castle and its courtyard had been a bustling hive of activity. Everything had been better when his mother was alive – without a doubt for his father, but also for him, his brother, and the kingdom. There was a time when the realm had been harmonious, and for all his pretence to please his father, by the gods did he miss those days.

"If it comes to it, then yes. To protect Bastian, I would kill my father. I am hoping there is another way though. For all his many flaws it would still be sad to see it come to that in the end. I do not believe anyone is past redemption."

As Nico trailed off, Cyrus flexed his hand, turning it to examine his fingernails as he mulled over this information. When he lifted his head to meet Nico's gaze, he spoke intentionally slowly, to make sure the seeds were well and truly planted.

"We could take a little trip to the Glowing Isle, perhaps take the fae princess hostage. Then with King Emil's precious daughter in our possession, we would have leverage."

"Are you mad? That would just start a war."

Nico watched Cyrus contemplate his words. This, after all, was why he had come to him. Cyrus was strategic and cunning; his plans always came together perfectly.

"Perhaps, perhaps not. If we can convince them to surrender to avoid further bloodshed, they can keep their Isle. Maybe the king can even stay in the palace as its warden. But we regain ultimate control. We return his daughter, and everyone gets what they want. No harm done."

Standing, Nico began to pace again.

"And how does this help my brother exactly?"

"Well. If he were to become king, the realm would already be in a more united state, shall we say, and your father would be far happier than he has been in the last decade, you can't deny it. He's regretted the decision to let the fae leave, without some element of control over them, for years. You know he's paranoid. He's always talking about the possibility of invasion. This way, there is less risk of all-out war."

Pausing, Cyrus chuckled darkly to himself again.

"Plus, if you die, then when the king follows, Bastian can just rule everyone as he sees fit. Hell, he can even reinstate King Emil if he wants to. Give him his land back and all that."

A small sigh escaped Nico as he stopped pacing.

"Yes, that was his last shreds of humanity, wasn't it? Letting the fae leave peacefully."

Dragging a hand down his face so it came to rest at his chin, Nico mulled it all over for a moment.

"I suppose that is all plausible, if we manage to pull it off. Do you have a plan?"

Cyrus's fingers thrummed on the wood behind him while he leant against the desk, looking around the room, instinctively making Nico do the same. It was quite plain in comparison to the rest of the castle. The room was made of stone, like all the others, and there was some gold: a candlestick, the curtain rail, a small pile of coins that sat among the books. Most of the bigger items in the room, however, were made of wood. Cyrus had always been powerful, and clearly didn't need a lot of gold to recharge his powers. But then he was a few years older than Nico, and he had been known to dabble in alchemy and the dark arts. It was one of the reasons he had been plucked from relative obscurity and made an adviser in the palace. The man had an uncanny ability to manipulate everything around him. It could well be coincidence, but Nico did wonder if it was more than that – more like magic. Pushing off from the table, Cyrus stalked across the small space to meet Nico. Running the back of his cold fingers down the side of the prince's face, Cyrus eventually spoke.

"The annual ball they hold to mark their independence. I can go, I can blend in well. I won't be recognised."

"And if you are?"

Nico admired the man's faith in himself, his confidence that he could infiltrate the Palace undetected. More so the thought that he would then go on to kidnap the princess.

"If I am, then…"

Nico watched Cyrus. He didn't even blink. Clapping his hands together, Cyrus conjured a small plume of blue smoke, then vanished before Nico's eyes. Maybe this could work after all.

"Well played." Nico addressed the empty room. "So, what will it cost me?"

Cyrus's voice emerged from the shadowy edges of the room, his words laced with sarcasm.

"Oh, I'm sure we can come to some arrangement."

Chapter Four

It's Dirty Work but Someone Has to Do It

Kicking up the dust, Bastian grumbled as the brothers walked through the outskirts of the town, past their usual confines of the city walls.

"I still don't see why I had to come."

The further away from the castle they got, the worse the cobbled streets became, until they were little more than dirt tracks. Bastian kicked a rock, sending it flying ahead of them. He had been in a foul mood since he had heard of his father's order for him to accompany Nico in performing his royal duties. He wasn't altogether sure if it made him angry, sad – or was it that he was scared, perhaps? A gnawing feeling clawed at the pit of his stomach and wouldn't relent. Bastian had been a mess for the duration of their journey and, worse, despite his best efforts to hide it, he was pretty sure he hadn't fooled Nico.

"I would feel much better if we could just fly there. This is taking far too long."

"Brother," Nico sighed. "We can hardly shift back into human form and speak to this poor woman naked. If it makes you feel better, we can fly home. Although you *will* ruin your clothes. Besides, when was the last time you charged your powers? I am meant to be training you in case anything were to happen to me. It would be less than ideal if I had to tell Father you died falling from the sky."

Bastian laughed at that, an unnervingly hearty laugh that fell from his lips with ease.

"I could think of worse fates."

Several armour-clad guards accompanied them, staying several paces behind at all times to give the princes a level of privacy. As they approached the house formally owned by Robert Houston on the very outskirts of the town, Nico stopped. Turning on the dusty gravel path to face Bastian, his expression was pained.

"Please know that I do not want to do this, any more than you would."

Taking a tentative step back, Bastian looked his brother up and down. "What do you mean?"

He watched in alarm as Nico turned his back on him muttering, "You'll see soon enough."

He strode towards the door of a small stone building and banged on it harshly. Not the same kind of stone that the castle walls were made of, this was much more primitive. Scraps of stone stuck together with mud and clay. Bastian was shocked when a pale, slender lady answered the door. She was dressed in old, ragged clothes, and was the kind of thin that came from malnutrition.

"Are you wife to Robert Houston?"

The woman looked past Nico to Bastian, and then to the castle guards that stood waiting just behind them. A noticeable shiver ran through her as she nodded.

"Yes, I am."

"Then I regret to inform you that, at his trial, your husband was found guilty of treason and executed. In his absence, I am afraid the king has requested your family as forfeit. You are henceforth property of the crown."

Bastian felt his stomach turning over at Nico's words. The woman dropped to her knees, tears flowing freely as she screamed out her pain. After giving the widow a few moments, Nico spoke again.

"I am sorry, but I can only offer you two choices. The king has ordered that you are to come back to the castle, where you will live with the other women who vie for his attention as he searches for a new queen. The alternative, I'm afraid, is to face the same fate as your husband."

Moving before he could stop himself, Bastian was suddenly shouting his brother's name in horror, grabbing his right shoulder from behind. Nico spun on his heels to face him, grinding out his words as the widow grovelled on the floor, still screaming and crying as she begged for mercy. If not for her, then for her children.

"Remember your place, brother."

Nico turned his face to the guards behind them.

"Let her decide. Either way, the children are to be trained in the royal guard."

Bastian watched as Nico turned to face him again. Words were leaving his lips, but he could not hear them. It felt as if he had been submerged in ice-cold water, unable to breathe, as pressure built in his chest. As he stood struggling to grasp the true scale of what atrocities were being carried out in his father's name, Bastian felt a hand grab his wrist. When he looked up, he was being dragged away from the house by Nico, while the guards surrounded the widow wailing on the floor. Her three young children had appeared to see what was happening, only to be grabbed by guards too. Bastian tried to pull away, tried to get back to help them, but Nico held him fast. Pulling him into the dirt, Nico was down on his knees with him, grasping Bastian's face, his palms flat against his cheeks as he fought to keep his brother's eyes on him.

"Brother." His voice cracked, a small sob escaping. "I can only protect you so much, you must know that. You cannot behave that way in front of the people, but especially not the royal guard. People talk. Do you really want to be the next person tried for treason?"

Bastian remained mute, his eyes wide as the urge to fight or run warred inside him. He felt Nico shaking his shoulders, calling his name. Recoiling as his senses came back to him, Bastian pushed himself back onto his feet, allowing the tears to fall freely.

"I used to think it was just Father who had turned into a monster, but you are just as bad, carrying out these atrocities in his name. How do you live with yourself, Nico?"

Spitting the words, Bastian's voice was filled with venom as he turned and ran. He was aware of his brother calling for him, telling him to wait, but he never slowed his pace. If anything, he propelled himself harder, faster, finally throwing himself into the air. Tangerine scales rolled along Bastian's body as he shifted. He was stunning, streamlined and beautiful as he soared upwards. Bastian was not fierce as a dragon, elegant as opposed to deadly. It was another fact that had always riled his father. Looking behind him, he saw Nico follow him into the sky; he thought how Nico's dark red dragon form was far more terrifying than he would ever be able to appear. Like always, Nico looked sleek, but he was as fierce as the colour that covered him. He was as impeccable as a dragon as he was as a person. The perfect son that Bastian would never be. He thought of their father, and how he had always been treated as an afterthought. He thought of all the injustices in this broken kingdom, and the anger rose inside him.

Roaring like a wounded animal, Bastian increased his speed,

determined to make it back to the castle and prove Nico wrong. He was not the only one who charged his powers; when surrounded by scheming, backstabbing dragons, Bastian would have been foolish to let his reserves wane. They might think him weak, but he was most definitely not a fool. There was only one person he could think of that could help him now. Bastian didn't like him, and he definitely did not trust him; but he was the cleverest person that Bastian could think of, someone who might actually be able to formulate a plan to salvage this mess. Bastian needed help. He needed Cyrus.

Chapter Five

Smoke & Mirrors

Leaning back in his chair, Cyrus lifted his legs up onto his desk, crossing them over so that they rested on the mahogany-coloured surface. He held a red apple in one hand, a book of world history in the other. It was an old volume, bound in leather that was now well worn, and it had a musty smell to it, although that didn't bother him. For as long as Cyrus could remember, he had been obsessed with researching lost treasures of old, especially the relic. As he flicked through the pages, taking the occasional bite of his apple, he daydreamed of the kind of power that wielding the relic would lay at his feet – the kind of power gold couldn't buy.

Finding himself restless, Cyrus bounced his foot as he flicked through the pages, until hurried footsteps and ragged breaths caught his attention. The door to his chamber was abruptly thrown open. Before him stood the younger of the Castillo brothers.

Bastian was still half naked from his flight back to the castle. He had returned to his human form, regretting not having stashed some clothing outside earlier. Having found breeches in the laundry room, he had hastily hauled them on and run through the hallways. Bastian didn't care about his bare chest. His blond hair was a mess from the shift. His whole body was slick with sweat. Bastian struggled to catch his breath, panting out his words.

"I need your help," he said.

That surprised Cyrus, who didn't think the young prince was his biggest fan, and wondered what could possibly have Bastian turning to him for help.

"Do you now?" Cyrus replied, not moving from his seat. He took another casual bite of his apple, reclining further back in his chair so that he could look Bastian in the eye. "To what do I owe the pleasure?"

Watching as Bastian troubled to take the time to ensure the door was closed before speaking intently, Cyrus found his interest piqued.

"I need your help, Cyrus," Bastian said. "I cannot be what they are, what they want me to be. If I'm being made into someone fit to rule, I need a united kingdom to reign over. I do not hunger for war. I don't want to oversee executions and round up children to be made into soldiers. Do you know where Nico took me today? What I witnessed?"

Opening his mouth to reply, Cyrus found himself cut short as the door to his chambers burst open for a second time. Nico strode in, fully clothed. He had not run, but walked with conviction. The only thing that betrayed any emotion was the strangled cry that left his mouth before he could register that Bastian stood there.

"Cyrus, I need you."

Stopping dead when he spotted Bastian, both of them took a couple of steps back from each other as Nico slammed the door shut behind him. They both stared at each other, eyes wide. Cyrus broke the silence, his words silky, the little stand-off seemingly having no effect on him at all.

"Firstly, Nico, don't threaten me with a good time," he said. "Secondly, if you don't learn to knock, I'll be forced to evict you from my window – that goes for both of you." Theatrically tossing the remnants of his apple down on the desk, Cyrus uncrossed his legs, sliding them to the floor. Closing the heavy book, he got to his feet, dropping the large volume on the wooden surface, creating a small cloud of dust that rose from its pages. "Do take a seat, gentlemen."

Bastian stumbled backwards into the window seat on one side of the room, the light illuminating the beads of sweat that laced his skin, while Nico moved slowly, calculating the best place to sit, finally opting for a small chair in the corner. Grabbing one of his dark tunics from the chest of drawers, Cyrus threw it at Bastian.

"For the love of the Gods, get dressed."

"Distracting you, is he?" Nico snarked.

Cyrus cast a cutting glare in the prince's direction,

"Not at all," he said. "I just don't want his sweat on my cushions."

Irritated, Cyrus sniffed the air, while Nico struggled to keep a straight face. Bastian, now dressed, had drawn his knees to his chest. He looked lost, like a child, and Cyrus wondered if Bastian was contemplating fleeing from the room. The stand-off was still clearly in progress.

"So, is anyone going to enlighten me as to what's going on?"

Eyes shifted in all directions, with none of them daring to speak first.

Nico eventually offered, "Why don't you take the floor, brother? After all, you were here first."

Peeking up from behind his knees, Bastian eventually straightened up enough to speak.

"I want peace. I want to unite the kingdoms. I will not become our father, Nico. I can't. If anything were to happen to you, and I were to be named king, I would not have a war-torn realm."

Nico stood, and walked over to Bastian. He dropped onto the cushion next to him, placing an arm around his shoulder. "I know, brother," he said. "We will find a way."

Bastian nodded tentatively. "I don't doubt it."

"Touching as this is, where do I come into it?"

The princes looked up to find Cyrus studying them, already formulating a plan that would satisfy them both. While he was at it, he might also be able to find out if the fae knew more than the dragons did about the lost treasures of old. Eyes on the prize, he reminded himself, always eyes on the prize.

"Cyrus and I discussed this earlier, to a degree," Nico said. "It would mean trusting each other implicitly and working together. Do you think you can do that, Bastian?"

Nodding with conviction for the first time, Bastian relaxed his grip on his knees, looking more at ease than he had since he entered the room. Nico gave Cyrus a curt look that implied he should tread carefully, as Cyrus began to outline a plan. Not *quite* the plan he and Nico had discussed earlier, but it would be sufficient nonetheless.

"We could convince your father that we want to go and gather intel on the fae to find out the weaknesses of the Glowing Isle, so that he can wage war. We could even suggest that, while we are there, we could kidnap the princess. But what we would actually do is use the time we are in Viriador to try and forge an alliance. Perhaps with their help we could overthrow Dracul and unite the realms."

The look in Nico's eyes told Cyrus that this was not likely to be the way that their venture panned out. He knew that what they had discussed earlier was more how Nico would want to play it. There was no leverage in making allies, but Bastian didn't need to know that. Not until the last moment, when it was too late. Until then, Cyrus thought the sliver of hope he was offering was enough to get Bastian on board. After all, that was what Cyrus was good at: he was all smoke and mirrors. Planting seeds, leaving trails of breadcrumbs. If he gave someone enough rope, they would hang themselves eventually. It was what had got him this far. Bastian nodded again, a small smile playing on his lips now; he seemed to like the idea. Tentatively he offered, "The Independence ball at the palace is coming up. Anyone who is anyone will be there. Perhaps we can find a way to speak to the princess or her parents directly."

"What if we are recognised?" Nico ventured, clearly more worried than he had been earlier, now that it would no longer be Cyrus going alone.

"How would anyone recognise us? We have never been to the Glowing Isle, and you were mere children when they lived among the people of Predoran. We just need to assume reasonable aliases. I am sure we will be fine. Failing that, I could get us all out, at a pinch, I suppose," Cyrus added, rubbing his finger and thumb along his jaw line as he mulled it over. Bastian's face betrayed him, his features crumpling in disgust.

"And how exactly do you propose that you will do that?"

"Oh, ye of little faith."

Clicking his fingers, Cyrus was suddenly surrounded by plumes of dark smoke, a mixture of purples and blues. The smoke crept outwards, quickly engulfing the whole room. Cyrus could feel his magic starting to drain away. They would have to be careful; he couldn't use vast amounts of magic and shift in quick succession. It was definitely something they would have to consider. Despite the fact that Cyrus had honed his power, only needing a small amount of time and gold to recharge it, he was still vulnerable under the right circumstances. Ever the showman, Cyrus clapped his hands, vanishing along with the smoke.

"Like that."

His voice echoed around the room, and while Nico was well adapted to Cyrus's showmanship, Bastian was not. All he could manage was the smallest "Oh."

Chapter Six

Phantom Pain

Wren blinked slowly, the blue sky above him swimming back into focus. He registered the cold, wet sensation of his saturated clothing, as the breeze bit into his skin. His brain struggling to wake, he gradually roused himself, one sense at a time; Wren registered the salty tang in the air around him – they had been at sea.

The wet sand was, in fact, a blessing he realised, as the day wore on and the warmth of the sun overhead started to dry out his clothes and the sand surrounding him. Wren tried repeatedly to move his injured legs but couldn't even wiggle the toes on his left foot. The right one he could move, just about, but it was incredibly painful and there was no way he would be able to stand on it. His attempts to call out for help were quickly reduced to little more than a whimper; his mouth and throat felt dry, like all the moisture had been sucked away and replaced with sand. Tears streaked down Wren's face as he resigned himself to the fact that, having survived his ordeal with the sea, it still wasn't enough, and he would likely still die. It would never be enough where he was concerned. Wren was still just the weak little boy he had been back in the village, the children surrounding him, calling him names and throwing rotten fruit at him for fun.

"Melana, look over there."

Wren could hear footsteps fast approaching but lacked the strength to open his eyes again. He could feel their presence as two children knelt in the sand next to him, realising as they spoke that it was two girls, probably around his own age, that had found him.

"Is he breathing?"

"I think so."

"Do you think he's a shifter?"

"Don't be ridiculous, Astraea, he's far too young."

"By the Gods, Melana, look at his leg."

Wren took notice of that, and the horrified gasp that both the girls gave. He hoped that he was about to find out what had happened to his legs. Using the last of his energy, Wren let out a garbled cry that just about resembled, "Please help me."

His hand reached out blindly to them, and one of the girls held onto it as his strength left him and his arm flopped back to the sand.

"What are we going to do with him? We cannot leave him here."

"Melana, we aren't meant to be down here. We'll get in trouble."

"We can't just leave him here, Astraea; he will die when the tide comes in, if he doesn't before then. I'll go and get Mamma."

"Fine, but if anyone asks, it was your idea to come down here. He's lost a lot of blood so don't dally."

As Wren drifted in and out of consciousness, he felt the girl – Astraea, her friend had called her – squeezing his hand. She spoke quietly, reassuring him that all would be well. Telling him how brave he was and how she wouldn't let anything bad happen to him. She stroked circles on the back of his hand while they waited, and eventually, Wren let everything whirling in his mind fade to black.

* * * * *

Sitting up, clutching at the white bed sheets, Wren gasped in panicked breaths. Sweat soaked his skin as images of the ill-fated voyage flashed before his eyes. The shame and guilt rushed to consume him. He had not been able to act when it had counted, his feeble body betraying him. The dream had felt so real, Wren could have sworn he'd heard the wind whistling by and the birds calling out to each other above him. He thought that he could still hear the noise the sea made as it lapped the shore, the gentle roll of the waves licking over the rocks upon the beach where he'd lain.

Dread rose as Wren felt himself trying desperately to lift his body, failing miserably beneath the overwhelming wave of pain flooding through him, emanating from his left leg. A noise somewhere between a sob and a guttural cry slipped from his lips. It was as though it was still there, pain tearing through the mangled flesh. This was what they had all thought him: weak and useless, a pathetic excuse of a man. That's what they had told him when he was barely more than a child.

When Wren's breathing finally calmed, the pain in his phantom limb fading, he rolled over and buried his face in the pillow, so that he could scream unheard. The last thing Wren needed was anyone barging in to check on him. Knowing the next day was going to be a long one, he attempted to get back to sleep, and failed miserably, worrying the whole night that he would not be able to protect the princess, that he was not good enough for the important role he played. Eventually, Wren threw his pillow across the room, frustrated. Some soldier he was.

CHAPTER SEVEN

A Great Gift

The wooden carriage made its way from the palace, along the winding path that led away from the city. Two of the finest brown dapple horses pulled it, trotting methodically as their manes blew in the cool breeze. In front of them, several guards rode ahead to ensure their safety. The carriage itself was ornate and beautiful. The body was shaped like a huge pumpkin, suspended in the air above four large wheels. It was rose gold in colour, with silver leaves that entwined as they crept up the sides, meeting at the small stalk on the top.

Inside, Melana sat next to Wren, who was attempting to read a book of mythical tales to pass the time. According to him, they were based on old truths. Melana watched the princess stare out of the small window as she sat opposite them. Leaning against it, Astraea was rolling the fingers on her right hand in frustration, causing small sparks of white flame to emerge from her palm. This seemed only to frustrate Astraea further. While she held some sway with water, and could make flowers bloom, Astraea struggled to create or control flame, and could barely manage to whip up a breeze. Wren, on the other hand, had been gifted the power to control fire and manipulate the air around him. Whereas, when Melana had aged into her power, it had seemed the elements had more control over her than she did of them, several emotion-fuelled incidents occurring before her true nature was revealed. Like the time she had accidentally set a bed aflame during a row with another maid… It had not mattered in the end, as it turned out that her real gift was something very special indeed. She was a seer. While she could not control the elements the way her friends could, Melana held one of the most special gifts a fae could possess. The visions were not something she could control, but when she had them, they allowed her to see into the future. Sometimes these visions came to pass as she had seen them, although the future was not set in stone. What Melana saw could sometimes be what *would* come to pass, if steps were not taken to address a chain of events that were set to unfold.

It was a rare gift and one that Melana was extremely proud of, but also one that she did not advertise to those she did not know well. In the wrong hands, that kind of gift could prove deadly, and not just for her.

Astraea had stopped trying to make flames, and now a small plant was uncoiling in her palm as she stared at her friends, an irritated expression on her face as she chewed at her bottom lip. Melana watched as the plant that stood in Astraea's palm withered and died. The book Wren had been reading dropped onto the seat next to him, breaking the deafening silence between them all. Melana jumped slightly at the noise as he spoke.

"It could be worse, you know."

Astraea clenched her fist, giving him a piercing look that would have sent others scurrying – not that there was anywhere Wren could have gone, even if he'd wanted to.

"Technically, he is right." Melana kept her voice gentle as she spoke.

"Thank you for your input, but neither of you knows what this actually feels like, do you? I never asked to be a princess, I don't want to rule a kingdom, and I definitely do not want to go and sort out neighbour disputes, of all things. I'm pretty sure other royals have servants to deal with this kind of thing."

Wren snorted as Astraea finished her grumbling.

"I think you're being a bit of a brat, personally," he said.

Gasping, Melana let Wren's name slip between her lips in warning.

"What? The kings of old would have been going off on crusades across the lands, and she's moaning about this?"

Moving across to sit beside Astraea, Melana took hold of her hand, stroking it gently as tears threatened to spill from Astraea's eyes.

"It will be OK. I understand. It all just gets overwhelming sometimes, doesn't it, lovely? Wren, I think you need to apologise."

Wren rolled his eyes, but he quickly offered an apology.

"I'm sorry, you know I didn't mean it like that. It's just one little inconvenience. We go, we make our presence felt, you say a few words, we leave. It's only as difficult as you make it."

"Wren, Astraea can't help that she gets worked up going out into the realm and speaking to the people. She can only just about manage to sit in the throne room when her parents call an audience without ending up making herself sick. Her anxiety is not her fault."

Hugging her friend close to her, Melana found Astraea leaning in to rest her head on her shoulder.

"I'm sorry," Wren said. "It's just frustrating sometimes. There's so much out there to discover in the world, and you're always missing out on it all, Astraea. I just— oh, I don't know."

"I would *love* the life you live, Wren. And I would probably feel a damn sight braver if there wasn't so much expected of me. I know this only seems like a small task to you, but it doesn't end there. It will never end. Not until I cease to walk this earth."

A small sob escaped the princess as she sat up, looking Wren in the eye, her own still damp and red rimmed.

"Sometimes I feel like we were all dealt the wrong cards."

Melana watched as Astraea turned away sadly, tucking the ringlets behind one of her pointed ears. Going back to watching the varying shades of the leaves on the trees that passed by, she returned to her original seat. Melana took the opportunity to smack Wren's thigh just above his prosthetic, making him wince. She gave him a look, the one where she didn't need to use words to convey her feelings.

No one spoke again for a while. The only sound was that of the wheels as they rolled along the path, and the horses' hooves as they continued on. Astraea's tears had stopped and she did not look quite so troubled as she fiddled with the tassels on the little cream curtain that hung by the window, eventually dropping it and turning to look at them. Finally, Astraea offered an olive branch.

"You're right, Wren. I was being a brat. I'm sorry for my behaviour. Sometimes I just don't know how to control the feelings that creep up inside me. It feels a bit like drowning."

"You don't need to apologise to me, Astraea. I just worry for you. I feel like sometimes you're your own worst enemy."

As Astraea released her breath in a heavy sigh, Melana saw a chance to salvage the situation.

"We're here to look after you, neither of us would ever let anything happen to you, Astraea."

The fleeting look that passed over Astraea's face had Melana's heart breaking.

"If only you could save me from myself. Sometimes I feel as if the very air we breathe is trying to suffocate me. I know it's difficult to understand when it's not something either of you feel yourselves."

"I get it," Melana said. "Your entire life is mapped out, everything is out of your control. You're not even allowed to dress yourself. I am not at all surprised you struggle. I know you say that if the roles were reversed, one of us would be more suited to your life, but we will honestly never know. You were born into this life; you didn't choose it. Your family has had to deal with so much conflict, and found strength in creating a new life for their people. Nothing has been easy for you. We cannot even begin to understand how it must feel to know that this is all your life will ever be."

"You could just run away."

"WREN!"

Both ladies shouted in unison, turning to look at him as he earned another bash on his thigh from Melana.

Rubbing the top of his leg Wren grumbled, "What? It was just a suggestion."

The carriage started to jolt as the roads became more like dirt tracks, the temperature increasing the further they got from the palace. Melana was pleased that the trio were back to talking normally, their squabble seemingly forgotten. When the horses finally ground to a halt outside the dwellings, Melana held Astraea's hand, waiting while she took several deep breaths. Letting go, Melana watched Astraea's mask slide into place while Wren fiddled with the lock. Eventually he opened the small door onto the steps at the side of the carriage. Peering out first – and only when he was satisfied by the guards' presence as they lined up either side at the bottom of the stairs – Wren motioned for the ladies to descend.

CHAPTER EIGHT

Nothing More Than Feelings

What to do. What to do. There were so many options. On the one hand, Cyrus could help poor young Prince Bastian, who seemingly struggled with every obstacle in his path. There was no way that Bastian would be able to cope with all that would be expected of him should he ever have to take the throne. Then there was Nico; he liked Nico. Not only was Cyrus his most trusted adviser, but the older prince had taken him to his bed on more than one occasion. Cyrus's loyalty to him had not wavered, until now. Especially with the possibility that, when Nico's time came to claim the crown, he may be in a position to rule at his side. Cyrus liked him well enough to play the part of his consort. He admired Nico's character, and no one could deny that he was nice to look at. Platinum hair and sharp features combined with ice blue eyes – the prince was stunning, and he knew it. There were definitely worse ways Cyrus could spend his life; but this was an opportunity too good to let slip through his fingers. With his main goal of finding the relic seemingly always just out of reach, Cyrus decided he could help execute the plan that they had previously concocted, or he could do one better. If he went to Dracul and warned him of the plot that was being set in motion by his sons, of the impending betrayal, then he would be in the king's good graces, furthering his position and influence within the castle. Or he could play Dracul, warning him of one plan while executing another.

Pacing the floor of his chambers, Cyrus pondered it all. He had never been known for altruism, quite the opposite in fact. Did he truly believe the princes would be able to emerge from this victorious, or would the king be the one to remain on the throne? Tempting as it was, Cyrus struggled to shake the feeling that this could become a suicide mission. At this very moment, Nico was reporting to his father, their king. That fact alone left Cyrus's mouth dry. This all hinged on whether they could trust one another, and trust was something that did not come easy to him. Cyrus could easily see this ending with one or both princes dead. Whether that were to be by Dracul's hand, he could not be sure, but his priority now was weighing up his own chances of survival.

If there was one thing that Cyrus was certain of, it was that he hadn't got as far as he had in this life to throw it all away now. Bastian was not a problem; Cyrus was not close to him at all. If anything, he found the young prince little more than an irritation, a thorn constantly wedged in Nico's side. And as much as it pained him, if he had to sacrifice Nico, he would. Despite his fondness for him, Cyrus wanted power, he wanted it all. In this game they were about to play for the throne, collateral damage was inevitable – although Cyrus was sure the princes would argue that they were gambling everything they had for the greater good, so that the people of Predoran could be free of their tyrannical king.

The youngest of seven children, Cyrus had not had an easy life. Far from it: most of his childhood had been spent hiding away, avoiding the beatings his stepfather doled out under the guise of shaping Cyrus into a better man. But it did not matter how well they behaved; he always found a reason to beat them all. His mother had stood up for them at first, but had soon turned a blind eye to their suffering to avoid beatings of her own. As children, they never should have been subjected to the horrors that Cyrus and his siblings had endured during their short lives. Consequently, he had still been so very young when he committed his first heinous act. Unquestionably, it had been his stepfather's own fault. And Cyrus had mocked him, telling him so as he gargled on his own blood. As if the abuse he had already suffered was not enough, the man had taken a liking to hurting him in other ways, to gain his own pleasure. The day Cyrus finally snapped, he had felt nothing but pure joy as the carving knife grasped in his small fist slid between the man's ribs like they were little more than a slab of butter. It was one of Cyrus's fondest memories, one that had spurred him on, keeping him moving forward every day since. Shock had been written all over the man's face as he dragged the knife from his chest. He certainly had not seen that coming. Cyrus had watched the pathetic excuse of a man as he fell to the floor, choking on his own blood. Crouching next to him as he died, Cyrus had revelled in his own euphoria as the light slowly left the man's eyes, vowing there and then that no one would touch him without his consent ever again. It had been twenty years since that night, the night Cyrus had fled his home. And he had never once felt the need to look back.

When the reality of his actions hit him, he was already long gone. Feeling no shred of remorse, only a resounding sense of peace that came with knowing that he had spared his siblings. It had been easy to blend in with the many others attempting to flee their land. Whispers had been on the breeze for a long time now. War was coming. Cyrus had been thankful initially that he had only been traveling for a few days when he was taken. Quickly realising that he had been captured by the enemy, his relief had curdled into fear. Once the prisoners were rounded up, soldiers took them on the journey to their new 'home'.

Traveling hundreds of miles across the ocean to a foreign land, chained in the belly of a large wooden vessel. So many people had been crammed into that space. Some were sick or injured, not all of them had survived the journey, but they had all stayed there in chains regardless.

Cyrus would never forget that voyage. The fear he had felt surrounded by all those people, crammed in so tightly that he had thought he might suffocate; all the while Cyrus had felt so overwhelmingly alone. The screams as those around him lost loved ones, then had to watch them rot. And the smell, gods the smell. It all haunted him.

His mind had slowly started to heal when he was taken in, raised by the Royal Guard, in Predoran. The place he now called home. Apparently no longer a prisoner, there was still a fair share of hardships for him to overcome, but Cyrus delt with them, getting his vengeance in opportune moments as the years passed by. It had not been long before memories of his old life began to fade, and now Predoran was all Cyrus really knew. Part of him wished he could see that his siblings were safe, but he was the youngest: he should never have had to be their keeper, and yet he had been the one who freed them all.

The older he got, the more responsibility was given to him in his role. Training daily to make the cut, at the age of fourteen he was finally allowed to go with the guard, to fight across the sea in foreign lands, seeing firsthand more and more war-torn countries. He had spent a good deal of his life in the royal guard before being promoted to his current role of adviser in the palace. But he had seen the civilian losses firsthand, pulling the limp bodies of women and children from the rubble on more than one occasion. And it had changed him, leaving a scar on his soul that no one could heal.

It was not long before Cyrus became consumed by a desperate need for vengeance. Both for those he had been made to destroy, and his own people, who had long since fallen to the Predoran army. Over the years, Cyrus had observed the fallout. It was everywhere, even in nature. After a storm, trees came down, buildings were destroyed; sometimes they even claimed lives. Collateral damage was everywhere you looked, if you paid enough attention; the only difference was that this time the storm would be of his own making.

Pulling on his cloak, Cyrus made his way to the throne room to request an audience with Dracul. His pace was intense, his feet pounded through the castle corridors. He wanted to get this done before he changed his mind. When he made it to the large golden doors of the throne room, Cyrus was dismayed to find that Nico was still in audience with his father.

Pacing back and forth in front of the guards that flanked the huge doors, he reminded himself that this was the only way. Leaning against the wall, Cyrus finally managed to pull himself together while he waited. And when the doors were eventually thrown open, he spoke with his usual calm demeanour, nodding his head in acknowledgment to the prince.

"Your Highness."

Nico took a few steps towards him, before leaning in, his voice low.

"That went better than expected."

Eyebrows raised, Cyrus replied, "We're on, then?"

"It would seem so. Were you waiting for me?"

A smirk lingered on the prince's lips, and Cyrus shook his head. A cruel smile creeping from the corners of his mouth.

"No, I just need to discuss some things with Dracul. We all need to book an audience, it seems."

He chuckled darkly as Nico's lips formed into their own sinister smile, his hand patting Cyrus on the back in confirmation of their plan. There was no denying this was just another moment that made his current predicament worse.

Watching as Nico took off along the hallway, Cyrus found himself contemplating how much he would miss him, if something were to happen to the heir. Perhaps he should reconsider. Perhaps he should see what the king made of the plan Nico had put to him and go from there. Now irritated, he spoke to the guard and requested his audience. A few moments later he strode towards the king with purpose.

With the sudden attack of conscience tugging at his heart strings,

Cyrus warred in his mind as he approached the dais. He could not give up that control. His lust for power. He would not. Having the urge to lose himself in Nico was one thing. Their encounters were laced with danger, forbidden and exciting. But he would not allow himself to succumb to the temptation. Not when he had worked so hard all his life for this.

Fucking feelings.

Chapter Nine

Seeking Solace

Reaching his chambers, Nico threw the door wide open. Once, he thought, he would have flinched at the sound the door made as it slammed into the stone wall and echoed through his rooms and the castle corridor. Not anymore. Life had done this to him. Chewed him up and spat him out. To all the realm he was Nico Castillo, crown prince, heir to the throne of Predoran. Wealthy and educated; privileged, with the world at his feet. Outwardly he appeared cold and ruthless like his father, but it had not always been that way. Stalking across the room to his desk, Nico grabbed the cut-glass tumbler that sat next to a decanter of whiskey. Leaning over, he poured himself a glass and knocked it back before pouring another, slumping into the chair next to him.

The knots coiling in Nico's gut started to unravel as the sweet caramel liquid burnt its way through his insides. Worrying was not something he was known for, and yet it was something he did more often than not. It irked him. It was well known that worry led to distrust in the gods, and that in itself was a sin. But with his brother and his lover stepping into danger, how could he not fret?

Chewing the skin at his fingertips, Nico pictured his father's cruel smile and cold eyes as he had laid out their plans to him. It sickened him that Dracul held such blatant disregard for Bastian; and though he knew it was likely to be harder than he'd originally thought, Nico had to protect his brother at all costs. He would understand, eventually.

Cyrus, on the other hand, was smart and talented in many ways, and while Nico was sure Cyrus could take care of himself, these days he found himself thinking more often that, maybe, he wanted to be the one to take care of him. He certainly seemed to underestimate how much Nico enjoyed their time together. There was something Nico loved about how sharp and witty Cyrus was, his dark, dry humour soothing Nico's frayed edges. However, it seemed that, despite his intelligence, Cyrus could not sense how much Nico wanted him. He craved him. Cyrus was his confidant, he made

Nico's life make sense, and that in itself unnerved him. To have that level of trust in another being was to risk disaster, but Nico just had to hope that, in the end, Cyrus would be able to see the bigger picture.

The further down the decanter Nico sank, the more he relaxed back into the chair, until his worried mind slowed enough for him to contemplate what they would need for the journey. It would have to be a conventional trip across the sea. They could not arrive at the Glowing Isle in their dragon form without risking detection before they had even landed. He would instruct Cyrus to get them on a ship that could deposit them somewhere along the coast. Close enough that they could return to the city on foot, but not so close that the vessel would be easily noticed when it docked. What the ship did after that, Nico did not care, as long as it got them in. Mentally searching his wardrobe, he started a list of items to pack, already deciding what he would wear to the ball. Black trousers, a dark shirt and tie with a matching jacket. Black shoes were a must, too. Smart enough to get him in, but not so elaborate that he would be overly memorable. Nico planned to slip in unnoticed, allowing Bastian be the peacock. Plain tunics and slacks with boots, he thought, would work well for the rest of their stay.

Mulling over the options, Nico poured himself another glass of whiskey. He wanted to seek out Cyrus before his movements became too clumsy from the drink. He knocked back another glass of the dark liquid, which burnt his throat as he pushed himself to his feet. Moving through the castle corridors towards the other man's chambers, he could feel his limbs growing heavy. Nico was still moving fluidly, just about. It wouldn't be obvious he had been drinking, unless anyone stopped him, but the alcohol was starting to make its presence felt.

Throwing the door open wide, he strode in, kicking it shut behind him.

Raising an eyebrow at the prince, Cyrus got to his feet.

"Tell me what it was I said about the next time you forget to knock?"

He didn't have the chance to utter another word. Before he knew what was happening, Nico was pushing him backwards, until he was pressed up against the cold stone wall. Ripping his shirt free, Nico's fingers ran over the toned ridges of Cyrus's chest, his hands working their way up until they came to rest at the back of his neck. Hesitating for the smallest moment, their eyes met, and when he was satisfied that he saw no objection in them, Nico claimed his mouth. Feeling the man's heartbeat race as he kissed him back, Nico bit at his bottom lip, making Cyrus moan into his mouth. Sliding a hand around to his throat, Nico squeezed, tightening his hold, keeping him firmly in place. The rush of ecstasy within him at that moment was exquisite. Grinding against him, Nico could feel his erection pressed against his thigh. Relaxing his grip, an animalistic cry escaped him as Cyrus bit his way down the skin at the side of Nico's neck. He sunk his teeth into Nico's shoulder, before pushing them both away from the wall.

Guiding him backwards through a purple velvet curtain that divided the living quarters, Cyrus pushed Nico down onto the bed, and they fell in a tangle of limbs onto the soft mattress. Items of clothing landed on the floor as they undressed each other ravenously. Cyrus spat in his hand before palming Nico's aching cock. His grip was firm as he worked Nico slowly, teasing his thumb over the head, beads of liquid forming at the tip. It was only when Nico began thrusting up into Cyrus's hand, trying to gain momentum, that he quickened his pace. When the jerky movement of the hand gripping him stopped suddenly, Nico cried out in protest, but was relieved when the bare feeling of its absence was quickly replaced by the blunt pressure of a finger easing its way past that first ring of tight muscle.

Allowing his head to fall back onto the feather pillows, Nico looked up at Cyrus, whose skin glistened with a fine sheen of sweat as he worked a second finger into Nico's tight hole. The sight only further fuelled the burning need building inside of him. Grabbing a chunk of Cyrus's hair, he pulled his lover down to meet him. Their mouths collided, all teeth and tongues, as Cyrus blindly lined himself up, thrusting inside Nico in one fluid motion that had his eyes watering. Pain became pleasure as they chased solace together. Cyrus leant back, taking Nico in hand once more and working him to match each thrust of his hips. It wasn't long before Cyrus came, buried deep inside him, in turn tipping him over the edge, warm, salty liquid coating his chest as Nico found his own release.

Afterwards, they lay together, tangled between the sheets, for so long that the candles burned to stumps. All the while Nico listened to the steady beat of his lover's heart, his head resting on Cyrus's bare chest. Neither of them spoke, simply enjoying the feeling of being sated in one another's arms, until Cyrus finally broke the silence.

"Are you ready for the journey?"

"I think so. I would be lying if I said I didn't have reservations about it though."

"I know what you mean. Dracul did not seem as excited with our plan as I hoped he would be. How did he take it when you spoke to him?"

"Good to know you are thinking about my father after you have just fucked me."

Cyrus's brow wrinkled.

"Gods, don't say that."

Leaning down he planted a kiss on the top of Nico's head.

"He just seemed off, that's all."

"What? My father being anything other than his usual vicious self? Never."

"There's no need to be sarcastic."

Giving Nico a playful shove, Cyrus rolled him off before he manoeuvred himself to face him. Icy blue eyes stared back at him. Nico's expression was unreadable, as it often was.

"Dracul was fine with me. No different to normal. I thought he seemed quite pleased at the thought of a kidnapping and hostile takeover. Maybe he was just bored hearing the same plan twice?"

Rolling his eyes at Nico's jovial tone, Cyrus flicked his chest. Usually he was so uptight, the same vicious streak he had clearly inherited from his father coming out to play. But when they were alone, he wondered if Nico was capable of being serious. Perhaps it was the drink, but he seemed calmer when they were together, a light-hearted humour running through their interactions. The exception being when he was worried about his brother.

A dark chuckle emerged, vibrating through Cyrus's chest. Leaning in, he started to kiss his way down Nico's neck, then bit his way along his collarbone, both of them moving until the prince was pinned and writhing beneath him. In between panting breaths and needy kisses, Nico looked up at Cyrus, smiling at the intensity of his honey-coloured gaze.

"Hurt me, Cyrus. I want to still be able to feel where you've been tomorrow."

A sadistic smile crept across Cyrus's face, his features darkening.

"As you wish, Your Majesty."

Chapter Ten

Secrets & Betrayal

Relief flooded Astraea as they headed for home, her tense limbs loosening the nearer they got to the palace. Listening to Wren and Melana tell her how well she had done, she found her breathing starting to calm. The dispute had been relatively easy to resolve in the end. It had turned out that the problematic neighbour was keen to please when it was revealed that she was the princess. Whether that would last, only time would tell.

The carriage bounced on the uneven road, snatching Astraea from her thoughts, where she had been replaying the exchange on a loop. Even though she was relieved to be on the return journey, a new kind of anxiety threatened to take hold. Chewing her lip, she worried on what she could have said or done differently. As if worrying after the fact would make any difference at all.

"I did tell her it would be fine."

Looking up, Astraea was just in time to see Melana smack Wren's prosthetic, just as she had done when he spoke out of turn on the journey into town.

"Will you stop doing that, Mel? For the love of the gods, you know how much it hurts."

"It's alright Mel, leave him, he's fine."

When the white walls of the palace came into view, Astraea smiled, diverting their conversation to a topic she found more enjoyable.

"I'll tell you how you can make it up to me, Wren. When we get back, I would like to visit your chambers."

The smirk that graced her lips was hardly appropriate, but Astraea couldn't help herself, breaking into a laugh as Melana's eyebrows shot up in alarm.

"Relax, I am not propositioning your brother. I was merely going to suggest we visit Tormund upon our return."

Pleased to have a reason, Astraea let another hum of gentle laughter escape her chest. Laughing harder when both Wren and Melana visibly relaxed, chuckling along with her. Astraea was not the least bit offended. While she could acknowledge Wren's good looks, warmth and great humour, she loved him like a brother and nothing more.

* * * * *

The cedar door slid open silently, revealing Wren's modest room. He did not have a lot in the way of material possessions, but at the far wall was a charming bed with four tall wooden posts. Intricate carvings trailed along the wooden frame. A light green and silver canopy was suspended from the posts, with curtains that fell to the floor. All the bedrooms in the palace had them, to keep in the warmth at night.

The sun shone through the window at this time of day, hitting the bed right in the centre, making it a magnet for Tormund. As if on cue, a furry ginger face popped up from his resting place in the middle of the mattress on hearing their approach. The fluffy orange cat got up, stretching dramatically, then excitedly pawed at the blankets, pleased his fae had returned to him. Wren sat on one side of the cat, ruffling the fur on his head, planting several kisses on the top of it. Astraea sat on the other, gently running her fingers through his fur while fussing over him.

"Who's a good boy? Is it you? Yes, it is."

Astraea continued to praise Tormund, and the cat responded by rolling over to show her his stomach. As she tried to stroke him there, Tormund playfully grabbed at her hands with his paws, retracting them as her hands retreated, only for her to ruffle the fur on his belly again moments later. He never failed to make her laugh, no matter how many times they repeated this game. The cat always looked truly stunned that she had dared to touch him there. Astraea could see why Wren loved Tormund; he was a gentle being. More often than not, the animal had the appearance of being slightly startled, but he was always pleased to see Wren. And Astraea found herself wishing that she had a bond like that with someone, even if it was a cat.

For a while she allowed her fingers to tease their way through Tormund's fur, his purring lifting her mood considerably. The thought of having a day to herself tomorrow made all her worries begin to slip away. It would be good for Melana and Wren to have some time for themselves, too. Astraea always worried that they worked too hard. Even when the pair had time away from their duties, they were never far away. She would have felt sad if the selfish part of her hadn't found it so comforting.

Lost in thought, the princess was brought back to reality as Tormund let out a loud yowl. Her fingers had only paused in his fur momentarily, but it was long enough that he felt the need to make his objection heard. Rolling over, he started to headbutt her shoulder, causing her to start fussing him again. The creature's eyes grew wide as Wren came up behind him, scooping the fluffy cat into his arms like a baby.

"Who's my fatticus catticus? Is it you? Is it you?"

A giggle escaped Astraea. She turned to find Melana had joined her on the bed. It was strange to her, seeing her friend dote on his cat the way he did. Having seen him fight, she knew he was fierce, in more ways than one. When Wren had lost his leg as a child, he had worked hard to recover, but now he was an able soldier. In fact, he was one of the best; he had to be for Astraea's parents to have promoted Wren to her personal guard. Yet here he was, cradling Tormund like an infant, not the animal he was.

"You know, most people have a cat to keep rats out of the kitchens."

Although she had a point, Melana's tone was jovial. No one was entirely sure where Tormund had appeared from. One day he had just followed Wren back to his chamber, and had never left. There was every chance he was meant to be one of the cats that lived in the palace to keep the rodent population down. It was more than likely, because he was too well looked after to be a street cat. Rolling his eyes at his sister, Wren looked back down at the fat ginger fluff ball in his arms, cooing.

"Don't you listen to her, my boy. You are far too beautiful to be traipsing around in dirty places trying to catch rats."

Astraea couldn't help but smile at her friend as he hugged Tormund, planting another firm kiss on the animal's head. Most cats would have run a mile by now, but not this one. He was sprawled in Wren's arms, loving all the attention. Meowing loudly every time there was an interlude in the affection being lavished upon him.

"You know you actually need to escort the Princess back to her chambers, right?"

"Oh leave him Mel. Look how happy the pair of them are."

Sitting there for a moment, they watched Wren tell Tormund how he was his baby, and the princess thought that this probably was the happiest she had ever seen him. For a moment Astraea could have sworn she saw the fluff ball smile at her. She was clearly going mad. It was funny the places people found their happiness, but if one thing was certain, it was that Wren's was in the form of a daft ginger cat.

* * * * *

Later, alone in her suite, she embraced the silence. Unlike many others, Astraea thrived on her own company. Alone, but never lonely. If anything, it served to reset her mind, silencing the chaos that whirred through her head daily. Reclining in the plush rose-patterned chair that sat in the corner of her room, Astraea closed her eyes. Enjoying the moment, she soaked in the peace, until a firm knock at the door had her eyes flying open.

Quickly sitting up straight, Astraea fanned her skirt around her, smoothing it down in an attempt to look presentable as she replied, "Come in."

The door opened slowly. One of the queen's servants peered round it tentatively before stepping into the room. She was a slight lady in a pale green dress. Her long blonde hair pulled back off her shoulders, falling freely down her back.

"I'm sorry, Princess, the queen has asked me to fetch you. She wishes to speak with you."

Her words were softly spoken, sounding genuinely sorry to have had to disturb her. And rather like she would prefer to be anywhere else right now. Letting out a pained sigh, Astraea responded.

"Give me a moment."

Rising in a leisurely manner, she gently slid her shoes back onto her feet one at a time. All the while, the lady stood fidgeting with the seams of her dress, anxiously scrunching the fabric into little balls between her fingers. Something felt off. Her mother could be formidable, but the servants were not normally this jumpy – although the queen never usually sent her personal ones to find Astraea. While logically it made much more sense this way, usually it was a bizarre chain reaction, their servants, alerting Wren or Melana to her parents' requests, then one of them, usually Wren, fetching her to the throne room. Just the thought of them overcomplicating the task exhausted her.

Staring at her reflection in the mirror, Astraea straightened her tiara before giving herself one final look up and down. Taking a deep breath, she motioned to the young lady to lead the way. She followed the servant, hands clasped and spine stiff as they left the room.

* * * * *

Astraea approached, sweeping her way through the throne room with grace, while Queen Briana sat upon her silver throne. A shiver shot through her. It was a lot colder here at the palace's core, compared to the rest of the building. But then it was on the ground floor, the centrepiece in a maze of marble rooms, that sealed in the cold. Curtsying as she reached her mother, Astraea gently said, "You summoned me?"

Her mother looked taken aback for a moment, her hand reaching up to grasp at her neck as she inhaled sharply.

"Darling, can a mother not simply call upon her daughter for company? Come, sit with me."

Now Astraea knew something was amiss. Her mother was nice enough, as parents went. But she was a powerful woman who had no time for weakness, and as far as Astraea could tell, tolerated her these days at best. Nevertheless, she found herself lifting her dress daintily to ascend the steps, taking a seat next to the queen.

"How are you, my love? Fetch some tea, please."

Her mother spoke to her affectionately, while gesturing to the serving girl who had escorted Astraea in. She barely took a breath to break up her words, not bothering to address the woman separately. The maid curtsied. Leaving the room, she took the back stairs two at a time to get away. Astraea wondered what on earth was going on.

"I am well, mother. And you?"

"Yes, yes, quite well. Your father and I decided we need to talk to you."

Feeling herself pale, Astraea's brows pinched in concern, her lips pursing as she uttered, "Oh?"

The queen turned to face Astraea, grasping her hands within her own.

"Where is Father?" Astraea asked. "If you both need to speak to me?"

"Sweetheart, he thought it best I speak with you, since it is a delicate matter."

Astraea's lips began to tingle, as her breaths came out in tiny staccato bursts. She felt her blood run cold as she quickly lost the battle to remain calm.

"What do you mean?"

The queen stared at her for a moment, Astraea could not tell if it was pity or contempt that flitted across her features. It alarmed her even more.

"Mother?"

Her voice was strained, barely a whisper. In the silence that followed, Astraea found her mouth suddenly dry. It was as if the queen looked through her, nothing but an unfamiliar coldness residing behind her icy blue eyes.

"As you know, we will not live forever. You are of an age now where we must find you a suitor, someone who will be your prince, and one day your king. You must rule our land together. Your father and I, we have decided that at this year's independence ball, we will arrange for you to meet the most eligible men in Viriador. It will then be up to you to choose who you will be betrothed to. You may have a long courtship if you must, but the decision you make will be final."

All Astraea could do was gape at her mother.

"Come, Astraea, don't look at me like that. All the finest families are invited. We are sure to find you an excellent match."

Astraea felt sick. She had known this day would come eventually, but to have it sprung on her like this, with the ball only a couple of weeks away? It was too much.

"An excellent match? An excellent match? And what would you say makes an excellent match, Mother? How long will you give me to decide my fate? An hour, two? Or am I to believe I will find my love at first sight?"

Anger was creeping in, replacing the emptiness she had first felt at her mother's words. Someone was screeching, but Astraea did not care, even when she realised that it was her own voice ringing out around them.

"Has anyone ever stopped to think of my feelings? Who or what I want?"

"Oh, come now, dear," her mother cut in, "don't be so dramatic."

"Dramatic? How could you? I don't even know this man, and you tell me in a matter of days I am to be betrothed to him?"

Screaming now, salty tears streaked down her face.

"Is this why you summoned me alone, without my friends, because you knew they would object? Or did you just not care at all for my feelings?"

All traces of concern were gone now as her mother gripped her hands hard enough to make her fingers burn.

"It is not our fault you find friends in unsavoury places. Do you see myself or your father befriending the staff?" Briana said to her through gritted teeth.

Astraea pulled her hands away, clasping them to her face so that she could sob.

"Enough, child. It is decided. That is the end of it."

Without another word the queen got up, walking away just as the skittish young servant returned with a tea tray, dithering in the aisle clearly unsure what to do. The queen did not bother to stop and address her. Gasping in ragged gulps of air, tears continued to flow through Astraea's fingers.

"P—Princess?" The servant stuttered, still clutching the silver tray. "Are you alright?"

"No, no I'm not."

Still sobbing as she got to her feet, Astraea was blinded by her tears. Running past the woman, head still in her hands, she disappeared from the throne room alone.

Chapter Eleven

The Jasper

Below deck, Bastian lay cocooned in blankets, pretending he was asleep; all the while his gut churned with anxiety. Worry of what would happen on their mission consumed him. The smell in the hull did not help, either. It was a stale mix of salt water and rain that had crept below deck over time. Combined with the odour emanating from the ship's cargo, it was too overwhelming for him. The barrels surrounding them held a mixture of alcohol and spices that all had their own distinct aromas. Bastian couldn't face small talk to pass the time when he was feeling so jittery. He would have felt better about the plan if it were just him and his brother; Cyrus had the ability to make Bastian feel stupid and like an inconvenience more often than not. He still wasn't entirely sure he trusted Cyrus, but it was too late for that now. They had managed to secure passage on the *Jasper*, a trade ship, whose course would pass Viriador. Nico had paid the crew handsomely for agreeing to let them off on the shores of the Glowing Isle.

Sitting on a barrel in the corner, Nico leant back against the wooden hull. From where he lay, Bastian cracked an eye open, noticing how tense his brother seemed. Nico's jaw was too tight, his gaze steely as he ground his teeth. The golden dragon on his finger chased its tail as he turned the ring repeatedly. Cyrus, on the other hand, seemed totally at ease, reclined in a hammock, his hands clasping the edges of an old book that rested on his chest. Bastian thought he looked *too* relaxed, watching the hammock sway gently with the rolling movements of the Jasper.

Letting his eye slip shut again, Bastian pulled the blankets tighter around himself, hoping the ship's motion might rock him to sleep. He started awake a while later when a quiet voice whispered into the darkness. Unsure how much time had passed, Bastian's ears pricked up, and he found himself suddenly alert. As he lay there, he heard Cyrus carefully climb down from the hammock, before making his way quietly through the barrels. Risking another glimpse, Bastian saw Nico hop down from his perch, sliding down the wall to sit on the floor next to Cyrus, who had done the same thing a moment before. It was unsurprising if they wanted to have a conversation in private, but Bastian did have to stifle a gasp, watching as Nico took Cyrus's hand in his, running his thumb over the backs of his fingers before pulling his adviser into his arms, their mouths colliding in a needy kiss that had Bastian squeezing his eyes closed again.

Now he could add the shock of that to his never-ending catalogue of emotional turmoil. Of all the people for Nico to be involved with, Bastian couldn't quite believe it was that arsehole. Anyone with half a brain cell knew that Cyrus only cared about himself. That man had clawed his way to where he was now, not caring who he'd had to step on to get there, his reputation for ruthlessness preceding him. What was his brother thinking? Although, he supposed, at times his brother could be just as bad.

Their voices resumed, drifting through the darkness, and Bastian found himself straining to hear them as he lay there trying to keep his breathing steady.

"This would be so much easier if it was just us."

A sharp stab of betrayal hit Bastian at his brother's admission.

"It will be alright. I won't let anything happen to him, Nico. You have my word."

The pair sat gazing fiercely into each other's eyes.

"That does not stop me worrying. I fear for you, too."

"I will be fine, I assure you. I'm more powerful than any fae, and so are you. If only Bastian wasn't so weak... He is a liability, you know."

Bastian's blood ran cold as he lay there feigning sleep, attempting to eavesdrop on the pair's true intentions. His heartbeat slowed, fear creeping in, until he heard his brother come to his defence.

"Cyrus." Nico's voice growled with warning as he scolded the other man, but his tone softened immediately. "He is my baby brother. I couldn't bear it if something happened to him because of me – because of us."

"Nothing is going to happen, Nico. We will go in, get the girl, and get out as quickly as possible. We will be halfway back to Predoran before they even realise she's gone."

"I'm always going to worry, you know that."

A pained look clung to the prince's features as Cyrus reached up, running his fingers over the shell of Nico's ear, before letting them trail down the side of his neck.

"Yes, and I feel privileged to be one of the few that do. I bet nobody else would believe that you sometimes cry yourself to sleep over the things your father does. The people believe the apple has not fallen far from the tree. In that respect, you have been very convincing."

"Cyrus, please, don't ever compare me to my father."

"You know I don't mean it. Not like that. I know who you truly are. You and Dracul are nothing alike."

"Just don't get cocky when you're there."

Rolling his eyes Cyrus responded.

"Bah, me cocky? I don't know what you mean."

Nico laughed but his voice remained stern.

"I'm serious. I don't know what I would do without you, Cyrus."

Bastian felt so sad for his brother. He'd had no idea he was so affected by the things Dracul had made him do. Wanting to comfort him, he watched silently as Cyrus stroked the side of his brother's face tenderly. Leaning in, Nico rested his head on the shoulder of his adviser, before he in return leant into Nico as they got comfortable on the floor together.

* * * * *

The noise of the crew moving about loudly on deck woke Bastian with a start. He must have drifted off to sleep again after all. Rolling over on the hard floor, he saw that Cyrus and Nico were still huddled against each other, eyes closed. If it was anyone other than Cyrus, Bastian would have found it sweet, the way they were cuddled up, their fingers entwined. Stretching, he yawned loudly, but failed to get the pair to stir.

Once Bastian got to his feet, he debated waking them, but thought it might be wiser to use the time to recharge his magic. The last thing he wanted today was to be on the receiving end of Cyrus's sarcasm. Knowing that the man kept some gold coins in the bag that was still in the hammock, Bastian decided that it wouldn't hurt to have a quick rummage. He was only borrowing them, after all. After a quick search, Bastian retrieved several coins. Turning, he found Cyrus staring straight at him, his eyebrows raised, and an accusatory look on his face.

"What the hell are you doing with my gold?"

"Relax, I'm just borrowing it."

"What's going on?" Nico asked as he rolled his shoulders, stiff from his awkward sleep.

"Bastian was stealing my gold."

"I was *borrowing* it."

In a flash Cyrus was on his feet, crossing the space and squaring up to him.

"So you say."

"Look, I tried to wake you up, but you two were too busy snuggling in your sleep."

Nico stood up slowly, his face suddenly flushed with colour.

"Stop it, the pair of you. Here, have some of my gold if you want to charge your power."

Angrily shoving the coins at Cyrus, Bastian pushed his way past him, making his way over to his brother, who held out one of his own gold bars to him.

"You can keep it, as long as you promise to try and be nice to Cyrus."

Bastian's eyes grew wide.

"*Me* be nice? He started it."

Pointing across the hull at him, Cyrus snapped, "I think you'll find he did, when he went poking through my things."

Bastian's eyes shifted to slits.

"Got something to hide then?"

Looking down his nose at Bastian, Cyrus replied, his tone dripping with sarcasm.

"Only my gold, apparently."

Whirling to face him, Nico snapped, "Oh, do shut up, Cyrus."

Irritated by Nico's intervention, Cyrus flopped back into the hammock, huffing.

"Merely stating facts."

Taking the gold, Bastian placed a hand on his brother's shoulder. Leaning in he spoke quietly, "I knew you liked men, but…"

He trailed off, unsure of how to voice his opinion kindly. Nico smirked.

"I like women, too. What's your point?"

"It had to be Cyrus, didn't it? Seriously, what do you see in him?"

"Bastian."

"Fine, fine. I will be nice, jeez."

Rolling the gold bar in his palm, Bastian walked over to the other side of the hold. Pulling himself up onto a barrel, he sat, letting the energy it released flow through him. It was a struggle to ignore Cyrus and Nico mumbling on the other side, and Bastian was just about to moan at them when one of the crew shouted down to them,

"Land ahoy!"

Chapter Twelve

The Sun Will Set Eventually

Standing on the shore, Cyrus studied Bastian, the young prince watching as the boat sailed away from them. His gaze remained steadfast until it became little more than a speck on the horizon. Cyrus struggled, as he often did, to believe that a ruthless bastard like Dracul could father such a sensitive soul. It almost made him feel sorry for Bastian. Almost. Pulling the leather strap of the satchel over his head, he turned away, thrilled to see the back of the vessel. Cyrus had not enjoyed their voyage one bit. History made it hard for him; he still detested boats of any kind. The motion, the smell, the confined space. All of it. It had taken everything he could muster to keep himself composed. Surprisingly, he had found that it helped when he had gone to Nico. They had comforted one another, and he had found it had distracted him from worrying about their surroundings. Cyrus had been pleased when they had both somehow managed to succumb to sleep.

Still, Cyrus couldn't help but feel that they were both conflicted for very different reasons. He was confident in their mission, although still slightly rattled by the king's reaction to his presentation. If there was one thing Dracul did not do, it was sit on the fence. He always had very strong opinions, which he would voice loudly to any who would listen. Nico, on the other hand, was having a moral crisis over blindsiding his brother, and potentially having to plot his father's demise. A peaceful relief washed over Cyrus with the thought that at least he didn't have to worry about family politics. The only silver lining to come out of his traumatic childhood, he supposed. He would worry about the ethics later.

Thick green foliage paved the horizon beyond the sand. Nico stood facing it as he studied a creased and faded map, running his finger over it as he traced the path to the city. Peering over his shoulder, Cyrus said, "I think we can reach the city by nightfall."

"We could get there quicker if we just—"

Cutting him off, Nico balled his fists in frustration, crinkling the map's edges.

"No. We stay in human form. I'm not willing to risk shifting until we are leaving the Isle."

"Is that in case we are seen, or in case he runs out of power?"

Nico sneered as Cyrus smirked, motioning towards his brother. Instantly, Cyrus knew he had overstepped, again, not that he was all that bothered.

"Both."

The word was ground out so quietly, Cyrus almost missed it.

"This would be so much easier if we could all get along, you know. Are you two going to keep making it difficult?"

Cyrus could argue his point, but he didn't want to upset Nico further, and he did not want to offer an insincere apology – not to him. Taking a breath to compose himself, Cyrus simply pretended that that part of the conversation had not happened.

"So, what's the plan once we reach the city?"

Narrowing his eyes Nico sighed. He glanced back down at the map. Circling a patch with his finger, he offered, "We should be able to find somewhere to get a room for the night in the city. They must have taverns, and if not, I'm sure we can find somewhere to hunker down."

"And then?"

"Then we wing it. We need to get close to the princess, but we cannot draw attention to ourselves."

"And how do you propose we do that, then?"

Nico's head rose, biting down on his lip. Cyrus followed his gaze until it came to rest on Bastian, who was still watching the waves break on the shore.

Cyrus clapped Nico on the back.

"And they say I'm the clever one."

* * * * *

The heat of the midday sun was unrelenting. The three men pushed on through lush green foliage as they made their way inland. Sweat soaking their skin, their clothes clung to them. Cyrus wondered how true it was that the further inland they got, the cooler it would be. He really hoped the theory proved correct. At this rate, they would have to make camp for the night and try to push on tomorrow.

They were all used to the heat. In reality, Predoran was probably far hotter than this, but it didn't feel that way now. This was a wet heat, if such a thing was possible, and they were all struggling with the humidity. At least in Predoran the heat was as dry as the desert sand.

Up ahead, Cyrus could hear Bastian whining to Nico that he could not continue like this, and he was not wrong: the heat was stifling. Maybe they would have to shift into their dragon forms, to rest if nothing else. Might as well utilise their ability to make themselves cold blooded. Bastian had obviously come to the same conclusion and as much as it pained him, Cyrus agreed with the younger prince.

"Please, Nico, I can't go on much longer, it's too hot. I can't breathe properly."

"No, absolutely not. It is too dangerous."

"He's got a point, actually. Have you ever seen a sweaty reptile?"

Nico rounded on him, fists balled at his sides.

"Gods, Cyrus, whose side are you on?"

Cyrus smirked, much to Nico's irritation.

"My own."

"Well, you two do what you like. We've been here five bloody minutes and you're already trying to get us all killed."

Huffing, he walked towards the bushes. "I'll be over here."

Laughing aloud, Cyrus asked, "You aren't seriously hiding in a bush, are you? There's no one out here."

"Cyrus, I'm going to rest under that tree, and if anyone stumbles upon us, I'll be the first to be screaming 'dragon' along with the rest of them."

"Well don't mind us, we'll just be over here, happily regulating our body temperature."

Cyrus was too hot and irritable to care when Nico turned on his heel and stormed the few feet to the bushes, before sitting bunched against a tree. Nico pulled his limbs in tightly, wrapping his arms around his bent knees to hug them. Closing his eyes, he muttered something about the pair of them in exasperation.

Dumping his bag and clothing on the ground, Bastian shifted first. Orange scales rippled over his skin until only his dragon remained. Cyrus watched Bastian's posture visibly relax as he laid down in the shade. After stripping his own clothes off, placing them neatly to one side, Cyrus joined him.

Closing his eyes, he let the reptilian scales shroud him. They ran the length of his body, a combination of blue hues that shimmered in the light that broke through the leaves. His dragon was only slightly larger than Bastian's, but Cyrus positioned himself in front of him anyway, almost blocking the young prince from view. Feeling him stir, Cyrus spoke softly, "Relax, I've got you."

"Now what's going on?"

Obviously, he had not been quiet enough. Raising his head, Cyrus saw Nico staring at the pair of them intently, his nostrils flared. He looked angry – no, he looked hurt.

"I thought you didn't like him?"

"Not jealous are you, Castillo?"

"No, I'm just never quite sure what you're up to."

Cyrus let the sides of his mouth lift into a tooth-filled grin,

"Don't worry. I said I would keep him safe, did I not? And I am nothing if I am not a man of my word. Relax, go to sleep. I will look after him."

"Why do you always talk about me like I'm not here?" Bastian said.

"Because you are a liability. Now if you don't mind, I'd like to rest."

Curling up, Cyrus was satisfied to know he could still baffle Nico, even after all this time. There was something rather empowering about knowing he was probably lying there now, second guessing everything. A wry smile crept across his face at the sound of Bastian grumbling as he got comfortable. But the noise was soon replaced, their makeshift camp engulfed in little snores that Bastian unleashed onto the breeze.

As soon as it was cooler, they would move again. The sun would set eventually.

Chapter Thirteen
Pain Is Inevitable

No one came.

Her parents did not even bother to check if she was alright.

They had never had much to do with raising Astraea. They claimed they loved her, but evidently, they must have felt their job ended when the queen birthed her. Sadly, she still loved them both, and their indifference cut her deeply.

Laying on her bed, all thoughts of royal protocol forgotten, Astraea sobbed into her pillow. Ripping the tiara from her hair, she flung it across the room. It landed noisily, sliding across the marble floor. She did not care if it was broken. Astraea did not want this. The throne. A prince. None of it. One day, she wanted to get married, but to someone she loved. Not now. Not like this. Her whole body shook as her tears consumed her.

"It's not fair. It's just not fair."

Sobbing into her pillow, she was only thankful that her friends were not here to see what she had been reduced to.

Chapter Fourteen
All The Little Lights

The afternoon sun shone high in the sky above them as Melana and Wren bounced down the palace steps, fully intending to embrace a rare day off together. It was a treat, this close to the palace, to be able to feel the sun warming your skin. The Glowing Isle had a strange climate: the east coast was always very hot, but then Melana supposed it was because it was the closest point to Predoran. The further inland you got, the colder the weather seemed. Especially heading out of Viriador towards Carpathia. The city centre was cold – not bitterly for the most part, but snow fell on occasion, and sunny days were unusual to say the least. Wren always teased her that it was because the lands were enchanted, for it was a well-known fact that the fae favoured the cold here over the heat of the lands they had left behind.

Racing down the narrow lanes that wound through the city, Melana could hear Wren somewhere behind, shouting for her to slow down. But it was such a lovely day, and running through the streets in the glorious sunshine made her feel so free. Eventually, she slowed enough for him to catch up as they neared the main square, the Lunar Cathedral coming into view in all its glory. Whirling on Wren as he reached her, Melana grabbed his hand, dragging him out of the lanes into the main square.

"I love this place. I still find it so enchanting, even after all this time."

Beaming up at him, Melana waited for a response, but Wren was still trying to catch his breath. She was somewhat breathless herself, but he was panting. Wren was a warrior: fast, physically fit, and surprisingly agile, given the disadvantage of a wooden leg; but he was clearly not built for long-distance sprints.

"Architecturally, it is a marvel, I agree."

His breathing began to slow as Melana gave him a small snort of disgust.

"Do you not feel it is so much more than that? Every time I see this place, our people, our cathedral, I feel like I am seeing it all for the first time."

Scrunching his nose, Wren replied with indifference.

"The building is beautiful, I agree. But other than that, it is just another fancy marketplace."

Melana gestured around them, arms wide, spinning with her face turned to the sky, as the sun warmed her skin.

"Oh, Wren open your eyes, it's so much more. When I am here, I feel alive."

The cathedral towered over the square. It had three sweeping archways at the front. Each one had a large circular glass window and was decorated with carvings of flowers blooming skyward, each with their own unique, detailed pattern. In the centre were huge wooden doors, and high above them was the real marvel. The main window, housed in the very heart of the building, the glass-encased symbol of their kingdom. An upturned crescent moon that held the sun and, either side of it, a star. The crystal used for the design sparkled in the sunlight. Continuing for several more stories, the building climbed towards the clouds. Small windows were cut into the stonework, and on either side of the cathedral stood two heavily decorated turrets. On each pillar, suns were carved in the east, to represent the rising of the new day; the west had the moon to complete the cycle. In between them at north and south were hundreds of cut-out stars, letting the sun- or moonlight pass through the turrets as the hours passed. That was Melana's favourite part to look at, but she also loved the words carved just over the door: 'Greatness does not lie in wealth or power, but in love, kindness and compassion. We are all born with the same blank slate. Use the time you have wisely.'

Even the market here enchanted Melana. Everywhere was lit up with little lanterns that ran on lines between the stalls, so come nightfall, it looked simply serene. The stalls themselves were little wooden huts that had small sloping roofs; the fronts came to waist-height, so that the wares available were on display inside.

This market was definitely Melana's favourite one. There was nothing wrong with the finery available at the stalls selling their wares in the courtyard of the palace, but it wasn't the same. The items on offer here were the type of things both her and Wren had grown up with, as well as some finer specimens. The pair milled between the huts, seeing what stock they held. It wasn't long before Melana had Wren offering to carry her bag. It held a new skirt and some foods she had picked out, along with a couple of books that he had picked up.

They wandered for a while longer, looking at materials, silks and satins on reels, spices that had been imported, and jewellery. Melana had just finished filling a bag with fresh fruits when she heard Wren inhale sharply, making a sound somewhere between a gasp and a sigh. Handing over coin for the fruit, Melana wandered the couple of stalls over to where she found Wren stroking the hilt of a finely formed dagger.

"Now, that is beautiful."

Wren's voice was silky; he clearly dreamed of owning the dagger at his fingertips. There were many swords on display too, but he already had one of the finest around. Even now it was at his side. Its scabbard rarely left his hips, even for a simple trip into the city.

"Do you really need it? You already have a fine sword, Wren."

"I don't need it, per se, so much as want it."

"Would you add it to your scabbard?"

"No."

Melana could swear she saw his eyes glitter, his pupils shifting slightly, but it must have been a trick of the light.

"I'd attach it to my thigh. Handy backup should I ever need it."

Wren winked at her, eyes back to normal, and Melana shook her head, thinking that the unusual heat must be getting to her.

"Shame I cannot afford it. Do you want a drink? I'm parched."

Nodding, Melana found herself saying, "You go on, I just need a moment. I want to look at some silks."

She did not turn to look at the silks, instead watching Wren walk towards the small stall that sold refreshments. Melana waited until she was satisfied he was out of earshot before turning back to the blacksmith's stall. Stroking her fingers over the cool metal, she could not deny that the dagger was well crafted. The hilt itself was made of gold, with a small dragon's head pressed to the blade. Either side of the hilt, two pieces stuck out, crafted as wings, and a small tail coiled the length of the handle. It was a strange piece – something that would not normally be seen in these parts – but she could see why he liked it. Once Melana had caught the vendor's eye, she asked, "How much for this?"

"A hundred gold pieces, Miss."

Sighing, Melana reached into the money bag at her waist. This was most of her savings from the last few months. But it would be worth it to see Wren's face light up when she gave it to him. Besides, what else was she going to spend it on? Handing over the gold, Melana watched the blacksmith put the dagger into a small wooden box, then place it into a cloth bag, before handing it over to her.

"Many thanks, lovely."

"And many thanks to you."

Smiling at the man, Melana turned to find Wren, relieved to see he had not gone far. Still at the drinks stall, he waved her over, offering her a tankard with some kind of red wine in it.

"Wren, that's hardly going to hydrate us."

"No, but it will make us have more fun."

He nudged her, dragging her over to sit on the little stone wall on the outskirts of the square. The pair sat there for a while, laughing and joking as they drained their tankards.

The evening drew in, the little lanterns glowed, illuminating everything around them now; burning like hundreds of fireflies trapped in glass cages. Once Melana's cup had run dry, she retrieved the wooden box and presented it to Wren, her smile radiant and sincere despite the alcohol.

"I got you something."

Carefully, he took the box from her, stroking the wood, eventually peeking inside and then quickly dropping the lid closed again shocked.

"Melana, you didn't."

Wren's eyes were wide as he opened the box again, this time placing the lid on the wall next to him. He let his fingers brush along the golden dragon that was part of the dagger's hilt.

"Call it an early birthday present."

"Thank you."

"You're welcome."

"No, really, Mel. Thank you. It is wonderful."

Wren's eyes filled with tears as he leant in, planting a kiss on her cheek and hugging her tightly. He whispered into her ear, "Thank you."

But as he pulled away, retrieving the dagger from its box and holding it across his palms to study it, Melana could have sworn she saw his pupils change again. Just for a split second. She really should not have had wine in this heat, but it had been far too long since they had spent a few hours having fun out in the world together. Melana was about to suggest they get some food from one of the vendors, to try and soak up the drink, when Wren froze. Goosebumps trailed along his flesh despite the heat, making the hair on his arms stand on end. The colour drained from his face, turning his skin ashen.

"Wren?"

"Can you feel it?"

"Feel what?"

Melana watched Wren's eyes flicker madly across the market square, as he searched for something, or someone. She was not sure which.

"Someone's watching us. I can feel it."

"I think you've had too much to drink."

Laughing, Melana stroked his arm, attempting to get up, but Wren pulled her back down.

"No, really, Mel. It's like I can feel them in my mind, watching me. Does that make any sense?"

Melana eyed him warily. A concerned expression creeping across her face.

"None at all."

Standing, she started to pull Wren up with her.

"Come on, put the fancy knife back in its box. We're going to get some food, and then we can head back and find somewhere quiet to relax in the palace. I think we've both been out in the heat too long."

Chapter Fifteen

Enchanted

When Cyrus woke, the temperature had dropped, and though it was still humid, it was bearable. Aware the young prince still slept soundly beside him due to the flurry of small movements and noises Bastian made as he dreamt, Cyrus decided he should wake him. They would have to get moving soon. Opening his eyes to check on Nico, a small rumble of laughter rolled through Cyrus's chest. The space where the crown prince had been propped up was now vacant, but it did not take long to spot him. Clearly, he had thought better of staying in his human form, as protruding from the bushes next to them was a large, scaly snout. Given the sheer size of Nico's dragon, Cyrus was amazed that he had managed to conceal himself at all.

Drawing his dragon back from the surface, Cyrus morphed, pulling his black tunic over his head as he made his way over to Nico. Sitting down beside him, Cyrus stroked the red dragon's snout. After a few grumbles of irritation, the animal opened its mouth and yawned. Suddenly, the scaley nose surged forward from the bushes, and his reptilian eyes scanned the area wildly.

"Hey, down here. It's just me."

Nico retracted his dragon in a fraction of a second, probably the fastest Cyrus had ever seen him shift, leaving Nico stood naked before him. His pupils were dilated, and as much as Cyrus would have liked to think it was because he was there, it was most likely the adrenaline rush of impending danger. Laughing quietly, he picked up the pile of clothes next to them, offering them to Nico.

"We should get going while we've got the light. Get dressed. I'll wake Bastian."

Nico reached over, stroking the stubble that lined Cyrus's jaw.

"Try not to give him a heart attack when you do."

As it happened, he didn't have to do much to wake Bastian. He was already yawning, scratching an itch on his neck like an oversized dog, when Cyrus leant in to tell him they were leaving. After a bit more fidgeting, scratching, and another dramatic yawn, Bastian eventually joined them, pulling his clothes on as the pair discussed where they would head next.

Poring over the map, they quickly realised they had actually covered more ground than they had initially thought. If Cyrus was correct, they should start coming across some form of civilisation soon. And as much as he hated to admit when he was wrong, Cyrus could see that the trio had been lucky to not be discovered this close to a settlement. Nico was right: meat suits only from here on out.

Pressing on down the overgrown path they hoped would lead them towards the city, the men were all more at ease in the cool evening air. Finally, as the hours wore on, they found the outskirts of the city. Everything here looked so fresh, so clean. They passed rows of houses, the light-coloured buildings practically glittering in the sunlight. The closer they got to the centre, the more people they came across, their idle chatter growing louder. Cyrus mused at the stark contrast between the two lands. The women they passed were dressed in long floating dresses, bangles and decorations laced over their skin. They moved gracefully, practically gliding as they made their way along the smooth streets. The men's clothing was similar to their own, although their tunics were mostly lighter in colour. Everything here seemed to have a light and airy feel.

When they reached the outskirts of a bustling market at the centre of the city, Nico placed a hand on Cyrus's shoulder.

"Do we need any supplies?"

"Not really. A good meal would be nice though."

The pair turned to find Bastian marvelling at the lights, enchanted by their beauty in the gathering dusk. When he saw them staring at him, he snapped, "What? They're twinkly. I like them! Why don't we have anything like this back home?"

Cyrus rolled his eyes.

"Liability."

"Yes, you keep saying that."

Cyrus turned to Nico, dismayed to find him irritated again.

"Well, I am right, am I not?"

Growling, Nico moved to his brother's side, leaving Cyrus smirking to himself.

Meandering through the stalls, Bastian's expression was one of wonder. Taking it all in with a reverence usually reserved for the gods themselves. He made them stop to look at swords and clothing, full of awe. In particular, Bastian was taken with a stall that sold jewellery, of the kind that everyone around them seemed to have decorating their skin.

While he attempted to persuade Nico to let him buy a bangle, Cyrus followed his nose. There was no doubt there was an exquisite smell in the air. Freshly baked bread and spices clung to the warm evening air, filling it with a fabulous aroma, but that wasn't what had caught Cyrus's attention. Wandering through the rows of wooden huts, he found the smell that had been calling to him. A vendor was selling beef stew that came swimming in a giant fluffy pastry, the likes of which he had not seen before. Splendid. Cyrus looked over his shoulder to check the brothers were still where he had left them. Seeing them still in debate, Bastian holding up a bangle, he got himself a plate of food. Sitting on a nearby bench, Cyrus ate while he waited for them.

Tucking in with vigour, he quickly decided that whatever this crispy dough was, it was one of the best things he had ever eaten. He had almost finished devouring the meal when the hairs on the back of his neck stood on end. A strange feeling crawled its way over his skin. Cyrus could feel his dragon stirring, which it rarely did on its own unless he was in danger. But this felt different. His dragon was crying out, agitated, fighting him as he tried to sooth it back to sleep. Looking back to the others, he could see they hadn't moved yet, and Nico was handing over money, meaning Bastian had got his way. *Of course he had.* But there did not appear to be any sign of imminent danger. Warily scanning the marketplace, his gaze eventually came to rest on a young man some distance behind him, seated on a wall with a female companion. His breathing slowed as Cyrus allowed his eyes to wander over the man. His light brown skin was flawless, and his dark hair hung in curls that framed his face. Cyrus felt a million butterflies unfurl in his stomach. *Curious.* The longer he stared in their direction, the more unnerved he felt; especially when the man suddenly turned, looking around as if he could feel his gaze on him. Cyrus quickly turned away. Could it be that the fae sensed him watching, the same way Cyrus had felt his presence? Well, this was an interesting development.

Before he'd had time to think on it too much, Nico and Bastian joined him. Bastian talking too loudly, and Nico scolding Cyrus for eating without them. They eventually went to get some food of their own, leaving Cyrus to his thoughts once more. When he glanced back, the man and his companion had gone. Shaking off the strange feeling, Cyrus allowed his dragon to settle once more, while he finished his food.

Chapter Sixteen

The Path of Least Resistance

Knocking at Astraea's door, Melana had a huge smile on her face. Giddy still from their day of freedom, gallivanting around in the city. Wren was pleased for her; he had enjoyed himself too, despite the unnerving moment when he was sure he was being watched. Not that he could explain it at all well. Melana had dragged him back to the palace, making him go and sit down before bringing him cold water to calm him. It had been a strange feeling, like someone was calling out to something deep in his soul. That was what had unsettled him the most: the feeling that something was trying to claw its way inside his mind.

A shudder rolled over him, and Wren's attention was drawn back to the present as Melana's smile vanished. She was now banging harder on the door, calling out to Astraea.

"Princess? Are you in there? Please open the door."

Wren's hand dropped to his sword, drawing it from the scabbard as a shrill voice rang out.

"Go away!"

"Astraea, it's just us. What's wrong?"

"I said go away."

Melana looked at Wren, panic-stricken at the distress in Astraea's voice. Scenarios of intruders, the princess being held at knifepoint, flashed through his mind. He didn't hesitate. Sword drawn, he barged into her chambers, looking around wildly, only relaxing when he was sure she was, in fact, there alone. Satisfied there was no threat, Wren sheathed his sword again, furious that a guard had not been stationed at her door in his absence. Melana bent down to their friend, who sat staring into space.

The princess was a mess. She sat on the floor, head leant back against the wall. Her hair was all over the place, her eyes puffy, face red. Melana's hand left Astraea's shoulder as she reached out to the princess's tiara that lay on the cold marble. Wren watched anxiously as Melana's fingertips brushed the tiara. Lifting it to look at the diamonds' reflective surface, she gasped in a breath, a few moments passing before she placed it back on the floor. Pushing it away, Melana leant back, her bottom resting on her heels.

"They didn't."

Astraea looked up to meet her friend's gaze, tears still rimming her own, her bottom lip wobbling.

"They did."

Melana pulled her into a tight embrace, causing Astraea to sob again. Wren was not sure when it would be appropriate to ask what was going on. He was pretty sure this was not the time, but he needed to know what was happening here.

"Do I need to kill anyone, Princess?"

The question only seemed to make her cry harder. Melana looked back at him over her shoulder, hissing.

"Unless you fancy killing her parents, I suggest you stay quiet."

Astraea pulled out of Melana's embrace, wiping the tears from her face with the backs of her hands.

"Leave him, it's not his fault."

"No, you're right, it is no one's fault but theirs. Honestly, I don't know where they keep all their audacity. They don't speak to you from one week to the next, and then this?"

Sitting down beside them, Wren took Astraea's hand, smiling when she turned to look at him.

"I'll still kill them if you want me to."

Wincing as Melana smacked the join of his prosthetic, he still managed to wink at the princess.

"They are marrying me off."

"Oh." Wren squeezed her hand. "Well, wherever you go, Princess, I will be at your side."

"As will I," Melana agreed.

"I don't think I'm going anywhere."

Astraea flung her arms about in theatrical fashion as she spoke.

"They want me to marry a high-born fae, so that one day I will have a king to rule Viriador at my side. They want us to live here as prince and princess until their deaths, and then we will ascend to the throne."

"Do we know who this man is? Can we find out about him? It might make you feel better."

A fresh wave of anger swept through Wren. How dare they? Why couldn't her parents just let Astraea meet someone and fall in love in her own time? Why couldn't they just give her this small slice of normality? What was the sudden urgency? He fumed at their need to control everything, watching Melana stroke their friend's arm as she tried to soothe her, before she answered in her place.

"At the next ball, there will be eligible young men presented to her. Then she must pick one. Is that right?"

They both watched Astraea nod silently. Wren thought it could be worse, but didn't dare voice that.

"How about we make a list of the sons from the high-born families? We can write out pros and cons for each one."

"Wren."

Melana's tone told him he was overstepping.

"Please don't hit me again, Mel. I'm only trying to help."

"Actually, that's not a bad idea."

Astraea straightened herself a bit, her breathing settling down as her tears finally stopped.

"Perhaps I should control what I can, if the rest is out of my control."

Chapter Seventeen

Eligible Bachelors

The three friends sat on Astraea's oversized bed, making lists of the eligible high-born fae who were likely to attend the ball.

Handing some parchment and a quill to Astraea, Melana said, "Shall we start with Jeffery? I am sure he will be top of your mother's list."

"Ugh, Jeffery. Do we have to?"

Astraea rolled her eyes, while Wren wrinkled his nose in disgust.

"I can give you all the cons," he supplied enthusiastically.

"Jeffery will never love anyone but himself. He thinks he is incredibly good-looking. He is arrogant and has no sense of humour."

Frowning, the princess looked as if she might cry again.

"A total catch then."

"Wren."

Melana glared at him with intent.

"There must be something nice about him."

"In fairness, I can't think of anything either."

Shrugging her shoulders, Astraea sighed. Flopping back onto the bed dramatically, she announced, "I'm doomed."

"Stop being dramatic, the pair of you," Melana blurted at them.

"What about Henry?"

Wren quirked an eyebrow.

"King's guard Henry?"

"Why not? He is a hard worker, he's kind, and he is also pleasant to look at."

Melana feigned irritation as Wren rolled his eyes again. She knew he'd had a crush on Henry for years. Not that it was ever reciprocated, to her knowledge.

"I'm pretty sure he doesn't like ladies."

His voice mumbled so they could barely hear. Astraea bounced up onto her knees in response.

"Oh Wren, you didn't. You dark horse. Do tell!"

"We only kissed in the stables a couple of times, there is nothing to tell really. It's not like we are together or anything like that."

Exasperated, Melana forcefully placed a hand on each of their shoulders.

"Please focus. Do you have anything helpful to add, Wren? Does he like women too?"

"I can't say I've ever asked him."

Now she was rolling her eyes as he blushed, colour filling his cheeks.

"Alright, who else will be there?"

"Kevlar?"

Even as he said it, Melana could see the shudder that rolled over Wren, who quickly added, "Perhaps not."

"Brody?"

"Brody does have potential," Wren mused.

"Don't you think he's a bit of a drip?"

Astraea glanced between her friends, a pained look marring her features.

"I mean, I think he just needs a little shaping."

Melana could see Wren was trying to be helpful, but truth be told, she could see where Astraea was coming from.

"So, positives for Brody?"

Astraea wrote his name at the top of the page hesitantly, while Melana reeled off a list of his good points.

"Brody is kind, he is good to his parents and his sister. He is not too bad to look at."

"He reads," Wren added, knowing that would tick one of Astraea's many boxes.

"He has a horse."

Astraea added that to the list herself. And it made her smile. It was the first thing that had genuinely made her feel any better about the whole situation. Perhaps it would not be so bad.

"So, bad points?" she asked.

The situation really was dire, Melana thought, if Brody was the best of this bad bunch. Surely there were more men out there, better suited to the princess. Sure, Brody was a nice boy, but she doubted he wanted to be a prince any more than Astraea enjoyed being a princess.

"He is a bit of a mummy's boy," she suggested.

"I think maybe you are just best to wait and see. Surely your parents will not make you choose at the ball?"

"Oh, I think they will," Astraea muttered sadly. "Father didn't even bother to show up. He just left it to mother to speak with me."

"I am sorry, Astraea."

"So am I," Wren added, and Melana was pleased to hear him sound sincere.

"Not as sorry as I am."

She was pleased to hear a bit of fight back in Astraea's words. It would all be alright in the end. It had to be.

* * * * *

The list now abandoned, it lay on the floor with Astraea's tiara. So far, they had been unable to coax her into putting it back on. Melana watched Wren as he gushed over his new dagger, proudly showing it off to Astraea in an attempt to take her mind off it all. Tentatively, she stroked the golden hilt, running her fingers over the small dragon's head pressed against the blade, then allowing them to glide the breadth of the wings.

"Why a dragon, Wren? Of all the things you could have on it."

"Why not? I like him, he's cute. Besides, when was the last time anyone saw a dragon round these parts?"

"Next you'll be naming it," Melana scoffed, making Astraea giggle too.

"I have, actually. I thought I'd call it Fury."

Both girls looked at him, then erupted into fits of giggles.

"What?"

It only made them laugh more when Wren looked at them completely dumbfounded. Snatching the dagger up from the sheets, he stretched out his leg. Rolling up his breeches, Wren attached it to the little holster Melana had allowed him to go back and purchase for it before she had dragged him back to the palace. When he had strapped it tightly to his prosthetic, the blade sat on the left of his leg just below the knee. Melana had advised him not to strap it to his thigh, as his regular sword would bang against it. And for once, to his credit, Wren had listened.

Astraea had stopped laughing. Rubbing Wren's leg, she said, "I'm sorry. It is very pretty, Wren."

Slinging an arm around him, Melana gave her brother a warm hug. "We're only messing about. Do not take it to heart."

She was pleased when he hugged her back, a lopsided grin on his face. Melana could not imagine her life without either of them now. Especially her idiot baby brother. Blood or not, they were family, and she loved them both unconditionally.

Chapter Eighteen

Drowning In Darkness

Eyelids heavy, but not enough for sleep to claim him, Wren tossed and turned between his cotton sheets. The feeling of goosebumps erupting over his skin tormented him. He would never be able to explain to anyone what he had felt in that market square. If only briefly, Wren's magic had thrummed in his veins. Someone close by had been calling out to him, he was sure of it.

Rolling onto his side, Wren felt the mattress dip under Tormund's weight as the cat leapt up to join him. Plodding around on the covers, the animal's purr rumbled as he attempted to get comfortable. Reaching an arm out of the sheets, Wren ran his fingers repetitively over Tormund's head, the cat nibbling at them, his purr reaching a crescendo. As always, Wren found Tormund's presence soothing, and despite the cold night air on his face, it was not long until his breathing evened out.

Although sleep continued to evade him, his mind too busy to let go, it pleased him that the ginger cat remained snoozing blissfully at his side. But when the darkness that surrounded him finally took Wren under its spell, he slept fitfully. Plagued by his own turbulent past, he threw himself about the bed as he slept.

The waters had grown rough as the hours pressed on, the small vessel thrown from side to side. Panic had broken out in the hull, so many screaming people. Wren could practically smell their fear. The impact when the boat collided with the rocks was sudden, but not entirely unexpected, given the raging storm around them. A huge hole was torn in the side of the ship, and screaming families were instantly sucked out into the unforgiving sea. Freezing water rushed in, the boat was obliterated in seconds, battered against the rocks. The hull disintegrated around them, the ship destroyed entirely. Wren was pulled under, dragged from the surface in the turbulent waters. It was only as he managed to kick his way skyward, breaking the surface, gasping for breath, that Wren woke.

Shooting up in bed, his eyes snapped open. Shaking, cold sweat beaded over his skin. Wren's lungs burned, his heart pounding behind his ribs. The vivid images began to fade as he glanced about the room, his ragged breaths slowed when Wren realised he was safe. It dawned on him that he must have been holding his breath while trapped in the nightmare, and had startled himself awake.

Balling his fists in frustration, Wren punched the mattress. An alarmed ball of ginger fluff whipped his head up to see what was going on. Tormund yawned, no sense of urgency about him, as he checked all was well; stretching dramatically, he curled himself back around into a bagel formation.

Drawing his knee to his chin, Wren wrapped both arms around it. Gritting his teeth, he allowed his forehead to rest against his thigh. Nightmares had plagued him on and off for years, but these last few weeks had been something else. He had no idea why they were suddenly so intense, but with all that was going on, he could hardly worry the princess or his sister with his problems.

Chapter Nineteen

Don't You Just Love It When a Plan Comes Together

Leaning back in his seat, Bastian made a point of observing his brother and Cyrus. Slouched in their chairs, they drank ale in a carefree manner while speaking with one another. The tavern seemed unnecessarily loud to him, especially as time passed and people became progressively more drunk, the volume increasing further as a result. Left to his thoughts, Bastian unwrapped the bangle he had begged Nico to allow him to buy, under the table. He didn't want any snide comments if Cyrus clocked what he had purchased. Nico had not understood why Bastian would want such a feminine item of decorative jewellery. Hence his reluctance to loosen the purse strings. Like many other things, Bastian was not trusted with the gold. But he was far from stupid. He had already decided that if he could win the heart of the princess, then maybe he could save her. Hopefully save them both. But that really was wishful thinking. His father would kill them if they were caught. That was if his brother and Cyrus didn't beat the king to it. As far as he was concerned, it was the perfect betrayal. That would teach them all for plotting behind his back.

The bangle, he intended to wear, until he gave it to the princess. It was silver with little leaves that trailed the length of it, and winding around the arm at either end was one big leaf. It would fit right in, here. Carefully Bastian wrapped the item again, placing it in his bag under the table. He hoped that the princess would like it. Thankfully, his brother had secured them a room for a few nights to tide them over until the ball. It was handy, one less thing for him to worry about.

"Another drink, brother?"

The grim smell of ale and sweat invaded his nostrils, but Bastian nodded. He would be pleased when they could leave this place. He found almost everything about it assaulted his senses. Without hesitation, Nico swooped a hand in front of him, grabbing his tankard before disappearing to the bar. Leaving him alone with Cyrus, who was now staring at him intently.

"What's up, Cyrus? Run out of insults to throw my way?"

"Just trying to work you out kid, that's all."

Gods, Bastian wished he could wipe the smug grin right off of Cyrus's face, but now was neither the time nor the place. Instead, he narrowed his eyes.

"I am not a child, Cyrus."

"Relax, it's just a turn of phrase. I just don't get you, that's all. You are so… different. I can see bits of you in Nico, but he also has a cold, ruthless side if provoked. You don't. You are just so… soft."

Cocking his head, Bastian stared him down in an attempt to be as intimidating as he could. His next words were deliberately slow.

"I don't know, Cyrus; anyone can turn with the right provocation."

The sinister grin Cyrus gave him was alarming.

"That would be interesting to see. In fact, I would pay good money for a front row seat to that show."

Bastian scowled, ready to retort, when Cyrus broke off. Nico had returned with their drinks.

"You'll never guess what I've just heard from a couple of drunkards over there."

"Try me," Bastian said sulkily.

"The queen has announced that the princess will be choosing her future prince at the next ball."

Both sets of eyes swung to Bastian. Kicking back in his chair, Cyrus rocked on the two hind legs, overconfident as always.

"That makes things considerably easier. How convenient. Plan's coming together perfectly, I'd say."

It did make things considerably easier, Bastian supposed, lost in thought, oblivious to the discussion that was now underway as to what high-born fae he should pretend to be. Could he really do this? Run, betray his family? All to save a woman he did not even know. Listening to Cyrus planning to kidnap some poor high-born so he could take their place, he made his decision. He could do this; he would do it to spite them. Bastian watched the pair clack their tankards together, Cyrus shouting, "Don't you just love it when a plan comes together?"

Arrogant arse. Bastian was going to show them. He would show them all.

* * * * *

By the time they were staggering up the stairs to bed, Bastian was shattered. And nowhere near as drunk as his brother or Cyrus were. To his absolute horror, when he opened the door to their room there was only one large bed. Dragging Nico past him, Bastian stood in the doorway, jaw slack with disbelief, as Cyrus pulled his brother down onto the mattress, passionately starting to remove Nico's shirt with his teeth. There was absolutely no way he was sharing that bed with them, and now Bastian felt the very real need to gouge his eyes out.

Making his way back downstairs to the bar, Bastian nearly folded in on himself when he found out the inn was full. It had been bad enough watching the pair of them cuddle on the ship, but this was something else. Slowly climbing the stairs again, Bastian debated sleeping in the hall. But on discovering that he could still hear his brother's cries from the top of the stairs, his knuckles turned white where he gripped the banister.

After a brief, traumatic moment of deliberation, Bastian decided that he would go for a walk. There would be no sleeping through that racket anyway. Leaving the inn, he wandered back towards the square where the market had been, delighted to find it still in full flow. Sitting on the edge of the fountain in the centre, he took it all in. Hundreds of lights twinkled like stars against the night sky, filling Bastian with wonder. Viriador was so pretty. How could his father want to destroy such a lovely place? What had gone so wrong for him that he wanted to wipe an entire race from the map? He just could not fathom it. What must it be like, to be consumed by that kind of hatred?

He was so glad that the fae had managed to rebuild here. Away from all the chaos and destruction. As he sat watching the world go by, Bastian realised for the first time ever, as a shiver rolled through his body, that he was cold. The evening had brought with it an icy breeze that rustled through the trees. And when it became too much for him, Bastian walked back to the inn, thankful to find his brother and Cyrus had fallen asleep. Creeping through the room, he made himself comfortable, curling up on the chair in the corner. Looking at the pair sleeping, Bastian thought they actually made a nice couple. Although he still couldn't stand Cyrus's frequent rude behaviour towards him. As long as he made his brother happy, he supposed. Daring not to think of what would happen if their father found out. Nico was expected to produce a line of heirs. No, he was not even going there, it was not his problem to solve. Instead, Bastian rolled himself into a ball and turned to face the window. Gazing out at the dark night sky, he sat mesmerised, staring up at the stars, until he fell into a dreamless sleep.

CHAPTER TWENTY

Descent Into Madness

The day of the annual ball had arrived. The day Astraea was to become betrothed to a virtual stranger. Part of her was still distraught at the thought of marrying at all, while another part just hoped for a good match. Someone considerate and kind. Then there was that little voice in the back of her mind that dared to dream that this could be it, she could find love and be happy.

Melana fussed around her, breaking Astraea's train of thought, as someone knocked at the door.

"Enter."

A young serving girl with a pitcher of dark liquid and a platter of fruits and pastries opened the door. It was clearly a peace offering from her mother, sent to sustain them while they got ready for the evening's events. The girl breezed through the room, placing the tray on the dresser before cheerfully informing them that the liquid was a spiced berry wine, and asking Astraea if she would like a glass poured for her. The princess's eyes darted to Melana. Was alcohol being served to them before the ball a good sign? Something to relax her, or was it merely another attempt to keep her compliant? Finally, Astraea found her voice.

"Yes, please, and a glass for Melana too, if you do not mind."

The girl seemed flustered at her request. She was slight, and pale, with a mane of tumbling red hair, and now her cheeks flushed almost red enough to match it. Chewing her bottom lip she begrudgingly obliged, pouring out two glasses.

"Can I be of any further assistance, Princess?"

Astraea sighed, irritated at the way the girl glanced between her and Melana, like their friendship was scandalous. She could not help but wonder if this was her mother's doing. Their last conversation played through her mind. *Do you see myself or your father befriending the staff?* Astraea's next words were cold and clipped, her mood souring.

"If you could draw me a bath, that would be wonderful. Then you may leave us."

Keeping her eyes downcast, aware of the obvious change in the princess's mood, the girl quickly curtsied before making a swift exit, leaving for the bathroom adjoining the chamber.

Melana placed a warm hand on Astraea's shoulder, smiling as she handed her a glass.

"Do not let others spoil this night for you."

Astraea turned to face her friend, dabbing at her glistening eyes.

"You are more family to me than any of my own. You do realise that, don't you?"

Melana grinned at her, wiping a rogue tear from Astraea's cheek with her fingers.

"And you are like a sister to me, too."

Wrapping an arm around Melana's shoulder, the princess let a few more tears fall. Squeezing her gently, Melana stroked her arm as Astraea tried to calm her breaths.

"No more tears. You need to meet this challenge head on, wherever it may lead. I will be by your side, as will Wren. Now, we are going to make this a night to remember. It will go down in history. After all, it is the night the princess will choose her prince. You are the future, Astraea."

Grabbing her glass from the table, Melana clinked it against the one that was still held aloft in Astraea's hand. Lifting it to her lips, she encouraged the princess to do the same. Both of them letting the warm, mildly spicy liquid slide down their throats before embracing each other in a hug.

* * * * *

The princess daydreamed, staring at her reflection while her friend styled her hair. Melana had helped her into the bath before retiring to dress herself for the ball. It gave Astraea time to relax in the hot water, it might as well be a baptism. When Melana returned with soft, fluffy towels, Astraea had felt like she was being reborn. A new version of herself evolving. Now, as she stared into the mirror, she felt more sure of herself. After all, this man would not know her strengths or weaknesses; she could use that to her advantage. All Astraea had to do was act the part, then she could be whatever version of herself she wished to.

The dress that had been picked for her was beautiful. It was blue, with hues of green that ran down to the floor from her waist. Backless, with tiny sleeves that held the corset of the dress in place. That part was a blueish grey, with silver flowered patterns covering it, cut just low enough to tease a view of her breasts. It was stunning. Suddenly her head tugged back; Melana apologised, while still pulling part of her hair so that the top of it met and was tied behind her head. The rest still hung in loose ringlets, apart from two pieces that had been tightly curled, either side of her face.

Affectionately, Astraea stole a glance at her friend's reflection. Melana had chosen a champagne-coloured gown. It had flared sleeves that reached her wrists, and the dress itself flowed straight to the floor, with a slit in the side that reached the top of her thigh. The garment showed off her figure beautifully, clinging in all the right places while still remaining elegant. Her dark, frizzy curls sat framing her face, and as always, she radiated natural beauty.

For the first time in as long as Astraea could remember, a wave of calm washed over her. She felt beautiful, and somewhat empowered. The choice tonight was hers, after all. There was another knock at the door, but this time they both knew who it belonged to.

Wren strode into the room. He had kept his usual high leather boots, but wore cream trousers beneath them, with a knee-length golden tunic that fitted him well. His black scabbard hung at his waist, holding his sword. His eyes roamed innocently over his sister and Astraea.

"You look lovely, Princess. You too, Mel."

Smirking, Melana looked him up and down.

"You don't scrub up too badly yourself."

Trotting in, Tormund yowled, just in case the ladies had not seen him arrive. Astraea took a small pastry. Breaking some off, she offered a piece to Tormund. The cat stalked up to it, sniffing at it to check it was indeed edible, before snatching it with his paws, hastily devouring it. Looking up, Astraea found Wren grinning at them.

"I am honestly surprised you did not fashion him his own outfit for tonight."

Melana laughed aloud.

"Could you imagine it?"

Tormund who had now finished his treat, looked between them all, a curious expression on his face. Astraea could have sworn it turned into a scowl as he turned and strutted back to Wren, weaving himself through his legs, until the fae bent to scratch behind his ear.

"Are you both ready to go down to the great hall?"

Was she? Astraea took a deep breath, steadying herself while Melana settled a reassuring hand on her shoulder.

"We are with you."

She turned to face her friends. Looking between Melana and Wren, she smiled, sucking in a breath.

"Thank you. I am ready."

Leaving the suite, Wren was ahead, with Tormund running alongside him, quickly descending the first staircase. Once at the bottom, Melana went ahead, gracefully making her way down the ballroom staircase alone, so that she could announce the princess's arrival. Wren waited at Astraea's side until the ornate doors opened. She no longer cared that her parents did not approve of her friends. These were the people who mattered to her. Those who were always there for her, by her side no matter what. Even Tormund, who Astraea was sure would have her mother spitting feathers when he entered alongside them. But this was her chosen family, and for better or worse, there were no others she would rather have at her side.

Astraea could feel her heart beating too fast, a lump forming in her throat, until Wren took her hand in his, squeezing gently.

"Ready?"

Sucking in one more deep breath, and raising her chin, Astraea looped her arm, offering it to Wren. She replied, plastering a false smile on her face, "Ready as I ever will be."

All eyes were on them as they slowly descended the grand marble stairs together, a fluffy ginger cat beside them.

Chapter Twenty-One

The Art of Impersonation

It turned out to be surprisingly easy to find a suitable candidate for Bastian to impersonate. There were many suitors headed to the palace to vie for the princess's hand. Some of them, as luck would have it, were staying at the same tavern as them. They were exhausted, enjoying a well-earned rest, having travelled miles across Viriador to visit the palace. It turned out, they were also incredibly loud when they became intoxicated, leaving themselves open for the trio to identify an easy target. The man Bastian had chosen, Lord Abernathy, was similar in appearance to himself, apart from the ears; but Cyrus said he had an enchantment that would rectify that. As easily inebriated as he was loud-mouthed, and arrogant, it had not been hard to ply the arse with drink. With a little help from Nico and Cyrus, they had overpowered him. And if luck was on their side, it should be a few hours yet before he was discovered, bound and gagged in a wardrobe. By which time the ball would already be well underway.

When they had arrived at the palace, 'Lord Abernathy' and his brother, with their newly enchanted ears, were taken at their word, and had no problem gaining entry. It was only Cyrus who had to find his own way to slip inside undetected. As usual, he had managed it with ease, using his magic. He found them again as the ballroom began to fill. Having been instructed to stay put, Cyrus was to keep an eye on Bastian, while Nico scoped out the palace. Typical, Bastian thought, that Nico had felt the need to leave him with a babysitter. Before he had too much time to dwell on why his brother did not trust him to be left alone, Bastian found himself being swept along into the small crowd of men who were there to present themselves to the princess.

The palace herald, a short portly fellow, ushered them into a line near the foot of a stunning marble staircase. Vines of silver and rose-coloured gold wound their way through the bannisters, and up the supporting pillars. Bastian marvelled at it. The decoration was detailed compared to his own castle. Back home, it was all cold stone, gold, and moody candlelight. Here, there was a vast glass dome that covered the centre of the ballroom. Natural light poured in, and once the evening passed into nightfall, it would make for a beautiful starlit centrepiece. Candles were indeed lit around the room for when the darkness crept in, but it was nothing like what he was used to at home. Everything felt somewhat lighter this side of the Barren Sea.

As they waited patiently at the foot of the stairs, Bastian found himself wondering if he had done enough with his chosen outfit. Although, he thought, it blended well with those around him. The jacket Bastian wore was long, the coattails falling to the backs of his knees. The fabric was an ice-blue brocade, his shirt white, and a cream silk cravat sat at his neck. Paired with dark blue trousers and plain shoes, Bastian thought it was just enough to be eye-catching, but not so over the top that he looked to be actively seeking out attention. Although he supposed that, in reality, that was exactly what he was doing.

The chatter that had rumbled through the line ceased as footsteps clattered quickly down the steps. Bastian noticed that even the king and queen, who were sat on their thrones to the side of them, stilled when a pretty, dark-skinned fae appeared, quickly making her way over to the herald. Bastian's brow furrowed; he knew that was not the princess, but everyone had fallen so still around him. Thankfully, his confusion was short-lived. The female passed along the line of males, stopping a few paces behind him. Watching the doors, as many others in the room were, waiting for the princess to make her entrance. The herald made his announcement.

"Ladies and gentlemen, it is my pleasure to announce the Princess, Astraea Thandal."

The princess began to descend the staircase slowly. When she reached his line of sight with her head held high, Bastian took her in. A natural beauty, Astraea's skin seemed to shimmer in the light. She was petite, but well proportioned, and Bastian thought she was his idea of perfection. Butterflies pooled in his belly, his breath catching in his throat, as he could already imagine her wrapped safely in his arms. Bastian could only assume the man guiding her down the steps was some kind of personal guard. A fine sword hung at his side, and while his clothing was not elaborate enough for a royal, it was also not the same as the other guards he had encountered. Already, Bastian felt a pang of jealousy, seeing Astraea's arm laced through that of another.

When they reached the bottom, her guard moved to stand to one side as the princess walked the length of the line, taking a good look at every male presented to her. Some she stopped in front of for longer than others. Bastian felt like she hovered near him for an eternity as their eyes met, but in reality, it was a mere fleeting moment. He exhaled heavily as she walked along the line, taking in the person next to him. Just as Bastian was starting to second guess himself, wondering if he would indeed be able to pull this off, the princess spoke to the herald.

"The Princess has chosen. For this evenings first dance, Astraea has selected Lord Rosindell."

Bastian watched as the man stepped from the line, a smug expression on his face, side-eying his competition. Walking up to the princess, he took her hand, kissing the back of it, before leading her to the centre of the dancefloor. Bastian felt dejected, making his way back towards Cyrus, who lingered at the edge of the room. His shoulders slumped as he watched happy couples making their way to join the star attraction on the dancefloor. Looking him up and down, Cyrus said, "What's the matter with you?"

Bastian glared back at him.

"What do you think?"

Bastian's eyes flitted over to where Astraea and Lord Rosindell danced. A smirk slowly drew across Cyrus's face, a wry chuckle slipping between his lips, and Bastian could not help the anger building within him.

"You do know that is just a first dance, right? You have all evening to try and win the princess's favour. She will not choose her prince until the end of the night. So cheer up, and monopolize some time with her, will you?"

Now Bastian felt foolish, but less morose than he had a moment ago. A spark of hope reignited inside him. Although he still wanted to punch Cyrus. That feeling seemed to be a permanent fixture lurking in the back of his mind these days. Regardless, he grumbled his thanks, wandering back into the crowd.

Waiting on the fringes of the dancefloor, Bastian had to bide his time. He let several others dance with the princess for what seemed like an age, watching the couples twirl about the dancefloor, before he finally amassed the courage to move in. When the music ended, he cut in, addressing both the annoyed lord who had just finished dancing with her, and of course, Astraea herself.

"May I have the next dance?"

Bastian was both pleased and relieved, when the lord stepped aside, lips pressed into a thin line. The princess smiled at him, colour flushing her cheeks. The quartet began the next piece of music, and Bastian led her round the floor in time with it.

"Thank you for rescuing me. Lord Norveile was a terrible bore. I am sorry, I do not know your name?"

"I am more than glad that I could aid you, Princess. I am Lord Abernathy."

Heart racing, Bastian smiled as Astraea peeked up through her lashes at him, her cheeks growing pinker, the colour spreading until it reached the tips of her ears as they continued to dance.

Chapter Twenty-Two
What A Tangled Web We Weave

The ball was well underway. Melana was relieved that Astraea looked happier as the evening progressed. Even more so since she had begun to dance with one blond-haired young man in particular. The princess had indeed turned down two offers of a dance from others since, and Melana watched curiously as the pair continued to chatter while gliding round the inner circle of the dancefloor. Wandering over to the nearest attendant for a drink, she chose a glass of mulled wine. It was lovely to be allowed to attend an event like this as a guest, even if she was mostly hiding in the fringes of the activity. But that was her choice. It was still a novelty not to have to think of her duties. Swaying to the music with her drink, Melana listened to the band play. There was an elderly gentleman with a cello, two older ladies on violins, and one younger lady who stood playing the viola, just behind the seated trio. They were all dressed up in their finest garments too, and Melana wondered if they were as thrilled as she was to be there.

Swirling the liquid in her cup, she took a mouthful, then foolishly gazed down at its reflective surface. Melana had only wanted a quick look, just to see who Astraea chose. But as was most often the case with her gift, she could not control what she saw, and this time was no exception.

Iron bars caged her in. The floor bare except for dirty straw. An older man with snow white hair sneered at her through the bars, spitting insults at her while she wept on the ground. Then there was fire. Fire, and so much blood. They were here in the palace, blood coated the marble floor. Suddenly she found herself in a much happier time, watching as Astraea spoke with the young man that she currently danced with. They sat by a fire under the night sky, smiling wryly at each other in the ambient glow of the flames. Her body started to shudder uncontrollably, as the vision dug its claws in, refusing to let her go. Dragons. Flames. Smoke. Thick, black smoke rising from ruins. And then she was in a castle. A male, remarkably like the one who danced with her friend, but taller, slimmer, his hair cut short. He was there with her, speaking softly to her as he grazed his fingers along her cheekbone affectionately. She wore a fine green dress. Much finer than anything she owned at present. Melana barely recognised herself as she glowed under his touch. In a heartbeat, her second sight had ripped her back to smoking rubble, when a hand softly gripped her shoulder.

"Mel, are you OK?"

Melana felt her body relax, the vision ending abruptly. It had been erratic, jumping about, giving her different snippets of the future. It left her reeling, with no idea what to make of it all. Wren took her weight, letting her lean on him, supporting her until she recovered. Waving her hand, she attempted to pacify him.

"I'm fine, honestly."

"Are you sure?"

Wren sounded worried, and now Melana wondered how obvious it had been that her mind had wandered of its own accord. Not that there was anything wrong with having the rare gift that she possessed, but she did not want to ruin anyone's evening. Once the night was over, Melana would tell her friends what she had seen. Then they could attempt to unpack it all together.

"You were shaking."

He stared down at her, brows pinched with concern.

"Honestly, Wren, I am fine. It was just a bit longer than I am used to."

"Alright, let's find you a seat for a while though, just to be on the safe side."

It was comforting that Wren felt the need to guide her across to the far wall, where there were several chairs and tables set up for those tired of dancing. Still a little shaky, Melana eased herself down into the chair that Wren had pulled out for her. Ever the gentleman, she thought, taking care to make sure the bottom of her dress fell in a proper manner. The large slit that went from her thigh to the floor left Melana feeling slightly exposed. Even though she had done her best to cover it, the dress was not designed for sitting in.

Wren hovered at her side, silently watching over her. Thankfully, he looked a little less concerned than he had done moments before. It was then that Melana saw a man approach them. He was incredibly pale, especially against his attire, his hair as black as the clothes he wore, and dark stubble lined his jaw. Now as she paid closer attention to him, Melana noticed his mouth was parted just a little as he moved towards them. His gaze trained on Wren, the stranger's honey-coloured eyes boring into him intensely. When he reached them, the man hesitated. Melana watched his chest heave with each breath he took; she could only assume it was nerves, his fingers twitching animatedly at his sides. Leaning in, the man practically whispered into Wren's ear.

"May I have this dance?"

Wren looked to her, unsure, but Melana dismissed him with a flick of the wrist. Nodding, she smiled at them both, pleased to see him gain some attention that he might actually enjoy. After all, it was Wren's night off too. Invited, like herself, as Astraea's friend, and not in any official capacity, even if he had escorted the princess into the hall. But Astraea had asked him to accompany her, as a favour to steady her nerves, and Wren had happily obliged. Watching as they began to dance, Melana felt soft fur press against her exposed calf as Tormund brushed past her. Sitting beside her foot he watched his master, head bobbling along in time with the music, almost as if he understood it was for dancing to. Finding it hard not to smile at them, despite her disturbing glimpse of the future, Melana remained cautious. So far, the night had played out perfectly – but it was still young.

* * * * *

Cyrus had sensed that the man from the market was there somewhere. He had felt nothing but the same prickling sensation coating his skin since he had set foot in the palace. As soon as he laid eyes on him, and if he was being honest, probably since that moment in the square, Cyrus knew. He was not sure quite how, but he knew. That was his mate. His fated flame. Every nerve ending tingled, desperate to be close to him. Every fibre of his being ached, with a desire that Cyrus had not realised was possible. He only became aware that his feet had begun moving of their own accord when he was already over halfway to the other man. Cringing inwardly, Cyrus wondered what on earth he was doing. But it was too late to turn back now. Cyrus spied the tips of his ears. Pointed. He was indeed fae. Curious, then, that they had this connection. Although now his mind raced, wondering if the fae could feel it too. Perhaps it would not be reciprocated, and that possibility terrified him. Closing the gap between them, Cyrus marvelled at how wonderful the other man looked. The golden tunic he wore was not really a garment designed for a ball, but then his sword still hung at his waist, so the man had clearly not let his guard down fully. Interesting.

"May I have this dance?"

The words had left his lips before Cyrus even realised that his mouth had moved. He hated that he felt so out of control. None of this was him at all. And yet, it was.

The male had looked to his companion for approval. She seemed more than happy for them to dance. It was as if Cyrus's body moved without his brain's consent. He felt like he was floating, this moment too surreal. It was too good to be true. This kind of thing happened to others, not him. Never him. Cyrus knew he did not deserve happiness – and yet here it was, dangled in front of him.

As they started to waltz, Cyrus looked deep into the fae's eyes, swallowing hard; they were the most dazzling emerald pools. His fingertips tingled, aching to be able to roam his skin. It looked so soft and inviting, Cyrus found himself yearning to go somewhere more private. The way the man's eyes roamed over him, he thought the feeling seemed mutual enough. At worst, even if he couldn't feel the mating bond, Cyrus could tell from the primal way his eyes raked him that there was definitely a physical attraction there, if nothing else.

"I'm Cyrus, by the way."

His voice was still barely a whisper as the air left his lungs.

"Wren."

Cyrus swore he felt his heart stutter when the corners of Wren's lips drew into a smile. Raising his hand, he ran his fingers through the side of Wren's hair impulsively. When Wren did not stop him, he still found himself apologizing.

"I'm sorry, was that too presumptuous?"

Wren offered him a half grin, appearing suddenly shy.

"It's alright. I like it."

"You do?"

Wren nodded cautiously, looking past him to his companion, and the cat that sat at her feet. Cyrus's brows furrowed.

"She's not...?"

"No, no."

Wren laughed, cutting him off.

"That's my sister, Melana, and that", he gestured to the cat, "is my little buddy, Tormund."

Cyrus looked between him and the cat quizzically.

"You keep him as a pet?"

Between the twinkle in Wren's eye and that grin, Cyrus thought this fae would be the death of him. His heart began to race, his mind drifting, inappropriate thoughts creeping in.

"I would say he more decided that I am his fae. He turned up one day and never left, and now as you can see, he follows me everywhere."

"I see. How strange."

Mulling over how he did not in fact understand the unique relationship at all, Wren caught Cyrus off guard as he changed the subject inquisitively.

"So, whose party do you travel with?"

"Lord Abernathy's," Cyrus drawled in a manner more expected of someone from a high-born's household, even if it was the staff.

"I am something of a personal assistant, I suppose. What is it that you do?"

"I'm Princess Astraea's personal guard."

"Well, I bet that's an honour."

And also incredibly convenient for their mission, Cyrus thought. Wren nodded his agreement, his cheeks flushing pink at the compliment.

"It is an honour to be able to keep the princess safe. I guard her with my life. I'm also very fortunate to call her a friend. It's how I came to be invited tonight, actually."

Cyrus led as they continued to waltz, talking into the next dance. He noticed Wren occasionally glancing over to Astraea, seemingly happy that the princess found herself occupied with Bastian, which was an added bonus. Pulling Wren a little closer as they continued to dance, his hand started to stray from the fae's waist while they spoke.

"They saved my life when I was young, Mel and Astraea. I don't think I would still be here if it wasn't for them finding me."

"Ah, I see: you owe them a debt. I also had a rough start in life. I had to work hard to gain my position."

"Hard work does pay off. My parents always say you never get something for nothing."

"Wise words."

Cyrus smirked, satisfied when Wren's head leant against his shoulder. Their waltz had turned into something of a slow shuffle, with Wren edging himself further into Cyrus's arms, until he was pressed flush against him. He wondered, would it be appropriate if he asked Wren to take his leave and spend the evening with him? But, when he saw Wren quickly glance around, once more checking on his sister and Astraea, Cyrus knew that would be a fruitless quest. At least until the ball was over.

While the logical part of his brain understood that he and Wren had just met, there was also the part of him, deep in his core, that knew this was it for him. He wondered what would happen when the fae discovered what he was. Cyrus hoped that it would not matter to Wren, for it mattered little to him that they were different. As far as Cyrus was concerned, the gods had still destined them to be together – although he might have to work harder to explain to the fae who he was and why they were there. The deception was already niggling at the back of his mind. Gods, how was he going to explain this to Nico? Logically, Cyrus knew he had to. He also knew he was going to cause the prince a good deal of pain in doing so. The thought of the conversation he had to have hurt for many reasons, but mainly because he cared for Nico. His intention had never been to hurt him. If Cyrus and Wren had never crossed paths, there was every chance he would have stayed with Nico, drifting comfortably for as long as he had wanted him by his side. The other concern that plagued him was one that anyone would have felt in his position. You did not go out of your way to upset a dragon. Especially a royal one. But Cyrus had always known that he was playing a very dangerous game. He had just not expected it to end this way.

Hands snaked their way up to the nape of his neck. Cyrus dipped his head in return, ready to press a chaste kiss to the lips of the beautiful fae before him, but a loud screeching stopped him in his tracks. Everything seemed to happen in slow motion. Wren stiffened in his arms before wrenching himself away, ready to defend Astraea, Melana, and the cat. Frightened whispers became suddenly quiet, an eerie stillness descending; even the quartet fell silent one by one. Another piercing screech filled the air. Astraea clung to Bastian, who held her firm in his arms, a knowing look of horror twisting his features. Melana was on her feet rushing towards them, fear etched on her face. Cyrus could not see the cat anymore. Then everything whirred back to life. He knew why Bastian looked horrified, why people were now scattering, screaming as they pushed and trampled each other trying to escape. This was not their plan. Something had gone horribly wrong. Cyrus looked up just in time to see Gerritsen smash through the dome above them. Glass flew in all directions, a giant tooth-filled snout invading the centre of the ceiling. Cyrus tried his best to shield Wren, but he was already on the move as he attempted to reach his friends. Looking around at the chaos, he saw the king trying to usher the queen away to safety, but she refused, standing defiant at his side. Soldiers started to pour in the main entrance, while the angry black dragon that was Gerritsen screeched through the hole in the dome, thankfully too large to enter, in his dragon form at least. Cyrus scanned the carnage looking for Nico, but he was nowhere to be seen.

CHAPTER TWENTY-THREE

Long Live the King

Roaming the darkened halls, Nico found that, save for the odd candle, he had been able to blend seamlessly with the shadows that lurked in the deserted corridors. He had been trying to get a feel for the place, while those who would usually frequent the halls were otherwise distracted. Reasoning to himself that having findings he could relay to his father, should things go sideways here, would be as good a contingency plan as any.

As the years had passed Nico by, he had frequently questioned his loyalty to his father, the brutality the king often displayed grating on his fractured soul. It had always been drummed into him that blood was thicker than water, but if Nico was honest with himself, he had never been sure that he quite believed it. His conscience had still been at war over their latest endeavour when he heard the dragon's battle cry. It was the moment he knew what a damn fool he had been for ever confiding in his father. Clearly, Dracul had never intended to let them gauge the lay of the land for invasion, nor had he ever intended to let them kidnap the princess. This had been his chance to prove himself, and now he had even been denied that.

Part of him feared the bloodshed that was to come. Bastian would most likely want to kill Nico for deceiving him. Especially as he had got it in his head that he and the princess would be able to unite the realms in some kind of fairy tale happy ever after. Would Cyrus believe that he had had no idea this was about to happen? Nico felt like he had betrayed them all, and there was him worrying that Cyrus might have had ulterior motives. Unless this was his doing. It very well could be, but Nico did not want to believe that.

The building shook, and screams echoed through the hallways as the dragon screeched again. The faint whiff of smoke curdled the air as those lucky enough to escape the ballroom began to run towards him. Footsteps echoed as they thudded his way, and their cries filled the darkness as they attempted to flee. It would do them little good in the end, Nico thought. The fae, with all their magic, were still no match for dragons. Fury simmered inside him. Nico could smell the fear leaching from their skin. Furious as he fought his way through the screaming fae towards the epicentre of the chaos, Nico could feel his blood boiling. He had to control the urge to shift in the confined space. It would be no use anyway. If he stood against his father's army, he would be destroyed. They would take Nico home and put him down – an example to the people of what would happen if you crossed the king. He was no good to anyone if he was dead.

By the time he reached the ballroom, the king of the fae had been brought to his knees. Now they were at the mercy of Gerritsen, who stood before them in his human form, his armour as black as his soul. Soldiers surrounded those trapped in the room. Bastian had the princess. Together with Cyrus and a couple of others, they stayed huddled together, somewhere in the middle of the swarm of people. Nico caught sight of the group. He hoped that their own side would not knowingly harm the young prince, but he had seen battle before. There was always collateral damage, and right now his brother was lacking in armour. Though his worry was eased slightly by the fact he could see Cyrus close by. Careful to stay silent, Nico shuffled his way slowly along the wall until he reached the alcove, managing to press himself inside just enough that he would be obscured from view for the majority of the room. From there, he had a pretty good view of the events currently unfolding in front of him. Straining to hear what Gerritsen was saying, Nico attempted to make it to the next alcove. He wanted to get closer, to gain a better chance of hearing what was happening, but he need not have bothered. The king spat in Gerritsen's face, and the dragon retaliated, dragging Emil to his feet by his long greying hair.

"You hear that?"

The general of the dragon army addressed the room loudly.

"He will never yield. Will never accept the one true king. He would rather die. Well," a grim chuckle escaped him, "that can be arranged."

With that, chaos erupted as Gerritsen drew his sword, skewering the king through the gut, before ripping it away viciously. In a moment forever frozen, Emil clutched at the wound left behind, crimson seeping from beneath his hands as it spread outward across the front of his shirt.

The air was filled with gasps and screams of disbelief. The king still tried to form words as bubbles of blood dribbled from his lips, reaching out to his wife with bloody hands, his eyes wide, before he collapsed onto the dais. The queen wailed, falling to her knees. She pressed her hands to the wound in an attempt to stem the blood flow, but it was futile. Her husband raised a hand, tenderly stroking her cheek, staining her skin red as he ran his fingers through her tears. Then Emil's hand dropped, all the life leaving him as he fell still. Briana was left sobbing over his lifeless body, his glazed eyes staring back at her long after he took his final breath.

Bastian had to hold the princess back. She struggled frantically against him, desperately trying to reach her parents. As fight-or-flight took over, it seemed the fae were not willing to go down easily. Chairs and tables went flying as people fashioned makeshift weapons. And several already had their own weapons drawn as soldiers confronted them.

Deciding to make a break for the others, Nico pushed himself from the alcove. He was halfway across the ballroom when a small dragon screeched, crashing its way in through the empty space that had once been the centrepiece of the ballroom. The ceiling shook so profoundly that a couple of the fixtures securing the marble pillars began to crumble. One immediately crashed to the ground, smashing into pieces, taking with it the surrounding floor. The other wobbled for a second, and for a moment Nico wondered if it would stay standing, but the force of the other pillar hitting the floor had this one crashing to the ground too. Dust filled the air as large chunks of marble scattered, blocking Nico's path. Part of the ceiling in front of him began to cave as the creature clung to the edge of the hole by its talons, swinging from it like a bat. Whoever the imbecile was, not only was he causing the ceiling to cave in, he was also shooting flames from his perch, causing pandemonium. No longer sure what parts of this display were intentional, Nico growled, his frustration reverberating in his chest. His father did like a good show, but he was not here to witness it.

Or was he?

Clawing his way up the smoking pile of rubble, Nico was shocked at how many were already dead. Bodies lay strewn across the ground, his dragon kin and fae alike. The floor was awash with blood, and littered with charred corpses. Gerritsen had the queen in chains, dragging her away from the fray and her fallen husband as the fighting continued. Nico tried to cry out, tried to let them know that their youngest prince was in there. He needed the dragon to cease spewing fire, but the smoke was thick now, and through the madness he could no longer spot Bastian or Cyrus. Feeling sick, he tried to throw himself over the remnants of ceiling and pillars, coughing, and choking, as the smoke grew thicker by the second. Flames now surrounded the circular tomb, all the decorative curtains were ablaze. Spreading, the fire took wood and fabric alike, before catching the bodies strewn around the floor. It trapped them all.

Just as he thought he would lose consciousness, Nico looked up, catching sight of Cyrus running through the smoke-filled room. He had never seen him look frightened before, but he could see that he was now. Why had he not gotten them out yet? Nico tried desperately to cry out to him, but it just made him cough and wheeze. Finally, he doubled over, the effort of trying to breathe in the hot, debris-filled smoke too much for him. As the fringes of his vision grew hazy, something sharp pierced Nico's shoulders. Pain exploded through them as he felt himself being dragged to his feet. Someone was hauling him up. Gusts from a dragon's wings surrounded him, and then he was weightless, as he was lifted skyward, dangling from jagged talons. The world below melted away. Nico watched the smoke and crumbling ruins blur as the ground below them grew distant. And then there was nothing.

Chapter Twenty-Four

Into The Fray

Their world imploded the moment Astraea's father drew his final breath. Wren looked on helpless as all they knew ceased to be. He had to get them out of there. He had to get Astraea and Melana to safety. Thankfully, Wren had Bastian there, helping him to restrain the princess while they watched their king murdered at the hands of the dragon scum. There was no way he could have done it alone. Astraea had fought against them both valiantly, before finally slumping distraught into Bastian's arms as he hauled her away.

The real panic commenced now. People fought for their lives, everything around them engulfed in smoke and flame. The dragon that was the cause of so much chaos began to fly in circles above them, bursts of flame raining down around them. The slain lay scattered all around. Ushering the group under the dais, Wren hoped that in all the commotion they would remain undetected. There was a small doorway hidden behind it for exactly this kind of emergency. Debris rained down on them while Wren held the small curtain back, beckoning Melana and Bastian, who dragged Astraea along, holding her in his arms, through and into the tunnel. Cyrus was just making his way under when Wren tried to run back into the fray. Grabbing him by the wrist, Cyrus spun him around, shouting above the noise.

"What are you doing?"

Wren tried to wrench his arm free, but Cyrus gripped it tightly.

"I need to find Tormund."

Cyrus's brow wrinkled, shouting at the fae angrily.

"You intend to risk your life for a cat?"

"You don't understand. He is not just a cat, he is family."

It was then that Wren saw Tormund, backed up against the wall. Flaming curtains framed him on either side. His eyes wide, fur standing on end, the animal's usually-orange coat already blackening with soot. The stench of smoke, blood, and charred bodies filled Wren's nostrils as he tried to sprint away, but Cyrus dragged him back.

"Don't you dare. I've only just found you. Get under there and look after the others. I will get the bloody cat."

Wren looked on, tension holding his limbs in place, as Cyrus ran back out into the chaos, vaulting over piles of smouldering rubble to reach the cat. Narrowly missing being impaled by a dagger as it spun through the air, Cyrus cursed through gritted teeth. Tormund looked around, eyes dancing wildly, before making his decision and leaping onto Cyrus's shoulders. The man let loose a tirade of curses as Tormund latched his claws into his skin, deep enough to draw blood. While Wren stood rooted to the spot, watching anxiously, flexing his fingers around the hilt of his sword. Melana joined him at his back, watching the scene unfold. A jet of fire spewed towards Cyrus, and Tormund flattened himself so determinedly against his neck, he looked like a scarf. On their way back to the dais, a soldier attempted to take Cyrus out, causing Melana to scream loudly in Wren's ear. But Cyrus reached inside his jacket, retrieving a dagger, and thrust it into the side of the man's neck. Just before he reached the relative safety of their hiding place under the dais, Cyrus slipped. Thrown forward, he skidded into Wren, entirely exasperated to find that he had yet to move from the spot where he'd left him.

"Gods, come on! I have the cat, let's go."

They pushed Melana in front of them as they bundled into the tunnel. Cyrus, already breathing heavily, cried out when Tormund jumped into Wren's arms, blood visible where the cat had clung to him.

"You're welcome."

Cyrus rolled his eyes at the cat, who was now rubbing himself all over Wren in an elaborate display of affection, leaving a fresh trail of soot all over him. Leaning against the wall to catch his breath, Cyrus was surprised when Wren launched himself into his arms, wrapping his own around him and squeezing hard.

"You saved him. Thank you so much, you have no idea what he means to me."

Smiling down at the fae, Cyrus replied, "Any time. He might need a bath though."

They embraced each other tightly, Wren returning his smile.

"I think we all do. Come on, we need to get moving."

Tormund jumped up, settling himself on Wren's shoulder, while

Bastian lifted Astraea off the ground, half dragging her along. The princess's tears still fell in rapid succession, with no sign of stopping. They hurried Melana along ahead of them, pushing her forward as she stumbled along the uneven earth in the tunnel. Wren was worried by how pale she looked. Muttering, her teeth chattered as she walked.

"Didn't realise. Should have said something. The smell."

Wren squeezed her shoulder, her last words escaping as a sob. She was right though: the smell of burning flesh had followed them, and now filled the air.

Somewhere behind them a dragon roared, the ground shaking once more. Melana screamed, ducking down, while Bastian had to pull a dazed Astraea into him so that her head was protected under his arm as earth started to fall, blocking the way back. Their fate now sealed, the only way out was through. If anything had happened to the tunnel further down, this would become their tomb. Not that any of them would have wanted to head back to the palace. Not now. They no longer had a home. The group pushed onwards, the sound of dragons and the screams of the dying growing more distant until they disappeared altogether. And then they walked on in silence, save from occasional sobs, shocked and unable to believe what had happened. Wren took comfort from the fact that the other men had been there with them. Thoughts scrambled in his mind, only quietening when Cyrus grasped his hand, gently squeezing it from time to time as they walked. Wren doubted that he would have managed to save both Mel and Astraea if he had been alone. The colour started to return to Melana's skin the further they got from the palace, and her teeth no longer chattered. The shock must have started to wear off, much to Wren's relief.

The closer they got to the tunnel's exit, the colder the air seemed to get. Finally, after what felt like an age, they made it out. The tunnel ended in a small cave, on the bank of a river. The air here smelled of dampness and vegetation, the chill of the night air cold against their skin. Wren thought it was a vast improvement on the lingering odours that clung to them. There was no doubt in his mind that the smell of burning flesh would haunt them all one way or another, for the rest of their days.

The vast difference in temperature was quickly becoming more and more apparent. Wren watched as the ladies began to shiver, and found it was not long before he joined them. Knowing they needed to stay warm, he thought their best hope would be to get a fire lit as soon as possible.

The small cave, he hoped, would conceal them enough that the flames would not be visible from the sky. But then he doubted the army would come out in this direction anyway. It was the wrong way. Far from the city, and from all they knew.

Wren mouthed to Bastian to stay with the ladies. The man was doing well attending to Astraea, who remained distraught as she mourned her father. They sat on a large rock, just under the overhang at the cave's entrance, Melana the other side of the princess, holding Astraea upright as she sat, dazed, staring into space. Tormund curled up at their feet, keeping watch, and offering comfort in his own way.

Motioning for Cyrus to follow him, Wren climbed up the bank, away from the mouth of the cavern.

"We need as much kindling and firewood as we can find."

Wren was already bent over, starting to gather twigs from the woodland floor while he spoke, checking they were dry before adding them to the pile he was collecting. Cyrus joined him, snapping a larger stick he had found into smaller pieces. He stopped after a moment, turning back to face Wren, watching the fae with a worried expression.

"Wren. Are you alright?"

Cyrus asked his question tentatively. He was not sure why he had asked; he already knew the answer would be 'no'. Taking an uncertain step towards him, something tugged at the void in Cyrus's chest. He did not know how to offer Wren comfort, aside from folding the fae into his arms where he could keep him safe. But something told him the sentiment would not be appreciated right now. Dragons had done this. His people had done this. Cyrus did not know how he was ever going to be able to make this right, but he wanted to. For the first time in his life, he wanted to be able to fix this, for Wren. Straightening, the fae turned to face him, his light brown skin still blackened with soot. Fury shone in his bright green eyes, and there was a brief moment where Cyrus could have sworn his pupils flickered into slits, but it happened so fast there was no way to be sure what he had seen, so Cyrus said nothing.

"What is there to say? We are all fugitives now."

Cyrus offered the most sympathetic look he could muster, while Wren continued.

"I just don't understand. They have left us alone all that time. All that time."

Trailing off, Wren bowed his head shaking it, wiping his eyes with the back of his hand, leaving small streaks in the soot that clung there. Pulling him in close, Cyrus rubbed soothing circles on Wren's back, as a small sob escaped him. This, he could do; he could allow Wren to grieve, to let himself fall apart without the others there to see it.

"There is nothing more you could have done. There was no way you could have known what would happen. Besides, you rescued the princess. That counts for something, right?"

"Right."

Voice breaking as he forced out the word, Wren pulled away. Turning silently, he went back to gathering wood for the fire. Following close by in case Wren should need him, Cyrus collected his own. Reluctant to let his mate out of his site now that he had found him, Cyrus felt a wave of relief crash into him. They were alive. They had made it out. There was still a chance for a future where he and Wren could simply be. And it was then that he remembered Nico. Fuck. Where was Nico?

Chapter Twenty-Five

Harsh Reality

Flames licked the air in their makeshift camp. While more smoke was the last thing Astraea wanted to smell right now, she was grateful for the warmth the fire provided. Wren and his pale companion had returned a little while ago, building the fire and igniting it. Meanwhile, she had remained seated, still in the same spot where they had left her. The darkness that surrounded them felt like it seeped from Astraea, radiating how hollow her insides felt right now. Her damp eyes stared into the void, where the flames fought against one another to climb the highest. Orange flecks danced in their glassy reflection. If she closed them, all Astraea could see were her father's final moments playing on a loop behind her lids.

In the opposite corner, Wren tugged at a loose stone, eventually pulling it free from the wall, revealing a hidden chest. Leaving Melana with her, Bastian went to help, prising more of the stone away with his fingertips as they tried to work the chest out of its hiding place. Wren spoke of how her parents had hoped such provisions would never be necessary. Yet here they were. Still, Astraea stared into the flames, Melana never leaving her side. While Wren handed out practical clothing, food, and coin to sustain them, for now at least. Without a word, Bastian brought their share over, but he did not push Astraea to move as she sat there in her tattered gown. Instead, he simply piled the items nearby. Meanwhile, Tormund had crept closer to the fire and was now sat cleaning himself. The motion of his head as he licked at the long fur on his back made his whole body rock. Astraea's senses came back to her briefly, allowing herself a half smile at the cat, who swayed wildly with every lick of his coat.

Looking past the flames, her attention snagged on Bastian and the man who had danced with Wren. Not having been introduced yet, she did not know what to call him. Whoever he was, he clearly knew Bastian well. Their voices were hushed, and she watched as Bastian grabbed him, pulling him against him aggressively, so that his jaw was aligned to the pale man's ear when he thought no one was looking.

"What do you think you are doing?"

The man smirked at Bastian, amused.

"Trying to keep everyone alive, the same as you."

Grabbing his shoulder as the man turned to walk away from him, Bastian snarled, "No you don't, you know exactly what I mean, Cyrus."

So that was his name.

"Look." Astraea watched his shoulders sag, a seeming look of genuine remorse flitting across his features before he continued. "This development is regrettable, truly. But I cannot walk away from this, Bastian. You know how rare it is to find your fated flame. Even if I stayed with Nico, my mate's call would be in the back of my mind now. We would have to live the rest of our lives knowing Nico was second to somebody else, and that is not fair on either of us."

"Not if you never tell him."

This time it was Cyrus who placed a hand gently on Bastian's shoulder, his face a mask of pity. And Astraea knew in her gut that the look was not really for Bastian's benefit. It was far off and whimsical, meant for another.

"Bastian. I would have told him tonight if I'd had the chance."

His fists balled in anger, through gritted teeth, Bastian quietly spat his next words.

"Just remember that you had him, and he was not enough for you."

When Bastian spun on his heels to join her once more, Astraea jumped at his sudden display of aggression. She hoped that he had not noticed, and thankfully, it seemed that he had not. His features were soft once more, as his gaze traced every inch of her face before reaching her eyes.

"Princess?"

The single word held the weight of every unspoken question between them. And yet he had said it with caution. Aware of the pain and emotion in every moment she had lived since the horror of what had played out mere hours ago. Looking down at her once-beautiful dress, now dirty and torn, Astraea traced her fingers along a section splattered with blood. Wondering who it had belonged to, the realisation hit her then that she was unsure of exactly what had occurred after her father had fallen. It had all been such a blur. The blood could have been anyone's.

Trying to remember all the times her mother had drilled her for a situation like this, Astraea attempted to keep her breathing steady. It had been drummed into her so many times that she must stay strong. She was to maintain composure and dignity. If both her parents were lost, she had a kingdom to rule. Only they were *not* both lost – not yet, anyway. As for the kingdom, Astraea thought if she had her way, she would let the dragons keep it. This had always been a possibility, but not one she'd thought might ever come to pass.

Her father had always told her that the world was a treacherous and unforgiving place. Naively, she had always thought him overly dramatic, despite the many stories she had been told over the years. Tales of war, secrets, and betrayal. These were the kinds of scenarios she'd imagined happened to others, but she had never truly entertained it happening to them. Never in her wildest dreams did Astraea think that she, of all people, would become a character in one of these stories, but now – now she believed her father. The world was a cruel and rudderless place. When her eyes met Bastian's again, there was a glint of something else. Something other than her suffering resided there now.

"I am fine."

Shrugging Melana's arm from around her shoulders, Astraea rose. Not once taking her eyes off of Bastian. Her friend moved aside to give her space.

"I would like to change my clothes, please."

He looked puzzled, tilting his head as if to make her out, and she wondered what was so hard to understand.

"Wren handed them out, did he not?"

Bastian rose to meet her. Taking her hand in his, he brought it to his lips, tenderly kissing the back, before clasping it within his own.

"I am here, Princess. For as long as you want me here, I pledge my sword to you."

The gesture caught her off guard. Blushing, she replied awkwardly, "Thank you, that's very kind."

Walking away, Bastian left the ladies to change into their fresh clothing. Astraea could not help but wonder who this Nico was, and what Cyrus had done to him. While in a way she felt reassured to have Cyrus and Bastian there with them, there was something niggling in the back of her mind. None of them actually knew these two men; they could be anyone. Still, she supposed there was safety in numbers, and Lord Abernathy would have been her choice to present to her parents had the night ended differently, not that he ever needed to know that.

A brush against her shoulder had Astraea turning to find Melana gesturing for her to follow. The pair stepped outside of the cave's entrance, discarding their dresses in a heap against the jagged rock face. The pair entered the frigid water, washing blood and soot from their skin. The night seemed too quiet now, silent save for the occasional bird's cry. The sky starless, but the moon bright, illuminating the river where they bathed. Eventually Melana broke the silence.

"I am so sorry, Astraea. I can't imagine how you must be feeling."

Astraea felt another wave of grief wash over her.

"Honestly, I do not know what feels worse. That my mother is held captive by dragons and I may never know what happens to her, or that they slaughtered my father as I stood by, helpless to do anything to save him. How will I ever sleep again, knowing that when I close my eyes, that will be the scene that plays out in the darkness of my mind?"

Melana's face crumpled as she replied.

"All things heal with time. I know it does not feel like it now."

The silence between them spoke volumes.

"I'm sorry if that is of little comfort to you."

More silence stretched between them in the darkness. Finally, the princess spoke quietly.

"Do you think your parents made it out?"

Melana blinked at her.

"They were not there, Astraea. They were not invited."

Biting her lip, Astraea replied, mumbling, as if she were talking to herself, "Yes, but if they took the palace... No, you are right. I am sure they heard all the commotion and got out just fine."

When they had finished bathing, the pair waded back to the riverbank. Another tense silence hung in the air between them, as heavy as Astraea's limbs felt, neither of them apparently able to articulate anything more as they dressed in the clean clothing they had been given. Too numb to continue a charade of normality, Astraea returned inside the cavern, curling up facing the fire in her clean, dry clothes. She lay watching the flames dance once more. Melana sat nearby, uncomfortable as she leaned back against cold rock. Wondering now what had become of her parents, while she watched over her friend.

Astraea found it comforting that Melana and Wren were there with her. She listened as Melana argued with the males in their party. Insisting to them that she was taking the first watch. Fierce as ever. After much deliberation, they begrudgingly agreed to let her. Getting Melana a sword from the chest, Wren kept his own at arm's length as he lay on the floor opposite her. Astraea watched as Cyrus curled himself behind him, pressing himself flush to his back, slinging an arm lazily across Wren's middle as they got comfortable together.

When Bastian lay down behind her, Astraea could feel the warmth of his breath against the back of her neck. He was so close they almost touched. Realising what she craved most right now was simply to be held, Astraea selfishly pressed herself back into him, feeling him stiffen for a moment before he allowed his body to melt against hers. Wrapping an arm around Astraea, he pulled her back to meet him, her back pressed firmly against his front. Bastian's warmth enveloped her, and she realised with a fresh wave of guilt that this was the most wanted she had felt in a long time. It wasn't that she had had a bad life, just that at times she had felt neglected. As much as Astraea had loved her parents, as she had grown older, she had found they had less and less time for her. If it had not been for Melana and Wren, Astraea thought she would have been very much alone. Lying there in Bastian's arms, it pained the princess to acknowledge that she was comforted by his presence. It felt much like when she wrapped herself up in a large blanket. Safe and satisfying. The goosebumps that seemed to have plagued her flesh for much of the night finally receded.

There was no point worrying about feelings for now. She could drown herself in what-ifs, but there was no way to change the past. All she could hope to do was help shape the future. Sighing, Astraea realised she was going to have to find a way to dig deep. She needed to find some courage and stay strong. One way or another, there were dragons that needed slaying.

Chapter Twenty-Six

Isn't It Ironic

Everything hurt.

Pain shot down Nico's spine as he tried to move, his vision exploding in blinding whiteness. Doubling over the side of the bed, he vomited onto the flagstone floor. This was a fresh kind of hell. Ironic, Nico thought, after all these years of being sculpted by someone so vicious.

His thoughts drifted to Cyrus and Bastian, his mental anguish colliding with his physical pain. While he was not surprised, the sting of betrayal from his father was the final straw. It was too much for Nico to bear.

Falling back, he closed his eyes, waiting for darkness to consume him once more. Part of him hoped that this time, perhaps, the abyss might claim him forever.

Chapter Twenty-Seven

Everybody Hurts

Hugging her knees close to her chest, Melana wallowed in self-loathing. This was all her fault; she had squandered her gift, and allowed this to happen. Leaning back against the cold jagged rockface, Melana knew it was her silence that had betrayed her friends. But her visions varied from minutes to years into the future: there was no way she could have known it would have happened *then*. Still, it ate away at her regardless.

Her companions were asleep now. Even Tormund, who had been snuggled against Wren's chest, had sensed her distress. Moving to lie next to her instead, the cat allowed Melana to stroke his belly until he fell asleep. She did not know what to say to Astraea to try and make her feel better; she hadn't even tried to pacify Wren yet. And who knew what had become of their parents? Astraea was right: if dragons had taken the palace, they had probably taken the surrounding area too. Would they have done that before or after their attack at the ball? Melana didn't have a clue. But if there was one thing she was certain of, as she kept watch by the light of the fire, it was that she would never let them down again. And if that meant sacrificing herself, then so be it.

Chapter Twenty-Eight
A Man of My Word

The floor was cold and hard beneath him. Still, a warmth coiled in Cyrus's core, his blood thrumming through his veins, his dragon radiating its happiness at finding its other half. Although, he couldn't quite fathom how it was possible. The phenomenon was rarely found, and when it was, it was something that, to his knowledge, only existed for dragons. Although apparently not, because the man in front of him was no more a dragon than Cyrus was fae. Although he could have sworn there was that moment last night when Wren was upset. His pupils had changed, Cyrus was almost sure of it. Even if it was only for a split second. Either way, he did not care what Wren was; he belonged to him regardless. Now as the fae's chest rose and fell rhythmically, he drew circles across it with his fingertips, content. It had taken a long time for sleep to come to his mate, and Cyrus had no intention of disturbing him now, despite the fact he had not been able to sleep himself.

The uneven ground digging into his hip, Cyrus was not only uncomfortable but also distracted, his mind a hive of activity. He needed to know what had happened back at the palace. Had Nico betrayed them after all? No, he would never have knowingly put Bastian in harm's way. What in hell's name had made Dracul allow them to go on this little quest if this was his plan all along? Cyrus clenched his jaw in an attempt to contain the building anger within him. What if they had all been killed? He might mean nothing to the king, but surely his sons did. Well, one of them at least. What was he playing at?

Mulling it over, Cyrus found himself a new suspect. Was it viable? Or was this his mind's way of clearing Nico? Gerritsen could have gone rogue. The bastard was almost as vicious and unpredictable as Dracul; it certainly was not beyond the realms of possibility. An image of icy eyes and platinum hair drifted through his mind. He was desperate to know what had happened to Nico. Despite having found Wren, Cyrus still cared. It would pain him if anything terrible were to have befallen his friend, his lover. Although he supposed he was not the latter, not anymore.

Feelings were something that thankfully did not trouble him often, but Cyrus felt every conflicting emotion in spades now. Perhaps he *was* the terrible person everyone thought him to be? More so, because there was a small part of him that simply did not care what happened now, because he had found Wren. Selfishly, despite all the bloodshed that had occurred and the inevitable heartbreak he would inflict on Nico, Cyrus still found himself smiling as he nuzzled into Wren's neck, inhaling his scent. He smelled of earth, and sunflowers, and fallen leaves. It made him think of Autumn. While Cyrus lay there, his pale face pressed against Wren's neck, sleep finally found him.

* * * * *

The first rays of sunlight painted the ground at the entrance to the cave. Cyrus's sleepy eyes flickered open. He could feel Wren stirring in his arms, and while more sleep would have been welcome, he was already too emotionally invested in his fae to let him stray far from his side. Melana and the princess, on the other hand, still slept soundly on the other side of the dying embers.

The air was damp with fresh morning dew, the temperature not much higher than it had been the night before. Their fire had burned out at some point during the night. He looked up to find Bastian sat keeping watch at the mouth of the cavern, staring out over the river. He had not noticed the pair stir.

While he had slept, Tormund had returned to Wren's side. The last time Cyrus had seen the cat, he had been curled up in a ball near Melana, as if he was offering her comfort, which he found most curious. Arching his back, Tormund stretched, as Wren squirmed, walking the tightrope between sleep and consciousness. The cat eventually sat up and stared at Cyrus for a while, before flinging his head back in a dramatic yawn. He watched, intrigued, as Tormund strutted right up to Wren's face before rubbing his whole body against it. The fae mumbled in protest, but the cat just began to nibble his fingers instead, and when that did not get the desired response, he bit the tips of his ears. Cyrus debated shooing him away, eventually deciding it was not his place to interrupt Wren and Tormund's bizarre morning rituals. Sliding himself back so he could get up without disturbing Wren (any more than he was already being disturbed), Cyrus wandered over to Bastian's side, quickly realising how tired and achy he felt. The adrenaline of yesterday's events had well and truly worn off. And now, in the harsh light of day, all that was left was an anxious pool in the pit of his stomach. The reality of their situation hit him. They were fugitives. If they went back now, he had no doubt Dracul would have them killed.

Bastian barely acknowledged him as Cyrus coughed, leaning against the rock beside him.

"Go on, Bastian, go and get some sleep."

The young prince swung himself around so quickly it caught Cyrus off guard. Their gazes collided. The young prince's eyes were icier than usual; they were almost grey. Swallowing hard, Cyrus braced himself, taking a moment to acknowledge the way Bastian glared at him angrily. His lips were drawn into a thin line, brow furrowed. Now he looked threatening, much more like his brother.

"Why? Are you going to keep watch for us?"

Bastian kept his voice little more than a whisper, but spat the words at Cyrus, causing him to frown, confused.

"I was, actually. I'm already awake, so what is the point of us both being up when the others are still asleep?"

Remaining hostile, Bastian eyed him warily. While the pair disliked one another, Cyrus had never heard the prince speak with such venom behind his words.

"How do I know that you didn't do this Cyrus? Tell me, was it you, or my brother – if I can even call him that anymore." His jaw clenched, and he ground his teeth, nostrils flaring as his chest heaved with every angry breath. "And if it wasn't him, then why wasn't he with us? Where was he, Cyrus?"

Allowing his shoulders to sag, a small sigh escaped Cyrus. Once he had glanced over to check the rest of their companions still slept, he responded.

"I did not do this. You have my word, for all it is worth to you. But I am nothing if I am not a man of my word. As for the rest, I honestly do not know any more than you do."

Bastian regarded him, narrowing his eyes with suspicion while trying to decide if he believed him or not. Cyrus felt sorry for the young prince.

His distrust was no more than Cyrus deserved. If the roles were reversed, he was sure he would feel exactly the same.

"I know you have no reason to trust me, Bastian, but I made a promise to Nico that I would never let anything happen to you. Regardless of everything that transpired yesterday, I intend to keep it. I do still care for him, whether you believe it or not."

Huffing, Bastian got to his feet, glancing over to where Wren slept, before grumbling back at Cyrus, "Bloody looks like it."

Walking straight over to the ladies, Bastian didn't even grace Cyrus with a backwards glance as he adopted a position on the floor at Astraea's side. Grimacing, Cyrus made himself as comfortable as he could, resting against the rocks. All the while, he could feel Bastian's eyes boring into the back of him from where he lay. It sent a cold shudder down his spine. He would have to watch his back. For the first time in as long as he could remember, Cyrus felt unnerved and out of control. And while he sat there, he used the time to try and form some semblance of a plan for what they should do next.

Chapter Twenty-Nine

Desire & Despair

After what felt like the longest few days of his life, Nico had finally recovered enough to be brought before his father. His vision was clearer today, but he was still lightheaded and agitated. It had been obvious that he was in uncharted waters as soon as he had woken properly for the first time. He had found a guard stationed at his door. It was not someone he knew, and despite his best efforts, Nico failed to get the guard to speak with him.

Now, as he was marched down the chilly hallways towards the throne room by two more, the fear of what was to come made his limbs heavy. Butterflies swarmed in his gut, while bile rose in his throat, until they reached the foregone conclusion of their short journey. Abruptly, Nico found himself on his knees before his father, after a booted foot found the back of his legs. It startled him, but he quickly braced himself for the onslaught he knew would follow, keeping his gaze fixed firmly on the stone floor.

The king stayed seated without making a sound for so long the silence became deafening. With a nod, he dismissed some, but not all, of the guards surrounding them. Nico could feel his breathing becoming erratic, a tremor ran through his arms as he waited for pain to be inflicted. But it never came. When the king finally spoke, Nico found his tone alarmingly jovial.

"Rise, my boy."

Still shaking, Nico tentatively got to his feet.

"Tell me how it is that your brother has made off with the Princess of the fae?"

Nico flinched at the implied accusation.

"I did not know that he had, Father, I swear."

"Look at me."

Dracul cut him off, tone changing in an instant, causing Nico to jump. There he was: the person Nico feared. Rising slowly from the throne, Dracul's voice boomed as it echoed around the grand space. Reluctantly Nico met his gaze.

"Do you seriously expect me to believe that you knew nothing of this? Was it not your plan all along for Bastian to get close to the princess and kidnap her?"

"Yes, Father, but the intention was always to return her here, to you. If we had only had more time. We did not know of your plans…"

"My actions are irrelevant. Gerritsen led our men to take Viriador. Your brother and your adviser have both aided the princess's escape. They could have brought her to me, and yet they ran. They have the sole heir of the bastard race, for fuck's sake. They have ruined my plans. It is their actions that are inexcusable."

Flinching at his father's wrath, Nico felt the butterflies swarming his gut drown one by one as his insides became acidic.

"There was no way any of us could have foreseen your plans—"

"It is treason!" Dracul bellowed, cutting him off.

Nico's throat constricted. He did not like where this was going. Struggling to force words past his lips, eventually he managed, "What would you have me do?"

The hairs on the back of Nico's neck stood to attention as the king made his way down the stone steps towards him. His mouth was twisted into a snarl, feral rage etched on his face. As his father came to rest, his face an inch from his own, Nico found himself holding his breath. Suddenly the king lurched forward, grabbing Nico's collar, and tugging at it violently.

"I want you to bring your brother back to pay for his crimes. Cyrus too, filthy blood traitors the pair of them. I want the princess as well, and any other bastard fae that fled with them."

Nico sucked in a breath when Dracul let go of him and pushed him away. Stumbling in an attempt to stay upright, but failing, Nico was relieved at least to have some distance between them again. Trying desperately to stop his body shaking as adrenaline coursed through him, Nico found his words stuck for a moment. Swallowing hard, his mouth suddenly felt drier than the parched land outside. It took him a moment, but Nico manoeuvred himself to kneel before his father once more.

"What would you have me do, my King?"

The king, who had started pacing manically, stopped dead. His footsteps echoed loudly against the hard floor before he crouched down, pressing his face so close that Nico could smell his wine-sodden breath. Spit flicked against his skin as Dracul spoke each word in a staccato that made Nico squirm as he attempted to hide his fear.

"I do not care how you bring them to me. I would prefer them alive; I want them to know the consequences of their treachery. I want them to suffer."

There was a glint in his eye that had Nico holding his breath.

"But, dead or alive, I suppose it matters little. They will all pay in the end, one way or another. You will have men at your disposal. Do not fail me again."

Returning to his throne without giving Nico a second glance, the dragon king shouted for the guards to turn him loose. As those who remained stood down from where they had flanked his sides, Nico got to his feet again. Stumbling as he ran from the room, he was only relieved that he had not been beaten, or worse.

Running through the hallways, he passed a small group of the castle maids. They turned their heads, whispering to one another at his apparent distress, but he did not stop. If anything, Nico picked up the pace, his feet pounding all the way to the courtyard, where they crunched against the gravel. Shedding his clothing, his dragon burst forth as he took to the skies.

* * * * *

Circling his father's kingdom, the midday sun was unforgiving, even for a dragon. Nico looked down at the world below. This was his birthright. But gone was the land of plenty. All he could see was the dried-up landscape that surrounded the city. This was what was left of Predoran. This was what was to be his kingdom.

He could not believe that his brother, and Cyrus, had put him in this position. And as it was, their lives would now be forfeit. Unless... unless he killed his father. How he was going to accomplish that, he did not know. He would have to take down Gerritsen as well, so that he could command his father's army. While the law clearly stated that Gerritsen would have to serve under him in the event of his father's death, Nico was no fool. He knew that if he murdered his father, his faithful commander would avenge the king, or die trying.

What on earth had the pair of them been thinking. If it was just Bastian, Nico's guess would have been that he hadn't been thinking at all. But Cyrus – he was always so precise in the execution of his plans. It troubled Nico that he had not stayed with their kin, that he had fled with his brother. None of it made sense. How had it all gone so awry? Unless his father was wrong… Could it be that they had become separated in the chaos? Perhaps one of them was among the injured, or worse. No. They would have searched the injured and the dead thoroughly, knowing the three of them were among the crowd. Wouldn't they?

The more Nico replayed everything in his mind, the more his father's betrayal stung him anew. Despite Dracul's blatant disregard for the lives of those around him, Nico had always thought that his father valued his. Because, if nothing else, he was the heir to the throne. The realisation that no one, not even his father's heir was indispensable, left a sour taste in his mouth.

Nico had been deep in thought for so long his wings had begun to tire, his reserves running low. It seemed madness to him that his father's dreams were an echo of desire and despair. What he wanted was unobtainable, and as a result, the whole kingdom had suffered at his hands. As Nico doubled back to return to the castle, he knew he had to get word to his brother or Cyrus somehow. He would have no choice but to launch a search for them – but if the gods were on their side, at least they could be prepared. The thought of willingly offering them up to Dracul made him feel sick, and while he had no intention of letting his father kill either of them, he had to be careful. He did not want his life to be forfeit either, if he could help it. There had to be another way.

Chapter Thirty

The Laughing Fox

They had argued the best way to proceed for much of the next day. Melana, in particular, had really struggled with the suggestions that had been bandied about, calling them all suicidal fools on more than one occasion. Finally, with a little nudge from Cyrus, it had been decided that they would hide in plain sight.

That was how they had come to be at The Laughing Fox. The smell of ale and stale sweat hung in the air, Bastian's nostrils flaring at the offensive odour. He felt ill at ease with being this exposed, even as he sat beside Cyrus, raising a glass of berry wine to his lips. Swilling the liquid in his mouth, Bastian had to admit that staying here had made the most sense of all their ideas. It was a better option than staying in the cave, that was for sure. For one thing, it was warm in here, a large open fire heating the tavern, and each bedroom housing its own fireplace. After their night in the cave, the temperature in here was perfection. Mostly, Bastian was just excited at the prospect of retiring upstairs, to wash in warm water. He hoped Cyrus was right that the last place their army would hunt for them was in public, among the fae. A strange feeling lingered regardless. It seemed too perfect a plan, and that was what worried him.

The pair had been in the bar of the tavern for a few hours already, waiting as their companions indulged in warm baths, while they waited their turn. It had already been decided that the ladies would share the room next door to them. Bastian had objected, with fears for their safety, but they had dismissed him. He was not thrilled with the prospect of having to share with Cyrus and Wren, either. Especially when there were only two beds. It did not help that Cyrus, who was now slightly inebriated, would not keep his damn voice down. Not that he was saying anything that was likely to give them away, but Bastian thought the whole purpose of coming here had been to lay low, not draw attention to themselves. Irritated, Bastian unfolded a map that he had managed to obtain from one of the bartenders. Smoothing the creases out with his fingers, he tried to work out a plan for them going forward.

* * * * *

Leaning on the bar, as people jostled around him, Bastian waited for the next round of drinks. While he stood there, a portly man turned, catching him in the ribs with his elbow, causing him to elicit a low growl. And it was then that he realised just how tired he truly was. Normally Bastian would have reacted in some way, even if it were just to tell the man to be more careful. Instead, he simply found himself sighing as he paid for the drinks, carrying them back over to the table.

Bastian caught sight of Cyrus, and to his horror, several strangers had now joined him around their table, and a game of cards was well underway. For the love of the gods, he had only left him alone for a few minutes! And Cyrus called *him* a liability. This was ridiculous. Rolling his eyes, Bastian took a seat. Watching Cyrus play, he had to admit that, despite being drunk, the dragon was pretty savvy, winning several rounds. Bastian kept a watchful eye on him as he raked in the coin. He supposed it would be handy to have more gold. The prince was unsure what bothered him more: Cyrus's uncouth behaviour, or the fact that he found himself admiring his skill. Relaxing into his seat, Bastian let himself soak up some of the conversations going on around him. Mostly, people spoke sombrely about the massacre at the palace, and what this would mean for their people. Rumour was spreading of how the dragon soldiers were moving outward, taking some of the smaller surrounding villages, and there was much debate about where people would head when it was no longer safe to stay in Viriador at all. His attention was dragged away from the gloomy surmising when he heard a man excitedly telling his companion the tale of a local bard, Foxglove Whitethorn.

"Legend has it, his ghost haunts the watchtower in the wailing woods, singing ballads of love and loss to those who cross his path."

"That's stupid, ain't no such thing as ghosts. Why's his spirit meant to be restless anyhow?"

The men slurred their words as they bantered back and forth.

"No one knows. Some say he lost his bonny lass there, and that's why he's stuck, always searching for her."

The man visibly shuddered.

"Bull crap."

"It ain't. Old Oberyn swears he's seen him himself."

"That old git don't know his arse from his elbow half the time, Ned."

The man swayed as he gestured, arms wide, his ale spilling over the top of his tankard as he continued.

"It's a strange old place anyhow. Centuries old it is, all crumbling stone. Who builds a twisted old stone tower in the middle of the forest anyhow?"

"Bloody odd, whoever built it, if you ask me."

Bastian sat up straight, rummaging in his pocket to retrieve the map. He had seen this place, the wailing woods. It wasn't too far away. Here was somewhere they could go. The ghost story, they could spin to their advantage, to help keep people away. Bastian did not believe in spirits, so that did not worry him, but convincing Astraea and Melana that this was their next destination did. Not that the wailing woods sounded a particularly welcoming place. But needs must.

* * * * *

Another hour passed, with Cyrus still drinking and gambling, and Bastian decided he was done for the night. Bidding Cyrus goodnight, he retired to their room. Standing near the fire as the water warmed in the hearth, he was happy that he would be the one able to keep them all safe – if they agreed to his plan. Even if it was only for a little while longer. Absentmindedly removing his clothing before pouring hot water into the copper tub, Bastian stepped in, letting the warmth seep into his skin. It felt marvellous. He hardly ever felt cold, but when he did, he hated it. Not that he had felt cold in the crowded tavern, but as a general rule, the warmer he was, the better he felt. Something that came with having dragon's blood flowing in his veins, he supposed.

As he lay there, Bastian felt his muscles begin to relax, but his mind would not rest. Despite his dire need for sleep, he kept thinking of the princess and her friend in the next room. As the water grew tepid, he decided that, however unwise, he would spend the night guarding the ladies' door. After all, he could sleep when he was dead.

Chapter Thirty-One

The Beauty in Others

Vulnerability was a feeling Wren hated. He had rarely had to worry about removing his prosthetic at night. The privilege of living within the palace had afforded him that, but he knew that he could not sleep in it again, despite the imminent danger they were in. When they had spent the night in the cavern, Wren had decided to keep the false limb attached in case they had needed to flee. A decision he had since regretted. The skin at his stump, although still intact, already felt irritated. And while the hot bath he had soaked in earlier seemed to have helped the soreness greatly, he knew that the more he slept in the prosthetic, the more it would continue to rub. Broken skin would lead to infection, which was something he could not afford right now. In the end, he opted to swallow his pride, propping the false limb next to the bed within easy reach, so that he could get a comfortable night's sleep.

From where he lay, Wren stared at the empty bed across the room. Bastian had left already, declaring that he would keep watch outside the princess's door. Even though Wren had objected, offering his services more than once, the man had still insisted. Relief flooded him. He would be able to sleep soundly knowing his friends had someone watching over them, and that Cyrus had his own bed for the night. Wren had managed to avoid his leg, or lack of it, from being noticed until now. Changing his clothes in a dark corner, he had just about gotten away with keeping his secret, under the guise of modesty. While he was not ashamed of his disability, it was not a conversation he wanted to have, less than two days after meeting Cyrus. Just thinking about him now was enough to send butterflies sprawling in the pit of his stomach. Wren did not want to ruin things between them before they had even begun. He just hoped that his beautiful stranger could accept him exactly as he was.

* * * * *

Wren heard Cyrus before he saw him. Metal grated against metal as the man struggled to align the key in the lock. After a beat of silence he managed it, and Cyrus stumbled through the door. The moonlight illuminating his features, Wren found it hard to look away. Beneath the stubble that lined his face, was a strong jaw. His nose was smaller, more delicate than many males. His lips curled in a feline grin, smiling to himself as he started to undress. Wren's eyes roamed the length of him, his heart beating faster as Cyrus fiddled with the buttons of his shirt, painfully slow as he undid each one, until he discarded it in a heap on the wooden floor. Wren's breathing hitched, as he took in the chiselled planes of his torso. In this light, Cyrus's skin was so pale it looked almost alabaster. It was only when the man dropped his black linen trousers that Wren forced himself to look away. Closing his eyes, a flush crept up his neck, spreading across both cheeks.

When the mattress dipped suddenly under Cyrus's weight. Wren froze. Sucking in a breath, he opened his eyes to find Cyrus gazing down at him, that smile tugging at his lips.

"You're so beautiful."

Stifling a nervous laugh, Wren replied, "And you are drunk."

Running the backs of his fingers down Wren's cheek, Cyrus chuckled darkly, making Wren's throat bob as he swallowed hard. A shiver ran through him. He felt at once both exhilarated and terrified. Whispering into the darkness, "There is a perfectly good bed over there, you know."

Cyrus did not falter; leaning in, voice low, he replied, "Did you really think I was going to pass up the opportunity to share a bed with you?"

He hovered for a moment, leaving mere inches between them, before leaning the rest of the way in until their mouths pressed together. Their tongues colliding in the slowest, deepest way possible. Apprehension forgotten, Wren's arms snaked around Cyrus's neck, his fingers weaving through his hair. He could feel Cyrus's hands roaming his chest, his fingers fleetingly grazing against his nipples as they worked their way down. Cyrus moaned into Wren's mouth, making him whine a string of frustrated little noises that emanated from the back of his throat. The heady mix of Cyrus's scent, combined with the taste of wine on his tongue, was intoxicating. It reminded Wren of the cathedral; it was incense, and the pages of old books, and he clung to the reminder of home.

Rolling Wren beneath him, Cyrus stalled, looking puzzled. Wren could feel his face heat, his cheeks turning red as he watched the other man in his drunken state, try to fathom what felt off. Equal parts amused and self-conscious, he took Cyrus's hand in his own, guiding it down his thigh until it reached the stump. A small 'o' formed on his lips, as he joined the dots in his mind. Wren was relieved when Cyrus brought his arms up, resting them either side of his head, running his fingers through Wren's hair affectionately while his lips sought his. They kissed until the edges of their vision darkened, and they had to stop for air. He could feel Cyrus's solid erection pressing down, slotting against his own, and while the thought of more made his skin buzz, he was relieved that Cyrus seemed content to let his hands explore higher. Trailing kisses down his neck and across his collarbone all the while he did.

It was a refreshing change from some of the near-feral exchanges he had had with other men. This made Wren feel truly wanted, in a way that his liaisons had so far lacked. When their fiery kisses turned into a somewhat lazy exchange, they relaxed, melting into each other. Getting comfortable, limbs entangled. Wren rested his head against Cyrus's chest, and suddenly he seemed more sober than Wren had thought him mere minutes ago.

"Who did that to you?"

Wren scoffed, "Do you mean, who wielded the blade, or who made it necessary?"

Cyrus ran a finger under Wren's chin, tilting his face up until their gaze met.

"Both."

Wren sighed. The memory was never any less painful for him. Squeezing his eyes shut as he lay in Cyrus's arms, he recounted it.

"When I was a child, my family had to flee from Predoran due to the growing unrest. We had lived there happily before that. On the crossing there was a terrible storm, the ship was wrecked. My family didn't make it. When Melana and Astraea found me washed up on the beach, my leg was too damaged to save."

Trailing off, he added sadly, "Dracul Castillo cost me everything that day. I lost my family, had to rebuild my whole life."

"I'm so sorry. Do you remember much of them, your family?"

Looking away, Wren stared at the wall, trying to keep his tears at bay.

"Many of my memories were lost that day. I would do anything to see their faces again. It's like they are always there in the fringes of my mind, and just as I think I will be able to see them clearly someone drops a pebble into the pond, and they are lost again."

Fingers gently threaded through Wren's hair, moving down to caress the back of his neck as Cyrus asked, "So, Melana is not really your sister?"

"Not by blood, no. Her family took me in and raised me. Astraea and Melana have been by my side since the day we met. I owe them a great deal. I would not be where I am now if it was not for them."

The irony of his own words was not lost on him, as Cyrus hugged him tightly against his chest. His honey-coloured eyes were glassy, and Wren could have sworn, as he whispered into his shoulder how sorry he was for what he had been through, that he felt a single warm tear drip onto his skin.

Chapter Thirty-Two

To Dwell in Darkness

The acidic feeling still burned in Nico's gut as he prepared the cells ready for a fresh batch of prisoners. Dracul had ordered the previous residents' execution that morning, his expectations for Nico's mission resonating loud and clear. The only person still remaining was queen Briana, chained in the middle of the smallest cell, with the least amount of light. Chewing his tongue as he laid fresh straw, Nico ignored her whimpers. This was punishment for his failings.

Panic crept from the depths of his stomach, clawing its way up, into his mouth, his tongue starting to tingle as the world grew hazy at the edges. There was no way he could bring Bastian and Cyrus back here to be caged like animals. They would be tortured intermittently, until his father was satisfied with the pain he had inflicted. Ultimately their bodies would give out; or he would eventually sentence them to death. As his vision blackened, Nico grabbed the bars to steady himself, sliding to the floor. His breaths came in short bursts, heavy, as he tried to draw in air, and his chest burned as it moved in rapid succession. Pressing the palms of his trembling hands against his eyes, Nico cried out in frustration. He could not save them. Not without giving his life as forfeit. And when it came down to it, Nico was uncertain whether he would find the courage to make that sacrifice. On the other hand, he could never be the son his father wanted. All these years, he had played his part well. With his constitution hardier than Bastian's, he had fooled his father – hell, perhaps even himself – into believing he was something he was not. There was a time when he had been oblivious to Dracul's cruelty, slowly learning that he was expected to thrive on it. However, it had not taken Nico long to realise that, in reality, despite how he had been forced to present himself to the world, he would never be the man his father craved as his successor. Nico had failed them. He had failed them all.

Nico had forgotten he was not alone, letting the tears fall freely – jumping, startled, when a shaky voice called out from behind him.

"It's good to see that at least one of you has a semblance of morals."

Nico sniffed, pressing his sleeve to his eyes as he turned in the direction of the voice, while he fought the urge to vomit. The queen of the fae sat against the wall. She was dirty, her dress torn. Hair that would normally have been pristine hung limply, framing her face. The crown that she had worn at the ball, nowhere to be seen.

"Quite some fall from grace you've had," Nico said. "I hope you were not looking to me to save you. It would seem I can't even save the lives of those I love."

His voice was raspy as he tried in vain to control his laboured breaths. Briana's lips quirked into an intrigued smile. Moving to lean on the bars of the cell, she spoke with an air of curiosity.

"Interesting. You are the prince, are you not?"

Nico shuffled closer to her cell, nervous in case they were overheard. Knowing that he could not waste this opportunity, as there may not be another. And now his interest was piqued, despite his anxiety.

"I am."

"And which one are you?"

"The heir."

"Ah."

Her features changed then, twisting slightly. Nico was unsure if it was a look of pity, or something else entirely.

"You must be Nico, then. May I say you are not what I expected? Though you look just like your father when he was your age."

"You knew my father well?"

At that her head tilted to one side.

"You really have no idea who I am do you?"

A small laugh slipped from her lips, though her brows pinched, and her lips drew tight before she spoke again.

"I knew him well enough; we were lovers for a time. Before he turned on my kind."

Nico recoiled as if she had struck him.

"You lie," he spat.

The queen's smile twisted into something cold and cruel.

"Do tell me then, young prince, why *did* your father turn on our people? Has he ever honoured you with the tale?"

Kneeling up, Nico grabbed the bars of her cell. Pushing his face obnoxiously close to hers.

"He was betrayed by your kind."

At that, her smile turned into a satisfied grin.

"So then, tell me, what was this great betrayal? What could have happened to make him erase half his kingdom in retaliation?"

Nico stalled, realising that he did not have an answer. He always thought his mother's death had had something to do with the king's banishment of the fae. And the pure hatred Dracul held for hybrids – well, he had never truly worried over it. His father never spoke his reasons aloud, and everyone knew better than to question the king. Even him.

Kneeling there, attempting to formulate a sentence, his mind flooded with images of his childhood. Nico remembered when his father had issued the commands banishing the fae and ordering the execution of hybrids. He had been old enough to remember, but only barely. Bastian had not been born yet. If that many years had passed, then perhaps… no, surely not.

"Are you trying to tell me that this whole mess is because of you? Because you refused to continue to lay with him?"

Her smile faded in an instant.

"Do not make it sound like I am some common whore. I was forced into my relationship with your king, but I never loved him. I refused to marry Dracul because I loved Emil. I chose him. I chose to fight for love."

"So, this is because you rejected his proposal?"

Brianna looked right at him. Her eyes felt like they were trying to bore their way into his soul. A sadness swept over her features.

"You should ask him. There was more to it. It was never simply because he loved me and I did not feel the same for him. I gave up too much to be free of him, but what happened, after…"

Briana's face contorted, her eyes glassy as she stumbled over her words.

"I think it is best you ask your father. You would not believe me, even if I told you."

Nico stared at her dumbfounded.

"Love. Are you trying to say he did all this because of unrequited love?"

Her features softened.

"Don't sound so surprised. People have razed whole kingdoms to the ground for less. There is an exceptionally fine line between love and hate, and you would be surprised how quickly one emotion can bleed into another."

Rendered speechless, Nico sat on the cold stone floor in a daze. The thought of his father falling apart, because the fae before him refused to return his love, was insanity. And what did she mean there was more to it? He thought of Cyrus. How could such hatred have spawned from love, even if it was not returned?

Briana was speaking again. Nico could see her mouth moving, but he could not hear the words that passed her lips. His mind felt fuzzy, a darkness looming over him. Getting to his feet, he turned, slowly walking away from the cells. The queen shouted after him frantically as he left. Nico could hear the noise as he descended the staircase, but the words were just a jumble of sound.

Walking through the castle, a feeling of numbness took over. Arriving at his quarters, he made certain the door was locked before collapsing in his favourite chair. Reaching for the decanter and pouring himself a drink, Nico began to laugh. Starting as a low chuckle, it wasn't long before it filled the space around him, reaching a manic crescendo before his voice broke, and the crown prince began to sob. Head in his hands, Nico's chest heaved with the effort.

Knocking back one glass after another, he repeated the cycle in an attempt to quell his hysteria. Finally, his body felt warm, his limbs heavy, and he could no longer tell quite what had made him feel so unsettled in the first place. The heir to the throne of Predoran, coping in the only way he knew how, did what he did best. He closed his eyes, and let the darkness take him.

Chapter Thirty-Three

The Way of Prophecy

"We have to find the relic. It is the only chance we have of defeating the Predoran army. Otherwise, I am afraid we can kiss Viriador goodbye."

Looking around at the unlikely group, Cyrus smiled when Wren gave his hand a comforting squeeze. Astraea sat on the bed opposite them, head leant on Melana's shoulder. Each stroked the other's hair, petting one another in small gestures of comfort. Bastian, on the other hand, stood rigid, arms crossed as he glared out of the window. Turning his head sharply, he re-joined the conversation.

"I thought you knew magic, Cyrus. My brother seemed to be under the impression you were some kind of great sorcerer."

Exasperated, Cyrus replied with all the restraint he could muster.

"While I have read every text I can find, my practical capabilities are somewhat lacking, in comparison to my knowledge."

"That's not true. I've seen you do magic with my own eyes," Bastian insisted.

Cyrus rose from the bed, walking to Bastian's side. Placing a hand on his shoulder, he replied gently, "That is nothing more than misdirection, my friend. Sleight of hand. It is all smoke and mirrors. I merely distort situations and turn them to my advantage. The relic would allow us to use true magic. We would wield real power, and have a greater chance of success. Anything less, and I think we are looking at a suicide mission."

Bastian shrugged him off.

"Do not call me 'friend', you have not earned that title."

Cyrus let the jibe roll off him unfazed. To his knowledge, the relic was more of an amplifier than something that possessed magic of its own, but that was alright. He had made sure to keep to himself his own minor flares of magic. They were small, but they were there, and he could control them. Sometimes, he would make flames appear at his fingertips; other times he would make plants grow to full maturity from seed in minutes. Not that either of those talents was likely to help them in their current predicament, but they were sparks of true power nonetheless. The magic had always been there, for as long as Cyrus could remember, although he was not sure how. His parents, Cyrus was almost certain, were both from pure dragon bloodlines. But then there was always the little voice of doubt that niggled at him. In their absence, he could neither confirm nor deny his troubling thoughts. The fewer people who knew what he could do, the better.

His attention snapped back to the present when Melana stood, pacing in front of them.

"I can help. I can see things. Although granted, sometimes it is quite hit and miss. But I can at least try."

Wren hurried over to Melana, at the same time as Astraea scolded her.

"You should not have to force it, Mel," Wren said. "The visions happen as they are meant to."

"Wren's right, you shouldn't push yourself. It makes you faint, and we can't have you weak."

"What's the point of being a seer if I can't use my gift to try and help our situation? You both know you would be the first to volunteer if it was you who possessed this gift."

"She is right."

All eyes turned to Cyrus as he spoke.

"At the moment, she is the best chance we have of remaining undetected. Any insight would be helpful. Is there anything you have seen already, Melana?"

Astraea sat back on the bed, worrying her lip between her teeth as her friend spoke.

"Not really anything that can help us yet. At the ball, I, urm—"

Melana stopped, biting her lip, she dropped her gaze to the floor.

"Go on," Cyrus coaxed.

"I saw the dragons. I knew something bad was going to happen. But I did not realise it was all going to play out so soon, I swear. Sometimes I see things that will not happen for months, sometimes years. Occasionally they do not come to pass at all."

Astraea's skin seemed to have turned a putrid shade of grey. All of them slipping into stunned silence. Looking at them each in turn, Melana mouthed.

"I am sorry," her voice barely a whisper.

Wren stood, embracing her.

"There is no way you could have known, Mel."

"You understand why I have to do this though don't you? No matter what I see. I need to try."

Wren hugged her tightly as she clung to him.

"I understand."

Cyrus watched them, an unwelcome spike of jealousy piercing his chest. It was irrational, since Wren had told him only hours before that Melana was like a sister to him. He could see that he loved her, even if it was as family. It still made Cyrus feel uneasy. His dragon stirred somewhere deep within him, telling him in no uncertain terms that Wren was his. Rolling his eyes, he interrupted their display of affection.

"Yes, yes. Very touching. Tell me what you need in order to… see."

Melana offered him a cautious half smile.

"Fetch some water for me."

Obliging, Cyrus filled a bowl, carrying it over to her. He sat it on the small table that was by the bed.

"You're sure?" Wren asked her, worry wrinkling around his eyes.

Melana nodded. Sitting on the edge of the bed, they all watched, on tenterhooks as she stared into the water. Her breaths lulled into a gentle rhythm, remaining that way for some time, until the vision took hold.

Moving so that he stood next to him, Wren grabbed Cyrus's hand, holding on to it tightly. A warmth bloomed in Cyrus's chest, and a pang of guilt crept in, at the way the reassuring gesture made him feel. Especially because of the scene playing out in front of them. Astraea leaned against Bastian, the pair speaking words of reassurance to one another, though they were lost to everyone else in the room.

It wasn't until Melana's sounds of distress had Astraea burying her head in her hands that Cyrus could see the fear written on Bastian's face. Though he had to agree that this was not pleasant to watch, what worried him more was how reactive Wren and Astraea seemed. Especially as they were used to witnessing Melana's visions. Melana's body started to shake violently, pain etched into every fibre of her being. Her head was thrown back, only the whites of her eyes were visible. Astraea screamed as the physical intensity of the vision played out, but Cyrus was mesmerised. This was both a terrifying and fascinating phenomenon to witness. He wanted to know what she was experiencing. Only, perhaps he didn't.

They did not have to wait long; as quickly as the vision had taken hold, it was over. Melana's eyes rolled as they returned to normal, a haunted look plagued her as her friends held her upright. They all waited expectantly, eyes wide, until Melana opened her mouth to speak. The physical toll the vision had taken on her was evident, but she managed two words, sending the room into panic.

"They're coming."

Chapter Thirty-Four
Too Late to Turn Back

That had been Melana's most volatile experience with her visions to date. It had started outside. Running through trees, hundreds of acacias as far as the eye could see. She had to run. She had to get away. A dragon began to screech, deafening her, and then the vision changed. Now she was back in a cell, hungry, dirty, filled with despair. The older man was there again, hair as white as snow. He screamed insults at her till she wept. His eyes had been wild. The feral rage that had possessed him frightened her. Her vision shifted: she could see the open planes of a battlefield, but she did not recognise the land. Though she could hear the screams of the injured and dying, it was the metallic smell of blood that overwhelmed her. Suddenly, the younger man, with his beautifully sharp features, icy eyes and chiselled jaw, was there with her. Now he was her jailer, cold and distant. Very different from how he had been with her in Melana's last vision. The timeline jumped again. This time she was dressed in fine clothes, looking clean and well fed. Still with the young blond, but this time he held her close in his arms, as if she meant something to him now.

Then everything changed, and she instinctively knew that this was happening now, somewhere close by. The young man haunting her visions led around thirty men. They were hunting them. Melana heard his voice as he told them, "He's more likely to hide them in plain sight. Cyrus knows we would have soldiers swarming the countryside trying to find them." She could see them searching taverns, causing unnecessary distress and destruction as the men tore towns apart in their search for their small party. Then there was the now all-too-familiar screech of a dragon, and she could feel her mouth moving, its own entity, as the vision drew to a close.

"They're coming."

As her consciousness returned to her, Melana watched any remaining colour drain from Astraea's face. They clung to each other, each holding the other upright. Bastian was on his feet, shouting obscenities at Cyrus,

Wren trying to push the two men apart. Melana grabbed Astraea's hand; her friend lifted her head to look her in the eye, but seemed unable to speak.

"We need to leave."

She tried to pull Astraea up with her, pushing herself up off the bed. But Melana was dizzy, unable to achieve the volume she needed.

"We need to leave."

The shouting around her continued as the men argued. Bastian told Cyrus it was all his fault. They kept shouting about Nico, and Dracul, and Gerritsen. It was so loud, her head hurt, and Melana lost count of the times Bastian called him a bastard. Summoning all her strength, she shouted as loudly as she could manage, emphasising each word.

"We need to *leave*. We need to leave *now*."

Everyone fell silent for a moment before the men started each pulling what few belongings they had together. Wren grabbed Tormund, who had been curled up asleep on the floor, shoving him into the cloth bag he had slung across his shoulder. The poor bewildered animal stuck his head back out, looking around startled.

It was mere moments before they were out of the room, grabbing the ladies' bags as they passed their room, before descending the wooden staircase, feet clattering heavily as they went. Stopping dead at the bottom, Cyrus flung his arms wide, pushing them all back. They listened as raised voices carried above the din from the bar. Looking out across the open tavern, Melana spotted the man from her visions. A few dozen soldiers were with him, all of them well built and muscular, unlike the blond man. He was tall, slim but toned, with pale skin and that platinum blond hair. His features just as sharp as she had seen in her mind's eye. She could hear Cyrus swear, Bastian muttering, "Nico."

So *that* was Nico. Now she knew what she had to do. If she stayed with the group, she would only slow them down. To give them the time they needed to escape, Melana was about to gamble with her life, uncertain if it would pay off. While she knew that only time would tell, everything seemed to make sense to her now, fragments of her vision falling into place. It would be alright – and if it wasn't… well, she would worry about that then.

Grabbing hold of Astraea's hand, Melana turned, speaking directly to Wren.

"You have to look after each other. You have to keep her safe. Keep them alive, Wren."

Then she was pushing past Cyrus, before any of them could react. Wren clung to Astraea, holding her back as she tried to chase after her friend, both of them shouting her name after her. Melana cut a path, weaving through the tables of patrons as she made her way through the area between the stairs and the bar. It was not too busy, as it was still early in the day, but there was a buzz of noise regardless. Above it, Astraea screamed her name. Cyrus shouted, instructing them to get out, to get to safety, he would get her and catch them up. Only, Melana knew that he wouldn't. Cyrus was behind her moments later as the patrons started to fall quiet one by one. Turning her head back to them briefly, Melana saw Bastian taking off towards the back door with Wren. They dragged Astraea between them as she fought to get free. It was the most animated Melana had seen her since they had escaped the palace, and she could not help the small smile that crept on to her face, glad that her friend's fire had not gone out.

Melana's eyes locked with Nico's for a split second. And then he was looking past her. Cyrus. The penny dropped; she only had to see the way Nico looked through her to know what Cyrus was to him. Chaos erupted once more. Commands were shouted, soldiers gave chase to her friends, following them outside, while Cyrus squared up to Nico, pulling her behind him.

"Cyrus."

Nico breathed his name like a plea, taking a step towards him.

"Why did you run? Do you have any idea how bad things are now? Dracul wants you all dead."

Throat bobbing in response, Cyrus stared at his former lover pitifully, as he reached into his jacket, letting his fingers rest on the hilt of his dagger.

"I can't let you hurt them, Nico. I made you a promise that I would protect Bastian, and I meant it. I *will* protect him, even if it is from you."

Shoulders sagging, Nico raised his hands as he spoke, gesticulating wildly between them.

"Do you really believe I would hurt either of you? You know as well as I do that I am not here because I want to be. I am just a pawn in Dracul's game. The same as any of us are. If you come back of your own free will, I can make him see that you were only trying to protect Bastian. Please, just let me save you. Let me try."

His eyes glistened, wet with tears that had yet to fall. Nico's voice caught on a strangled sound as he tried to speak, and Melana suddenly wished she was anywhere else, as they shared this awkwardly intimate moment.

"I'm so sorry, Nico, but I can't do that. I met my fated flame."

Squeezing his eyes shut tightly, Nico's eyebrows dropped. His lips parted, mouth falling open slightly.

"It is him I ran with. I am sorry."

"No, no, you can't be serious."

"I really am sorry, Nico."

Opening his eyes, only steely resolve remained. The mask Nico wore for the rest of the world had fallen firmly into place.

"I am giving you a chance; you can rule by my side. I will talk to my father. You have not worked so hard all your life to lose everything now. You have a choice, Cyrus. Please."

Looking to the wooden floor, nostrils flaring, Cyrus brought his gaze slowly back to meet Nico's.

"How many of us are lucky enough that they can say their mating bond fell into place when they were not even looking? I choose him. I will always choose him, and if that means returning to the gutter, then I'll gladly do it, as long as he is by my side."

Drawing himself up straight, Nico clenched his jaw, his eyes focused and deadly as he spat, "Well then, I hope you're prepared to die beside him too."

Staring each other down, their gazes intense, Melana could tell that Cyrus still cared a great deal. But she could also see Nico's expression flitting between emotions. Hurt flickered across his features, then rage. Then his eyes were empty pools, frozen over. Pushing her way past Cyrus, Melana stood between them.

"Let them go, take me instead."

Nico continued to look straight through her, while Cyrus addressed him, pushing her behind him once more. Taking off his jacket, he was prepared to shift if he had to. The gold-handled dagger remained gripped in his palm as he spoke.

"Don't make me do this."

"Then choose me. Choose us."

His gaze filled with sadness and a hint of regret; Cyrus gave the only response he could.

"The right one won't run, Nico. Remember that."

Melana pushed her way between them again. Growling in irritation, Nico acknowledged her presence this time. But Melana knew what Cyrus was now. Quickly turning to face him, she spoke so that only he could hear.

"Get them out of here. Take to the skies if you have to, but get the others somewhere safe."

Spinning back around, she punched Nico square in the face, sending him stumbling backwards. Rubbing her knuckles, Melana watched as he toppled backwards over the chair that had sat behind him.

Cyrus remained frozen, blade drawn.

"Go!" Screaming at Cyrus, Melana gave the startled man a shove, pleased when he co-operated. His limbs finally catching up with the weight of her words, he started to move. Cyrus ran, and Melana watched, relieved, flexing her fingers as he disappeared through the open door.

Slowly, Nico got to his feet. Clasping a hand to his nose, as blood trickled through his fingers. Squaring up to him, Melana did her best to be intimidating, but even drawing herself to her full height, she knew she was outmatched.

"I said, take me."

"You fucking bitch."

Springing forward, he spat the insult, grabbing Melana by her hair, making her cry out loudly as strands were ripped from her scalp.

"Who the fuck do you think you are?"

Her friends all she could think of, Melana cried out again, her words ground out through the pain.

"I will die before I let you hurt any of them."

Tugging hard, Nico dragged Melana against him, his blood smearing the length of her arm where it had begun to dribble down onto his shirt as she struggled in his grasp.

"I do not know who the fuck you think you are, or what exactly you think you are going to achieve here, but I can promise you, you are going to pay for that."

Melana gasped as Nico grabbed the sword that hung at his waist, pulling it from its sheath. He brought the butt down hard across her skull. As she slipped to the ground disorientated, Melana realised quite how foolish she had been. Her actions had been too rash. To think she could know this male's character from the few snippets that had played out in her visions had been madness. In any case, it was too late to turn back now.

Chapter Thirty-Five

Friend or Foe

Reverberating footsteps pounded the dirt paths, cold air whipping against Astraea's cheeks as they ran through the trees. Trying desperately to stay silent but failing, she cried out every time she stumbled over a root or slipped on damp leaves. Dragging her along, Bastian hauled Astraea to her feet every time she fell. Setting the pace just ahead of them, Wren led the way. Zigzagging through the evergreen fir trees, she realised there were too many soldiers on their tail. Astraea fell once more, her trousers now sodden. Crying out, she begged Bastian and Wren to carry on without her. Any hope of them all getting away had diminished; she just wasn't fast enough to keep up with them. At least if they left her behind, she would stop slowing them down.

Above them a dragon screeched, the gears of time seemed to grind into slow motion. Wren gasped, fleeting expressions racing across his face; shock, fear and finally resilience. Reaching to draw his sword, he prepared to defend them to the death, while Astraea braced herself for whatever terrifying ordeal would come next. She could only hope that, one way or another, it would be over quickly.

Squeezing her eyes tightly shut, Astraea held her breath, thinking that the only one who had not looked terrified was Bastian. But before she could process anything further, a clawed foot swooped in, grabbing her from the forest floor. Astraea screamed until her lungs were raw. The wind hit her, like ice piercing her skin, as they hurtled through the air in the monster's grip. She was aware that Bastian was hunched over her, his arms wrapped around her shoulders as he tried to shield her face from the elements. Looking over at the creature's other foot, Astraea could see Wren stowed safely in its claws. One arm clutched the bag across his body as if his life depended on it. It was quickly apparent to her that the animal held him just firm enough to keep him still, but not hard enough to hurt him as Wren struggled against its grip. With the realisation that the dragon might be trying to help them, Astraea wished she could simply ask Bastian the questions that raced through her mind. But the dragon's wing beats were thunderous in her ears, so instead she relaxed into his arms, allowing him to casually manoeuvre himself so they could sit more comfortably in the creature's clasped claws. She mused on where the dragon had come from, while Bastian snaked an arm around her waist, holding her firmly against him. The gesture made her feel at ease, and her fluttering pulse finally began to even out.

The further they flew, the safer she felt, and Astraea no longer thought it was one of Dracul's men. Eventually, even Wren gave up struggling, going limp against the creature's huge claws as the flight continued. Astraea watched, laughing despite their situation, as Tormund's furry face poked out of the bag in Wren's arms, only to instantly disappear again. She did not blame him. The only thing she could do now was to pray they would land safely, and that the creature was, as she suspected, friend, rather than foe.

* * * * *

The dragon started to descend, the beats of its wings less rapid now. Astraea felt a euphoria wash over her as the creature started to glide. Up here, she felt a strange sense of freedom, which was ironic, seeing as they were held captive between taloned bars. A stone tower came into view, surrounded by trees as far as the eye could see. This was the place Bastian had told them about. A partially enclosed staircase twisted around it all the way from the ground to the sky. The tower loomed above the woodland, dominating the skyline. That must be where they were headed. Abruptly her thoughts were cut off as the dragon paused in the sky. Its mighty wings flapped to stop them free-falling, but it drew itself upright. Astraea squealed, holding on tightly to Bastian as the creature made a jerky descent. Landing in a gap between the trees, the beast let them go as it hit the ground. The impact sent the trio, and the cat, tumbling from its talons.

When she looked up, Astraea's breath caught in her throat. The dragon was beautiful, a truly magnificent creature. Shimmering blue scales glistened the length of the animal's body. She was awestruck that the creature had decided to help them. Seduced by its beauty, she could not understand how the feud between their people had come to pass. The dragon grunted, tiny smoke rings puffed from its nostrils, but it made no move to attack. This was not the beast that her parents had warned Astraea she should fear. Tormund, who had taken one look at the creature, instantly burrowed back into the canvas bag that now sat on the forest floor.

Before she could get to her feet, Wren was up, standing between her and the dragon, sword drawn. Screaming at him to stop, Wren was distracted long enough for Bastian to tackle him. Taking him down, they hit the floor like a sack of potatoes. And moments later, both Wren and Astraea found themselves struck dumb. The dragon had shifted. Before them stood a very naked Cyrus.

"You have got to be fucking kidding me."

Shouting as he got to his feet, Wren lunged at Cyrus. Astraea ran towards them, placing herself between the two men, grabbing her friend's shoulders.

"Wren, stop. He saved us."

Bastian quickly threw Cyrus spare clothes from his bag. Thanking him, Cyrus pulled them on. As the tunic came over his head, Astraea turned slowly to face him.

"Where's Mel?"

Flinching, Cyrus's brows knitted.

"She fell behind."

Wren unleashed a guttural cry from somewhere behind her, and Astraea became aware from the noise he made that Bastian was having to restrain him again.

"What do you mean, she fell behind?"

Astraea's blood turned to ice in her veins. Wren screamed a continuous string of insults at Cyrus, as she stood there demanding an answer of the dragon-shifter.

"Melana told me to save you. She knew what I was, and she knew she would slow us down. She begged me to save you all, to take to the skies and get you to safety. It is regrettable though; she would have been an asset to us."

"An asset? An *asset*?"

Breaking free of Bastian's grip, Wren smashed into Cyrus, the pair crashing to the floor, Cyrus pinned beneath him on the hard ground. He grabbed his shirt with both hands, lifting him by it, shaking Cyrus frantically before smashing his skull down onto the solid earth. It was only when Wren raised his hands to his throat that the dragon tried to fight back. Clawing at them, Cyrus struggled, the lack of oxygen debilitating, as his windpipe was crushed. Wren continued to squeeze tightly, then reaching down with one hand, he unsheathed his dagger, pressing the blade to Cyrus's throat. He hurled more insults his way before asking, "Give me one good reason why I shouldn't just kill you now?"

Astraea thought for a moment that Wren might actually do it, as she hovered, unsure how best to help. Then, to her relief, Bastian was back, dragging Wren off of him. Cyrus lay on the ground, coughing as he tried to force air back into his lungs. The smallest trace of blood visible, beading where the dagger had pressed into his flesh moments before.

Moving towards the scrapping pair, dirt and dust filled the air where they struggled. Astraea wrapped her arms around Wren, holding him tightly, until he eventually fell still.

Cyrus called out, voice croaky from where he lay massaging his throat in the dirt. "She punched Nico in the face, you know. I think she may have even broken his nose."

Astraea felt the moment Wren gritted his teeth, his face resting against her, jaw grating on her shoulder as she held him.

"That bastard's going to kill her."

He spoke so that only she could hear, his voice breaking on a sob.

From beyond him, Bastian's eyes searched hers. He looked ashamed, and maybe a little broken.

"You're one too, aren't you?"

Turning away, he was unable to look her in the eye when he replied, "I think you already know the answer, Princess."

Cyrus was on his feet now, coming to stand beside Bastian.

"Who are you?"

She did not recognise the voice as her own. It was loud, angry, and filled with disdain. All the while, her hands never stopped moving through Wren's hair in an attempt to placate him. When Bastian did not reply, Cyrus stepped forward, theatrically introducing him.

"Prince Bastian Castillo of Predoran."

The anger she felt towards them began to diminish when Bastian smacked the underside of Cyrus's head, causing the dragon to curse. After all, the pair had, for whatever reason, aided them; but they had also deceived them.

When Bastian's gaze rested on her once more, he offered, "I swear to you, Nico will not hurt her. I know him, he wouldn't. Although I can't speak for my father."

Astraea narrowed her eyes, lines pinching the corners.

"What is he to you?"

Her words were slightly less venomous now, but they were still a far cry from civil.

"He is my brother."

In her arms, Wren let out another cry against her chest. The moment the sound left his lips, she thought Wren sounded less fae, more beast, wounded and feral. Pulling him in, Astraea held her friend tightly against her. Cyrus watched him, fidgeting uncomfortably as if Wren's anguish pained him. She felt a little sorry for the man. Astraea could not see a way back from this for either of them. Releasing a long drawn-out breath, she addressed them.

"Then I swear this to you. If any harm comes to her, I will flay the skin from his bones, and I will revel in his screams."

As Wren continued to sob, Astraea shuddered at the way her own voice sounded. It was detached. Cold and concise. Shivering, she no longer knew what frightened her more, the burning rage that was consuming her from the inside, or how terrified she was at the thought of all that could befall Melana.

CHAPTER THIRTY-SIX

No More Lies

Moving quietly through the forest, Bastian was pleasantly surprised at the evergreen firs that grew there. Trees in Predoran did not tend to bear much in the way of foliage. Those that did, mostly bore leaves in warm shades. Hues of red and orange kept the land in a frozen state of aesthetic Autumn.

The bow in his hand felt foreign. Although he had been taught to shoot, Bastian did not recall being much good at it. Growing up he had been schooled in a range of combat. As an adult, his weapon of choice was the sword; nothing compared to the power he felt, wielding it.

The thought of the group relying on them for food did not have him filled with confidence that they would eat tonight. Especially since Wren had insisted that Astraea accompany him, which he found odd. Perhaps the fae had wanted to spend time alone with Cyrus, although after his earlier outburst, Bastian doubted it. Perhaps Wren would permanently silence him in their absence. Bastian could only dream. Either way, he did not imagine the princess to be at all skilled at hunting. A flash of brown fur caught his attention, bringing him to a sudden halt. Turning to Astraea, Bastian raised a finger to his lips, motioning towards a tiny fawn that had wandered from between the trees ahead of them. Pulling an arrow from the quiver on his back, Bastian took aim. They did not have many arrows between them. He knew his sword would be no use to them out here; this shot had to count. Taking several steady breaths, confident the small creature was firmly in his sights, Bastian loosed the arrow. At the same moment, he felt Astraea nudge the bottom of the long bow, tipping the arrow skyward. The rustling as the arrow disappeared among the trees sent the fawn bounding away. Spinning to face Astraea, Bastian found her grin wide. She was pleased that the fawn had escaped.

"What in Dios Drago's name is wrong with you? Do you *want* to starve?"

Smirking at him, Astraea's eyes flicked back to just over his shoulder.

Bastian turned to see the fawn reuniting with a doe, nuzzling into its mother's side as its tiny tail waggled happily. Slightly nauseous from hunger, he was not sure how this was supposed to make him feel any better. Folding his arms over his chest, he snapped at her, irritated.

"That was our bloody dinner."

Tilting her head to the side, she squinted at him, contemplating his outburst before rolling her eyes.

"Don't worry, I will get us something to eat."

"Like what? Do you expect us to survive on nettle soup?"

Throwing his hands up, Bastian looked around at the surrounding earth. He doubted she would even manage that, here. Given that they had not spoken properly since the revelation of what he and Cyrus were, it felt awkward for him to be the one in an unbridled temper. But the fact remained, they were hungry, and in his opinion, she had been ridiculous in sparing the fawn. At this rate, they really would starve.

Her eyes softened, "Just have a little patience."

"Fine."

Biting his tongue, Bastian stormed off, exasperated. He found a thick trunk to lean against. Resting his back on it, he refused to let her out of his sight. Even now, as heat pulsed in his veins, Bastian could feel a pull towards the fae, urging him to be the one to protect her. Sulking while sat on the uneven earth, his gaze remained firmly fixed on her, just in case danger lurked nearby. Even if, in his irritation, his eyes remained angry narrow slits while he watched her work.

* * * * *

Kneeling, the stoney dirt scraped against her knees, and Astraea found herself wondering if Bastian thought her incompetent. Thankfully the ground here was softer than that by the tower. The smell of damp earth lingered in the air as Astraea pressed a second stick into the mud near the base of a tree. The fabric at her knees grew damp as she looped cord between the two. She had set several of these snares now, so that any rabbits or squirrels unfortunate enough to try and pass through them would become their evening meal. It was satisfying when Astraea noticed, after a couple of the traps were set, that Bastian had stopped watching her with disdain, now studying her with intrigue as she worked. While she did not enjoy hunting the animals of the forest, it was now a necessity – although she would be damned if she would have knowingly allowed any of them to separate a mother from its child, when there was other fresh meat available to them. And she was confident they would catch it in due course.

Groaning as she got to her feet, Astraea motioned for him to join her as she crouched behind a fir tree. Bow out and arrow drawn, they waited. They did not have to wait long before a small brown rabbit stopped to sniff the air nearby. Astraea did not hesitate. A second later, the rabbit fell to the ground, dead. An arrow pierced its chest near the animal's shoulder. It was not a perfect shot, but it had done the job regardless. Dropping the bow to her side, Astraea rose to collect her prize. It was only as she offered the still-warm animal to Bastian that she noticed him gawking at her, jaw slack. A satisfied half smile quirked her lips.

"What?" Astraea stared back at him, laughing as she spoke again. "Don't tell me you have never seen a lady shoot before?"

Clutching at her neck in mock horror, Bastian thought she looked every inch the scandalised maiden. Her laugh was beautiful, her smile reaching her eyes. It was the first time he had seen it. Bastian allowed his gaze to roam over her slowly, taking her in, as if he was seeing her for the first time.

"A female? Yes, many. But never a princess."

Astraea snarked at him, "Oh, really? Do you know many princesses then?"

She tucked herself back behind the tree and they lay in wait for another rabbit. A few minutes of silence stretched between them before Bastian inquired, "Who taught you?"

His breath was warm as it brushed the skin at the back of her neck. Swallowing hard, it took Astraea a moment to compose herself.

"Wren taught me, growing up. He still takes me hunting sometimes. Well, he *did...*"

Hearing her own words drift away sadly, Astraea readied her bow again. She did not want to dwell on before. Nothing could be gained from it now. The girl she had been back at the palace had died there. That version of her would not have been compatible with the world they now found themselves in. The woman she was now, above all else, wanted to survive.

"Please believe, I had no idea what was going to happen. I wanted to unite our people."

Slowly turning to face him, Astraea struggled to keep the emotion from her voice. It crawled its way up her throat from the pit of her stomach, threatening to overwhelm her. If she let her tears fall now, she feared they would never stop.

"I think it is too late for that now, don't you? It's not that I am sad you lied to me, Bastian, although I suppose I am; it is more the fear that I will not be able to believe what you tell me from now on."

"Would you have ever entertained me, had I been honest with you? How would I even have made it to your court?"

Bastian raised his hand, brushing a loose strand of hair that had broken free of the braid behind her ear. She grabbed his wrist and they both froze, staring into each other's eyes. Astraea's mouth suddenly felt so dry she struggled to swallow, yet she gulped hard, her whole throat heaving as her eyes became glassy.

"Deceit, no matter the reason, is dishonourable, Bastian. Don't you see that this one lie, no matter your reasons, will tarnish a thousand truths you might tell? Why would you pretend to be something you are not? Are you ashamed of what you are? What did you possibly think you could gain by lying to me?"

"I am not ashamed of who I am, but I am ashamed of what my people are capable of. I have read the history books. And yes, I knew you would find out eventually, but I hoped by then it would not matter. If I ever thought for one moment that my father's army was going to attack, I swear I… Do you know what? I do not know what I would have done differently, but I would have tried. I would have done something."

Looking down, Astraea took Bastian's hands in her own before raising her eyes to meet his once more.

"There is never a better reason to lie than there is to tell the truth, Bastian. What is done is done, nothing can undo it now. Just promise me, no more lies."

"No more lies," he echoed as she let his hands fall from her own.

Slipping back into a more comfortable silence, they waited for another unfortunate animal to cross their path.

Chapter Thirty-Seven

Strangers Once More

The silence between them spoke volumes. Wren had not so much as spared him a glance since finding out his true nature, and it stung. All his life, Cyrus had made a point of keeping an impenetrable shield around himself, his sole focus obtaining the relic while climbing ranks until he was in a position of power. Nico had slipped through the net to some degree, but otherwise, there were no others that truly knew him. He had almost made it, despite a lifetime of pain that had hardened him beyond anything Cyrus now recognised. He was just a shell, a carcass, hollow inside. Even the relic seemed to be slipping to the fringes of his vision, as the longing for the fae in front of him gradually dominated his entire consciousness.

Digging his fingernails into his palms, Cyrus sighed as he turned away to gather more wood for the fire. His whole life he had felt he had been moving forward, but the path he walked snaked, ever moving. The closer he got to any kind of happiness, the more he seemed to fail. It sent him spiralling over and over again. As a result, he would get the pleasure of revisiting all the trauma he had endured through his life, and all the emotions that came with it. Cyrus knew he was an awful being. From the moment he was born he had been cursed. It had been stupid to think he could have that kind of connection, something so pure, a blessing from the gods. No, nothing that good happened to him. Still, at least Wren had stopped trying to kill him. That was something, he supposed.

* * * * *

Relief flooded Wren when he saw the others return from their hunt, a small selection of rabbits carried between them. It was about time. He'd had enough of the awkward silence that loomed between himself and Cyrus. It had been a long drawn-out afternoon for him. Ignoring him had been painful. Wren could feel Cyrus's sadness seeping into his own soul, but he was still furious with him, vowing to himself that he would not back down. It was still too raw, and he was far too angry, possibly enough to cause Cyrus harm. But, at the same time, he could not bring himself to hurt the dragon. Physically anyway. Wren still had no plans to speak to him any time soon. Saviour or not, he had left his sister behind. Cyrus had left her with those monsters, and regardless of what Wren felt for him, that was the act he could not forgive. That, and his cavalier attitude. The worst part was that when Wren looked at him, he found himself wanting to both simultaneously kiss Cyrus, and wring his neck. It was too much. He hated the fact that he could not control his feelings for the dragon-shifter. Wren found himself consumed by him, and he loathed it.

Even the simple act of lighting the fire had led to a whirlwind of emotion. As Wren had bent, trying to create an ember, Cyrus had placed a hand on his shoulder, stopping him mid-motion. There was no time to object as he watched Cyrus summon flames from his fingertips. They rushed forward into the kindling, igniting it instantly. Wren looked away from the flames, squinting back at Cyrus, finding him hopeful, a half smile on his face, a peace offering. Through their bond he felt the pang of rejection emanate from Cyrus, his face falling as he realised Wren was not about to yield.

* * * * *

As the darkness crept in, the group sat huddled around the fire, rabbits cooking on spits over the flames. The understanding that they were going to have to work as a team to survive had slowly sunk in. None of them would be able to make it alone. As a result, the mood in their makeshift camp was somewhat improved. Of course, it had helped greatly that Bastian and Astraea had used their time wisely, hashing out some of their issues with each other.

Wren did not care though. He decided that he would be civil to Cyrus at best. There were too many unanswered questions whirling in his mind to ignore the man completely. The main one was, how had Cyrus used magic? Having heard him denounce the ability in front of them all, it was curious then that Wren had watched him produce flames from his fingertips. Despite being no expert, Wren was pretty confident that regular dragons could not do that. Yes, they could shift between their dragon and human form. But as far as he was aware they held no other magic. That in itself was intriguing. Coupled with the fact that Wren now felt any remaining malice melting away as the hours passed, he found the entire situation frankly infuriating.

The stone tower loomed above them, a pillar of darkness against the stars that twinkled in the night sky. That was not only where they would sleep, it was also how they could keep watch of the skies for unwanted company. While Astraea had tried to proclaim that it made more sense for most of them to stay on the ground, saying that only one look-out need climb the elevated platform, it was eventually decided, much to Cyrus's delight, that they should all stay together, in case a quick getaway was needed. Although he would need much longer to recharge his power if they had to flee. At a push, Cyrus supposed he would have to conjure enough distractions to give them the leeway they would need to escape.

Listening to Bastian waffle on as he tried to woo Astraea, Cyrus thought his ears might bleed, while his companion spoke of his lonely childhood. Having spent most of his imprisoned, he held no sympathy for laments and wistful memories. He only wished that at times he could forget his own misery.

As they ate, he watched Wren. The dancing flames made his skin glow. Cyrus longed to trace his fingers over Wren's features again. But as he sat, taking small bites from the rabbit's flesh, the fae still refused to look in his direction. Cyrus was a moth drawn to a flame, and there was nothing he could do to stop it. No doubt he would get burnt, perhaps they both would, but the feeling was too overwhelming to ignore.

It was only when Bastian went to take up watch at the top of the tower, Astraea deciding to join him, that Cyrus once again found the pair of them alone. When the chatter faded as the others ascended, the silence left behind was deafening. Risking a glance in the other man's direction, Cyrus studied Wren while he sat there in the fire's glow. He really was an exquisite creature, beautiful even in his fury. They stayed a while longer, Wren still refusing to acknowledge his existence, the ginger cat sitting loyally at his feet.

When the fae eventually rose to join the others on their watch, Cyrus found himself on his feet, rounding the fire to meet him. His hands were on the nape of Wren's neck in an instant. When he didn't move to stop him, Cyrus crashed their mouths together, their lips colliding in a kiss that quickly had Wren whining from the lack of oxygen. Moaning, Cyrus bit down on his bottom lip, hard enough to break the skin, causing red beads to rush to the surface. Sucking the blood from Wren's lip, he felt delirious. Growing hard from the coppery tang that coated his tongue, Cyrus ran his fingers the length of the fae's jaw, his other hand snaking its way up to grip his throat. Feeling Wren's hard length pressing back against his own, the only barrier between them the thin material of their breeches, Cyrus pulled back. He had to stop this before he lost control.

Gasping in hurried gulps of air, Cyrus could see Wren's pupils were blown wide. Before he could stop himself, he slid his palm down Wren's chest, bringing his fingers to rest over his heart. Their eyes connected for a moment, both still panting, filled with longing. But there was something else that lingered behind Wren's eyes. A trace of uncertainty: something was holding him back. As Cyrus revelled in the feel of the fae's chest rising and falling, his heart beating steadily under his palm, he wondered if Wren feared him. And then the delicate but deadly fae was pushing him, shoving Cyrus so hard he almost fell backwards.

"Please, Wren, I do not want us to be strangers again. I don't think I could stand it." He readied himself for a verbal assault as Wren's nostrils flared, his face scrunching in barely contained anger.

"Well, you should have thought of that before you left my sister behind."

"I did try—"

Wren cut him off. "You did not try hard enough."

He knew this was not the right moment, but Cyrus had to know.

"Is it that? Or is it because I have dragon's blood?"

Wren's fists balled at his sides.

"You are un-bloody-believable, you know that, right? I hate this. I hate that I feel like I cannot breathe unless you are near me. I hate that you were the one to let me down. You lied to me, and you left my sister to be captured. But most of all, I can't bear the way my body betrays me when you're close. I despise it. Because more than anything, I want it. I want us, but I can't. So no, it's not that you are a dragon, Cyrus."

"Wren, please, do you even realise what you are to me?"

"Don't you get it? I do not care what *we* are, I care who *you* are."

Gesturing wildly between them, he continued.

"Unless you can prove otherwise, how can we be anything to each other? Whatever we might have had, it was built on deception. Created from a pack of lies."

Cyrus could feel his heart plummeting in his chest. This could not be over before it had even begun. It just couldn't be. The way they responded to each other was visceral, primal. He craved Wren in a way that made Cyrus think that if the fae continued to reject him, his heart might stop beating of its own accord. Whining, he made a final plea.

"You don't mean that. I know you can feel it too. Wren, please."

"I don't give a fuck what I feel anymore. I can't. I just can't, Cyrus, please just stay away from me."

Pushing past him, Cyrus reached out grabbing his arm. Spinning Wren around to face him, the fae's eyes were dark and full of anger as their glassy surface glittered in the moonlight.

"What is it you want from me, Cyrus? You had your chance and you blew it."

Biting down on his bloody lip, Wren was on the verge of losing it. His eyes glistened, all pupil, as he warred with himself. Cyrus searched them for some sign that he had not lost him, any sign at all that there was a chance to redeem himself. But there was only painful loathing staring back at him.

"Don't you get it, Cyrus?" Wren's voice began to crack as he spoke. "It's all just words now. There is nothing you can say that will make me believe you can be better. I need to see it. And for the record, I really do mean it. I hate that I want you."

Shirking his arm free Wren muttered, "The next time I feel butterflies, I am going to drink enough to drown them. Come on, Tormund, let's go."

Disappearing up the staircase to join the others, he left Cyrus standing dumbstruck by the fire, alone.

CHAPTER THIRTY-EIGHT

Salt in the Wound

As morning light broke over the distant snow-covered mountains, Bastian's eyes blinked open at a glacial pace that mirrored their frosty caps. The wind whipped around his face, and he smiled when he saw Astraea had moved closer to him during the night, her body fighting in sleep to keep the chilly night air at bay. Only Cyrus and Wren remained a good distance apart, still feeling the strained aftermath of the dragon's monumental revelation. Bastian mused how the fae looked stubborn, even in his sleep. Smirking, he found it satisfying that at any rate, Wren would give Cyrus a run for his money. The cat was now curled into a tight ball in Wren's arms, purring happily, even as he squinted open one eye slowly, checking who it was that had stirred.

Restless as he laid on the cold uneven stone, Bastian's mind was too active now to allow him to sleep again. When the others woke, they would have to formulate a plan. No matter how safe they felt here, they could not stay forever.

Sitting up, he looked out at the snow-covered peaks in the distance. Carpathia lay just the other side of those mountains. Bastian wondered if they would find any help with the elves or if his father had destroyed that alliance long ago. He had seen Carpathia before on Cyrus's old maps, so he knew where it lay geographically, but he had never seen the land himself. He looked forward to it, having heard tales of its beauty.

The group began to stir one by one, making their way down the crumbling structure to the clearing below. Animals that had been milling about, enjoying the peaceful morning, scattered as the group appeared from the entrance. The only thing that continued unaffected was the birdsong. When Wren appeared in the stone archway, Cyrus reached out to him. Bastian thought he looked tired, the underneath of his eyes marred with dark rings, his skin paler than usual.

"Wren, please can we talk?"

The fae crossed his arms tightly over his chest at the words.

"I thought I made myself clear last night."

Bastian chuckled to himself, watching as the fae stormed away, disappearing into the trees with a ball of ginger fluff and its dancing feather duster flapping at his heels. Cyrus exhaled loudly, folding in on himself defeatedly as he sank down to sit on a rock.

"I've really messed this up, haven't I?"

It wasn't a question – he clearly already knew the answer – but Bastian took great joy in replying anyway.

"I mean, you are an insufferable arsehole at times, Cyrus, so he was bound to see it eventually. Besides, there are far more pressing matters. We need to work out what route will get us all safely to Oldir."

Cyrus couldn't hide his irritation, his eyebrows rising till they were dangerously close to getting lost in his hairline. But he did not disagree. Instead, he simply replied, "Have you ever thought that perhaps I don't know how to be anything else?"

From behind him, Astraea placed a gentle hand on Cyrus's shoulder.

"I will go and keep an eye on him, don't worry."

And then she too disappeared in the same direction that Wren had headed in. Being stuck with only Cyrus for company had never been at the top of Bastian's list of his favourite things to do. In fact, normally he would have debated if more fun could be found rubbing salt into an open wound, but somehow now it did not seem quite so bad.

"So, what is the plan once we get there? How do we get this relic anyway?" When Cyrus did not answer, he found his chest growing a little tighter. "You do have a plan, don't you? You always have a plan."

When all that emerged from the man was a small burst of hysterical laughter, Bastian felt himself visibly deflate. Dropping down to join Cyrus on the rock, he sighed. "Marvellous."

Tilting his head, Cyrus turned to study him. "You worry too much. We have to get there first. Worry about that before you worry about anything else."

Tutting, Bastian rolled his eyes skyward. "I take it you have a route planned out, then?"

"Not exactly. When the others are finished gallivanting about in the woods, perhaps we can all discuss it together."

Fidgeting, his fingers tangled in his lap, Bastian huffed. "Hopefully they won't be long."

Now it was Cyrus who rolled his eyes. "Yes, with any luck."

* * * * *

The others did not return for hours. When they did eventually traipse back into the camp, night had almost fallen. Bastian had contended with Cyrus, spending most of his afternoon talking him out of searching for Wren. While they waited, the pair had explored their surroundings, gathering enough wood to keep the fire going for the rest of the night. As an observer of their predicament, Bastian thought it was obvious that Wren had left to get some space away from his newfound mate and allow himself to process everything that had happened. It was a lot to take in, and besides, Astraea was with them, and the cat.

When the wanderers finally returned with game from the snares, the fire was already alight. Night had fallen by the time they sat eating their meal of roasted squirrel and rabbit. Tormund hovered at Wren's feet, disembowelling a small furry creature. Wren had started it off for him, ripping a hole in the animal's gut with his dagger. Not that the animal was not, in Bastian's humble opinion, perfectly capable of ripping the food apart himself. When Tormund looked up, incredibly pleased with himself, he had to stifle a laugh. The fur on his face was a bloody mess. In the firelight, he looked like a tiny lion devouring its prey.

Smoke swirled around them in the darkness, and while everyone was managing to be civil to each other, Bastian thought it would be good to air his ideas. He cleared his throat before beginning.

"I was thinking, if we head into Carpathia, we can see if the elves will pledge us their allegiance. If they will not, perhaps we can at least barter safe passage across the sea to Oldir from there."

Wren shook his head, his arms folding across his chest once more. "I do not like it. The elves only hide themselves away in Carpathia because of what past conflicts did to them. I do not think they will readily welcome what they will consider the enemy into their home."

Glancing sideways at Cyrus with a look of disdain, he quickly added, "And I do not blame them."

"I agree," Astraea said, sadly. "They have no reason at all to help us. Their trust is something we would need to earn back. I would not expect them to give it freely, not after all they have lost."

"Then do you have a better plan?"

Staring at their blank faces, Cyrus continued, "Going through Carpathia makes the most sense, even if we try to slip through undetected. It would take too long to go around the mountain pass, and we would still have to enter their lands to find a port. We might as well just go the whole hog."

Pleasantly surprised, Bastian smiled at him. It was a rare thing for the pair to be pushing the same agenda. Next to him Astraea hugged her knees to her chest, while Wren warmed his hands near the flames, staring at Cyrus defiantly.

"After what your people did to them, they will kill you if we are caught. Hell, I would be surprised if they didn't kill us all."

Stroking the stubble lining his jaw, Cyrus mulled over the fae's warning, taking his time to respond.

"We are all guilty in our own way."

Letting the weight of his words hang in the air for a moment, Cyrus finally continued, "I know I am as guilty as the next person. I've crawled up from the gutter to get to where I needed to be, knowing full well I have trodden on anyone I needed to on my way up the ladder." He laughed to himself in a moment of wistfulness. "For all the good it has ended up doing in the end. I lived in the castle, had everything I could have ever wanted, but I just couldn't let it go. I still allowed the guilt to eat away at me."

Unsure what Cyrus was talking about, Bastian cocked his head to the side like an inquisitive animal. But the man continued, as if the rest of them were simply not there.

"For me, this was always about avenging my people, and my stolen freedom. The resentment I've held for Dracul Castillo has festered within me for so long, I didn't know how to be anything other than this embodiment of rage, but now—" Cyrus's voice threatened to break on him as he choked back a small sob. Bastian felt terrible. There was a whole other side to Cyrus, one that he had not even known existed. Come to think of it, he knew nothing much of his history, he had never *wanted* to know, until now. It wasn't long before he found himself wondering if Nico knew what Cyrus was talking about, but he was quickly pulled from his thoughts. He watched the other man, his eyes reflecting the flames they stared into, no longer acknowledging anyone else's presence. The next words to leave his mouth made Bastian shudder.

"I crave power, too. At least I did. Maybe I still do, I don't know." His gaze flickered to Wren for the briefest of moments before he continued. "My mind feels a little fractured right now. But I do know that vengeance isn't enough for me, not anymore. I don't think it has been for a while. Now I am not sure what exactly it is that I do want."

Bastian risked a glance at Wren and Astraea, relieved to find they also looked unnerved by Cyrus's statement. Lost in the flames he continued to whisper, "It was only when I stopped being afraid that I realised I too could become something to fear. And he will fear me, in the end. That much I can promise you."

CHAPTER THIRTY-NINE

Not So Different After All

It was with discouraging slowness that Cyrus raised his head. It took a while, but he eventually acknowledged that Bastian was asking him a question. He wondered how long he had drifted in his own world. The information he had just divulged had been a hard truth to swallow, but it was the most honest Cyrus had been with himself in a long time, never mind with anyone else. There was little point in keeping secrets now. As time went on, he knew that Bastian would begin to question his obsession with the relic, just as Nico had. If there was any chance of defeating Dracul, of becoming more powerful than an army of dragons, then this was it. It was their one shot, and Cyrus was going to make damn sure that he would be the one to take it. This, after all, was the culmination of his life's work. Funny, he thought, how his miserable existence had come to this.

Fingers tugged gently at his sleeve in a childlike manner. Cyrus's eyes darted to them, then he looked up to find Bastian, his eyes wide and startled as he asked, "What happened to you, Cyrus?"

A hollow laugh escaped him. "How long have you got?"

Wren immediately straightened from where he sat hunched on the other side of the fire, his interest piqued. A log popped loudly as the flames consumed it, and Tormund, who had moved to sit in his lap, washing himself in an overzealous fashion, jumped with a start. The cat's eyes grew wide as he shot up, climbing Wren's chest and snaking his way around his master's neck like a scarf. The fae did not so much as flinch, and Cyrus could tell from the looks the group now gave him that none of them would take no for an answer.

"Oh, we have all night."

Sighing, Cyrus thought he would probably live to regret this at some point, but it was about time he told his story. It was only fair, after all, that Bastian learned why he was always such an 'insufferable arsehole', as he had put it. More than that, he wanted Wren to know his truth, especially if it held any sway over whether he would ever forgive him.

"Where do I start?" Clearing his throat, Cyrus decided against his better judgement, that the beginning was probably the best place. "I was still a baby when my father died, and my mother remarried. There were seven of us altogether, I was the youngest. Given any excuse, that man would beat us. And if he did not have a reason, he would make one."

Pausing, Cyrus sucked in a deep breath, his hands starting to shake. "I was six the first time he hurt me. I had been asleep in my bed when he came in. He did things to me that no child should ever have to experience. I bled for days after, didn't even try to hide it, but my mother turned a blind eye to all of it. I don't know if he did that to the others. Everyone was so busy trying to pretend none of it was happening."

His head dropped into his hands as he continued, staring at the floor, not wanting to see the pity that was no doubt written on the faces of his companions.

"I was seven when I killed him. He tried to take me across the kitchen table, but someone had left a knife there, and it was all over so quickly. I wish I could say I regret it, but I don't. Then I fled. I knew my siblings were safe, so I turned tail and ran like the coward I was. I tried to make it to the port, to barter passage to a better place, but the Predoran army had already taken some of the land nearest the coast and I was captured. They would not tell us what was happening or where we were going. They threw us into caged carts."

Pausing for a moment, Cyrus's palms pressed into his eye sockets. "I tried my best to be brave, but all choice was taken from me. It was not long after that that Oldir fell. When I heard, I knew I would never see my family again. I don't even know if any of them made it out alive."

When he looked up, Astraea was curled into Wren's side. Both had glassy eyes, and Cyrus could not tell if the cause was the smoke or their sympathy for his former self. If he stopped now, he knew he wouldn't continue, so he pressed on.

"They chained us in the hold of a ship. Packed us in so tightly that we could barely move. People died on that voyage, and they just left them with us as they started to decay. I can't even tell you how terrified I was. We were all convinced we would die. No one knew how long we would be there. And the voyage was not smooth. Those of us who did survive it were forced to join the royal guard, or were taken as servants in highborn households. Children were split up accordingly, whole families divided. After all that, my choice was join them or die. Can you imagine it?"

The further into the account Cyrus got, the higher his voice pitched as he neared hysteria. "Some men refused, and they were executed. After that, most of us fell in line and joined quietly. It's hard to put up a fight when the penalty is death. I quickly realised that even though I could not control what was happening to me, I could use it to fuel the fire in my heart. But what I did not know was that the harder you fight for something, the more you want it, the more it seems both unobtainable and consolatory in equal measure. The longer you fight for it, the more priceless it becomes. It will drive you to obsession."

Cyrus sighed, pausing for a few moments to gather his thoughts. The memories of his childhood were painful, but the faces surrounding him were emotional and invested. Bastian remained focused, intent on learning his truth. Astraea's eyes were wide with horror, but Wren – Wren's expression killed him. The fae looked utterly horrified, his eyes wet, brows pinched, mouth parted as he listened. For him, for his mate, Cyrus forced himself to continue. Wren deserved to hear it, deserved to know all that he was.

"I spent years training with the guard, but I also ran errands, gaining trust within the castle. I passed much of my free time with the old librarians. These were valuable years for me. I like to think that I utilised them well, given the circumstances. I was cared for by my superiors, if you can call it that, as were all the children who had been obtained as prisoners of war."

Throat bobbing, he swallowed hard. "I was beaten often, raped by some of my supposed comrades, but I was also trained well. I made sure that those who had it coming paid dearly for what they did to the ones who had not been able to defend themselves in the beginning. It was quite easy, actually, to dispatch them during the fighting. I was no longer a prisoner by then: I was a citizen in my own right. But all I really yearned to do was go home. To a land that no longer existed. Not as I would have remembered it, anyway. It fuelled my thirst for knowledge and power. I wanted to be able to search for my family or avenge them. Over the years, the more I travelled with the army the more horrors I saw. In the end I lost count of the places we invaded, but the civilian losses were always haunting. There were so many bodies, women and children we pulled from the rubble after attacks. I tried to save so many, but most had already passed. And what was I saving them for, really? So they could be slaves to Dracul? So they could be forced to fight for him? In the end they were all I could see when I closed my eyes at night. For such a long time, sleep evaded me. I had learned by then that my life had a tendency to fall apart in my waking hours and it haunted me. In a lot of ways, I feel like it's all I deserve now…"

Trailing off, Cyrus swallowed, trying to keep his breathing even, hands still shaking as he struggled to keep himself from falling apart. His story had never been spoken aloud, and he had underestimated how much hearing the words come from his own lips would affect him.

Bastian placed a firm hand on his knee, spurring him on to finish.

"Once I was promoted to the king's guard, we still committed atrocities under the banner of the dragon, but now they were much closer to home. As soon as I could get out, I did, earning my promotion to adviser in the palace. That was when my search for the relic really began. I had always thought it a legend, little more than a bedtime story, but texts I came across in the library suggested otherwise. I became consumed by a desperate need for vengeance, more so than I already felt. I wanted to avenge the people we were made to destroy over the years, all those who had fallen at the hands of the Predoran army."

Silence fell around the fire, until he added, "Yes, I think that just about covers it. Now you all know why I am the way I am."

On the other side of the flames, he could just about make out the tracks where tears stained Wren's skin. Tormund, still curled around his neck, watching him, his eyes beady slits, while Astraea clung to Wren, tears falling freely down her cheeks. Bastian's hand had moved to his back, and Cyrus noticed that he was rubbing it in circular motions, as if he were soothing a child.

Looking up to meet his scrutiny, he was shocked when Bastian said, "Cyrus, you are a good man. A good man that bad things have happened to. You don't have to let it define you."

Choking, Cyrus replied, "Well, those are words I never thought I would hear you of all people say." A small smile tugged at his lips. "But if you think I am a good man, then you clearly haven't been paying attention."

Chapter Forty

Butterflies

They stayed by the fire until its embers started to die. All arguing the best route to take, eventually they decided they would proceed through Carpathia with caution. Astraea was pleased when Wren suggested they stay on the ground for the night. They fed the fire again before they settled in, to give them the warm and somewhat comfortable night's sleep that they all desperately craved.

It had been worth the risk. When the first morning light came through the trees, they all roused slowly, reasonably refreshed. Astraea made sure she had an additional dagger strapped to her thigh, like Wren, as she readied herself to travel. Keeping the quiver on her back and bow in hand, she was ready should they need it. Bastian had his sword but also carried a bow, and even Wren carried his sword in addition to his concealed dagger. But, she noted with curiosity given all she now knew about Cyrus, that he only kept a pair of daggers, which he stowed somewhere inside his jacket. Interesting, given his military experience, that his weapons of choice were those requiring the closest contact.

As they gathered their meagre possessions, Astraea watched Wren usher Tormund back into his bag. The animal initially resisted but eventually complied, poking his head out to survey his surroundings once he was safely stowed.

Relieved to sense a definite break in the tension that had been plaguing them, Astraea let out a huge sigh that felt like it had been weighing her down. It had taken her a while to get her head around the whole situation. While she could see that Bastian's reasons made sense, it had not made it any easier to accept. It had certainly changed things between them. While Astraea liked him, he was still a dragon. The sting of betrayal was still fresh, especially given what his people had done to her father. It was compounded by the fact that she still did not know the fate of her mother or Melana. They could never be anything more than friends. Their positions in their rival families would never allow a union.

Bastian's dream had been a wonderful one, but it was just that, merely a whimsical fancy that in reality could never come to pass.

Watching him interact with Cyrus, it was clear he had a newfound respect for the man. It made her smile, pleased that no matter his race, he did indeed seem to have a kind heart.

They travelled on foot for a few hours before Astraea turned to look at the watchtower behind them. It was still impressive, but did not look anywhere near as formidable from this distance as it had when they had slept below it last night. Beyond, the mountains still looked so very far away. Listening to the birdsong, Astraea readied her bow, drawing an arrow so it was ready to fire. It would not be too long before darkness crept in and they would have to camp for the night. She reasoned that they might as well have food ready to cook on the fire they would inevitably set in just a few hours' time.

A flash of orange moved in her peripheral vision, as Tormund leapt from Wren's bag, a blur of colour shooting after a rabbit that had crossed their path a moment before.

"Tormund!"

Following as fast as she could manage, Astraea watched Wren disappear through the trees. Cyrus was close behind him, shouting for her friend to slow down. It was not long until she couldn't hear the rustle of them pushing through the dense forest, or their feet thudding on the earth. There was only the pounding of her heart, as Astraea realised that she and Bastian had been left behind. They could only guess which way to head next.

* * * * *

Wren careered through the trees, green flashing around him in all directions. He was vaguely aware that Cyrus was not far behind him, shouting his name. In the distance he could hear Astraea shouting for him too, but he could not lose Tormund. The silly animal would not know where he was out here. If he lost sight of him now, he could lose the damn fool for good. The tips of the firs scratched at his skin as he pushed on, refusing to slow his pace. The fluffy orange shape ahead of him kept up its speed, and now Wren panicked as his breathing became noisy and shallow.

"TORMUND!"

The rabbit continued to zigzag across the landscape, not even slowing as it reached a muddy slope that took out Tormund's back end for a moment before he gave chase again. Wren's boots skidded and he slid most of the way down the small hill, praying his feet would manage to stay on the ground. Behind him he heard Cyrus shout as he slipped in the mud, turning just enough to see the man sliding down the slope on his arse. A smirk crossed his face but soon faded as the gap between him and Tormund grew substantially larger. One more burst of adrenaline had him sprinting. Wren could feel his heart pounding in his chest, his heavy footfall reverberating through him.

Before his brain could register the change in the earth under his feet, Wren was falling. The ground beneath him had simply ceased to be. Landing awkwardly, he let out a cry, cursing the gods. *Tormund.* His eyes began to fill with panic-laden tears, as Wren realised that while the hole he had fallen into was not deep, he could not climb out alone. At this rate his furry friend would be long gone. He would be frightened and alone in the wilderness, and there would be nothing Wren could do about it. Just as the tears threatened to spill, Wren heard a yowl and looked up to find a startled pair of amber eyes peering down at him. Wren could have sworn he felt the physical weight of worry lift away. The cat stared down at him, meowing loudly in bewilderment, as if this had not been entirely his fault.

"Wren, where are you?"

Feeling rather grateful that he had managed to find himself a guard dog, even if it did come in the form of a sarcastic dragon-shifter, Wren cried out to him. "I'm down here."

It was only when he got to his feet that Wren felt the blood, wet at his thigh. He sent up a silent thanks to the gods that while the merlot slowly seeped through his trousers, it was in fact just a flesh wound. Reaching down, he retrieved Fury from where the blade stuck in the cold earth. It must have come loose, cutting his leg as he tumbled into the hole. It could have been much worse, but it was still less than ideal to have any kind of injury this far from civilisation. The other man's torso appeared, leaning over the hole. Wren's heart squeezed at the look of relief on Cyrus's face.

"Need a hand?"

Wren narrowed his eyes, the warmth that had hummed inside him evaporating as Cyrus added, "I sense you are feeling vertically challenged."

Wren's brows furrowed. "You know, I really can't tell if you are making fun of me, or you just have no idea of what's considered appropriate."

When Cyrus kneeled, leaning in to offer Wren his hand, the corners of his mouth snagged upwards, betraying him as he tried to stifle a laugh. That was enough for Wren to decide that it was both. Once he had been hauled back to solid ground he rolled, lying on his back in the mud, wincing at the sting in his thigh. Regarding him with concern, Cyrus crouched next to him, sucking in a sharp breath when he noticed the blood soaking the material at Wren's leg.

"Gods, you're hurt."

Still grimacing at the pain, Wren watched as Cyrus did not hesitate to rip a length of material from his own tunic, exposing the pale flesh of his stomach and a small trail of dark hair that led south. Gently, he lifted Wren's leg off the cold ground, his hands pleasantly if not surprisingly warm as he wrapped the fabric tightly against the wound. Wren found himself transfixed by Cyrus, his lips pressed thin, brows furrowed and face plagued with concern for him. When he had finished, Wren gazed at him breathlessly. It was only when Cyrus tucked a rogue curl behind his ear, before stroking his fingers down Wren's cheek that he remembered himself. Pulling away, Wren uttered his thanks. Waving him off, he refused to allow Cyrus to help him to his feet, using Tormund as an excuse to turn away.

Closing his eyes, Wren let his chest rise and fall, breathing deeply as he struggled to clear his mind. His leg was sore, but that was not what troubled him. Butterflies swarmed deep in his belly, and he was shocked to find he no longer wanted to drown them. Alarming thoughts stirred in his mind, and Wren had to remind himself that he did not want this. Thankfully a ball of muddy ginger fluff bounded up, leaping into his master's arms to distract him. Tormund purred so hard Wren could feel it vibrating throughout his body, and he smiled as the cat smothered him in little nibbles, butting his whole head against Wren's face with vigour.

"Yes, yes, I love you too, you little imbecile."

Eventually the cat resumed his position as Wren's personal neck warmer. It was only then that he realised Cyrus had been watching him.

"You stay here, I am going to find the others."

Nodding sheepishly, he watched the man walk away, covered in mud, as they all were. He was loath to admit that he was thankful Cyrus had been right behind him. Little flutters threatened to reappear in his core, but Wren squashed them down with thoughts of how they had come to be here in the first place. They had not covered nearly as much ground as he would have liked, and now that he was muddy and injured, he was fairly sure the rest of them would insist that they set up camp for the night. At this rate it was going to be a very long journey.

Chapter Forty-One

Falling

As predicted, Astraea and Cyrus insisted they make camp for the night so that Wren could rest his leg. When one night became two, Wren found himself pacing the makeshift camp in irritation. It was only a small wound, a cut really. He couldn't see what all the fuss was about. His ginger scarf was still wrapped firmly around his neck, purring loudly, as he had been at every opportunity since he had caused Wren to fall into the hole. At least they had now worked out that the trap had been used to hunt animals, although worryingly it had been freshly covered, which was why Wren had not seen it as he approached. Yet they had seen no signs of life other than the small creatures that littered the woodland.

The fire was dying now. It was the perfect opportunity to move on. Besides, Wren could not wait to reach Carpathia: with any luck they would have more than rabbits and squirrels on offer. If he never had to eat another small furry creature off a spit it would be too soon. Tormund, on the other hand, seemed thrilled with the menu.

When Wren emerged from the nest of trees he had been left to sleep under, his sword hung back in its rightful place, Fury now sat next to it on his belt. His bag of belongings was slung over his shoulder. Astraea nearly knocked him flying as she rushed over, fussing over him.

"Princess, I am fine. It is only a cut."

Patting him down as one would an injured child, Astraea said, "But it could have been so much worse. I have already lost Mel, I cannot lose you too."

Pulling her in for a hug he mumbled into her shoulder. "It wasn't, though. I am more than well, and we need to get moving."

Nodding at Bastian and Cyrus, he hoped they would back him. Bastian agreed with him readily, but Cyrus stared down at his boots, clearly not wanting to encourage the move.

"Oh, come on. This is ridiculous, Cyrus, it's a scratch."

The man sat up straight and cast a look over his shoulder, eyebrows raised, mumbling, "Lot of blood for a scratch."

Rolling his eyes, Wren retorted, "Seriously?"

Bastian chimed in, attempting to help the situation. "Look, can't we just see how we get on? If we head north and Wren struggles, then we can make camp again. If he is fine, then we have not lost anything."

Astraea was tight lipped as she contemplated his words. "That is true. We could do that," she eventually relented.

With three of them in agreement, they were soon on the move again, much to Wren's relief. Not wanting to be the reason they fell behind, he blinked away the pain as the wound rubbed on his dirty clothes. Even the fresh material wrapped around the cut was becoming marred by the grime from the rest of him, a bloody liquid seeping from where the wound wept. Wren was desperate to wash. They had been out in the elements too long already, their clothing becoming dirtier with every passing hour.

Astraea and Bastian tried valiantly to keep their spirits up. They sang, and Astraea taught them traditional fae songs from her childhood. Plodding behind them in silence, Cyrus's eyes never left Wren. He was clearly sulking, having moaned valiantly, arguing adamantly against their decision. But it had not changed the outcome. Even when Wren could not see him, he could feel Cyrus's eyes boring holes in his back. While it was unnerving, Wren could also feel a warmth spreading through his chest. He rationalised that it must be a result of the pain that he absolutely was not in, and nothing whatsoever to do with his growing feelings for the petulant man-child, feelings that just refused to leave him be.

As the moon began to rise, they found a secluded cluster of trees and set about making a fire. Wren felt unusually tired, but at least the burning sensation where his wound had rubbed was easing now. As the others sat about the fire talking, Wren simply offered his apologies, telling them he was tired. Once he had said goodnight to the others he curled up under their green canopy, looking up at the starlit sky above them. His eyelids felt heavy as he marvelled at the stars' beauty and listened to his friends' idle chatter. And soon enough, Wren was fast asleep.

* * * * *

As they pressed on the next day, Wren found that the time dragged horribly. The pain was getting worse, bordering on unbearable. A thin sheen of sweat had begun to form on his skin. He was only thankful the others had not yet noticed how pale he had become as he continued to lead them through the forest. Even Cyrus, who skulked along behind him, had yet to notice anything was awry. Although he supposed there was no flesh at the back of him on show. They would rest soon, Wren told himself, as he fought to put one foot in front of the other. Longing for the light to fade so they could make camp, he began to regret his insistence on moving on. Still, Wren refused to be beaten. He could do this, he could make it.

Astraea's chatter filled the air, their footsteps crunching through the fallen leaves. It all sounded so loud to him now. It was then that Wren started to feel dizzy, his head swimming as black spots floated into his vision. The last thing he remembered was taking a few more steps, staggering as he moved. Feeling Tormund skitter to the floor in alarm, he could hear Cyrus's voice calling his name, and then Wren hit the ground. It was so cold against his hot, clammy skin. It felt lovely.

Hands grabbed at him, rolling Wren onto his back. He could hear voices, but it seemed like a tangled web of noise. They were incredibly loud, and yet they felt so far away. It was as if someone held his head underwater. Before he allowed his eyes to close for a final time, Wren smiled as Cyrus's face loomed over his, blissfully oblivious to the chaos that erupted around him.

* * * * *

"It's going to be alright. You have to be alright. Please, just stay with me, Wren. I promise it will be OK."

Wren forced his eyes open at the fear that leeched from Cyrus's voice. His gaze locked with Cyrus's for a moment before his lids closed again. Wondering what it was that could have the dragon so riled, somewhere in his subconscious Wren registered the other man's honey-filled eyes. They had been wet and wide. Cyrus had looked terrified, and Wren could not fathom why.

In an instant he was falling. No, he was flying. Air rushed past his hot skin, his limbs dangling limply. Wren was vaguely aware of a feeling of weightlessness. Then they were falling. The impact was jarring, his body tumbling across the forest floor. It hurt but he did not cry out.

The pain seemed otherworldly, coursing through his entire body, emanating from his throbbing thigh. There were strange voices: he could hear Bastian shouting, Astraea screaming. Wren thought he should try and defend them, but he was so tired. Too tired. His body shivered, teeth chattering as he lay somewhere between this world and the next. With his last moments of lucidity, Wren wondered if this was what dying felt like, but he was too far gone to fight it.

Chapter Forty-Two

The Villain

The sensations were truly overwhelming. Voices boomed nearby. Melana flinched as her senses began to return to her. Lying on her side, the stone was cold against her skin, but the air was much warmer than she was used to. The smell in the air was not dirty exactly, but a mixture of straw and something that reminded Melana of cattle. She was still in the same clothes that she had been abducted in, the only difference being that now her loose-fitting tunic was stained with blood. Melana could only assume it was her own. Her eyeballs throbbed in their sockets, a pounding sensation behind them making her nauseous as she struggled to crack open an eye, slowly forcing her lids apart as a layer of grit threatened to keep them bound. Melana let the one closest to the floor stay squashed shut as she attempted to focus on the words being shouted nearby.

The light hurt, causing her to squint, but she could still make out Nico's outline, identifiable if nothing else by his short white blond hair and the sharp edges of his face. Melana had to repress her reactions, stifling a gasp when she saw the older man from her visions in front of him. It was the king. The man wore the Predoran crown, but this close it would not have mattered either way. Melana realised before she even saw the gold lining his head that it was, unmistakably, Dracul. Thinking he looked every bit as terrifying as his reputation proclaimed him, she wondered how she had not realised it before.

The way he spoke to Nico was almost as harsh as when he had threatened her future self.

"You might as well not have brought anything back at all. You have failed me. Again."

Watching the dragon king pace angrily back and forth like an animal in the confined space, Melana felt goosebumps erupting over her skin. All the while, Nico desperately tried to justify his actions. Melana quickly realised that in reality, Dracul was far more terrifying than she had always been led to believe.

"I did what I could. I thought you would be happy that we captured at least one of them."

"Happy?" A soft chuckle rolled from Dracul's tongue. "I would have been happy had you brought me the princess, or even your treacherous brother or aide. But tell me, what use do I have of that thing in there? I can't even take it as one of my whores. Just look at the state of it. What possible purpose could it have?"

"They will come for her, Father, I am sure of it. She gave herself up to save them, so she must be of some value, to them at least."

Melana watched as the king backhanded his son across the face. His jaw was tight with disgust as blood began to trickle from where his jewelled hand had collided with soft pale skin. Nico did not flinch but simply raised his own hand to his jawline, wiping at the blood that tracked its way along it, almost as if to check it was real. Looking at the blood on his fingers before flicking it away, Nico's eyes were glazed, an eerie expression creeping over him as his gaze returned to his father.

"She is nothing, you fool. Nothing. Do you hear me, boy? No one is going to come to the aid of a servant. I told you that if you disappointed me again you would be sorry. Now you can wear the scar as a permanent reminder."

Watching as Nico's body stiffened at the king's words, Melana almost felt sorry for him. Almost.

"What would you have me do with her then, Father?"

The king flew at Nico, and Melana feared he would strike him again. His voice was full of fury as he spat, "Kill it, put it to work, keep it as a pet. I do not care."

Nico's composure did not waver, even for a second. "As you wish." Bowing his head respectfully, Nico watched his father storm away. But he stopped abruptly in the doorway, and Melana quickly closed her open eye as the king turned, spitting at her cell before facing Nico again.

"One last thing. Until you have proved yourself, you can address me as your king. You are no son of mine until you can show me that you deserve to call yourself a Castillo." With that, he spun back around, his black cape billowing behind him as he left.

Melana cracked her eye open once more, watching as Nico's face dropped until he was looking at the floor. A sadness and vulnerability crept over him as his shoulders slouched. Running his fingers through his hair, he began to pace. She continued to lie there, watching him with one eye open until he finally leaned back, letting his body slide down the stone wall. The blood on his face had congealed into sticky lines, and as Nico brought his knees up so that he could lean his head against them, Melana wondered if he had forgotten about it or simply chose to ignore it.

It was only when she stirred, dragging her reluctant body up into a seated position that Nico raised his head again. Melana took him in. There was no way she could be certain, but she could have sworn there were tear stains on his face now, smeared amongst the bloody streaks.

Nico stared her down. His eyes were glassy, flecks of grey speckled in his blue irises. Melana shuddered, shaken when she found beauty in his eyes. They were like a perfect storm against a clear sky, cold but complex by nature.

"What the fuck are you looking at?"

Melana jumped a little in her own skin as he snarled at her. On closer inspection, she could see his eyes were indeed red-rimmed and puffy. Deliberating how she should play this for a brief moment, Melana decided that though she owed him nothing, it was not in her nature to ignore Nico's distress. After all, as her mother had always told her, kindness costs nothing.

Rolling herself forward onto her knees, Melana realised quite how much her body ached. Leaning in, her hands resting on the bars, she spoke to him. "Are you hurt?"

A sudden startled look crossed Nico's face before his expression turned into a scowl. Melana could tell that was the last thing he had expected her to say.

"What is it to you?"

"You just... you looked so sad after he left. I just... I don't know."

"I don't need your pity." Spit flew as Nico spoke, rage flaring in his icy eyes.

Melana replied softly, "You are nothing like him. I know you are not, because I have seen it."

He was on his feet in an instant and Melana found herself scrambling backwards into the hay as Nico bellowed at the top of his lungs. "You know nothing! Nothing! Do you hear me? You have no idea what I have had to endure. Who are you to say what it has or has not made me?"

Trembling, Melana got to her feet, taking a step towards the bars.

Close enough to make a show of defiance, but not so close that he could reach out and grab her.

"You are not the villain you try to make out you are, Nico."

Still shaking, Melana watched his expression grow cold and indifferent, a smirk spreading across his pale face as he chuckled wryly.

"I did not take you to be so naive. I took you as my prisoner. Knocked you out cold and brought you back here, knowing full well I could be carrying you to your death."

Gritting his teeth, his gaze arctic, Nico glared at her. Taking several steps towards the cell he continued, "And yet here we are. You refuse to make me a villain. You still fancy me a victim of circumstance. Poor Nico Castillo, taking orders from his abusive father." A small but manic laugh broke free from his chest. "Of course I am a villain. I had a choice the same as everybody else, but I have only ever wanted an easy life. You see, we are all the villain in someone else's tale. All it hinges on is who tells the story."

Melana tried to relax, remembering her visions. The way the prince had held her close, his warmth radiating, seeping into her skin. She had felt safe, cared for. She would not fear him. She refused.

"The only difference is that you *do* care, Nico. These things haunt you, I can tell. The way your father treats you breaks you a little more inside each time you clash. You can deny it all you like, but I see it as clear as day. You would not have been sat here crying if you were truly indifferent to the suffering he causes, and to what he would have you inflict on others."

Chewing her lip anxiously, Melana regarded Nico. A sadness washed over him for a moment as she spoke, but then his mask slid firmly back into place as he snapped, "Then it is a shame that I am already lost to darkness."

He was already turning to leave when Melana called out to him once more, determined that she would get through to him. She knew her life might very well depend on it. "There are always cracks, Nico. Everything has cracks, it is how the light gets in."

She watched him falter for a moment, then his shoulders rose and fell as he inhaled deeply, back straightening, before lifting his head high. Striding out of the gaol's only door, Nico let it slam shut behind him.

Chapter Forty-Three

The Cracks

The glass Nico had been holding a moment before collided with the stone wall, shattering into hundreds of tiny pieces. As usual, he had searched for solace at the bottom of his decanter, but this time he had failed miserably. The girl's words echoed in his head. If he closed his eyes, Nico could still see her warm chestnut eyes, pleading with him to be better than he was. She knew nothing. And yet she seemed to be able to look inside his soul. The way she spoke to him, like she had seen glimpses of his life, perhaps even his future, sent chills through his entire body. Lounging back in the chair, Nico let out a frustrated cry. Raking his fingers through his hair, he watched as droplets of the brown sticky liquid slowly ran down the wall into the sea of glass shards that littered the floor.

Having to decide a person's fate was an horrendous punishment. Nico thought of Queen Briana, who was now being held in the cells under the castle. Dracul had had Gerritsen's men torture her for information and, he was sure, in part for his father's amusement. As much as he hated how his father liberally doled out torture or ordered executions, this was somehow worse. It was Nico's decision to make and his alone. The only thing he could *not* do was free her. He should have let her go when he had the chance. He never should have brought her here.

After all the ideologies he had been raised on, Nico still found that it did not matter to him what she was. That was his father's crusade, not his. Despite it all, Nico did not want to hurt the girl. Killing her was out of the question: he struggled taking lives at the best of times, having to find a way to justify each act to himself, and if Nico was honest, he had always felt the same about torture. It was all an unfortunate but necessary evil. His indifference to suffering was a skill he had acquired to keep up his charade. Perhaps he could keep her as a serving girl, but then he did not really want her in his private space. It was bad enough that she had made him second guess himself. He could do without her seeing his weaknesses. Tonight, for example, it would not be him clearing up the mess he had made. Some poor girl or another would be along in due course to do his bidding. Perhaps he should just keep her caged as his pet. That probably was the easiest option for everyone.

It was easy to follow orders, but having someone else's life placed in his hands with which to do as he wished was very different. How could his father have done this to him? Maybe it was because he knew how deep his internal conflict ran. Perhaps he realised how much this task would affect him. Although Nico was sure that he had been more than convincing over the years, blending seamlessly with those around him who revelled in acts of brutality in order to survive. Was it possible his father saw right through him after all, just as the dark-skinned fae had? Reaching for the decanter, Nico dropped the crystal stopper on his desk. Tilting his head back, he sighed, lifting the vessel to his lips, slowly drowning out the voices in the darkness of his mind.

By the time the door creaked open, Nico felt much more at ease. He had drunk more than it would take to subdue a lesser man, but by now his body was used to it. A flurry of red hair came into view as Rae made her way through Nico's chambers. She had a pretty face, generous cleavage and ample thighs, while maintaining a well-proportioned waistline. Only just reaching his shoulder when they stood side by side, what Rae lacked in height, she made up for in personality. Nico could see why the guards fell over themselves to bed her. Especially since Rae was not just a pretty face to pass the time, she could hold her own in conversation, and had been trained in combat from a young age. She had a wise head on her young shoulders. Service had never been her first choice. Unfortunately, as it was for many in their kingdom, her place within the castle was the result of a debt that had needed to be paid. Stopping to look between him and the mess he had made, Rae rolled her eyes, placing a small tray of food down on the table. She scolded him as if he was a child. Bending to speak to him on his level, she placed a hand on Nico's shoulder.

"What on earth happened this time?"

He leaned back in his chair, gesturing with his right hand as he spoke. "Father happened. Oh, wait, I'm not allowed to call him that anymore. His Royal Highness happened. There you go, that's better."

Smirking, Nico leaned in to grab the decanter again, but Rae was quicker, swiping it straight out of his reach.

"You can't keep doing this to yourself."

Scowling, Nico tried to think of something witty to say. Rae was probably the only one of his servants he would allow to speak to him this way. With anyone else, he would have flown into a theatrical rage, sending them scurrying. But this young woman was capable of matching him at every turn, and for that he valued her. She did not fear him and she held a fire within her that could compete with the best of them. With her, he had dropped any pretence early on. Rae was one of the few who saw him as he truly was. She had even known about Cyrus. Ah, Cyrus.

"Did I mention that Cyrus ran off with another man?" The tips of his fingers scuttled along the desk miming a run. "I am having one of the best weeks of my life, truly."

As Nico raised an eyebrow sarcastically, Rae slid the decanter further away from him, placing it at the other end of the desk. He could see her looking him over, a pitying expression on her face. Nico wondered quite how dreadful he looked. Would he have felt sorry for him if he could see himself? Probably. But he needed no one's pity. About to snap at her, an idea struck him. Luck seemed to be on his side after all.

"I don't suppose you would do me a favour, would you?"

Rae's eyes narrowed to slits as she looked him over. "It depends what it is, although I can't really refuse you, can I, my Prince?"

"Don't call me that. I'm asking as a friend, Rae."

He was starting to slur his words now. Scrunching her face as she scrutinized him, Rae answered gingerly, "What is it you need?"

"Can you take food to the fae that is being held in the gaol? Not just scraps. Decent meals, please?"

Visibly relaxing, relieved that was all that was being asked of her, Rae replied with a smile, "Of course I can."

But she jumped, her limbs stiffening as Nico leaned in, grabbing her hands. "I do not want her to know it was me who asked you. Let her continue to think I am as bad as Dracul. Please, Rae."

Her wide eyes searched his. Her mouth forming little 'o's as she floundered, not knowing quite how to respond as he begged.

"Promise me, Rae. Please."

"Fine. I promise. But Nico, no one will think you weak for supplying her food. That's a basic necessity, to keep her alive."

"Ah, but that is how it starts. She knows about the cracks, you see."

"What are you—"

"The cracks. They're how it gets in."

He cut her off and Rae retreated, knowing she had lost him to his self-inflicted stupor. Bending with care, she cleaned up the mess Nico had made. He babbled nonsense about darkness and light while she gently reassured him that she would indeed feed the prisoner, and keep an eye on her on his behalf. It had been a long time since she had seen the prince quite so agitated, and frankly she found it alarming. Thankfully, by the time Rae left to head back down to the kitchens, Nico was slumped in his chair, snoring soundly.

Chapter Forty-Four

Measure of a Man

When Nico woke, his head felt like it was splitting. His whole body ached from the awkward night's sleep. Light poured into his chamber through the open curtain, hurting his eyes, and he cursed as his head continued to pound. The empty decanter in his peripheral vision reminded him of his troubles from the night before, and how his poor life choices had once again led him here. Groaning, he tried to recall the precise moment he had decided to fix all of life's problems with hard liquor as he cracked his neck from side to side, enjoying the feeling as his bones crunched. It was incredibly loud, but thankfully eased the ache in his spine to some degree. At any rate, he found it very satisfying, on both counts.

Stretching, Nico pushed himself up out of the chair, moving to look out of the window. He quickly realised that it was much later in the day than he had thought, as he watched Gerritsen run drills in the courtyard below. He vaguely recalled Rae having come to check on him last night, and there was a foggy memory of her cleaning something off the floor, but the whiskey ensured he could not remember any more than that. Had he spoken to her about his current predicament, the fae locked up in the tower gaol?

"Shit." Nico swore aloud, realising that no one would have checked in on the girl. Although had he asked Rae to feed her, or had he imagined that? Either way, he decided that he should go and make sure that she was alright, seeing as she was his charge now. Gods, he still had to decide what to do with her. Rolling his neck back, Nico stared at the ceiling for a moment in an attempt to compose himself. Why in the gods' names did he always feel the need to do this to himself? Wandering over to look for some clean clothes, Nico was comforted to find that at some point this morning someone, probably Rae, had left him a washcloth and a bowl of what was once warm water. Splashing his face with his hands he was pleasantly surprised at how nice the cool water felt on his skin. It woke him up a bit, making him feel fresher than he had moments before.

Deciding that the gaol was his next destination, Nico took his time but eventually managed to get himself washed and dressed.

* * * * *

As Melana laid on the floor of her prison, staring at the grey stone ceiling, she was relieved to find that the pain in her head was at least starting to subside now. It had been a day, maybe nearer two since Nico had left. No one had returned for her, though a guard remained stationed outside the gaol's door. Sitting up, she shuffled towards the bucket of water that had been left in her cell. Bits of hay and a solitary fly floated on the surface. Cupping her hands to bring some water to her dry lips, Melana stifled a gag as she forced herself to swallow the stale liquid. With any luck someone would bring her some fresh water soon, if nothing else.

Allowing herself to flop back into the hay once more, Melana sighed aloud. There was only so much silence one could take. She had been alone with nothing but her thoughts for company for hours. It had given her a good while to contemplate how her own stupidity had led her here. Perhaps this would be it: she would die alone, starved to death. Still, she hoped that at least the others would be safe. She wondered where they were and what they planned to do now. Maybe they really would find the relic and save the world from Dracul, but then, perhaps not.

The more time dragged by, the more Melana found herself questioning her gift. Having always thought some great good would come about because of it, she felt devastated that she had in fact just been complicit in a disaster. How utterly tragic it all seemed as she struggled to understand how she had come to judge the situation so poorly in all regards. Her visions were not normally wrong. And that was the one part Melana could not fathom. She had been so sure that Nico would not harm her, and yet here she was. Granted, she was still alive, so that was something, she supposed. It did not help that her head spun every time she so much as attempted to sit up. Although the pain had begun to subside considerably, some disorientation remained. Already filthy, Melana was in desperate need of a wash and terrified of vomiting with every movement, knowing that if she did, there was no way of washing it away. Instinctively she knew she had to rest, to let her body recover, if she were to have any chance of making it out of there. She had to try and fight. Yet Melana found herself wondering whether the peace and serenity of death would be more welcome to her now.

A voice broke the silence outside. Someone was coming. Cursing her aching body, she sat up, quickly regretting it as her head spun once more. Her insides relaxed and muscles she did not know had been clenching unfurled when she realised it was a woman's voice. It was only then that she acknowledged quite how terrified she had been that Dracul would come back for her. Especially now she knew the dynamic of father and son. If he came for her now, Nico would not be able to save her. She would be at the king's mercy. Nothing could be worse than that.

When the woman stopped for a brief conversation with the guard, Melana strained her ears in an attempt to overhear, failing miserably. The door dragged open, scraping against the flagstones before it was slammed shut behind her forcefully, a key turning loudly in the lock as the guard locked them in from their side. A woman around her own age walked towards her. Relief flooded through Melana. In one hand she held a fresh pale of water, in the other a platter of food. The woman stood for a moment at the bars regarding her. Then without saying a word, she unlocked the cell and entered.

Melana found herself lost for words; she would wait for the woman with hair as red as flame to be the first of them to speak. But she did not right away. Instead she placed the pale on the floor. Crouching down in front of her, she offered the platter to Melana to take. Shaky hands reached out, taking the tray. Nervously she took a bite of cheese, half expecting the food to be poisoned. All the while the woman watched her with fascination. It was only after the first mouthful that Melana realised quite how hungry she had been. Quickly she worked her way through a variety of meats, bread and cheese, slowing only when she reached the fruit at the far edge. Melana was thankful that all the while she stayed still it kept the nausea at bay, enabling her to enjoy this. As she chewed on a slice of spiced ham, she was debating whether to eat some of the fruit now, or see if the woman would allow her to keep some in her cell for later, when her visitor spoke.

"It's OK, you can save some for later if you like."

Nodding her head carefully, Melana continued to chew the pulverised meat in her mouth.

The woman smiled at her warmly, flashing her white teeth before she spoke again.

"You are very lucky the king let Nico keep you, you know. I was surprised when I heard he hadn't just had you executed, but then I suppose he thinks it some kind of punishment for Nico's failings, otherwise I doubt he would have let you live."

Melana just stared at the woman blankly, bristling inside at the echo of the king's implication that she was some kind of pet.

"Who are you?"

"Forgive me. My name is Rae."

Rolling her hands, Melana found herself gesturing for the woman to continue.

"And you are here because..."

"Oh, well, someone needs to keep you alive. I suppose I am what you would call one of Nico's personal servants within the castle, so, by extension, I get to look after you. Saves him having to do it. He has enough to worry about."

Melana's face fell as Rae spoke. She seemed so animated, as if she was talking about something that interested her, not her incarceration.

"And does he have many prisoners?"

She smiled again, and Melana felt a chill creeping up her spine.

"Look around, does it seem like he does?"

Rolling her eyes Melana, placed the large plate to one side.

"I mean, have you had to tend to many of his prisoners previously?"

"Actually, you are the first. Usually, it would just be the guards tending to the prisoners. Contrary to popular belief, Nico is not as terrible as people paint him. He is really quite sweet once you get to know him. Please don't ever tell him I told you that, he would skin me alive."

Melana felt her eyes grow wide as Rae chortled at her own flippant remark. Unsure if the woman was desensitised to death threats or merely joking, she made sure her next words were not misunderstood as her tone dripped with sarcasm.

"Mmhmm, he seems wonderful so far."

Gods, now the woman knelt in front of her. Her face so close Melana could feel her own breathing slow to small staccato bursts. Wisps of red hair dangled in her face, and Melana's spine stiffened as she wondered what on earth the woman was about to do. Rae looked directly into her eyes as she spoke, all pretence gone. She whispered so that the guard outside could not hear.

"He saved me from a life of… servicing the king's needs, shall we say. Claiming he needed his own servant when he was still merely a child himself. I can only imagine the horrors I would have had to go through if he had not. I would even go so far as to class him as a friend now. Nico is a good man, someone I would defend until my dying breath."

Ignoring Melana's wide eyes and slack jaw, Rae grabbed her hand and rose, pulling her to her feet too quickly. The room spun, nausea threatened to overtake her again, but Rae held her up, a small smile settled on her face. Thankfully for both of them, the feeling quickly subsided. Allowing Rae to lead her from the cell, she watched as the woman grabbed the stool that sat in the corner, dragging it over the drain in the floor.

"Take your clothes off, then sit here for me and I will wash you."

Melana began to protest but Rae cut her off.

"You can barely stand, please just do as I say. Besides I don't want you to vomit on me."

Slowly starting to shrug off her clothes, Melana muttered, "Don't you get all the good jobs?"

But she quietly did as instructed, sitting there naked, her back to the goal door. Rae, who had retrieved the old bucket of water from the cell, now stood scooping bits of hay out, flicking them off of her wet fingers and onto the floor. She rummaged in her skirt pockets, pulling out a flannel and a bar of soap. As she lathered up the material, Melana could not help but let her body relax. The soap smelled divine, like honeysuckle on a summer breeze. By the time Rae ran the cloth over her skin, washing away the grime and ridding her of the godawful smell that was starting to cling to her, Melana had almost forgotten where she was. Almost.

* * * * *

Deciding that he did in fact need to eat something before he could function properly, Nico made a slight detour to the kitchen, stopping briefly to devour some freshly baked rolls and a cup of fresh ginger and honey tea, before he headed up the winding stairs of the tower gaol. The guard at the door informed him that his serving girl was here with food, so he knew that the prisoner was not alone, but Nico was not prepared for the sight that greeted his eyes as the guard unlocked the door for him.

The fae was sat with her back to him, clothing nowhere to be seen.

Nico only had a moment to take in her curves and the dark complexion of her skin before Rae stepped in front of the fae, blocking the view. A flurry of dark curls bounced behind Rae as Melana turned her head, alarmed at the intrusion. Nico watched her desperately try to cover herself in his presence, before Rae squared up to him, pushing her face a breath from his own.

"Did you hear me? Let the poor woman get some clothes on. For the love of the gods. Nico, NICO! I said get out."

Recoiling from the sting as she slapped his cheek, Nico growled. Anyone else would have been backhanded across their face for that, but not Rae. Raising a hand to his cheek, a little taken aback, Nico simply grumbled, retreating to wait the other side of the door. Their voices still carried to him as Rae went about making her presentable.

"I can't believe you struck him. Will you not be punished?"

"Don't worry about me, I will be fine."

"I am his prisoner, he can do with me as he wishes."

Rae's voice grew hushed, but Nico could still just about make out her words.

"Frankly, I do not care. No matter who he is, the prince does not have the right to ogle you when we're here just trying to get you cleaned up. This is not a brothel. Even a prince needs to learn respect."

A flush crept up Nico's neck, spreading across his cheeks. He had to admire the brass on Rae; no one else would dare speak to him, or about him, in the way she did. Strangely, that was one of the reasons he trusted her more than any of his other servants. Ogling though, he most certainly hadn't been... had he? There was no denying there was a certain appeal to the fae, she did have a lovely figure. Now rid of the blood and dirt that had marred it, her brown skin looked soft and inviting. If he had to take her to bed, well, she certainly was not displeasing to look at. Shaking the thought away, Nico composed himself. Bloody women putting these ideas into his head. He was not his father; he did not have a collection of whores who he could take at a whim and do with as he fancied, and nor did he want them.

Mind wandering as the ladies grew quiet, Nico found himself dwelling on the memory of Cyrus. It felt like it had been an eternity since he had laid eyes on the face of the man he loved, but none of that mattered now, not anymore. Now all Cyrus would be was a memory. Unfortunately for him, some memories seemed unforgettable, remaining ever vivid. Nico could only hope there was some truth in the saying, that all things healed with time.

The door in front of him slowly began to open, saving Nico from dwelling on his memories. As he entered, he too was locked in by the guard, unable to help but wonder what they thought one girl would be able to accomplish in the way of escape with the three of them there. Not to mention the fact that she was still probably feeling quite fragile after her ordeal, Nico rolled his eyes at the ridiculous precautions. He turned muttering to Rae, "Lovely welcome. I suppose that is what I get for trying to be nice."

"I do trust you are satisfied I made your guest feel welcome."

Rae's words were sugar coated, sarcasm radiating, reflecting their usual rapport. Before he could think of something witty to fire back, Nico caught sight of the girl. Rae had safely deposited her back in her cell, like she might actually come to harm due to his presence. He would have to praise her for that little touch later. Nico couldn't fault Rae's work though. The fae sat on the stool, her hair and skin now clean. She wore a plain dress that covered her modesty. Letting his gaze rest on her for a long moment, Nico couldn't help but notice that the fae was very much a woman, and not the girl he had initially taken her for during their earlier altercations. Some light bruising still marred her face, but it was nothing that time would not heal – even if the sight of them did make him feel guilty. Nico hated when the innocent suffered under his hand, especially women. And after some reflection, what was this woman if she was not collateral damage? Just another by-product of a war he wanted no part in. Catching sight of the almost empty platter in the cell, Nico was quick to catch the smile playing at his lips, returning them to a thin line. The girl had been fed too. Excellent. Hopefully he could see what information he could find out now. Turning to face Rae, Nico did his best to sound threatening. He was not too fragile in his masculinity to admit that she really did scare him at times.

"Thank you. You may leave us."

Chapter Forty-Five

Muted Shade of Grey

Before she left, Rae had given her a warm look of encouragement. But as the door closed, trapping them within the gaol, Melana realised just how frightened by the prince's unpredictable nature she was. Despite the other woman's earlier warm words and praise for Nico, she could not help but feel he was volatile. There was no way she could trust him enough to lower her guard, not yet. After all, it was not him that had shown her any kindness thus far. Shivering, Melana pulled her arms around her chest, allowing herself to rock gently in a soothing motion, watching him with reserve. His cold eyes searched hers as he seemingly tried to gauge what she was thinking. Eventually he offered her one word.

"So."

"So."

Melana found herself echoing him. Trying to summon her normal confidence that had been lost somewhere along the way. At least having been washed and fed she felt more herself, but she still warred with her nerves regardless. Foot tapping on the floor at a manic pace, Melana tried her best to remain calm.

"I'm Nico, but then you already know that. What should I call you?"

Melana eyed him suspiciously; pleasantries would get them nowhere.

"What is it you want from me?"

Nico smiled, unnerving her. His eyes lit up.

"The way I remember it, you were volunteering yourself to be my prisoner. Why don't you tell me what I should do with you?"

The smirk that lingered after his words had Melana gasping, her breath caught in her throat. Replying, she rasped, "—to save my friends."

His eyes danced now. A chill ran through Melana's body as the thought crossed her mind that perhaps they had never gotten away. What if they were being held elsewhere? Panic seized her, her voice coming out as a whisper. "Did they make it? Did they get away?"

Chuckling, Nico grabbed a chair from the far wall, pulling it up to the bars of her cell. Straddling the seat, he leant with his arms resting on the back of it. Making himself comfortable as he continued to watch her.

"What is your name?"

Her eyes frantically searched Nico's, his face suddenly serious. The prince's features were drawn tight, and Melana could tell she would get nothing further from him unless she answered his question.

"Melana. My name is Melana."

"There, that wasn't so hard, was it? Yes, they made it. My men lost them. Tell me about them, your friends."

The tense worry Melana had carried for her friends uncoiled at his words. Her body visibly relaxing at the news, she noted the smile that crept back onto his face, responding, "What is it you want to know?"

"The princess, what is she to you?"

Relief rolled over her. This she could answer with ease.

"We have been lifelong friends. My mother attended Queen Briana."

"And the boy?"

Melana felt her brow furrow, immediately regretting showing any emotion to Nico's line of questioning.

"He is my brother."

"I see."

Watching as he cricked his neck one way and then the other, Melana shuddered. This was almost too easy. Her stomach began to churn, butterflies running riot with the anticipation of where this was going.

"And I don't suppose you have any idea why my brother and Cyrus ran with you the night of the ball?"

His brother. Of course, it was his brother. She could have kicked herself; the likeness was uncanny. Melana had realised what Cyrus was to him back at the tavern, and now wondered if this would be where the trouble began.

"Bastian wanted to defend the princess. I think he was quite taken with her. And Cyrus… well I think you know the answer to that already, don't you?"

Nico's smile turned sinister, his gaze icy. His eyes narrowing as if he thought she might lie to him. The look Nico wore chilled her to the bone. Realising that the prince looked murderous, Melana was suddenly frightened for her brother, forgetting that she was in a very dangerous situation herself.

"Ah, but I want to hear your version of events."

Stalling for a moment, Melana looked all around her, stuttering and gesturing with her hands as she tried to find the right words.

"I think they were connected somehow. They were drawn together."

Her admission found Melana staring at the flagstones on the floor, suddenly unable to meet Nico's gaze.

"Curious is it not, that a dragon and a fae should share that kind of connection? Do you not think Melana?"

"I... I do not know. I have never had real cause to think about it."

An uncomfortable silence fell between them. She could feel Nico watching her, but she did not dare look up again. It was obvious from his tone that the mere mention of them caused him an incredible amount of inner turmoil. A pang of guilt hit Melana. It was a physical twinge, a sadness emanating from somewhere in her chest. She felt as if she was intruding on his privacy, which was ridiculous given the circumstances. Cyrus had obviously meant a great deal to Nico, and Melana found herself genuinely wishing she had something more she could offer him. If she had known what the bond between Wren and Cyrus was, she would have told him. Anything to rid him of the pained look he wore currently. It hurt, Melana realised, to feel for him when she should not. But she had seen things, snippets of their future, the way he had treated her – would treat her – with kindness and affection. Now Melana just had to wait for Nico to collide with her on that timeline. Who knew how long it would take, or what would happen to her along the way.

Suddenly the floor was rushing up to meet her as a fresh vision tore through her already fragile mind. Wren was trapped in a cavernous space, water rising around him, and she could see Cyrus there too. The orange cat was paddling in circles, as Wren screamed that they were going to die. And they were – they were going to drown. Then she was back in a cell, and Dracul spoke of her execution. Another. A man struck Melana hard, knocking her to the floor. She cowered as tears fell. The scene faded away until all she could see was sky. Nico shifted, soaring up to tackle a large black dragon. Hearing her own screams, she opened her eyes.

Nico sat on the floor of her cell. The door was wide open. His brow pinched in concern as he held her, her body draped across him, head supported in his arms. Melana could feel her mouth opening and closing, like a fish out of water, as she struggled to find words. Melana could feel her cheeks grow red, embarrassed that she had fallen to the floor. These last few days had clearly left her rather more fatigued than even she had realised.

"You're a seer."

The secret was whispered, suspended in the air between them. The weight of a single word, it hung there, frozen in time for a terrifying moment. Melana was only able to nod, her mind reeling as her thoughts raced. The thumping ache inside her skull reached a crescendo as the fringes of her vision faded to black. White bursts, like shooting stars, danced behind her eyelids as they grew heavy, she could feel herself fading.

"It's going to be alright, I've got you."

Nico's voice was a soft caress, his fingers stroking the length of her face in an attempt to sooth her. A million miles from the person he had been moments before. All Melana could feel was the warmth of Nico's body against hers as he enveloped her in his embrace. Realising that it did not matter how morally corrupt he had been, the fact that he sat here now, on the cold and dirty floor comforting her, was proof that he could be better. A small, delicate smile graced her lips, colour fading from her vision, Melana found herself thinking how much she liked this muted shade of grey.

Silence descended like fog as she allowed her eyes to close. Her thoughts, his touch, the warmth of their bodies pressed close together. Melana wondered if Nico could feel it too. He was safety and comfort, and he felt a lot like home.

When Melana opened her eyes again, she was still on the stone floor, this time shrouded within a pile of soft blankets. But now, she was alone.

Chapter Forty-Six

A New Can of Worms

Raking a hand through his hair, Nico blanched. The fae was a seer. This opened up a whole new host of problems. Throwing open the doors of the castle library, Nico paced the wooden stacks, his chest tight. It was a beautiful room, the walls decorated with swirling gold patterns. A large red-patterned runner ran from the ornately carved door, covering the wooden floorboards of the walkway between the stacks. Atop the doorframe a lone dragon watched over its domain. Nico had always thought there was a certain irony in the fact it guarded a room of tinder. Having spent many hours in there with Cyrus while he poured over ancient texts, there had been many occasions for him to contemplate why someone had placed the gilded creature there in the first place.

What Nico would not give to have Cyrus there with him. He would have known exactly what to do. But he wasn't. Nico was alone, and now he had to decide how to proceed. Whatever he did, his next move would have to be made with caution. Melana was exhausted, fragile. If he was going to keep her alive then she needed to be properly cared for. If anyone found out about her gift, they could both find themselves in a lot of trouble. Searching the leather-bound texts for anything that might help, Nico felt bile rise in his throat. He wasn't even sure exactly what he was looking for. It was unlikely he was going to come across a book called *How to Nurture Your Seer*. Eventually, after a frustratingly unfruitful search, Nico decided the best thing he could do was to go and find Rae. After all, she was one of the few people that he trusted implicitly.

Almost an hour later, after searching most of the castle, Nico found her. To say he was irritated was an understatement. The woman was bent over a large cauldron, her red hair tied back out of the way. Holding a ladle to her lips, Rae sipped at the stew she had been nursing as it cooked in the open fireplace. Nico's lips quirked in amusement when the woman made a noise of satisfaction in response to tasting her own cooking. The aroma of it filled the air, and if it tasted as good as it smelt, Nico hoped that he could persuade Rae to let him have some when it was ready. The prince crossed his arms over his chest grumbling, "Why is it you are always in the last place I look?"

Jumping, Rae turned quickly to face him, raising a single eyebrow.

"Well, people don't usually continue to search for something once they have found it, so that is kind of how it works, Your Highness."

Nervously, Nico glanced about the large kitchen. It was a homely sort of place. The brickwork remained bare, but a selection of copper pots and pans hung on a rail for decoration. Herbs and spices were in racks that dangled precariously from the ceiling.

"I trust we are alone?"

Rolling her eyes, Rae looked about the room theatrically.

"Unless there is someone hiding in the stew…"

Trailing off, she noticed Nico's clenched jaw. It moved slowly as he ground his teeth, his hands restless as he spun the gold dragon on his finger repeatedly.

"Then there is no need to be so formal."

A large wooden table with benches either side dominated the centre of the room. Seizing the opportunity, Nico hopped up, perching on the end of the table. The way he sat, still spinning his ring with his shoulders hunched, worried her.

"Is everything alright? Are you quite well?"

Nico spoke, his tone sour.

"I am fine. The girl not so much."

Rae's eyes widened.

"God's Nico, what did you do?"

Running his fingers through his hair, fingernails scraping his scalp, Nico crumpled. Curling in on himself he hugged his knees.

"No, I mean she is fine. I have not hurt her, but I am going to need your help. There is something you should know."

Looking up, he searched Rae's face, unsure what he was looking for. The last thing he wanted was for her to come to harm because of him. Was telling her the right thing to do? If anybody found out they had kept this secret… well, what his father would do did not bear thinking about. Walking over to him, she placed a hand on both shoulders squeezing gently.

Narrow green eyes searched his, her nose scrunched, as Rae worried her lip, waiting for him to speak.

"For the gods' sake, Nico, spit it out."

Taking a deep breath, Nico pressed his palms hard against his eye sockets. Slowly releasing the air from his lungs, he allowed the words to escape with it.

"The girl is a seer."

Rae's eyes widened. She relaxed her grip on him, her hands slowly sliding down the length of his arms.

"Oh."

Nico's fingers pinched at the bridge of his nose.

"Yes. Oh indeed."

Hopping up to sit on the table beside him, Rae looked his way. Noting he still looked incredibly severe, she asked gently, "So what do we do now?"

"Well, it is only the three of us that know, and we cannot let anyone else find out. I dread to think what they would do to her if they knew. Can you imagine my father?"

A little shudder rolled over him as Nico did indeed imagine his father forcing prophecies from Melana, stopping himself before he could imagine what other horrors he might force on her.

"For someone with no heart, you seem to care an awful lot about what happens to the girl."

Jumping down from where she sat, Rae shot him a smile over her shoulder. Heading for the hearth, she stirred the stew while Nico scowled at her.

"I never said I don't have a heart."

"Actually, you do, frequently. I believe I have also known you to question if your soul is as black as the clothes you favour, or perhaps I imagined that too."

Nico allowed a little laugh to tumbled from him.

"Was I inebriated when I said those things, perchance?"

"You might have been."

She quipped back over her shoulder, smirking at him as Nico became embroiled in his thoughts. Rubbing his chin, he contemplated why, after the stunt his brother and Cyrus had pulled, he did in fact care so deeply about ensuring the wellbeing of his prisoner. Despite the fact that he did not know her, there was something Nico found he quite liked about the woman. Not that it mattered much. Nico knew they would come for her, and he had no intention of returning her in anything less than one piece.

"I would not wish my father's wrath on anyone undeserving. Besides, you know as well as I do that, as we speak, her friends are probably trying to work out a plan to rescue her. Given that they have Cyrus and Bastian to help them, I would wager they may actually be successful. If she is important to the princess, she will be important to Bastian by default, chivalrous as he is. I don't want to be the reason anyone else has to walk away from this string of disasters with a broken heart."

"Oh, Nico, come on. You can do better than that backstabbing weasel. It is a lucky escape if you ask me."

"Perhaps," he mumbled refusing to meet her gaze. "Don't suppose there is any whiskey down here?"

Shooting him a disapproving look, she sipped the stew once more. Unperturbed, Nico tried again.

"Brandy?"

Storming back across the room to meet him, Rae waggled a finger in his face, as if he were a disobedient child, all the while scolding him.

"Don't. You will sit there all night sinking further into your sea of self-loathing if you start drinking now. Besides, I will have to clean up after you."

"Fine," Nico growled. "Can I at least have some stew then?"

A laugh punched from her chest, echoing around the deserted kitchen. The stew was almost done, so it seemed only fair. Grabbing two porcelain bowls from the cupboard, Rae swiped some fresh bread from where it sat in a basket on the side.

When she was satisfied that the stew was cooked to perfection, Rae filled their bowls, carefully scooping the meaty gravy up with the ladle. As they sat to eat, discussing the predicament they now found themselves in, neither of them noticed the shadowy figure that lurked in the doorway.

Chapter Forty-Seven

The Shadow

The shadow left silently. Making his way through the castle corridors to the gaol, Anor walked with purpose, eager to test what he had just heard in theory. It was almost time for his watch to begin anyway. It was pure chance that he had heard what he had; Anor had only passed the kitchen looking for a snack for later. But this – this would sustain him for much longer than food. This information was so substantial that, for the first time in a long time, Anor felt he might have a greater purpose. Finally, he would be able to see his future within the house of Castillo.

Out of breath from climbing the tower's many stairs, he took a moment when he reached the top. Pausing, hands on hips, Anor sucked in much-needed gulps of air. Still breathing hard when he eventually rounded the corner, he bumped into Estrafin who confronted him jovially.

"Aren't you meant to be able to manage a few flights of stairs?" the man asked with a laugh. The hand that had been resting on the hilt of his sword relaxed.

"And I suppose you never struggle coming up here? Going back down is fine."

Laughing, Estrafin replied, "Clearly not as much as you. Perhaps you should reconsider your line of work."

"Yes, yes, very funny," Anor grumbled, looking at the guard in front of him. Estrafin was tall, slender but toned, with high cheekbones that made his face stand out from the crowd. His hair was short, brown and a little fluffy, and people often complimented his eyes, telling him how unique they were, although Anor had always found the silvery grey pools eerily serene, like the calm before a storm. The truth was, the other man unnerved him more than Anor would ever care to admit. There was something quite pretty and feminine about Estrafin. Sensitive in nature, the man wielded a surprising amount of fierce determination. Coupled with an unusual amount of physical strength for someone so delicate in so many other ways, the man was a maze of juxtapositions. Many of the

Guardians were still unsure how to accept him as one of their own. Although, if it bothered Estrafin, he didn't let on, performing his role with a diligence and ease that many of the other soldiers would have killed for.

Stepping forward, Anor slapped his fellow guard on the back in a friendly gesture.

"Go on then, I will take it from here."

Heading past him, pleased to be relieved a little early, Estrafin passed Anor the keys as he took up his position outside of the gaol door. His foot tapping impatiently, Anor repressed a scowl as he waited for the other man to leave, cursing internally, when at the last moment he turned to remind him that Rae would be along to tend to the prisoner in a few hours. And then Estrafin was gone, his feet clattering down the stone staircase.

Straining his ears while he waited, Anor listened until the footsteps had faded away to nothing. Leaving it a few minutes more, just to be sure that his fellow soldier had gone, he dug his nails into the flesh of his palms anxiously as the seconds ticked by. Peering out of the small, barred window, Anor watched as Estrafin exited the tower and crossed the courtyard, walking back into the castle.

Fingers twitching with excitement, Anor grabbed at the ring of keys. Picking the largest one that fitted the lock to the main door, his hands shook as he tried to line the key up with the hole. It took him a few attempts before he was eventually successful. Endorphins flooded through Anor's body as the key turned in the lock, the door swinging open to reveal the lone captive in her cell.

Wide brown eyes shot up to meet his. The seer was undoubtedly frightened, as well she should be. This was going to be a fun evening; he liked it when women were a little scared of him.

* * * * *

The sound of the key turning in the lock had startled Melana, she thought it was a little early for Rae to arrive, and she had been right. Instead, at the bars of her cell stood a slight man who looked like he had seen too few winters to be a soldier. A thick scar ran the entire length of his face, and she found herself wondering what he had done to earn it. Melana's blood ran cold as his dark eyes sized her up menacingly. She cursed herself as her body began to tremble. Whatever this man wanted, it could not be good. Sneering at her, the guard curled his top lip, revealing a row of uneven teeth.

"I hear you have a gift."

Eye's wide, she responded cautiously, "Where did you hear that?"

"Never you mind. What I want is for you to tell me what I need to do to get myself in the king's guard."

Melana's voice was breathless, betraying just how frightened of him she truly was. "That's not really how it works."

Somewhere in the back of her mind was the memory of Nico. Holding on to the way he had held her safe in his arms, Melana found herself wishing he was here. Although, perhaps it was his fault that this man was here in the first place? Someone must have told him, and Nico was the only one who knew.

"I will make this easy for you. If you cooperate, no one need ever know what happened here. We can keep it between us. Our little secret. If you don't help me, though, I will have no choice but to tell the king what you are. I doubt he will give you as generous an offer."

Feeling sick, Melana's voice shook as she spoke, her heart now pounding in her chest.

"You might not like what I see. I have no control over it, and I can't always make the visions happen."

The corners of Anor's mouth curled into a terrifying grin.

"Oh, you can. And you will."

The blood drained from her face, but somewhere deep inside her a spark ignited. She would not let them win.

"Fine. Don't say I didn't warn you."

Pulling the wooden bucket full of water towards her, Melana sat cross legged beside it.

"Stay out there. I can't do it if you come in here."

It was a blatant lie. Holding his hands up, Anor grinned at her.

"Wouldn't dream of it, love."

Taking a deep breath, Melana looked down at her dishevelled appearance in the water's reflection. When the vision took her, she found it substantially less intimidating than the man himself appeared to be. She quickly learned that he was deeply insecure. Desperate to prove his worth to his family. Always trying to get a woman, forever being rebuffed instead. Melana saw him in the armoury with his comrades; she also saw them when he was not there, him the butt of all their jokes. Perhaps if the man actually tried to be himself, instead of this persona he had adopted, he might actually get somewhere. Spending most of his time frustrated and lonely, she could not help but pity him. But that was no excuse for the way he treated people.

Unfortunately for her, there was not much more to see. There was no way of knowing if that was because Anor's path was yet to be determined by his actions, or that his future was about to be cut short. When her normal vision returned, she found the man clutching the bars, face pressed so hard against them, she imagined it would take a while for the indentations to fade from his skin.

"Well? What did you see."

A bead of sweat rolled down his brow. Anor was desperate. When she did not answer straight away, he shouted, attempting to shake the solid bars. Fearful he would hurt her, Melana knew she had to lie.

"I saw you as the head of the king's guard."

"Yes?" The man shouted, his eyes growing wide.

"Yes." Nodding, and stammering, Melana tried to keep up her pretence of terror. Her fear of the man in front of her fortunately somewhat diminished, she carried on,

"Yes. You lead the army valiantly into battle. The king's most trusted general. But—"

"But?" Anor cut her off again, his voice raising several octaves.

"But, you must be patient. I see you older, more mature. Ready for the…"

Pausing, she contemplated her words, much to the man's obvious irritation. If he stuck his face any further through the bars his head would get stuck.

"…honour, and responsibility, a position like that carries."

Pulling back, he regarded her, "You are sure?"

Melana nodded vigorously. Although the way her vision had gone, she had no gauge for judging if he would even last the night. Everything she had seen of the man had been past tense. Still, he never had to know that.

Standing tall, the man snarled at her, putting on his most frightening performance.

"If you tell anyone what happened here, I will kill you myself. Do you understand?"

Words failed her. Melana stared at him, mouth open, jaw slack, letting it wobble as her eyes grew glassy. She might not be terrified of him anymore, but Melana was pretty sure he would make good on his threat if it came to it, to save his own hide if nothing else. There was no good reason for her to divulge to anyone else what had happened here. Nico had clearly betrayed her. He must have told others in the castle what had happened to her on his last visit. And where was he now that she needed him? No. She owed him nothing. Unable to meet his gaze, Melana cast her eyes down to the floor, muttering, "I swear it."

As the door locked behind him, Melana could hear Anor take up his position on the chair outside. Her shoulders slumped as she allowed herself to fall in a heap. Sobbing as quietly as she could, Melana drew the blankets tightly around herself. The bastard outside did not need the satisfaction of her tears; he hadn't even given her the courtesy of a response.

It was utter madness to think that just a few weeks ago, she had been in a palace, resting her head on feather-filled pillows in a four-poster bed. How was this what her life had become? Pondering the devastation that had played out back home, Melana thought of the loss of the palace in Viriador. The death of the king. Closing her eyes, she relived the moment Emil had fallen. It was all so needlessly devastating. So much death and destruction, and for what? Astraea was on the run, and who even knew where the queen was, or even if she was still alive? It just served to remind her how quickly the mighty could fall.

Chapter Forty-Eight

A Day Much Like Any Other

It was a day much like any other. Listening to Dracul ranting about the need to keep bloodlines pure, Nico caught himself staring at his father with disdain. Sat there on his golden throne, with Gerritsen at his side, Nico couldn't help thinking his father had ruled for far too long. Despite telling him that he was no longer his son, until he earned his title as a Castillo, Dracul still expected Nico to keep up appearances for the sake of the kingdom. Made to attend his father's court, Nico's eye twitched as he endured what, in his opinion, was unnecessary noise. It was the same rigmarole, just a different day.

Nico's interest was suddenly piqued as the king addressed the court, expressing his plans to take Carpathia. Gerritsen stepped forward on the dais to explain their military strategy. The silence that descended on the throne room was eerie; you could have heard a pin drop. Gerritsen began, speaking of moves and counter moves for proposed attacks. If they succeeded, then the Glowing Isle would be completely under the control of House Castillo.

It probably shouldn't have bothered Nico as much as it did, but as the general carried on spewing war strategies to an eager crowd, he found his jaw tight. This was a war he did not want, knowing full well that after this victory, his father would not stop there. How far would their men be sent? How many would pay the ultimate sacrifice? Taking a moment to close his eyes, Nico breathed slowly, in through the nose and out through the mouth, as he had practiced so often. Saliva filled his mouth, but his tongue felt dry, nausea creeping its way up from the pit of his stomach. Frantically spinning the dragon in circles on his finger, Nico tried to calm himself. But when his tongue started to tingle, all Nico could think about was locking himself away in his chambers, where he could quell his anxiety with hard liquor.

If Cyrus had been here, he would have known what to do. Even if he hadn't, at the very least, he would have fucked him until his feelings were forgotten. The pain from their encounters was not something Nico enjoyed exactly, but it had a beautiful way of replacing everything, helping Nico to forget. It had always made all his worries melt away. There was no one to help him forget now, just good old Rae, always there to pick up the pieces.

* * * * *

From the sky, the world below looked beautiful, but insignificant. People scurried below him like ants as Nico flew high above the city. Even the buildings were merely shapes below him. Part of him had hoped that he might be able to forget his plight up here. The other part just wanted to leave, to hunt his brother and Cyrus down in the wilds. It did not matter if Cyrus did not want him, his brother would. And at least he would not be left alone to deal with his father.

Red scales glistened in the afternoon sun as the giant form of Nico's dragon shook its head dismissively. On reflection, he decided it was a bad idea; they could be anywhere by now. He would need to travel with gold to recharge his powers. Even with the enchanted ring that clung to his talon, the golden dragon as big as Nico in his human form, it was not enough. Alone, it just was not viable. Nico thought about asking Rae to join him, but he couldn't drag her into this; it would not be fair.

Letting out an almighty roar of frustration, Nico dove, pulling up just before he hit the ground. Staying low, he covered an expanse of fields. The crops flustering wildly under the beat of his giant wings, before he soared skyward again. Trying to burn through his rage, Nico found the physical exertion helped a little, but he still couldn't wait to drown out the pain. The thought alone infuriated him. Why was he like this?

Circling the castle, he made a point of passing the tower gaol. Melana should see him like this, see the beast that lay beneath the surface. Then she would know the monster he truly was. Passing the window, he had no clue if she had seen him or not.

Once he had landed, Nico dressed quickly, storming through the stone walkways of the courtyard before heading into the castle. Making his way to the kitchens, he searched for Rae, still feeling somewhat unhinged. He did not want to do anything stupid. Knowing what he was like, he kept searching when he did not find her there. The last thing Nico wanted tonight was to be alone.

* * * * *

The prince had been searching for Rae for a little while when he ran into Gerritsen. The man was a mountain. He was a good foot or more taller than Nico. With his added height, muscular build and broad shoulders, Gerritsen dwarfed him. A tiny black goatee sat in the middle of his chin, decorating his pale skin. His black hair was just long enough to scrape back into a band, the tuft sitting behind his head like a stumpy tail. Dressed in his armour, the man looked formidable. His sword, as always, was sheathed at his side.

"Ah, just the man I've been looking for," Gerritsen exclaimed loudly, making Nico jump. His eyes narrowed as he responded.

"Why would you be looking for me?"

Slapping the prince on the back, Gerritsen replied, "The king wishes me to help you finesse your swordsmanship."

Raising a brow, Nico gave the man his best bombastic side-eye.

"Why?"

Laughing heartily, Gerritsen turned him around, leading them to the armoury.

"We are to go to war! It is nothing to be sniffed at. We will be living in perilous times, Your Highness."

As they strode the corridors that led there, he expressed his growing excitement at the impending bloodshed, and Nico could only hope that his own enthusiasm for the subject would seem genuine. The armoury itself was a hexagonal room, every available surface covered in cherry wood. A small amount of light entered through three small windows at the rear of the room. Racks filled with hundreds of swords were hung on the walls, armour and shields had their own place to one side. The atmosphere in here was heavy. It wasn't like Nico had never been in the armoury before, but this time he felt a definite level of coercion. As he wandered the racks, selecting the best sword he could lay his hands on, Nico cursed himself for leaving his own sword in his chambers. There should have been no need for it today. Lifting a fine specimen from its place on the rack, Nico brandished the weapon, giving it a general swing as he got a feel for it. The rage he had felt earlier had well and truly dissipated, leaving Nico feeling uneasy as he selected a shield. Donning some armour slowly, he tried to stall for as long as possible.

Once Gerritsen had led him to the training area, he was relieved to find it was indeed just the two of them that would be sparring in the sandy arena. Nico was thankful this had not been an elaborate ruse to get him alone and dispatch him. There was nothing he would put past his father these days. But then Dracul would find himself heirless, now that Bastian had been declared traitor to the crown.

Nico found himself on the defence as Gerritsen launched his attack, blocking his swings and parrying them away. Ducking down, he rolled to the side, a cloud of dust billowing in his wake. He caught Gerritsen off guard as he launched his own attack. They found themselves in sudden close proximity, the handles of their blades clashing. Nico reached down, grabbing the blade he kept concealed in his boot at all times. It was small, but did the job. Pushing it up to Gerritsen's thick throat, he watched as the man's vein pulsed at the side of his neck. A bead of sweat trickled from Gerritsen's brow as his deep laugh echoed around the arena. The general offered Nico his hand, gripping it firmly as he shook it.

"Well played."

Nico wiped his own brow, pleased he had bested the man.

"Yes, you too. Before we go again, may I ask you something?"

Stabbing the tip of his sword into the dirt, Gerritsen rested his hands on the hilt.

"Ask away."

"Do you agree with my father? About the war, I mean?"

Dumbfounded, the man stared at Nico for a moment before answering.

"Of course I do. The elemental gifts, and their inclination towards healing, does not make the elves and fae strong. It makes them weak. Their kind have sullied our bloodlines for far too long. Their whimsical magic waters down our dragons'. Why do you think some among us need to recharge more frequently, and need more gold to do it? Honestly, I am pleased that Dracul is finally finishing what he started all those years ago. The fact that their kind was allowed to live disgusted me as much then as it does now. It was a moment of weakness on the king's part, and I believe that it has haunted him ever since."

Feeling the familiar wave of nausea creeping in, Nico feigned a grin.

"Good, I am glad we are all on the same page."

"Yes. Besides, it makes sense. Why take only one kingdom when you could have the entire realm?"

"Hmm, we have to be careful though. Just because we *can* conquer everything, does not mean we should. You can get anything you want in life, but still not have everything. Sometimes other things are more important than power."

Gerritsen slapped him on the back jovially.

"They are wise words indeed, but do not forget you are a dragon. You are the future of your house, the future of the Castillo name. Your very existence is power."

Nico felt his brow wrinkle. Quickly letting his face fall, he allowed a smile to creep in instead.

"Quite. I don't think I'll ever forget it. Shall we go again?"

Indeed, he would never be allowed to forget it.

As they moved into position to spar again, Nico thought of his position in the royal household. All it was now, was a burden he was forced to carry, and he found himself wondering if he really did want it after all.

Chapter Forty-Nine

Snowshine

Blanching, Bastian dropped to one knee, and then the other, kneeling on the muddy forest floor. Raising his hands in surrender, he could hear Astraea screaming behind him. Turning his head to look for her, Bastian saw that both Cyrus and Wren lay still. Elves surrounded them, arrows drawn. What had Cyrus been thinking, shifting this close to Carpathia? The answer was, he hadn't been. He had been trying to save Wren. Shaking his head, Bastian tried to calm the situation before it spiralled further out of control.

"Listen, we mean you no harm."

One of the elven warriors approached Bastian, the tip of their arrow sitting dangerously close to his neck. A woman's voice rang out, full of fury.

"You brought a dragon here."

Bastian swallowed hard; Astraea's cries had turned into sobs. His bow lay nearby snapped like a twig. There was nothing he could do but beg.

"Please, we came seeking your aid."

The archer lowered her bow, and Bastian let himself relax for a moment, dragging in a deep breath before she grabbed his hair. Yanking his head backwards, she asked, "Why should we believe you?"

Panicked, Astraea's shout was high pitched as she rushed to aid Bastian.

"I am Astraea Thandal, Princess of Viriador. Please, please help us."

The woman released Bastian, who sat back on his knees, eyes wide. His mouth hung open as he waited for the woman's response. The Carpathian warrior narrowed her eyes, turning towards the princess. The rest of her face was obscured by a snood. Pulled up over her nose, it covered the lower half, making it impossible to read her expression.

"What business do you have here?"

Tears rolled freely down Astraea's cheeks, her voice shaking as she spoke.

"The dragons invaded our realm. My father, the king – they killed him. They took our home. My mother has also been taken prisoner. Please. We didn't know where else to go."

The archer's eyes flashed with anger, her brows furrowing deep between her eyes.

"So then, tell me. Why are you with a dragon?"

The woman pressed her face into Astraea's, her chest rose and fell heavily as she barely contained her rage. There was not much Bastian could do now apart from draw her attention away. Pushing Astraea aside, he fronted up to the warrior, their faces so close, a trace of her breath was warm against his chin. They stayed there for a moment. His jaw tight, Bastian realised that once again she held an arrow to his neck, the iron arrowhead digging into his flesh.

"Two dragons. They travel with two of us."

Gasping, Astraea clutched at his arm, while Bastian continued as calmly as he could manage.

"We mean you no harm. Cyrus was just trying to help our friend, Wren. He is very sick; we think he might be dying. He only shifted to get us to Carpathia quicker. Please, help them…" Gesturing towards his motionless companions Bastian added, "Even if you will not help us. Please save them."

Bastian never thought he would see the day he begged anyone to save Cyrus of all people, never mind the fae boy he had only known for a matter of days. Bastian watched the woman signal with one hand, indicating for the other archers, who had them surrounded to stand down as she issued her order.

"Help them."

Watching as several of the elves marched forward to the injured men, Bastian's insides began to uncoil, relief replacing the turmoil that had been there moments before. He stroked Astraea's arm as she trembled beside him. The elves unpinned their olive-green capes, covering Cyrus with one in an attempt to both keep him warm and his modesty intact. After that, they created two makeshift slings in which to carry the men. As they placed Wren on his stretcher, Bastian saw a loaf of ginger fluff jump in with him. Rolling his eyes, Bastian thought, for better or for worse, that cat was with Wren to the end. Running to be at Wren's side, Astraea trailed behind them as the soldiers carried his friends towards civilisation.

His friends. He supposed that was what they were now, and Bastian found himself mumbling his thanks as the woman removed the snood. Blonde hair tumbled to her shoulders. She was petite, a good foot shorter than him, but still had a terrifying look about her. Dark grey eyes studied Bastian as she sized him up. He noticed that they were an unusual shape, lifting into distinct points at the sides; they matched the tips of her ears. The woman's ears were neater than Astraea's, more compact, whereas the fae's held more length at the tip. The elfish armour was also most unusual. It was delicate, not looking as though it would withstand much force at all. This was the first time Bastian had seen elves in the flesh, but he had heard the old tales. They were very similar to the fae, but whereas the fae used elemental magic to manipulate their surroundings, the elves were masters of a much more powerful magic. There was every chance the armour was enchanted. At any rate, it would be much easier to move about in it on the battlefield than the armour Bastian had been used to back home. Although he supposed it wasn't his home anymore. Not now. Voice shaking a little as he spoke, Bastian looked down, realising his hands were trembling too, as his emotions caught up with him.

"Where will you take them?"

Remaining tight lipped, the woman replied, "We will tend your injured. In the meantime, you and the girl can plead your case to the council."

"The council?"

Offering him her hand, she helped him to his feet. Bastian's legs almost buckled but the elf held him firm.

"It's always good to let them come back to life before trying to walk."

Bastian felt his face flush. Embarrassed he said, "I'm so sorry, they feel like rubber."

She laughed, a pleasant sound that seemed to tinkle in his ears.

"They probably will for a minute. I'm Aiko, by the way."

"Bastian."

Taking her hand in his, he shook it. Aiko pulled a strange face. Head tilted to one side, she looked him up and down.

"You really just want to help them?"

A half smile pinched one cheek, as he replied.

"I do."

Testing his legs to see if they worked, Bastian took them one at a time, flexing each leg at the knee. Gradually, Aiko released her hold on him, until he was standing alone.

"Come. Let's go and see how your friends are holding up."

As Aiko led him through the trees with the remaining soldiers, Bastian felt his skin grow colder. From where they stood the mountains looked formidable, towering above them, the peaks disappearing high into the clouds.

"Don't worry, we don't have to climb them."

Aiko laughed when she caught Bastian gazing up at the sky, his brow furrowed.

"I hadn't even thought that far ahead, to be honest. They are just so big. We don't have anything like that in Predoran."

Face falling, her lips pressed thin once more, before they rose gently at the sides into a sympathetic smile, she offered her sentiment.

"That's a pity."

Bastian nodded nonchalantly.

Continuing through the valley, the ground started to turn white. Bastian gasped. Looking back, it was as if they had crossed a barrier into a different world. The trail started to slope down. Below them, he could see hundreds of little log cabins, their brown wood a stark contrast to the blinding white landscape, their windows tiny specks of light on the horizon, curls of smoke rising from their chimneys.

In front of them sat several carriage-type contraptions, drawn by some kind of horse-like creatures, but covered in fur. They were very sweet, although Bastian was alarmed to see the big, spiney structures protruding from their heads. Looking down at the tracks that ran parallel in the snow, Bastian wondered aloud, "What *are* they?"

Walking up to one of the creatures, he gently ran his fingers through its dark brown flank. The animal's body radiated a comforting warmth, its fur soft against his skin. When it turned to nuzzle him back, Bastian decided he quite liked the creature.

Grinning at him, Aiko gestured towards their transport.

"He is a reindeer, and that is a sleigh."

"Why does the reindeer have bones on the outside?"

She laughed again, this time covering her mouth with her hand as she attempted to stifle it, and Bastian was pretty sure that this time she was laughing at him.

"They are antlers. It is how they fight for the females."

"Oh right, I see." Blushing again, Bastian gestured to the sleigh. "So, do we sit in it?"

Aiko smiled at him now as if he was daft, all prior thoughts of him being a threat seemingly forgotten. Apparently, she found him rather amusing.

"Yes, come on. Your friends have already gone ahead, we need to catch them up."

* * * * *

Sitting atop the sleigh as the icy wind cut into his exposed skin, Bastian pulled the red blanket around him tightly. There had been one on every seat, and now he understood why. This was the coldest he had ever been in his life, and it showed as he began to shiver. Aiko sat on the bench facing him, lips pursed, her own blanket wrapped firmly around her shoulders.

"Cold?"

"A bit. So, who are this council we are going to see?"

Reaching down, Aiko retrieved another blanket from beneath the sleigh's bench seat. Tossing it to Bastian, she replied, "We do not have a royal family here. They elect a leader instead, and then they have a team of councillors that advise them."

"Ah, I see."

Bastian pulled the second blanket across his lap. He thought the concept strange, not really understanding it at all. The logistics of what Aiko was saying made sense, but he still struggled to get his head around it. Who didn't have a royal family? But then the elves had always liked to do things differently, if the history books were anything to go by. Thinking about it, he was sure that he had read somewhere that they *had* had a royal family once, who had all been murdered because the people did not approve of the decisions they made. Allegedly, even the children were not spared. Bastian remembered thinking at the time that they must be utterly barbaric, but seeing the delicate female sat in front of him, he wondered how true any of it was. They seemed just like him, or Astraea. Similar on the outside – although obviously they held different powers within. Not really knowing what to say next, as they fell into a slightly awkward silence, he suddenly blurted, "Can you eat it?"

Looking utterly bewildered Aiko responded, "What the council?"

"Noooo, the snow."

Shaking his head, it was Bastian's turn to laugh at her. He could see her cheeks turning red, where they had already been pink from the cold.

"I mean, you can, but I would not recommend it. Especially if it is yellow; a reindeer has probably relieved itself in that patch."

Tilting himself so that he could see over the side of the sleigh, Bastian studied the snow's surface. It had looked so soft and fluffy when they were stationary. Now the glare was something else.

"Is it supposed to be sunny? Why does it turn sunny?"

Bastian looked at her totally perplexed. When Aiko burst into another flurry of laughter, he found himself sat there, blinking rapidly as he waited for it to cease.

"It is because it's white. Sunlight is white, and the snow is white, so it reflects it instead of absorbing it, silly. What did they teach you in school?"

"We do not have snow in Predoran, so I suppose they did not think it necessary knowledge. Besides, I had tutors." Gazing into the distance to observe the scenery that raced past, he murmured, "My education was quite specific I suppose."

Aiko scoffed, "Rich were we?"

"Oh, urm."

Bastian shrugged, feeling suddenly awkward given their earlier exchange, and the fact that she had held the arrow to his throat.

"Royalty, actually."

Bowing mockingly, Aiko laughed loudly.

"Crikey. I knew you were trouble. What a strange group of travellers. I dare not ask how this alliance came about. You can save that one for the council. I'm sure I will get to hear it then, anyway."

Pointing over his shoulder, she shouted against the wind,

"Look, we are almost there."

A feeling of dread resurfaced as Bastian thought of his injured companions.

"They *will* be able to heal them, won't they?"

Smiling at him reassuringly, Aiko simply said, "Have a little faith Bastian, you would be surprised at what us elves can do."

CHAPTER FIFTY

The Cat Has a Name

Sat at Wren's bedside, Astraea gripped his hand. It had been days now, almost a week in fact. A lot had happened in that time. Putting their case to the council had been a rather nerve-racking experience, that had spanned two days. Though it was something neither her nor Bastian ever wished to repeat, Astraea could not deny that the council building was a truly astounding place. It was no palace, but the building was large. Turrets sat at each corner, the main structure cream and rectangular. Simple enough, but behind it sat the snow-covered mountains. Astraea had found herself lost for words at the stunning view. After much deliberation, the council had eventually decided that they would help them. While they were not yet willing to send their soldiers to fight in a battle that was not theirs, they had instead afforded them two of their best archers to accompany the group on their quest.

Tormund had spent his days alternating between Cyrus and his master. The animal had a newfound affection for the man that had now saved both Wren's life and his own.

Cyrus had woken on the third day inconsolable that Wren had yet to regain consciousness. Desperate to be at Wren's side immediately, he was most put out that his healer refused to allow it. Instead, the old elf took great joy in reminding him that he had almost died himself. Cyrus had been far from an ideal patient. Especially as he now saw his bed rest as incarceration, which had made him by all accounts most cantankerous.

They had both been admitted to the infirmary on their arrival. At first, teams of healers had worked on them in rotating shifts, and early on they had been continuously monitored day and night. They had both been in a critical condition, Wren more so. But after they were stabilised, they continued to be nursed, just not as intensely. Elven magic had won out in the end. When Astraea and Bastian had been informed that both their companions would live, the pair had been ecstatic.

Jumping when Wren gently squeezed her hand, Astraea gave a small squeeze back. Watching, she held her breath as his eye lids fluttered until finally, he prised his emerald eyes open.

"Hi."

His gravelly voice startled her, but it was little surprise, having not used it for so long. Smiling to the tips of her ears, the princess responded, "Hi yourself."

Reaching for the jug on the small side table, Astraea poured her friend a glass of water. Wren was looking around, slowly taking in his surroundings before trying to wiggle himself to a seated position. The room that had been his home for the last week was rather plain. The crisp linen was as white as the walls. Setting the glass back on the table, Astraea placed her hands under his armpits, hauling him up. Supporting Wren's weight, she noted how light he felt after not eating for an entire week. Feeling a little tearful, she recalled the last time she had seen him like this. It had been when they were still children, after Wren had lost his leg. That ordeal had left him with many scars, both physical and psychological. While his flesh had healed, Astraea knew his mind had taken longer to piece back together than Wren would have ever admitted.

Once he was comfortable, Astraea passed him the glass. Wren took a tentative sip. Satisfied that it did not hurt, he took several small mouthfuls, passing the glass back to her.

"I'm alive then?"

Barely, she thought, taking in how pale his skin remained. Bruises littered Wren's body; the side of his face was no exception. It was several interesting shades, purples fading into yellows, changing daily as his skin fought to return to its normal pallor. Instead of saying any of that, Astraea mustered some enthusiasm.

"Oh Wren, you absolute idiot. You let your wound get infected. We thought you'd had it."

Allowing a stilted chuckle to slip free, Wren followed it up with a fit of coughing before muttering, "If it helps so did I."

Astraea knew if she allowed herself to dwell on how close a call it had been for him, she would cry again, so she continued rapidly.

"You've missed so much! Cyrus was amazing, you know. He carried you. Me and Bastian both offered to help, but he insisted. I don't think he trusted anyone else to keep you safe. When we realised that you weren't going to make it, he didn't even hesitate. We were all swept up in his talons before we knew what was happening. It was really quite something."

Wren could feel a warmth swell in his chest at her words, but he reminded himself that Cyrus was still a dragon. He had still betrayed their people. Wren would not allow himself to let it go. Turning his head away, he muttered sadly, "It doesn't change anything."

Clasping his hands in hers, Astraea leant into him a little, emphasizing her words as she spoke.

"Wren, Cyrus almost died. He didn't have the reserves left to shift, and he did it anyway. The only reason you are still alive, is because he almost died to save you."

The warm, fuzzy feeling threatened to consume him. The dragon had almost given his life for him. Wren was not sure he could put into words what he felt in that moment. Instead his eyes searched hers for any hint that she lied. But he knew Astraea, and Wren knew she would not deceive him. Finally, he managed, "Where is he now?"

"He is in another room. Cyrus used the last of his strength to shield us all as he crash-landed. It's why we weren't too badly injured. You were a little worse, because as he lost consciousness, you were thrown clear when his body shifted back. Cyrus was in quite a bad way too. Although he has been awake for a couple of days now. You both had a really close call, you know."

"Is he... is he alright?"

Wren's voice wobbled a little. This had all been his fault for being stubborn and letting his pride get the better of him.

"Oh, he has been creating merry hell, threatening to unleash his magic on everyone if he was not allowed to see you."

Raising his eyes to the ceiling, Wren muttered, "Gods."

"Indeed." Nodding in agreement, Astraea leant in and hugged him gently. "I'm so pleased you are alright; you have no idea how relieved everyone will be that you're awake."

As if he had read their minds, Tormund skidded into the room, his chest rumbling with loud purrs. Leaping onto the bed, the cat bounded up the covers, rubbing himself under the fae's chin.

"Wren!"

Adopting a comfortable position, the cat plodded happily, kneading Wren's flesh with his toes. At first, he did not react, simply turning his head to Astraea to say, "I think I might be hallucinating. Tormund just spoke."

Astraea chewed her lip, "Yes, about that—"

Tormund cut her off,

"Oh, you are in for a whole world of surprises."

Wren's eyes went wide like saucers. He had to be dreaming. Perhaps he was actually dead, and this was the gods' idea of a joke.

"So," Astraea began again. "It turns out Tormund is an elven forest cat."

"It's why I'm so big. Us elven cats are chonky."

Ruffling his head, Astraea scolded him,

"Tormund. We talked about this."

"Fine, fine, carry on."

Turning his bottom to face Astraea, Tormund's tail brushed her face, as he continued with his merry plodding.

"Charming. Anyway, as I was saying, it turns out that Tormund may have angered an elf who put an enchantment on him. That was why he ran away to Viridor. He wanted to start again somewhere new, because he could no longer speak."

"There was no 'may have' about it. I stole his goat and got caught."

Wren looked at the cat in alarm.

"You stole a goat?"

The cat looked unnaturally pleased with himself.

"What? I was really hungry at the time."

Wren blinked a few times as he tried to fathom whether any of this was real. It couldn't be real, could it? Astraea gave Tormund a warning glare, rolling her eyes.

"What did we say about easing this on him?"

"Actually, I believe it was more you, telling me I shouldn't speak much. There wasn't an actual discussion."

"He's not wrong."

Cyrus stood leaning on the door frame, arms crossed, brows knitted as he watched them all intently.

"Cyrus! He's awake!"

Tormund squealed excitedly, launching himself off of the bed to weave around the man's legs, still purring madly. Reaching down Cyrus ruffled the cat behind his large, pointed ears.

"I know pal, I can see."

The cat wasted no time, jumping back on the bed, headbutting at

Wren's hand to get more affection, all the excitement clearly getting the better of him.

Indulging the cat with the fuss he craved, Wren looked past him to Cyrus, allowing his gaze to roam over the dragon, taking in just how much damage he also appeared to have endured. His skin was covered in far more cuts and bruises than Wren's was, and the man seemed to be even paler than usual, if that was at all possible. Suddenly Wren scrunched his face in confusion.

"Hang on, so how is it that the cat is talking?"

"The cat has a name." Tormund sung, in between affectionate mews.

Relaxing his stance, Cyrus chuckled.

"The council discovered the enchantment and dissolved it. I have to say, as you can probably gather, Tormund is quite the character."

"I think I preferred him when he couldn't talk," Astraea muttered glancing at the ceiling, just as a nurse hurried down the hall and began to manhandle Cyrus back to his own room. As expected, they were met with a tirade of abuse, leaving Astraea looking smug.

"Told you so."

Tormund wiggled his furry brows at Wren in an overly human gesture.

"I like him."

"Wait, did you just... do you know what? Never mind."

Wren smiled. Butterflies spawned deep in his core once more. Fluttering their way up into his chest, they flew full pelt into his throat, stealing any words he might have had. Eventually he managed, "I like him too."

And he realised that despite everything that had happened, he really did. Cyrus had risked his life to save Wren's. The fae did not have the strength to fight the deluge of feelings that were swarming him. They had been locked away for too long and now he was too weak, both physically and mentally, for this to be anything other than what it was. Cyrus was his mate, and when all was said and done, Wren knew he was going to be a very addictive distraction.

Chapter Fifty-One

What Is Love

Several days dragged by at a glacial pace before Cyrus and Wren were well enough to be discharged from the infirmary, allowing them to join Astraea and Bastian in the log cabin they currently shared. With the four of them staying there, the little cabin quickly became extremely cosy. The exchanges between himself and Wren had been exceptionally awkward, and they spent much of their time skirting around each other in the confined space. There was a small communal area with a log burner, and a little room for each of them to sleep in. The beds were comfortable, but most importantly the cabin was clean and quiet. It was a safe space.

After some deliberation with the elves, Tormund had also been allowed to stay with them. Although Wren was still finding it difficult to adapt to the fact his furry companion now spoke. Cyrus, on the other hand, was building up quite the rapport with the animal, fully embracing Tormund's newfound skill.

The evening after they had settled in, Aiko had insisted they come to the tavern for dinner. After much pleading, Tormund was thrilled when he was finally given permission to join them, washing his coat thoroughly in preparation. As they left the warmth of their cabin to venture into Carpathia's snowy landscape, Tormund hesitated. Starring at the snow suspiciously, he tentatively dipped one paw into the white substance. A million tiny needles pricked at his sensitive toe beans. Beads of the stuff clung to his fur as he recoiled in horror, crying out.

"My toes. It ate my toes!"

Coming to his rescue, Cyrus scooped him up, wrapping his hand around the cat's foot, the heat of his body thawing the little balls of snow, leaving Tormund's fur soggy.

"There you go pal. Don't worry, your toes are still in one piece."

Cyrus tucked the perturbed animal inside his cloak as Tormund muttered a string of profanities. Smiling at the pair, Wren was quick to look away when Cyrus caught him looking.

They were all incredibly grateful. The elves had been more than kind to them. After arranging accommodation for the unlikely group, they had not stopped there, additionally delivering fresh clothes for each of them. Clothes that would keep them warm, designed for travel in the elements. Aiko had personally delivered to them olive green elven cloaks, including one for Tormund, for whom they had made a small replica, complete with a buttoned collar to fasten it about his neck. Even if he had refused to wear it this evening, insisting that he was not in fact naked, and that his fur coat would more than suffice, even in the freezing outdoor temperatures.

By the time the group flopped down onto the benches that matched the long wooden tables in the Golova Olenya, patrons already filled the venue. The tavern, like most of the other buildings in Carpathia, was wooden. Deer mounts decorated the walls, a large log fire roaring in the open fireplace at the far wall. Joining them tonight were Aiko and Dimitri, who they had just been informed would be the archers accompanying them on their journey. Around the same height as Wren, Dimitri was stocky with a strong jaw. His skin was tan, his eyes dark brown, with thick black brows that sat above them. Stubble lined his jaw and upper lip, and short hair the colour of coal sat atop the elf's head. Bastian was already well acquainted with them both, having been at somewhat of a loose end for the last week. Most evenings, he had joined them at the tavern simply to pass the time, but found he actually rather enjoyed their company. Now he sat next to Dimitri chatting heartily. A small fellow was stationed near to the bar playing lively tunes on an accordion, and Tormund who sat next to Cyrus on the tabletop, bobbed his head to the music.

On the menu tonight was roasted goose or goshawk. As they made their decisions, Bastian and Dimitri opted to each get a different dish so that they could share, chattering away like an old married couple. Distracted, Cyrus found his gaze roaming along the table, coming to rest on Wren. As the others mulled over their choice of game, Cyrus could feel his gaze growing hazy. The wanton feelings taking him over were primal, an animalistic need. Wren was his. Every atom of Cyrus screamed it. They belonged as one. Wren was meant to be loved and protected by him, and only him. Breaking his trance, Tormund rubbed his face against Cyrus's shoulder, headbutting it, he whispered to him.

"You're watching him again."

Cyrus glared at the smug ginger cat.

"I don't mean to pry; it's just I can feel how much you want him. It's rather distracting."

With that, Tormund pranced the length of the table, jumping onto Wren's shoulders and weaving himself about the fae's neck so that he could take a nap.

Trying to think about their situation on a deeper level, Cyrus acknowledged that he did indeed want Wren, possibly more than he had ever wanted anyone in his life. It was infuriating to him that his advances had been rebuffed since Wren had discovered Cyrus's true nature. Wondering what it was that drove people to want to share the most intimate parts of themselves with another. Cyrus decided that for him, it was the way Wren watched him when he thought that no one was looking. Both the shy little glances, where Wren's cheeks would flush red if he was caught, and the full-on glares Wren gave when Cyrus annoyed him. It was the endless shades of green that decorated his eyes, and the sound of his voice. A sudden longing took hold. To him, Wren was everything. All he wanted was to be able to hold the fae in his arms. Cyrus wanted to be his safety; he wanted to be Wren's home. Whether he could feel it or not, their souls cried out to one another. The dragon within him yearned for Wren too, making the situation even more difficult than it already was. Dragons did not like to be denied, and it only fuelled his belief that they shared a mating bond. He didn't just want to take him to bed, Cyrus wanted to claim his soul. His dragon longing to bury itself so deep inside Wren that they would become one entity. There was a reason Cyrus had risked his life to save him. Unsure why it had taken him so long to reach this conclusion, Cyrus felt his own heart shatter as the realisation dawned on him. Somewhere along the way, in the short time that they had known each other, he had fallen in love with Wren. Perhaps unknowingly, he had always had his heart, and now he had to face the very real possibility that it might remain unrequited.

When a plate dropped down in front of him, Cyrus was plunged back into the busy room. Looking at his food, he was pleased to see a generous helping of potatoes, vegetables and the breast of a goshawk staring back at him. Excited that the food smelt as good as it looked, Cyrus offered up his thanks to the gods. This was the first decent meal they had had in weeks. Glancing around the table, he watched as everyone tucked in. Even

Tormund had hopped back down onto the table to eat a plate of carved meat. Although, as Cyrus watched the cat, he had to wonder if 'inhaled' wouldn't describe the cat's eating habits more accurately.

There had been much idle yakking as they ate, but the party had also pieced together some semblance of a plan between them. As they finished their hearty meal, Aiko addressed the group.

"So, are we all in agreement. We will give it a few more days for these two to rest and recover. And when they are ready, then we will head out to the docks. From there, the council have granted us passage on one of their trade ships. Along their route they will leave us at Oldir."

General mummers of agreement rolled across the table. It seemed fair. Their injuries were healing, bruises fading. Bastian and Astraea especially were back to their usual selves. Cyrus could not complain too much, the elven healers had worked wonders mending his broken ribs. They had even given him and Bastian gold to rejuvenate their power. Wren's injuries had been the most complex. Where the infection had spread through his blood, it had taken days to fully draw it back from his body. But they had managed it, and he was thankful that they were all still here in one piece.

Really, they had Aiko to thank for it all. She could have just issued the order to kill them that day in the forest, but instead she had given them the benefit of the doubt. It was reassuring to know there were still good people in the world.

* * * * *

Lying on his bed that night, Cyrus reflected on what, in his humble opinion, was one of the best meals he had ever had. Admittedly, after eating rabbit and squirrel for days on end, it was hardly surprising. Unable to remember the last time he had felt so comfortable, Cyrus had even managed to get a glass of whiskey to finish the evening off. Leaning his head back, Cyrus melted into the soft bedding, his stomach pleasantly full. The only thing that could make the evening perfect would be if Wren was here with him. Wren, who right now was in his own bed, just the other side of the wall.

The minutes dragged by as Cyrus thought about the things he wanted to do to the fae, given the chance. Before he had time to overthink it, he was on his feet heading towards the other man's room. They could tip toe around each other forever, if that was what Wren truly wanted. But Cyrus knew Wren could feel it too, despite the fact he had told Cyrus to stay away. Whatever this pull was that existed between them, it went both ways, and it was too strong to ignore.

Pushing open the door, Cyrus swung it wide. Wren jumped, shooting upright in his bed, alarmed. Still fully clothed, he had been relaxing on top of the covers, reading a book. A flash of orange fur launched itself from the bed, making a quick exit before Cyrus kicked the door shut behind him. Closing the distance between them, he climbed on the bed. Taking the book straight out of Wren's hands, he smiled at the fae, who stared at him, jaw slack. The air between them simmered as he hovered over Wren.

"By the gods, I've tried. I've tried so hard to stay away from you, but I can't seem to stop myself wanting you. I'm so tired of fighting it. I'm sorry."

Wren gasped as Cyrus knelt before him. The man's composure breaking in front of Wren's very eyes, and in that moment, he realised they had been inevitable from the start, drawn together by some unseen force that was outside either of their control.

"Then don't."

It was all Wren could manage, breathless, sounding so full of longing for him. It had Cyrus choking back a sob,

"The things I've done, Wren. Terrible, unspeakable things. I'm not a good man. You deserve more than me, better than me. I am a monster—"

Cutting him off, Wren placed his hands gently either side of the man's face, gazing into his warm eyes. Swirling brown bled into amber, dancing around his pupils, as Wren said, "I know what you are, and I want you anyway. So what does that make me?"

Leaning in, Cyrus tucked a loose strand of hair behind Wren's ear, stroking the flesh there with his fingertips. Holding his breath, Cyrus let his lips brush against Wren's softly, feeling any resolve they might have had to fight their mating bond slip away. Deepening their kiss, Cyrus was pleased when Wren returned it with ferocity, his tongue exploring Cyrus's mouth, letting out a little moan when he tasted the smooth caramel whiskey still lingering there. Their kisses became brutal, starving the pair of oxygen. A few moments later, Wren pushed Cyrus away. He rested back on his heels as Wren manoeuvred himself so that they knelt mirroring each other. Their mouths collided again as Wren moved closer to him, snaking his arms around Cyrus, his hands coming to rest at the nape of his neck. Sliding his hands slowly down Wren's back, Cyrus dug his nails into the delicate flesh at the base of his spine. Wren jumped, and Cyrus pulled back sharply, his eyes wide, as they both gasped in hurried gulps of air.

"I'm sorry, did I hurt you?"

Wren responded by pulling Cyrus back into his arms, kissing his mouth softly before dragging them both playfully down onto the bed. Resting his head just over Cyrus's heart.

"No," he whispered, while listening to the dragons heartbeat thrum beneath his ear. "Not at all."

The world seemed to slow as Wren lay wrapped in Cyrus's embrace. After everything that had happened, he should feel guilty. This was wrong, it went against everything he had ever been taught to believe. But, as Wren listened to the steady rhythm of Cyrus's heart, all he felt was blissfully content. Lustful thoughts began to cross his mind. Brushing them aside, Wren decided that they could wait, there was no rush. They had time now. They had each other.

Chapter Fifty-Two

Worth the Wait

A cold breeze danced across Wren's skin. A woman's voice calling out to him through thick swirling fog. Slowly he turned, shrouded in darkness. Holding his hands out in front of him, Wren gasped. Where there had been skin moments before now were scales, hundreds of scales. Eyes wide, Wren gawked at them. As he turned his hands over, studying both sides in amazement, Wren was transfixed, unable to look away as his fingers morphed into talons. A silent scream tore from his throat as he broke into a run, unable to get away from himself. Trapped with the haunting voice on the wind, there was nothing but the darkness and the eerie white swirls within it.

Fingers stroked the length of his ribs, a kiss pressing over the fluttering pulse at his neck. A gravelly voice purred into Wren's ear, "Are you having a nightmare?"

Wren's eyes snapped open. Taking in several ragged breaths, he drew his hands straight to his face, and relief washed over him when he found flesh there. Rolling until the tips of their noses touched, Wren shivered in Cyrus's arms. Sleep-filled eyes, clouded with concern, found his in the darkness.

"It was just a dream. You are safe with me, Wren; I will never let anyone hurt you."

Burying his face into Cyrus's neck, Wren embraced the warmth of the man's body, until they both fell back into a deep and dreamless sleep.

When he woke, nightmares forgotten, Wren found that they had rolled again. Now he lay on his side, wrapped tightly in Cyrus's arms. Unable to help the smile that played at his lips, Wren let out a small sigh, content. The man's body pressed tightly to his own, a leg dangling precariously over his waist, pinning Wren to the bed. Every nerve ending tingled as Cyrus stirred next to him, his fingers lazily stroking the length of Wrens arms. Exhaling loudly, Wren snuggled back into him, feeling every hard inch pressed against him, as Cyrus trailed lazy kisses along his collar bone. His own erection throbbed at Cyrus's touch, but Wren wanted this to be something more. He did not want them to be a quick fumble, or a quick fuck. Wren wanted to savour every precious moment of exploration with Cyrus. Even if they had forever, it felt like any amount of time would never be long enough.

Rolling to face Cyrus, Wren pressed their lips together. The man responded by grabbing Wren's bottom lip between his teeth, biting down gently with a moan.

"Cyrus, please."

Wren's voice was a breathy whisper. He did not know why he had said please. Was he pleading for Cyrus to continue, or to stop? Kissing him back, Wren hooked his good leg over Cyrus's waist, his aching cock leaking between them as he closed any gaps that had remained between their bodies. Hands roamed his chest, working their way between their abdomens. Cyrus's fingers searched out the laced tassels that held Wren's tunic in place, loosening them before rolling the material up and dragging it over his head.

Heat radiated from Cyrus's body, his dragon starting to awaken. He pushed Wren away, so that he fell back onto the bed. A small gasp tumbling from his lips at the sudden loss of contact, as he lay there looking up at his man. Wren's gaze became dreamy. Sucking in a shallow breath, his chest slowly rose and fell with anticipation as Cyrus took his time, observing every inch of the naked body laid out before him. This did not feel real. What had Wren done to deserve someone who looked at him like they were about to worship him? The logical part of his brain knew that he should be bothered by all the things that Cyrus had done, all the lives he had taken, and the fact that he had been in part responsible for the loss of Melana. But none of it mattered, not to him, not anymore. Really, if he was truly honest with himself, for all his righteousness, none of it ever had. The pull that existed between them was far greater than he truly knew what to do with. Lips pressed against the spot over Wren's heart, before Cyrus used his tongue to trace the planes of his chest. Wren found himself moaning obscenely, while Cyrus grazed his teeth against one nipple and then the other. Heading south, Cyrus took Wren in his mouth in one fluid movement, which had his hips bucking off the bed as he cried out, a string of profanities tumbling from his lips. It was both too much and not enough at once. Cruelly, Cyrus had somehow managed to remain clothed, and as Wren wrapped his legs around him, he longed to feel skin on skin. The heavy prosthetic pressed down, resting against the other man's back, Wren saw him tense for just a moment, but then Cyrus quickened his pace. Relentless in his assault, until the heat of his mouth had Wren spilling into it. Panting, he watched as Cyrus swallowed every drop, before crawling up to claim his mouth in a dirty kiss.

Wren couldn't control himself; he tore at the man's clothes. Pulling his braies down just enough to free Cyrus's cock, Wren spat in his palm. Taking hold of it, Wren worked him hard and fast. Obscenities poured from Cyrus, as Wren jerked the sensitive flesh. When he was close, Cyrus leant in biting down on Wren's collar bone, hard enough to leave a mark, crying out as he spilled over Wren's palm. When they both fell back panting hard, Wren wiped the evidence away on the sheets. Breathless they stared at the ceiling, Cyrus eventually breaking the silence. Chuckling wryly, he tilted his head down to look at Wren, who burst into a flurry of giggles as their eyes met. Tucking himself away, Cyrus smirked, "I take it you enjoyed that."

Wren made a nonchalant sound, scooting over to lie in his arms once more.

"You're an idiot. It was worth waiting for, if that is what you're asking." Smiling he added, "You were worth waiting for."

"As were you."

Wrapping his arms around him, Cyrus dropped a kiss on the top of Wren's head, hugging him tightly to his chest.

"I have to admit, I've wanted to do that since the moment we met."

Wren laughed, rolling his eyes.

"How romantic. There was me thinking you would have wanted to make love to me."

Tilting his head to face Wren, Cyrus was not laughing anymore, instead he looked stoic.

"I do. I just wanted to make sure that, when we do, it is the right moment. I didn't want it to be the first lust-filled thing we did. I wanted to be sure you loved me too. Plus, you know, we are both still recovering. I didn't want to hurt you."

Searching for any indication that he had misheard, Wren stammered, "You love me?"

Nodding, lips parted, Cyrus's cheeks grew pinker. He looked fragile, like one wrong word could break him. Feeling heady, Wren gazed at Cyrus doe eyed, responding, "I—I don't know if I would call it love, just yet. But I do know that I can't ever see myself loving anyone else."

Face morphing, Cyrus grinned at him in a feline manner, his tone a caress that made the hairs on Wren's skin rise,

"Good, because I don't ever plan on letting you go."

Their lips found one another's again in a tender kiss. When they finally pulled apart Wren asked, "Why me?"

"I'm sorry?"

Cyrus pulled away, his brows pinched as he shifted position, turning until he faced Wren. Leaning casually, his head suspended on one arm.

"What makes me so special?" Wren pulled himself into a seated position facing Cyrus. Sitting cross legged, he lifted his knees, hugging them against his body. Looking away, he continued, "You could have had a prince, and you chose me. I just— I don't understand it."

"Wren, look at me."

Cyrus waited, silence stretching between them, as Wren lifted his gaze to meet his. When their eyes met, Wren's breathing faltered as he observed Cyrus. The man looked like a deadly predator, his gaze fierce. He looked ready to kill. Wren was unsure if he was aroused or terrified, and that in itself alarmed him. Taking Wren's hand in his, Cyrus pressed it over his thundering heart. His warm palm coming to rest over the same spot on Wren's chest.

"My heart never beat for him the way it beats for you. It yearns for you more than it ever has for another. My soul cries out for yours. I know you can feel it too. The thought of losing you, of something happening to you. It scares me. I love you, Wren."

Trying to think of a response, a way to match the sentiment, Wren blinked repeatedly. The bond between them was a feeling he would never be able to put into words. Wren knew he would love Cyrus, the same way he knew that this was it for him now. The dragon-shifter, this sarcastic, brooding man who liked to dabble in alchemy and illusions, was his. If anything were to happen to him, he might as well die too. A lifetime of feeling this connection with no way of satisfying the longing would be the end of him. The mere thought of them being separated now seemed impossibly painful. Even before this, when Wren had been happy to pretend he hated the man, even then he would have found it unbearable.

To lose him now would be like losing a limb – and he knew that feeling only too well.

A scratching at the door broke his train of thought. They both jumped, Wren grabbing his clothes, pulling them on quickly, while Cyrus hurried out of bed to see who was there. When he pulled the door open, Tormund marched in, tail floating high in the air. Of course it was the cat. Jumping on the bed, he stopped at the foot end, sniffing the air. Pulling a disgruntled face, he retched as if he was about to bring up a fur ball, mewing, "Well, I'm glad the pair of you finally got that out of your system. It took you long enough."

Not waiting for any acknowledgment, Tormund instantly curled up in a ball, beginning to purr loudly, apparently content. Cyrus looked at Wren. They were both mortified, red to the tips of their ears. The cat, oblivious to their embarrassment, was simply pleased that his two chosen masters were now united.

Chapter Fifty-Three

No One Asked You to Babysit

Sitting in front of Golova Olenya's roaring hearth, with their tankards of ale in hand, Bastian had been quizzing Dimitri about snow. Given he had now had a few weeks to get used to the foreign substance, Bastian still found himself mesmerised by it.

"Where do squirrels go when it snows?"

Dimitri laughed hard, spitting ale back into his tankard. He wiped the back of his hand along his chin to catch the drips.

"They have a nice long sleep for the winter."

Bastian's eyes grew wide in disbelief.

"The whole winter?"

Aiko, who had been sat quietly, staring into the flames, spun a dagger between her fingers. The last few days had been frustrating. As time dragged on, she had found herself repeatedly contemplating when it would be acceptable to encourage the group to start packing to leave. Chiming in on their inane wittering, Aiko corrected Dimitri.

"No, not the whole winter. They prepare well and get cosy in their nests, so they don't have to leave, but they do not hibernate."

Leaning towards her, Bastian asked intrigued, "Hibernate? What is that?"

Patting him on the back, Dimitri reiterated his earlier sentiment.

"A more literal nice, long sleep for the winter."

Bastian's head flicked between the two in amazement, his mind completely overwhelmed at the concept. Having never heard of hibernating, it sounded a lot like the sleep some entered before death. Still, sleeping for the whole winter sounded tempting. Bastian thought perhaps he should try it.

The more they spoke, bantering back and forth, the more irritated Aiko seemed, her jaw locked as she twirled the metal in her hands. After a while Dimitri changed the subject, curiosity getting the better of him. They all knew that Bastian liked Astraea, and Dimitri could tell that she liked him too, although she was clearly loathe to forgive the man's deception.

"So you and the princess seemed close the other night," he said. Wiggling his eyebrows suggestively, he added, "Any progress there?"

Bastian sighed, running a hand through his hair. He placed his tankard on the table.

"I don't know that she will ever forgive me. It is a shame, Astraea is sweet and kind, and fiercely loyal to those who deserve it…"

As he drifted off dreamily, Dimitri took the opportunity to cut him off.

"She's also not bad to look at. What more could a man want?"

What more could Bastian want? He pondered the thought a moment. Astraea would be a good match, a smart match. While he would most likely never be king, their union could unite the realms regardless. Politically, he thought it was an excellent strategy. Making allies of their enemies would benefit everyone. His father would not last forever, and the steppingstones to peace would be in place. But then what did he know? Bastian had made peace with the fact that they might never form a romantic union, but he still took comfort in the hope that, perhaps, they could still forge an alliance for their people. That was, if his father did not kill them all first.

"Mmm…" Bastian agreed whimsically.

Tutting, Aiko kicked her feet, swinging them down from the stool.

"Yes, what more indeed?" she huffed. "You men are such simple creatures. Did no one ever teach you not to think with your cocks?"

Blushing, Bastian apologised profusely, while Dimitri snickered into his ale. The dagger thumped, as the tip made contact with the table, narrowly missing Dimitri's hand, bringing with it the men's silence. Aiko stood over them, lips curled inward as her shoulders rose and fell heavily with every breath. Grabbing the knife back, Aiko stroked the blade. Jaw tight, she stared down at her reflection in the metal. Twisting it over and over in her hands, her nostrils flared as she spoke.

"You all need to sort your priorities out. If what you say is true, there will not be any kingdoms left to unite."

Pointing the shiny dagger in Bastian's direction, Aiko continued, "If your father has his way, we are all going to die, so I suggest you stop trying to get your dick wet and worry about us obtaining this relic instead."

Not appreciating the threatening gesture, Bastian's tone was clipped, as he added, "If it even exists."

Dimitri grumbled something into his tankard, earning himself a glare from the blond elf.

"Don't be shy Dimitri. If you have something to say, you can say it to all of us."

Glancing at Bastian nervously, Dimitri instantly regretted saying anything, and had the feeling he was about to be in all kinds of trouble. Ironic, really: two men scared of this petite woman. They both pitied the fool who underestimated her wrath; even if she was short and slender, Aiko was lethal with a weapon in her hands.

"I was only musing that you haven't said anything to the lovebirds, and they haven't left each other alone for days."

The blade danced precariously in the air as Aiko shouted at them, waving her hands about in an alarming manner.

"Gods, Cyrus and Wren are just as bad. I know they have spent the last few days joined at the hip, but it has to be better than the godawful pining that was going on. I would rather listen to them shag all day long than have that kind of tension hanging in the air. Besides, I was genuinely worried for a while that Cyrus might hurt someone, if anyone else went near Wren."

"Yes. I suppose you are right."

Bastian agreed quietly, nodding along to Aiko while she continued to speak.

"What we cannot have are any more distractions. Those two are evidently better together than apart. Separated, they are too pre-occupied with what the other is doing. I will do my best, but if you are all troubled by other things then keeping you safe on this journey will be a nightmare."

Feeling mildly irritated, Bastian pointed out, "No one asked you to babysit us. We only wanted somewhere safe for our friends to recover from their injuries. We were, and still are, more than happy to embark on this journey alone if we have to."

Slamming her palms down on the table, Aiko made everyone in the immediate vicinity jump. The circle of revellers surrounding them, who had turned to investigate what the cause of the outburst was, spread wider. A hush descended over them as the girl began to shout loudly.

"And where would they be now if it was not for us?"

Looking past the two men in front of her, Aiko noticed the hush was spreading. Some stared at her open mouthed, others whispered to one another. Those still enjoying their evening on the other side of the room seemed a whole world away.

"They would be dead, that's where! Is that what you want to happen to your friends?"

Slowly, Bastian shook his head from side to side. Glancing around at the astonished onlookers gawking at them, Aiko shouted again, "What are you all looking at?"

Suddenly it was as if nothing had happened. Over-animated chatter sprung up around them, heads swivelling back around to mind their own business. Bastian found it rather surreal. The fear and respect the tiny elf inspired was quite something. She was right though; they needed to move on from here. They needed to begin their journey, and they could not afford any more distractions. Every day they wasted was another day Dracul gained. Time was not on their side.

* * * * *

That night Bastian's thoughts drifted to his brother. He wondered if Nico was alright. Already having forgiven his betrayal, Bastian knew Dracul would have had something to do with the way everything had played out. Unsure if Nico was simply trying to do what he deemed as the right thing, or whether he was just following orders, deep down Bastian knew that his brother would never hurt him intentionally. Gods, Bastian missed him. He wondered how Nico was coping, now he knew that Cyrus had left him. Although, if he was honest, he had also grown quite fond of Wren – and who was he to stand in the way, if they truly were fated flames? Besides, the bigger worry was what his father was up to. Bastian truly hoped he would not hurt his favoured son and heir, but that was the thing with Dracul: you never could tell what he was about to do next. Praying to the gods, Bastian asked them to watch over his brother, and Melana. He desperately hoped that she would be alright; if anything happened to her, he knew Astraea would never forgive him. Knowing his last prayer was a selfish one, Bastian rolled over. Grumpy, a little drunk, and a little frightened of what was yet to come, he fell into a fitful sleep.

Chapter Fifty-Four

Fire & Ice

The metal stove had a fire burning in it. Astraea watched the logs as they slowly turned to ash, the black smoke disappearing up into the flue. She pulled her knees to her chest. The stove threw out enough heat that her body was comfortable, the flames popping and crackling as she sat close to them. But Astraea's insides remained cold. Wanting to be alone, she had refused Bastian and Dimitri's insistence that she should join them at the tavern that evening. Making an excuse of a headache, she had stayed behind. When the two men headed out to meet Aiko, Astraea wondered why it was that, when someone wanted to be on their own, they usually wanted to be alone, but not lonely. Although sometimes, she thought, the loneliest thing of all, would be to be surrounded by the wrong people. Thankfully, Astraea found she quite liked her own company – gods knew she had had enough of it over the years.

Rocking back and forward as she clutched her knees, a tear rolled down Astraea's cheek, her thoughts turning to Melana. Wherever she was being held, Astraea would have felt so much better if she could just have known they were treating her friend well, if she was injured, or frightened. Clinging to the hope that Cyrus and Bastian could be trusted, Astraea prayed that Nico would not see her harmed. It was not only the prince that worried her; the king was their biggest threat. The scene of her father's death at his commander's hands lived freely in her head, replaying at will. It was no better when she closed her eyes to sleep, the sight of her father being executed on the dais still there to taunt her. If Astraea had her way, both the king and his commander would die screaming. Revenge could wait though. Her most pressing concern was finding her mother and Melana. Praying to the gods daily, Astraea hoped to manifest her deepest wishes into reality. Was it so wrong to merely wish that those that she held dear that were still in this world, would make it through this unscathed? It was a foolish notion; she knew that the reality would probably break her, but Astraea refused to give up the hope that this could end in their favour. If she entertained any other possibility just yet, there was every chance that she would break completely. Should she feel guilty at the thought that the screams of Bastian's father, as he died slowly and painfully, would be music to her ears? There was part of her that thought she probably should – but the sad reality was, Astraea did not care anymore. If she had to be haunted by Dracul's actions, by seeing her father's death every time she closed her eyes, then she did not care what suffering his death might cause – even if it was to Bastian.

Murmurs reached her ears as Wren and Cyrus stirred in the other room. They had chased each other's shadows for days. It was quite evident that they were together now. Glaringly obvious, in fact, the pair glowed in each other's company, radiating their newfound happiness. Especially Wren; Astraea had never seen him smile so much. The way he looked at Cyrus melted her heart. She wondered if, in another life, that could have been her and Bastian – but that did not matter now. There was no point resenting his happiness, and Astraea refused to hold who Wren's mate was against him. After all, neither of them could help what they had been born. While she was pleased for her friend, Astraea couldn't help but feel a bit forgotten. Stoking the smouldering logs with a poker, she bit her lip. When they pored over ancient texts, as they had been for the past few hours now, there was never an invitation for her to join them. Even Tormund, who had often spent a lot of time with her when they had been at the palace, seemed preoccupied with his two new dads. Astraea was still struggling to come to terms with the fact that the cat could speak. And that he had an entire conscious thought process of his own, that he now relayed to them all with delight, and without an ounce of humility. Remembering all the times she had changed her clothes in front of the furry little man, she cringed inwardly. Always assuming there to be little more than cotton wool between his furry ears, she was mortified. Although thankfully, Astraea imagined that she was not his type, not being a cat and all. It was still a bit creepy though, when she dwelled on it, so she tried her best not to. There was enough to think about without worrying about a talking cat.

Any day now they would leave the safety of Carpathia. While she wouldn't be sad to see the back of the snow, beautiful as it was, Astraea knew she would miss the safety of the cabin they had come to call home, even if it had only been for a short time. Deciding she could no longer sit still, Astraea went to her room. Grabbing her fur-lined gloves that had been gifted to her by the elves, Astraea pulled them on gently, the rabbit pelt lining soft against her skin. Today she wore a simple cream gown; green and brown pleats hung at the sides and a brown corset was laced at her waist. Pulling on her cloak, Astraea ensured the garment was securely fastened about her neck before she ventured out into the snowy wonderland.

Kicking up the snow with her boots, Astraea was thoughtful as she weaved her way through the trees. The shrill screech of goshawks sounded overhead, and small children squealed happily nearby as they played in the snow. The air was crisp as Astraea wound her way further along the path. Already it stung her cheeks, biting her nose and turning it red. A low and husky warble sounded overhead; Astraea looked up to see a smaller bird perched on a snow laden branch, singing the song of its people. The sky was a beautiful shade of blue today, with a splattering of fluffy white clouds littered across the sky. Astraea would not be surprised if it snowed again later. It seemed to be a re-occurring pattern here: cold, clear days gave way to snow-filled nights.

The further from the path she strayed, the harder Astraea found it to move, her feet sinking deeper into the white powder with every step. Mind spinning, an ever-changing blur of worries, Astraea tried all the tricks she had learned over the years. Breathing in through the nose and out through the mouth, counting slowly. Finding things she could touch and smell to slow her racing mind. Astraea was desperate to be the strong woman her parents had fought so hard to forge her into. But instead, she found her thoughts spiralling, suffocating her.

In a moment of unbridled despair which bordered on insanity, Astraea unclipped her cloak, dropping it to the ground. Holding her arms out wide she began to spin, her dress billowing with the momentum. Eventually Astraea allowed herself to fall back. The snow cushioned her, but its iciness hit her instantly, claiming her breaths for a moment as water started to seep into the fabric of her dress. Unable to move for a long while, Astraea lay there staring skyward, marvelling at the way the snow clung to the branches, weighing them down. Twigs were bent out of shape, but the snow still managed to stick to them. A fresh wave of hysteria washed over her. Astraea found herself flapping her arms and legs in the snow, giggling like a child. When she did eventually stand, her clothes were drenched. She observed her snow angel with a smile. The prickling sensation that crawled its way over her skin was starting to work its way through the numbness she had felt.

Suddenly Astraea came to her senses, knowing that she would be in trouble if she did not get herself back inside where it was warm. The last thing they needed was another one of them to be incapacitated for any length of time. Even if she could rationalise that her actions were a direct result of their selfish behaviour, this was still her fault. She had come out here alone, lost her way, and thrown herself in the snow, without thinking about the consequences. Astraea knew her mind had been slowly deteriorating since they had all moved into the cabin together. It had not been quite so bad when it was just her and Bastian, when she had been preoccupied with the fact that both Wren and Cyrus had been so incredibly unwell. Since they had joined them there – but then effectively ignored her in favour of each other's company – Astraea had really struggled with her own intrusive thoughts. At points, thinking the group would just be better off without her. It was almost like she needed someone to remind her of her purpose. Of what she was born to do. Pulling the cloak tightly around her, Astraea started to shiver. Trying to make her way back through the thick snow as quickly as possible proved interesting. Following her footsteps, Astraea began to think that she had strayed too far and would not make it back to the town. But she did. Even if she did spend most of the journey cursing her fragile disposition. What a cruel trick the gods had played when they had made her – a princess, a sole heir – so unfit to rule.

* * * * *

Swinging the door to their cabin open wide, Astraea was shocked to find several worried faces there to greet her. As she stood on the threshold, they all gawped back at her, horrified. Astraea realised that she must have looked a bedraggled mess. Shivering, skin mottled, her wet hair clung to her skin. As she looked around the cramped space, Astraea was shocked to find Aiko and Dimitri there too. The female elf, especially, looked rather angry as she sat cross legged on the tabletop, arms folded tightly across her chest. Bastian hurried forward to meet her, throwing his arms around Astraea's shoulders.

"What happened to you? Where have you been?"

"I only went for a walk," Astraea attempted, through chattering teeth.

Stepping forward, out of Cyrus's embrace, Wren's eyes were puffy and red rimmed as they searched hers.

"Princess, you have been gone for hours. We thought something terrible had happened to you. We've been out searching all over town."

Hours. Had she really been gone for hours?

Ushering the princess towards the log burner, Bastian started to bark out orders. Aiko was sent for dry clothes, and emerged moments later from Astraea's room with a night shirt and a thick blanket. Wren was instructed to fill the kettle; sitting it on the top of the log burner, he got the honey and lemon ready.

Once Aiko and Bastian had argued over whether the men should leave the room while Astraea changed her clothes, Bastian stood rubbing her arms and back, lending her his body heat through her now-dry apparel. It was a fruitless argument: Astraea, infuriated by their shouting and growing shakier by the second, had started to strip off her garments in the presence of everyone anyway. The only person who left the room was Dimitri; he had remained reserved, hovering awkwardly on fringes of the group throughout the entire ordeal.

By the time she had recovered her faculties enough to really take in her friends surrounding her, Astraea was touched that Bastian had showed true concern. Wren on the other hand had been crying, racked with guilt. Cyrus stood behind him, with his arms locked fiercely around the man. Both he and Aiko looked at her like they wanted to carve her heart from her chest with a teaspoon, and Dimitri still had not returned. Tormund, who had until that point been curled up near Wren's feet, sat up, shook his head at her in disgust, before marching back into the bedroom, presumably to resume his interrupted sleep. Pulling the blanket tighter around her shoulders, Astraea apologised to her friends.

"I am so sorry I worried you all. I—I must have got lost."

"It's our fault," Wren choked out, "We heard you leave and looked out the window. We just didn't think any more of it till you did not return."

"Yes," Cyrus added through gritted teeth. "We have been most concerned for your wellbeing."

Huffing, Aiko hopped down from the table, where she had resumed her position, waiting while Astraea thawed her limbs by the stove.

"Speak for yourselves. From this point on I refuse to be held accountable for anyone else's foolish actions. I swear you all have suicidal tendencies, the lot of you."

"Nobody is blaming you, Aiko," Bastian offered sheepishly.

Dimitri's deep voice boomed from the doorway.

"Stop being a martyr, Aiko. Just because you don't like that you have been assigned this mission does not mean you should take it out on them. Nobody is holding you accountable for their safety. We have only been asked to help where we can, in their search for the relic. You are the one that has decided that keeping them alive is your responsibility. No one else has."

Scowling at him, Aiko drew her blade. Striding across to where the man stood, she held the dagger to his throat. For a moment silence fell, everyone waiting with bated breath as she stood with her lips drawn back in a snarl. Her chest heaved with the effort of restraining her anger. Dimitri remained eerily calm, refusing to back down; his gaze never left hers. Finally, she dropped the blade away from his throat, storming from the cabin. The silence left behind was deafening, no one daring to utter a word.

CHAPTER FIFTY-FIVE

Darkness Falls

Alone in her cell, Melana waited for him to come. Anor had used these past weeks to abuse her powers, causing her to spin a web of lies to placate him. On his latest watches, he had let a couple of his friends into the gaol, using Melana as an attraction. The passing of time had made Anor progressively braver, or in her humble opinion, more stupid. Taking money from his friends, forcing her to tell them their futures. It was so degrading. Melana's gift was valued in her homeland; here, they were using her like some kind of mystic at a fayre. At least thus far they hadn't felt the need to touch her.

Footsteps echoed outside. Melana listened as muffled words were exchanged between Estrafin and Anor. Their watch changing over. Melana felt a sense of hopelessness wash over her, wondering if she would ever be free again. Her experiences when Estrafin was on duty were preferable. The man did his job, letting Rae come and go with food, but otherwise she was left alone. The hours of silence were starting to border on intolerable, but it was nothing compared to the feeling of dread that came with knowing that Anor was her gaoler.

Darkness had fallen outside when the key eventually turned in the lock of the main door. The length of time it had taken Anor to join her tonight had Melana's heart racing at a maddening pace. Enough time had passed from the guards' switch that Melana had almost thought he was not going to torment her. It was cruel and calculated on his part, lulling her into a false sense of security. As the door cracked open, it was not just Anor who walked in. Melana's heart stuttered when she saw who he had brought with him.

The king stood before her, smouldering with resentment.

"For your sake, Anor, I hope she is as good as you say. The thought of having to take anything from this wretched creature turns my stomach."

Anor grovelled, physically folding in on himself in fear.

"I swear, Your Highness, you will not be disappointed."

Melana did her best to remain calm. Her mouth was suddenly dry, tongue tingling as her heart continued to pound. Her mind stalled. How had this happened? Anor had been terrified of Dracul finding out what he had been up to. Every time the weasel had visited, he had made sure to remind Melana of all the unpleasant things that would befall her, should she tell anyone. It must have been one of the others. The stupid, stupid fool.

Melana's shoulders started to shake as the king approached the bars of her cell. She tried to rein it in, but when Anor stepped forward and unlocked the door so that Dracul could enter, she found herself trembling from head to toe.

Striding straight up to her, the king grabbed Melana, pulling her towards him. They were so close that she could feel his breath, hot against her skin. Squeezing her eyes tightly shut, she tried not to vomit while he shook her savagely.

"How does it work?"

Gritting her teeth, eyes still pressed shut, Melana responded, "You can start by letting me go."

Not only did Dracul let Melana go, he also smacked her across the face, so hard she fell to the flagstones, whimpering when he spat on her.

"You are nothing more than a rancid smear on this world. I would say you need to know your place, but you do not have one here."

Gesturing to the blankets that lay on the floor behind her, he shouted at Anor.

"Who left those there? It does not get luxuries. Get rid of them now."

As the cowardly man scurried past her, Melana held a hand to her stinging cheek, watching as Anor balled the blankets in his arms, hurriedly removing them from her cell. Her most coveted items, gone. Melana sucked in small, startled breaths, wondering why Dracul had entrusted her life to Nico in the first place. Why not just kill her when he had the chance? He was the king; surely he could just do as he wished, anyway. His booming voice crashed into her thoughts.

"All I want to hear from you is my future."

There was fire in his eyes now. His lust for power coiled with his disdain for her kind. It was terrifying. Unsure which version of him frightened her more, Melana continued to tremble.

Stepping forward, Anor ventured, "If I may, Your Highness, she just needs to look into the water. You don't have to touch the girl."

A moment passed before Dracul's voice rung out across the gaol.

"Well, what are you waiting for then, girl? Get on with it."

Dragging herself over to the bucket, Melana could feel fury springing to life inside of her. Looking past the water's glassy surface, Melana only hoped she would see the dragon king die a slow and painful death – but that was wishful thinking. Swallowing her pain and frustration, Melana allowed the vision to take her.

There was a battlefield. Soldiers lay broken and bloodied, the smell of iron filled the air, the sound of the injured and dying assaulting her ears. The scene changed; back at the castle, the king argued with Nico, cursing Bastian and declaring his life forfeit. In a flash, she was in the dungeons, watching her queen, Briana, chained in darkness, bruised and bloodied as she wept alone. Dracul sat on his golden throne discussing war strategies with the head of the king's guard. The banner of the dragon was spreading across their world, the house of Castillo laying waste to the communities that inhabited these lands.

But that was all Melana saw. Nothing more specific to the king. Coming around, she wondered if this would satisfy him, or whether she should lie. Opting for the truth, Melana once again found herself face down on the cold stone. The dragon king shouting as he stormed away from her, "Is that it? Is that all you can tell me?"

Clutching her side, tears in her eyes, Melana blurted out, "I cannot control what I see!"

Leaving the cell, Dracul turned a final time, walking the length of the bars like a caged animal, hurling insults at her. While Anor, who had already begun apologising for her lack of competence, locked her back inside her iron prison. After a few more parting insults, Dracul spat at her, before storming from the gaol altogether. A terrified Anor followed, scuttling after him. Melana was relieved that, at the very least, the invasion of her privacy was once again over, for now.

Chapter Fifty-Six

You Went Too Far

Rae knew something was wrong the moment she entered the gaol. Sitting in the far corner of her cell, Melana stared at the wall. The blankets Nico had given her, gone. Opening the iron door, she set down the tray.

"Melana? Melana, I brought your dinner."

When the fae did not move, Rae came around to her side, gasping as she caught sight of her face. It was still damp from fallen tears, dark purple bruising spread across her cheekbone, the flesh around the eye swollen.

Grabbing her hand, Rae squeezed it tightly.

"What happened, Melana? Who did this?"

Melana did not reply straight away, looking past her with dead eyes. Eventually she mumbled, "I tripped."

Rae's brow furrowed.

"Melana."

"Please."

A pang of guilt ate at Rae's insides as the woman's voice shook.

"I fell, it was my own fault."

Raising a brow, she pressed on, "Then where are your blankets?"

A flicker of panic flitted over Melana's face, just for a moment. So fleeting that Rae almost thought she had imagined it.

"I—I don't know. They were gone when I woke up today. Somebody must have taken them in the night."

Getting up, Rae rolled her eyes.

"Liar."

Scrambling to get to her feet, Melana's voice was high pitched, "I'm not lying. Where are you going?"

Locking the cell again, Rae's gaze was sympathetic, and Melana knew the woman could see right through her.

"I am going to get Nico."

Throwing herself at the bars, Melana cried out, knowing if Nico got involved it was bound to make things worse.

"No, Rae. Please leave it."

Her voice was shrill. Hovering, Rae was conflicted. There was no way Melana was being honest with her, and Nico would want to know that the welfare of his prisoner had been compromised. She had to tell him, but that did not mean she could not feel bad for the girl, who clearly wanted this kept to herself.

* * * * *

Nico was exactly where Rae had expected to find him. In his chambers, working his way through a decanter of expensive liquor.

"Please tell me you aren't drunk."

Raising his glass, Nico grinned at Rae.

"Not nearly drunk enough."

Sat casually in his favourite chair, for once Rae noticed there was no hint of worry on his face. That made her feel worse, but he needed to know.

Sighing, she replied, "Good, we have a problem."

Placing his glass on the nearby table, Nico frowned. Familiar creases of worry decorating his brow.

"What is it?"

"It's the girl."

Nico looked at her blankly.

"Yes, what about her…"

Swallowing hard, Rae knew she was about to unleash Nico's fury.

"Someone's hurt her."

There it was. The moment the switch flicked. Nico's brow relaxed, but his jaw ground tightly as his nostrils flared.

"Who?"

His voice was commanding, and Rae flinched at his tone.

"I do not know; she would not tell me."

"How bad is it?"

Worrying at her lip, Rae spoke gently, her voice calm.

"I mean, she is quite bruised. Melana said she fell, but I do not believe her. She will live though, if that is what you are asking."

A loud growl rumbled in Nico's chest as he flew from the room. Rae could feel the molten rage coming off of him, his feet thundering against the stone walkways as he strode through the castle with intent. The black cloak that hung around Nico's shoulders flapped behind him formidably. Rae had to jog to keep up with him, shuddering as the light from the lamps that lined the castle walls illuminated his features. Highlighting just how fearsome the heir to their realm looked. Whoever had done this was about to pay dearly.

Reaching the gaol, Rae saw Anor get to his feet, eyes wide as he took in the prince's rage. Standing before Nico, his mouth opened and closed, like a fish out of water.

"Open the fucking door, Anor."

* * * * *

The man nodded, shaking violently, fumbling with his keys. As soon as the lock turned, Nico burst through the door. The food still sat untouched on the tray where Rae had left it. Nico's chest rose and fell heavily as feral rage consumed him. Defeated, Melana refused to acknowledge his presence, keeping herself curled in a ball, pressed against the far wall.

Once the cell was opened for him, he stormed towards her. When Nico faced her, he was relieved to find that she was not too badly hurt, and found himself pleased that her injuries were nothing that time would not heal. Crouching down, Nico used his finger to tilt Melana's chin up, so their eyes met.

"Who did this to you?"

Nico tried to keep his voice level, but it sounded terrifying, even to his own ears. Wide, frightened eyes stared into his own. Anger flared in his gut. Melana's eyes were so dull, all their usual fire gone. It had not occurred to Nico that he liked her usual defiance, but he supposed it commanded a certain level of respect, even from him. Now it was nowhere to be seen, and Nico was not sure how he felt about it. Melana was his charge; his father had told him she was his to do with as he saw fit. And his wish had been to take care of her. She might be a prisoner of war, but that did not mean she had to suffer for simply being. No one could help what they were born, or where they came from. Nico thought of his brother, out there somewhere with the others. Perhaps they should have pushed for peace, but it was too late for that now. All the time his father was alive their nation was doomed to repeat the same mistakes. Superficial, foolish species that they were.

"Who did this to you Melana?"

"I—"

She stammered, struggling to form her words as she lied to him.

"I fell."

Who was she protecting? It made no sense to him; there was no way her loyalties could lie with those who held her captive.

"Please do not lie to me, Melana. How can I help you if you will not tell me what happened?"

There was a brief moment where her eyes searched his; it felt to him like she was searching his soul. Perhaps she was. Nico was unsure quite how Melana's gifts worked. When she hesitated, chewing at her lip, Nico thought that she was about to tell him something. A clue that could lead him to the culprit, but instead she dropped her gaze to the floor.

"I tripped, walking over to the window. I like to watch you fly."

Fire stirred along his skin. Infuriated by the lie, it took him all his self-control not to shift right there and then. As hard as he tried, Nico could not stop a small dragon born from flames bursting forth from his palm. Melana drew in a loud breath, watching as the creature flew towards the ceiling, before petering out into nothing. Interesting, Nico thought, that she had seen him as the monster he truly was, and yet she still did not fear him.

"I said, do not lie to me."

Instead of moving away from him, Melana drew herself up straight. Body trembling, she bit the inside of her mouth as she met his glare. Lip wobbling, she refused to say any more, but she did not back down. There she was, the woman Nico had come to respect. Admiring her determination, he backed down. There would be nothing more to be gained, for now.

"Fine," he growled. "Have it your way."

* * * * *

Furious, Nico wasted no time in taking his wrath out on Anor. As soon as the gaol door closed behind them, he pinned the man against the wall, his bare hands holding him up by his throat. Rae squealed in alarm as Anor's legs dangled helplessly, the man kicking out wildly as Nico held him firm.

"Did you do this, Anor?"

The man tried to shake his head. His face was turning pale, the flesh taking on a blueish tinge as his eyes started to bulge from his head.

"Because if I find out you had anything to do with it, you will wish you had never been born. If anyone harms so much as a hair on her head, I will kill them."

Letting Anor go, Nico watched the man slump to the floor, clutching at his neck as he gasped for air. Not giving him so much as a second glance, he stalked away, feeling somewhat better than he had moments before. Running to catch up with him, Rae grabbed at his arm in an attempt to slow him. Abruptly Nico stopped, swinging around to face her.

"What was that?" she panted.

Curling his fists at his sides, Nico found the rage returning.

"What was *what*, Rae?"

Narrowing her eyes, Rae scowled at him like he was a naughty child.

"That, back there. How do you know it was Anor?"

The way she looked at him simply infuriated Nico further, and he ground out, "I don't."

"Then what are you playing at? You nearly killed the man."

The prince was taken aback, his shoulders jolting backwards in surprise when she shouted at him, and for a moment Nico simply blinked at her. She was right, he did not know – but he suspected. Besides, he was the crown prince. Who was she to question his actions?

"Are you really telling me you believe that slippery little weasel did not have anything to do with it?"

Rae slumped, defeated, quickly realising this was a losing battle.

"No, I never said that. But you have no proof it was him. Plus, I'm pretty sure you frightened Melana, which is ironic considering your outrage at her treatment."

Another rush of anger was building inside Nico.

"I'm angry, because she was put into my care. Mine – no one else's." The vein at his temple throbbed as he continued. "I stipulated exactly how I wanted her treated and my authority has clearly been questioned. If there is one thing I have learned about people, it is that if they have done something once, they will do it again. I am telling you, that man cannot be trusted."

Raising her brows, a smug look snuck across Rae's face. Crossing her arms over her chest she ventured, "Nothing to do with your feelings for the girl, then."

Nico's face fell. He felt as if the air had been sucked from his lungs.

"I don't have any feelings for the girl."

Her smirk turned into a full-blown grin.

"Oh, really."

"Yes, really. Tell me, what have I done to make you think that I might?"

His fists were clenching again, and Nico's head swum as he tried to calm himself. Meanwhile, Rae reeled off a list, ticking each item off on her fingers dramatically in front of him.

"Let me see: you had me wash her; you gave her blankets; you ordered me to take her proper meals; and, oh I don't know, you almost killed a man because you think he *might* have hurt her."

Rae's voice pitched so loud now, Nico thought half the castle had probably heard her. The corridor felt like it was closing in around him. Rage rippled inside him like molten lava, his dragon threatening to emerge unwelcome. How could she accuse him of lusting after the enemy? Not harming the fae was one thing, but this... well, this was something else entirely.

"Are you sure you aren't just jealous?"

He spat the words, jaw tight. He had to get out of here, before he lost control. Turning from his friend, he walked away as fast as he could manage without breaking into a run. Rae scoffed, shouting after him, "Don't flatter yourself, you aren't my type." After a short pause she added, "You went too far, Nico."

Stopping in his tracks Nico spun around, taking several steps back towards her, he pointed aggressively in her direction.

"And you forget your place."

Leaning in towards her, Nico could feel the vein at his temple pulse as he shouted, not caring when she visibly recoiled from him. He was too far gone now.

"What you are implying would be treason. I thought we were friends, Rae. Or would you see me dead at Dracul's hand?"

Nico did not wait for an answer. Heading straight for the courtyard, he broke into a run. Only just making it, scales shimmered along his body like dominos before he took to the sky.

Chapter Fifty-Seven

You Can't Change the Past

Soaring through the skies above the castle, most of the anger Nico had felt had now dissipated. The city was beautiful at night, thousands of lamps illuminating the landscape, helping calm him. Instead of rage, guilt was creeping in, his thoughts turning to his chambers and the decanter that waited for him there. Had he really frightened Melana? Nico hoped that he had not. Yes, he had been angry, but it was not directed at her. Was Rae right that he had feelings that he should not? Nico did not think so – but then found himself debating if he should go and apologise to Melana. His foremost thoughts were for her welfare. No, that did not mean he wanted her. It just made him a decent person, and he would have liked to have thought that, by now, Rae knew what lay beneath his façade. Most of all, Nico regretted the way he had spoken to Rae. The woman had always had his back, and he had dismissed her as if she were nothing to him.

The time Nico had spent in the air had made him evaluate his rash behaviour. He was always calmer up here. Feeling much more level-headed than he had earlier, Nico deeply regretted the way he had acted. Apart from what he had done to Anor. That man had got everything he deserved, and Nico was only sorry he had not hurt him more. Nico decided that, while he could not change the past, moving forward, he could learn from it. Resigning himself to the fact that he was about to grovel for Rae's forgiveness, Nico began his descent. During his flight he had also decided he would confront his father. But Nico had to patch up his relationship with Rae first. It was always a good idea, he had found over the years, to have her in his corner. And he really hoped that she would not hold a grudge – but then he supposed he was about to find out.

After scouring the castle for Rae, Nico hesitated outside the servants' sleeping quarters. Making his way through the tight walkway between the tiny rooms, Nico found himself on the receiving end of a few startled looks, servants staring at him in shock when he shuffled past them. One of the royals sculking around in the bowels of the castle was practically unheard of. When he finally found her room, Nico knocked, but was met with silence. After a moment, he tried again, relieved when a distant voice told him to go away.

"Rae let me in, please. I'm sorry."

Out of his peripheral vision Nico saw someone peering out of one of the nearby doorways. Glaring back at them fiercely, he knocked again.

"Please, Rae. People are ogling me out here."

The fierce redhead swung the door open, eyes puffy and red. She kept the door barred with her body, a hand on her hip.

"No one asked you to come down here."

"Please let me explain. I truly am sorry. I did not mean to hurt you."

"Fine."

Bowing mockingly, she stepped aside, allowing him to enter.

"Come in then, Your Highness."

Nico was horrified at the size of the tiny space; to say it was cramped would be an understatement. Along one wall was a bed barely big enough for one adult; at the end of it was a chest of drawers under what could only be described as a slit of a window. Beside the bed there was only enough room to shuffle along the wall.

"You live like this?" Nico asked, reeling.

"How else did you think we live?" Folding her arms across her chest, she delivered one of her more scolding looks at him. "Your father would hardly provide mere slaves with lavish accommodation."

"But this is your home. I—I don't know what I thought. I didn't think it would be this bad. Rae, I'm sorry."

Her eyes were icy now, chin tilted to the floor. Despite her height, she appeared to look down at him.

"You did not come down here to pity my living conditions. Now say what you wanted to say, and then please kindly do us both a favour and go back upstairs to your part of the castle."

Nico's shoulders slumped in defeat as he exhaled.

"I'm sorry. I'm sorry for my actions, and my words. I behaved like an absolute heathen, and I am ashamed of myself. Most of all, I'm sorry I upset you, and I want to make sure you are alright."

Watching her posture relax, Nico was pleased when she replied, "Fine, apology accepted. Now off you go."

Leaning one hand against the wall, his brows raised, Nico responded, "Oh absolutely not. You need to pack your belongings, you are coming with me."

He chuckled as Rae's eyes widened, her hands shooting to her hips.
"Excuse me?"
Nodding he replied, "You heard."
"Why?"
"There is no way you're staying down here."
Rubbing her palms down her face, Rae sighed loudly.
"Nico, you can't just barge in here and make demands—"
He cut her off.
"Actually, as your Crown Prince, I can, and I am. Now that I have seen it down here, I cannot unsee it. I am moving you upstairs and that is the end of it. Now get your things, or I will take them up myself."

Rae turned, yanking at the drawers, throwing several items of clothing on to the bed. Blushing furiously, she waved her arms around as she spoke.
"There. Are you happy now?"
"That's it?"
"Yes, that is it – all my worldly possessions."

Looking exasperated, she watched as he stood there, jaw slack, unsure of the best thing to say to her.
"You are a ridiculous spoiled rich boy, you know that, right? How did you expect servants to live?"
"Well, I mean, not quite like this. You might as well be in the gaol."
Rolling her eyes while bundling her clothes into her arms, Rae retorted, "Don't threaten me with a good time."

Unable to laugh, Nico found himself suddenly full of self-loathing. He really was an idiot. Rae was right: despite the issues they had with their father growing up, both he and his brother were spoiled. They had never known any kind of hardship, bar the loss of their mother. Nico held his hand out to her in a gentlemanly gesture.

"Rae, you have always been there for me. I promise I am going to look after you now. I am sorry it took me so long to see."

Hesitating, Rae looked around the small room that had been her home for most of her short life, before placing her hand firmly in his. They headed upstairs.

After having a bed moved into one of the partitions in his chambers, Nico left Rae to settle in, pleased that he could at least offer her this small luxury. As his personal maid, she was always around anyway, so it wouldn't make too much difference to him. If he was honest with himself, he only used that room to get drunk in anyway, and he could do that anywhere. Hell, now he might have someone to drink with.

If he could manage it, he was hoping to avoid his father finding out. A servant living in his private quarters was a conversation he could live without having any time soon. Although, where Dracul was concerned, any conversation they had to have would come too soon. Unfortunately, he had to seek him out tonight. Arriving at the king's chamber Nico knocked on the heavy wooden door. When he did not get a response, he let himself in. Nico hated his father's quarters. There was so much gold décor, and he had always found it garish. Staring at an elaborate gold frame that surrounded the mirror, he supposed there was no accounting for taste. Nico could not see the king immediately as he entered the ornate chambers, but several conspicuous noises gave away his location. Pulling back the velvet curtains to his bed chambers, Nico revealed two women, who squealed loudly, attempting to cover their bare skin with the bedsheets, while the king continued to thrust into a third, who was on all fours on the bed, her eyes wide and mouth open in shock at the prince's intrusion.

The sad truth was it was nothing Nico had not seen before. Even when he and Bastian were children, Dracul had always had a number of whores in and out of his chambers at all hours. It was something he found completely unsurprising now. The king barely spared the prince a glance.

"Wait outside."

Snorting in disgust, Nico pulled the curtain shut. Of course his father's whores were more important than his own son. Waiting at the desk in the king's study, Nico cracked his knuckles impatiently. Wanting to get this unpleasantness over with, he was relieved when the women finally emerged fully clothed. Making their way hurriedly from the room, closely followed by Dracul, whose shirt still hung open at the top, revealing his muscular chest. Nico had to admire him in that respect. Given his advancing years, his father had kept his body at the peak of physical fitness. It was only a shame that his mind did not match.

Striding towards him, the king poured himself a drink, failing to offer

Nico one. His actions were purposefully drawn out. So that by the time Dracul plonked himself arbitrarily into the chair opposite, Nico spun his ring wildly around his finger. Counting in his head, he tried to stop his anxiety getting the better of him. Without looking up, his father swilled the amber liquid round his glass before taking a sip.

"To what do I owe the pleasure?"

Exhaling slowly before sucking in a deep breath, Nico began.

"My prisoner has been injured. You placed her in my care. I wish to know who went against my direct orders. I assume you know, as you are the only one able to go above my head and revoke my commands."

Swilling the liquid in his glass again, casually Dracul replied, "How would I know. I have hardly been to visit the creature." Looking Nico up and down he continued, "Out of interest, why do you care? Its kind are scum. It hardly matters if the creature is injured."

Anger was once more threatening to take Nico over.

"Because you entrusted her to my care. MINE."

Slamming his hand down on the desk, he composed himself before continuing.

"What is the point of my being the crown prince if people can undermine me without consequence? It should not matter what it is regarding. What has happened to the girl is irrelevant, but I want the person who has gone against my command punished."

"That's the spirit."

Nico squinted, perhaps his father was drunker than he thought.

"*What* is the spirit?"

"I must admit I was disappointed to hear the girl was being well cared for. I thought perhaps you would at least leave her there to rot. But it is good to hear you talk like a true Castillo now. And you are right: no one should undermine you without consequence."

Nico slumped back into the chair, relieved his father was in a relatively good mood.

"So, you have no idea who did it?"

"Have you tried Anor? I would be surprised if he did not know. That man is involved in every shady dealing I get wind of."

Smirking at the memory of Anor pinned to the wall, Nico earned an eager smile from his father.

"What is so funny?"

"I damn-near killed the man earlier. I do not think he knows anything."

Nico watched as Dracul's eyes lit up, the king leaning forward in his chair with interest.

"Tell me about it."

Nico swallowed hard. Anor was one of his father's favourite guards.

"I might have strangled him."

Flinching, he waited for a blow that never came. Instead the king rose, patting him on the back in a congratulatory fashion.

"That's my boy. I knew you had not gone soft."

"Ah, so I am your son again, am I?"

"Of course, of course. Someone has to carry on our bloodline. I doubt your idiot brother will live long enough to produce any heirs."

Trying to stay calm at Dracul's flippancy, Nico concentrated on keeping his breathing even. His father poured him a glass of his favourite whiskey while Nico stammered.

"And there was me thinking you had gone off me."

Dracul placed the decanter back on the table, giving his son a half smile and offering him the glass.

"Come, come, Nico. You have always been the most resilient of my children. I have always been able to count on you."

Feeling uneasy at the way Dracul refused to even call Bastian by name, speaking so easily of his impending demise, Nico took the glass, clinking it together with his father's.

"Cheers."

How had he once cared for this man? It had been so long that Nico had almost forgotten a time when his father was what he would call a good person. After his mother... well, it had all gone downhill after that, and now here they were. Raising his glass, Nico wondered how quickly he would be able to make his excuses and leave. Unable to think of anything worse than an evening with just the king for company.

"Cheers."

Chapter Fifty-Eight

Beware the Black Dragon

In the dead of night, someone slipped into the gaol. Pressing herself further into the wall, Melana's heart thudded in her chest, beating so hard she could feel the rhythm pounding in her ears. The shadowy figure could not be up to anything good. They had not brought a lantern with them, instead moving quietly through the darkness. Holding her breath as the key turned in the cell's lock, Melana waited. The figure passed the door, gently closing it behind them as they approached her. Melana was about to scream when she realised they held a bundle in their arms. As the person got closer, she realised that it was the other guard – the nice one – it was Estrafin.

"Sorry, I did not mean to wake you."

He bent down to her, offering Melana the bundle.

"It's alright," she found herself stammering. "I couldn't sleep anyway. You just frightened me that's all."

"I am sorry, that was not my intention."

A pang of guilt tugged at Melana's heart, brows pinched with concern. Estrafin did indeed look terribly sorry. Feeling the item he had given her, she was thrilled to find that she now had several new blankets. These were even softer than the previous ones, the ones that had been taken from her. Pulling the fabric to her face Melana inhaled deeply: they were clean, a light floral scent filling her nostrils.

"Prince Nico sent them for you. He sends his apologies for frightening you earlier."

Melana bit her lip, chewing it slightly as she thought on what to say.

"Tell His Royal Highness that he does not scare me. If he really wants to apologise, then perhaps he should come himself. Although I don't see why he would feel the need."

She sensed Estrafin regard her for a moment.

"As you wish."

When he retreated, about to lock the cell door, Melana found herself on her feet.

"Wait."

The guard stopped fiddling with the lock, looking up at her.

"And can you tell him, 'thank you'... for the blankets."

The man smiled.

"Of course."

The lock clicked into place, then Estrafin was gone. It was strange knowing he was only the other side of the wall, and yet she was still painfully alone. The hours wore on, and sleep still did not find her. Melana swore a silent prayer to the gods that she would make it home again. Thinking about Wren and Astraea, she wept alone in the darkness. Her mind ran rampant in the hours that followed, all the ways her friends could have come to harm racing around in her head. It was all too much. The silence was suffocating. Melana felt as if she was drowning in it. After what seemed like an eternity, the first morning light crept in her window. Mercifully, this land was warm most of the time, but the early hours still seemed to hold a slight chill. Melana found she preferred this time of day; later on, it got too hot for her liking.

Making a bed out of the blankets Estrafin had brought her, she stared at the ceiling. If the dragons really were going to war, there was every chance Nico would go with them. At the moment, he was the only thing keeping her from coming to harm at Dracul's hand. Without him, she would be well and truly done for. A sudden need to escape gripped Melana; she just had no idea how to go about it. Rae flitted briefly into her thoughts. Would involving her be a gamble that would pay off? Even if she kept her mouth shut, it was risky not only for herself, but for Rae. The girl had been kind to Melana while she had been here, and she did not want to repay her kindness by asking dangerous favours.

Wondering if Nico suspected how she had come by her injuries, Melana got to her feet, making her way to the window. The sunrise was beautiful. Back home, she would have got lost in the way the world slowed as the sun peeked over the horizon. Even here, Melana enjoyed the sense of peace it brought, to know that it was a new day, a new chance to start over. Vowing that no matter what, she would fight. If her fate was to die at Dracul's hand, there was no way she would make it easy for him. Having entered this world kicking and screaming, if it came to it, she would leave the same way.

The door scraped open behind her, making Melana spin around in an instant. She had been so absorbed in her thoughts, watching the sunrise, that she had not heard anyone enter the gaol. Clutching at her neck, startled, Melana sucked in a nervous breath. It was still ridiculously early, but before her stood the prince. Dressed all in black today, with gold decoration that spiralled its way along the edges of his attire. A gold dragon earring sat at his helix, its tail winding its way down to his lobe. Rays of sunlight stretched across the cell, hitting his face, giving his skin a mild glow. For a moment, Melana struggled to tare her gaze away, thinking Nico striking, before she remembered herself.

"Sorry, you made me jump."

The prince stood, his eyes raking over her, regarding her as if he was seeing her for the first time. In his hands, Nico held a platter of fruits, bread, meat and cheese. Far too much for one person. Eyeing him suspiciously, Melana asked, "What are you doing here?"

"You told Estrafin that if I wanted to apologise, I should do it in person, so here I am. I wondered, actually, if I could join you for breakfast?"

Melana blinked several times in quick succession, maybe she was dreaming.

"Why would you want to do that? I thought I was your prisoner. Wait, are you even allowed to eat with me?"

Smirking, Nico responded, "I am the crown prince. I make my own decisions. The only one who can question them is my father, and as you can see, he is not here."

Her eyes widened.

"And what if he found out?" Melana asked, alarmed.

Smiling now, Nico replied, "He won't. Dracul is currently..." Nico mused on a polite way to tell her he had just seen several whores headed to his father's chambers, "...otherwise engaged."

Coming to sit beside her, Nico leant back against the wall, one leg bent, the other stretched out. Placing the plate in front of him, he grabbed a strawberry as if this was the most normal thing in the world. It would be rude not to join him, she supposed, especially as he had taken the trouble of coming here in person. Joining him, Melana sat with her legs tucked underneath her. This was definitely the most surreal thing that had happened since she had been brought here.

Tentatively leaning forward, Melana grabbed a slice of cantaloupe.

Biting down on the juicy flesh, she relished the sweet flavour. The mushy texture was perfect for chewing with her aching jaw and swollen cheek. Catching her wincing, Nico asked, "Does it hurt terribly?"

His question caught her off guard. Melana swallowed, meeting his gaze.

"Does anyone remember pain once it's over?"

A gentle chuckle rolled off his tongue.

"You are incredibly brave, you do know that, don't you?"

Melana found herself smiling.

"Or incredibly foolish. My mother says I am stubborn."

He laughed again, and Melana cursed herself for enjoying the sound that fell from his lips.

"Well, she is not wrong."

The pair slipped into a moment of comfortable silence as they ate. Taking a bite of a pastry, Melana still thought she might wake up and find this all a dream. Although if it was real, it proved that there was some good in the young prince. Melana had known she was right. As she sat mulling over the thought, rather pleased with herself, Nico broke the silence, shattering any thoughts of his behaviour being altruistic.

"I wanted to ask you something." Hesitating for a moment he continued, "Actually, never mind."

Placing a hand on his arm, Melana's eyes searched his.

"Whatever it is, just ask, Nico."

His worried gaze flickered across her features, brow deeply furrowed as Nico chewed at his lip.

"When you see things... Is there a way you could perhaps look for me?"

"You want me to look into your future?"

Melana was not sure why she was surprised; the breakfast had been a ruse, to use her gift.

"I just—" Coughing, Nico looked down, fiddling with the hem of his jacket. "I just want to see what happens, with my father, with the war..."

As he trailed off, Melana watched him look away with a sigh,

"None of it sits well with me. I do not want to go to war. This is to be my kingdom one day, and honestly, I could not care less if we shared it with elves and fae. I do not care if bloodlines are pure, as long as my people are happy. It all seems so meaningless in the long run. If our people have to go to war, let it be to defend our land, not because of one man's greed."

Nico looked at her, eyes pleading. Melana thought perhaps she had been too hasty to dismiss his motives, quickly making the decision to help him. After all, Nico was the first dragon to ask her permission for the use of her second sight. All the others had demanded it of her. Besides, he thought of his people, of the realm. How often would a dragon seek to pass over the chance of additional riches and power? How could she not help him?

"Alright, I will do it. Can you pass the bucket of water? I need it to see."

Letting out the breath he had held, relieved, Nico cocked his head to one side, "Really? You didn't before."

As he passed Melana the bucket, Nico shuffled closer to her, pressing against her side, so he too could stare at the water's surface. Smiling at the contact, she noted that unlike most she encountered here, he did not pull away from her. Nico smelled like soap and liquor, the deep spicy undertones comforting her. Unable to help the smile that curled her lips, she replied, "I only need the water if I bring on the vision myself. But sometimes they find me on their own. You won't be able to see it though; you will have to trust that I speak the truth."

Leaning in, Melana settled her hands either side of the bucket before looking in, her brow furrowed in concentration until the vision took her.

Suddenly, they were inside Nico's chambers. Rae was there too. They talked, laughed and joked; it was as if they were friends. Now they were alone, just the two of them, his fingers stroking the planes of her face. She wanted to see what happened next, but she was ripped away to a battlefield. People lay dying. And there was blood, so much blood, and the screams, they were haunting. But she could not see if Nico was among them, alive or dead. The scene changed; two dragons fought in the sky as she ran through the landscape below them. One red, one black. She knew the red one: it was Nico. They tumbled through the sky, droplets of blood raining down beneath them. Then the red dragon fell, plummeting towards the earth. Screams rang out inside her mind as she watched Nico fall to the ground. No one could survive that. She had just seen him die.

Melana opened her eyes, quickly realising the screams were her own.

Nico held her in his lap, just as he had the last time, cradling her in his arms in an attempt to soothe her. She pulled herself upright using his jacket. Their faces inches apart.

"Stay away from the black dragon! You have to stay away from the black dragon."

"Alright, alright, calm down."

She only gripped his collar tighter. Wide, frantic eyes, searching his. Looking back at her, Nico tried to hide his unease at her reaction, but even in her panicked state, Melana could tell he was unnerved.

"Promise me."

"Alright, I promise."

Melana could feel the panic in her chest, her heart beat wildly and she struggled to catch her breath. Closing her eyes, she could feel Nico soothe her brow with his fingers, before moving to her hair, gently stroking it in an attempt to calm her.

"Breathe Melana, we are fine. You are fine, just breathe."

When she did manage to regulate her breaths, Melana sat up, putting a small amount of distance between them. Nico's eyes searched her face for clues. Eventually he asked her what she had hoped he would not.

"What happened? Why were you so upset?"

For a moment Melana debated lying to him, but the only way she would get him to listen was to tell the truth. Whispering, she told him, "I saw you die. The black dragon killed you."

His reaction was one she did not expect. Nico snorted and chuckled darkly.

"Why does that not surprise me? Tell me, what else did you see?"

Wailing at him, Melana cried, "Didn't you hear me? He *killed* you. You died."

Nico looked into her eyes, searching the wide worry-filled pools, before whispering so that only she could hear, "But I am not dead yet, am I little doe? Now, tell me everything you saw."

Chapter Fifty-Nine

What Is There to Live for Anyway

For days, Nico had been mulling over the information Melana had given him. It surprised him that he was to die at Gerritsen's hand, but it did not shock him. Now his only question was 'why'. Melana had told him of their battle in the sky, and that he had fallen to his death. She had seen fields of battle, although they had not quite been able to establish where those were. And in an interesting development, she had seemed to be genuinely frightened for him. Although he was her captor, they seemed to be building a certain rapport, which could prove useful. At any rate, Nico had found that he enjoyed their witty exchanges. In many ways, she reminded him of Rae. Fierce, caring and loyal to those she thought deserved it. Musing whether she would fit in, should she join the servants in the castle, Nico decided he wanted her to be kept in a better manner than she was at present. He was not entirely sure why, but he found Melana seemed to bring out a certain kind of humanity in him. One that he did not often let people see. Although, he thought, at least the gaol offered her some form of protection. In his absence, Nico trusted Rae to keep an eye on her, and Estrafin was one of his more trusted guards. It was only Anor that was a problem. Perhaps Melana should stay there for now. The more Nico thought of her injuries, the angrier he became, starting to realise that perhaps his anger wasn't only because someone had questioned his authority. The image he conjured in his mind of her bruised face filled him with rage. And the thought that his feelings might point to something more was terrifying.

Stretching, Nico sat up in the chair. His shirt was unbuttoned at the neck, his hair messy, sticking up where he had run his fingers through it repeatedly as he contemplated his options. Hearing Rae enter behind him, he sought her council inquiring, "Good day?"

Coming around to take the seat in front of him, Rae smiled warmly. Reaching for Nico's decanter and a glass, she casually poured herself a drink from the prince's personal stash. Completely at ease, like it was a normal occurrence for a prince and his maid to share their personal time together.

"Better knowing I'm coming back to that comfortable bed for a good night's sleep."

Nico was pleased he had been able to give her that small comfort. As yet, no one had dared ask Rae where she had been moved to. It would seem that, having ventured into the depths of the servant's quarters, he had rendered the wagging tongues mute. The fact that he had taken her, he knew would be news, once the shock wore off. It was inevitable that it would eventually work its way around the castle. Especially if Gerritsen caught wind of it. If he realised that she was still present in the castle, but unaccounted for in the servant's quarters, then Nico knew the man would not hesitate to scurry off to his father with the news.

"Cheers."

She leaned in, clinking their glasses together, her ample cleavage threatening to spill from her simple robes, before she sunk back into the chair, making herself comfortable. Taking a sip of the dark liquor, she rolled her shoulders, sighing theatrically.

"Ah, this is the life. I could get used to this."

Setting his glass down, Nico allowed a small chuckle to break free. Glad that he had someone he called a friend to pass these lonely hours.

"Can I ask you something?" he ventured.

Rae lowered her glass, wary at his tone.

"Of course."

"The fae girl. She saw me die in one of her visions. Do you think I can avoid it?"

At that Rae sat up straight, lips pinched together, her mouth a straight line as she narrowed her eyes at him.

"Are you asking me if I think you can cheat death?"

Sighing, Nico let his head fall to his hands. Pressing his palms to his eyes, he eventually raked his nails across his scalp, sitting up before he responded.

"Perhaps. I was thinking, now that I know how it will happen, if I avoided the situation she spoke of, then maybe it would not come to pass."

Leaning in, Rae clasped Nico's hands in her own.

"I think we both know that is not how the fates work. Can you tell me what she told you? I need to get my head around the details if you want my help."

Nico nodded, taking a deep breath before launching into the description that Melana had given him.

"She saw two dragons fight in the sky. One red, one black. She knew the red one was me."

Rae cut him off, squeezing his hands tightly.

"How did she know one of them was you?"

Cheeks reddening at the question, Nico replied, "I may have landed near the gaol on a few occasions. I had the stupid notion that if she could see the beast within, it might scare her more. I thought it might make me seem more fearsome. It unnerves me that she can see through my mask. Not that it matters, it did not work anyway. Melana said she saw blood raining down. She was running through the trees below us, and then I fell. She said there was no way I could have survived from that kind of height. She saw me fall to my death, Rae."

As they sat there, an uncomfortable silence grew, stretching between them for just a few moments longer than it should have, before Rae's voice pierced it.

"Alright, so we are assuming that Gerritsen is the black dragon?"

Nico nodded. "I would say so, yes. He is the only black dragon I know large enough to best me in the air."

The tense muscles in Rae's face relaxed. Creases that had pinched her skin melting away as relief washed over her.

"Then the simple answer is, you do not upset Gerritsen. More to the point, you don't go out of your way to antagonise your father."

Nico raised an eyebrow quipping, "I thought you said that was not how the fates worked, Rae. I want to know why we were up there, why we were fighting in the first place. If I could only know that, then perhaps I could change something."

Rae stilled. Nico thought he saw some of the colour drain from her face, but it could have been a trick of the light.

"Did you say the girl was there?"

"I don't know if she was there simply because it was her vision, but it sounded very much like she did see it happen."

"Then perhaps you need to start there, Nico. Why was she running? How did she escape?"

"I do not know."

Slumping back in her chair, Rae took another mouthful of her drink, wincing as the liquid burnt the back of her throat.

"I think you need to increase the number of soldiers that guard her."

Nico lifted his glass, taking a mouthful of his own drink, topping it up again before he replied.

"I think perhaps you are right, but I do not want to arouse suspicions. No one else knows about this, just the three of us. It would have to be a subtle change."

Offering the prince a half smile, Rae eventually said, "Don't worry, we will think of something."

Looking around his chambers at the golden swirls that curled their way up the walls, Nico felt a sadness within him. Was this really going to be how it would end? All the privilege in the world would be unable to save him if the command Gerritsen acted on was the king's. Looking around at all his worldly possessions, his gaze came to rest on Rae. She studied him over the top of her glass, looking gloomy now as she attempted to hide her concern, failing miserably. If Cyrus was here, he might have been able to offer them some wisdom, but that was a bridge best left burnt. No one would save him now. Thinking of Bastian, Nico wished deeply that his brother was there with him. Not wanting to die without the chance to apologise or to say goodbye. He felt for Rae, caught up in their unusual friendship. Letting himself linger on all the pain and frustration he had endured because of his position, Nico thought perhaps death would be a merciful release for him, after years of pretending to be something he was not. No. Nico found himself clawing his way out of the darkness of his mind. He still had his brother. He still had Rae. He still had whatever it was that kept him going back to the fae. There was something he could not put a finger on. Something that intrigued him about Melana that he needed to pursue. Even Estrafin had proved his loyalty to Nico time and time again. And while he would not class him a friend as such, he supposed it counted for something.

Nico had always known that he liked the privileges that came with his life, the comfortable bed and hard liquor, but he had never enjoyed his position. Even though there was power that came with it, because of the way his father was, Nico felt almost permanently unsettled. He had been made to endure some terrible things. Even as a child, Nico and his brother had watched as his father had prisoners tortured or executed.

Seeing too many men go off to fight in battle, and too few return. Nico had lived this moment many times in his life, where he had contemplated whether death was a preferable alternative to living. But now, Nico realised, that while he was not afraid of death, he did not in fact, want to die at all. A shiver rolling over his skin, Nico acknowledged something that he could not voice, even to Rae. The fae that resided in the gaol was not just his prisoner. Having visited her several times since her vision, he had spent varying lengths of time with Melana, sharing meals with her and enjoying her company. Rae had been right. There was something there. Something dangerous and forbidden. Something that had the potential to get them killed if they were caught, and yet Nico could not seem to stay away.

Chapter Sixty
Reflections

Wandering the pathways that headed out of town, it was painfully obvious that Aiko was still furious with them all. Stalking ahead, she kept a hand on the hilt of her dagger at all times. Refusing to talk to any of them, even Dimitri, who had hung back, walking alongside Bastian, to allow Aiko to blow off steam alone. Looking around at the group, they were all in matching shades of brown and green. Bastian thought it seemed so strange to see them all dressed in the same clothing, especially Cyrus. The elves had provided them enough trousers, and tunics to keep them comfortable and clean. Each of them had also been given a pair of fur-lined black boots to go with their matching olive-green gloves and cloaks. Apart from Tormund, who currently looked as if he had been stuffed into an oversized grey sock. Tiny black booties covered his delicate paws, and his cloak hung around his neck, keeping him toasty warm. Dimitri had assured him it would keep his fur clear of snow and keep his toe beans safe. But the cat was not overly convinced, repeatedly announcing how ridiculous he looked as he trotted along, the little olive cape, billowing behind him in the icy breeze. Cyrus and Wren reminded him each time he objected that it was only until they reached the docks, telling him that once they boarded the ship, and were free of the snow, he could take it all off and be as naked as he pleased. Bastian had to hide his amusement, as the outraged animal had insisted that his fur meant he was not in fact naked. Cyrus took great pleasure in riling him up further, telling Tormund his fur did not count, and he would in fact, be a little naked boy.

Even Astraea, who had walked along silently by his side up until now, let out several small giggles, struggling to contain her amusement as the trio argued along the way. It was still strange to Bastian that the cat spoke, but then there were not any talking animals where he came from. Aside from dragons, he supposed. Evidently, it must have been the same for Astraea, who seemed to struggle with it far more than Cyrus or Wren. Although, Bastian imagined Cyrus would adapt to anything, if it meant making Wren happy.

The group each carried linen sacks across their bodies, apart from Cyrus, whose bag was made of tanned leather. The important documents for their voyage had been entrusted to him. Strangely, Bastian found he was not as worried about their choice as he would have been just a few weeks before. Somewhere along the way, he had begun to trust the man. Cyrus's bag held maps, a detailed book of dark magic that they had thought might prove useful, as well as ancient documents detailing the traps that they could expect to find protecting the precious relic. It also contained a compass and brass telescope to aid their navigation. The other bags all contained clothes and rations of food to last them several weeks.

The town had quickly faded into the distance behind them, the wind blowing fresh snow into their faces. Watching as Astraea attempted to pull her cloak up around her face, Bastian left it a short while before offering her help, pleased when she graciously accepted. It gave him hope when a pink flush spread across her cheeks to the tips of her ears, as he tipped snow from her hood. He brushed the white flakes from her hair, before pulling the hood up for her. Dimitri who had watched their exchange, patted Bastian's back when Astraea walked ahead to join the others.

"I wouldn't get your hopes up too much. Her skin is probably pink from the cold."

Striding ahead, Dimitri cast a glance back over his shoulder, waving Bastian on too. With a frown, he pulled up his own hood, attempting to pick up his pace while he trudged through the snow. Tormund had given up on walking, and now resided in Wren's bag, his fluffy face poking out of it, going cross eyed as he attempted to catch snowflakes on his tiny tongue. He purred in delight when Astraea tucked a hand into the bag, giving him some fuss as they walked.

Looking at the landscape surrounding them, Bastian was not thrilled when he realised there was only snow as far as the eye could see.

"Aiko, this is ridiculous. We need to shelter until the snow stops. We can't see where we are going."

Shouting ahead, he was disgruntled when the woman whirled around, her feet kicking up a small flurry of white powder.

"Tell me, young Prince. Do you wish to make it onto this ship?"

Bastian floundered. Of course he did. But the group were simply not used to this kind of weather, and it unnerved him that the dock was not yet in sight.

"Are you sure we are headed the right way?"

"Of course I am," she scoffed. "I have only lived here my entire life."

Huffing, Aiko turned to the others, hands on her hips.

"Look, do you trust me or not?"

Nervous faces nodded their agreement. Even if they did not, the elf was not to be trifled with, especially with the mood she was currently in.

"Good. There is a cabin halfway to the docks. At this pace we will be there by nightfall. Hopefully the weather will be better in the morning and we can make it the rest of the way in one go."

"There is no hopefully about it," Dimitri piped up. "If we do not make it to the dock tomorrow, we will miss the boat. It will be at least a week until there is another."

Cyrus shouted over the shrill wind, "That settles it then. Lead the way."

Whether they trusted her or not was irrelevant. No one had forgotten the incident at their cabin.

The hours crawled past as they trudged through the snow. No one dared question Aiko again. Bastian had never been more pleased when a glassy lake came into view, at its side a log cabin like the ones in Carpathia's city. There was no way they could swim in this climate; the only way was around it, much to everyone's irritation. So close and yet so far. But still, at least the end was in sight.

Willowy branches hung down to the water at the far side of the lake. The snow crystalised on their surface in a beautiful display. As they got closer to the cabin, the trees changed primarily to firs, hundreds of them surrounding the little wooden structure, each covered in their own coating of white powder. The scene looked like a picture out of one of Bastian's childhood story books.

They had only just made it through the door when a scuffle for beds broke out. Aiko claimed one bedroom, angrily slamming the door behind her, making it clear that no one else was welcome in there. With her volatile outbursts, the group were more than happy to give her the space she so clearly wanted. Tormund shot into another bedroom, closely followed by Cyrus and Wren, who quickly poked his head back around the door to declare that there was only one bed. That only left one remaining bedroom for the three of them to share. Bastian did the honours, sticking his head around the door frame to see what was left to them, confirming that this room only had one bed too. Although it was easily big enough for two, three would be a push. Quickly volunteering himself to make a bed by the fire, Dimitri scurried off to get the fire lit, leaving Bastian and Astraea in an awkward silence.

"It's not a big deal," she offered. "It's not like I've never shared a bed before. When we were younger, Melana used to stay with me all the time."

Bastian stared at his boots like they were the most interesting thing he had seen that day.

"I could, er, always go and sleep out there with Dimitri."

Astraea grabbed his arm as he turned to leave. Speaking softly she said, "It's only for one night. I am sure we can manage.

"Just for tonight."

Nodding, he echoed the words back at her. The pinkness was back, stretching across her cheeks, and Bastian could feel the heat spreading across his own face. It was going to be a long night.

Out in the open living space, Cyrus had helped Dimitri get the fire going. It crackled, roaring as they added alder logs to it. Feeding the flames that continued to grow until the room was pleasantly warm, their light, sweet smell filling the air around them. Aiko refused to leave her room, even when Dimitri attempted to talk to her, telling him in no uncertain terms that she should be left alone until the next morning. Wren emerged from their room soon after with a now 'naked' Tormund, who stretched before circling until he was sure the spot in front of the fire was comfortable. He proceeded to lay out like a small furry loaf, flexing his toe beans until he was content. Then he tucked his front legs underneath him like a chicken, closed his eyes and purred, content with the spot he had chosen.

They had sat there, eating some of their rations and getting warm for a while, when Bastian looked up in time to see Astraea slip outside, the olive cloak disappearing as she pressed the door closed behind her. After a moment's deliberation he followed her, having come to the conclusion that he didn't want a repeat of the other night. Aiko might actually kill them all if there was. As it turned out, he need not have worried. Sat on the little wooden bench at the front of the cabin was Astraea. Wrapped tightly in her cloak, only her face was visible as she looked out over the icy water.

The sky was serene tonight. Purples, blues and pinks danced in the night sky amongst the sparkling stars. It looked surreal, almost unnatural. As he slipped onto the bench next to her, Bastian thought the view bordered on perfection. Neither of them spoke for a while as they gazed at the night sky, and its reflection in the unmoving water. It was equally breathtaking mirrored in the lake's glassy surface. Eventually Astraea's quiet voice cut through the silent night.

"We aren't really cut out for this, are we?"

The words danced on a knife edge. They were both a question and a declaration simultaneously. Turning to look at her, Bastian responded, his tone kind.

"Does anyone ever really want to live through times of war and unrest? The way I see it, we have a choice to make. We can run and hide, or we can fight. We must obtain the relic; we have to use it against Dracul. It is where we can have the biggest impact. The relic could mean the difference between success or failure for the rest of the realm. It will level the playing field, that much is certain. We may not be taking up arms, but this – this is the part we must play. I am sure of it."

Astraea sighed, Bastian could see her steamy breath, hot against the frigid air.

"Do you honestly think we can do it, Bastian?"

He took her hand in his.

"We will, or we will die trying."

Frowning, she offered him a sad, fleeting smile that lasted only a second, as she murmured, "That is what I am afraid of."

The rest of the evening had proved no more fruitful. As the others went to sleep one by one, Bastian had awkwardly asked the princess her preferred side of the bed. They had retired shortly afterwards, to let Dimitri get some sleep, and now Bastian stood with his back turned while she changed out of her clothes. Opting to leave his braies and tunic on, he slipped between the sheets next to Astraea, alarmed to find that all that covered her skin was a scrap of fabric masquerading as a nightgown. Eternally grateful that she faced away from him, he felt himself grow hard at the thought of curling his body around hers, his hands longing to explore every inch of her pale flesh. But he could not. Rolling so that their backs now faced one another, Bastian closed his eyes. Letting his breathing form a lazy rhythm, eventually he relaxed enough to fall into a dreamless sleep.

Chapter Sixty-One

A Blurry State of Agitation

This was hard. So hard. It had been one of the longest nights of her life. Astraea had lain awake for hours, listening to the sounds Bastian made as he slept. The breathy little moans that crept from him during the night had exhausted most of her willpower. When the morning sun seeped in through a crack in the heavy curtains, Astraea realised that she had not had a single moment of sleep. As the light stretched, moving its way across Bastian's features, Astraea lay there, soaking in his beauty. His jaw was square but had soft edges, the shape of his face lacked the sharp planes that Nico's had. It made him look softer, kinder. She stared at his nose; it was cute, like a button. His pink lips were perfect, rounded and full. Astraea blushed as she found herself tempted to reach out and stroke the part of him she found the most endearing, the round tips of his ears, so petite and compact. Drawing a sharp breath, she rolled back as his eye lids fluttered open. Stretching with a yawn, his ice blue eyes met hers.

"Did you sleep well?"

"Yes," the princess barked out, answering too fast. She quickly added, "Did you?"

She knew full well he had slept brilliantly, frustratingly so. At one point he had even snored beside her, looking so content, while she lay staring at the wooden ceiling. Unlike her, Bastian looked refreshed. Astraea felt blurry, confused and agitated by her feelings for him. The lack of sleep compounded it. All Astraea wanted was to be able to switch her feelings off. It was not fair. Of all the people she could be attracted to, why was it the son of her father's murderer? Although he may not have been the executioner, they all knew that Dracul was the one responsible. And even if that was not the case, they did not have time for distractions. No good could come of what she felt for the youngest prince of dragons. But as Astraea hauled herself out of bed wearily, her stomach still managed to somersault when she caught sight of Bastian's toned chest. Standing by his side of the bed, he had slipped off the tunic he had slept in, and now rummaged in his bag for another to replace it. Evidently, he was completely oblivious to the effect he had on her. Dressing quickly, Astraea packed any remaining items in her bag. Lifting it over her head, she draped the linen strap across her shoulders.

Feeling like a ghost, she made her way out of the bedroom to warm herself by the fire. Putting on a false smile for her friends, she found Cyrus, Wren and even Tormund sat round the now-dying embers, soaking up the last of the fire's warmth. Dimitri was placing the last of his belongings in his bag when Aiko emerged from her room, ready and eager to leave.

Bastian stood just behind her. Astraea could feel his warm breath at the back of her neck as she loitered in the doorway, conscious that the room was fast becoming too crowded.

Sensing Aiko's eagerness to get going, Wren got to his feet.

"Do you think we will make it to the docks in time, Aiko?"

The woman scoffed, smirking as she replied.

"It is only a couple of hours' journey now, so we should make it in plenty of time."

"I thought you said we might not make it?" Cyrus cut in, his eyebrows raised in irritation.

"As if I would have given you our true timescale. Unlike you lot, I actually want to make it onto this boat. I couldn't cope if I was trapped here with you idiots for another week."

"Aiko," Dimitri growled. His tone held all the warning his words lacked.

"What? It's true. You clearly did not think that they would have made it here by nightfall if they thought they had another day to waste?"

Astraea jumped as Bastian joined in the conversation, his voice loud beside her ear.

"You have to give it to her; she is not wrong. We were ready to give up when we had only just set out yesterday."

Feeling a small stab of betrayal at Bastian's agreement with the petite elf, Astraea pursed her lips until her cheekbones tingled. Eventually she turned to Bastian, "That is not a reason to lie to us though, is it Bastian?"

There must have been enough angst in her words for Bastian to sense her annoyance.

"Don't take it out on me if you are upset with her," he argued.

Astraea mumbled, "I am not angry with her or him, I am annoyed with you. We said no more lies, and there you are condoning theirs."

Then she turned her back on him, striding forward, past the men, past Aiko. Hauling the door open, snarking, "Well, are you all coming then?"

Bastian looked around him, mouthing 'What did I do?' to the others, who, alarmed at her outburst, quickly gathered themselves before joining Astraea. Tormund trotted out remarking, "I'll never understand why people do not just say what they feel. At least Aiko does."

Which caused several confused whispers among them all, as it had seemed pretty apparent that Astraea had, in fact, said exactly what she had felt for a change.

Taking her position at the head of the group, Aiko herded them as they made their way through the snow-covered landscape. It was hard to imagine that anyone knew the way to anywhere in this barren wilderness.

Voices drifted on the wind, reaching Astraea's sensitive ears. Wren and Tormund were talking about her and Bastian. It made her cringe. Especially when the cat, with a smug glow of satisfaction, told Wren that the reason she was being snappy with Bastian was because Astraea had feelings for him. It only got worse when Tormund referred to her as transparent. She found herself having to take several deep breaths to keep from revealing her eavesdropping. According to the cat, he could just *sense* these things. Although, Astraea supposed, she could probably do a better job of concealing her feelings for the prince. But that was not the point. The fact that they felt it was acceptable to discuss her feelings among themselves vexed her. Even if they were correct, their speculation was all completely irrelevant, because unlike Wren, she would not act on her lustful impulses.

Trying to keep her footsteps even as she fumed silently was interesting, not helped when she tripped on a rock that had been concealed under the snow, only to find it was Bastian who grabbed her arm, righting her.

Murmuring a hurried apology, Astraea felt herself still as his hand lingered on her arm for several moments longer than it needed to be there. Turning to face him, she felt the concern seeping from him. Bastian's brow furrowed, pinched tightly as his eyes studied her, radiating a warmth she hadn't thought them capable of conveying.

"Are you quite well, Princess?"

Astraea cursed herself internally as she felt the redness rushing back to her cheeks, betraying her. Nodding vigorously, she replied, "Quite well. Thank you—" gesturing between her feet and the rock that now lay exposed, she added, "—for that."

It pained her when a warm, genuine smile tugged at Bastian's lips as he watched her flustered expression.

"Anytime."

They made their way onward in silence, but now both Bastian and Dimitri walked close beside her.

Chapter Sixty-Two

Rise & Shine

Melana's heart ached. Three days had passed since Nico last visited her. After the ill-fated vision, he had started to grace her with his presence regularly. Never asking her to look into his future; he simply shared meals with her, and stayed to talk. It felt like they had started to get to know each other properly. And then, just like that, he had stopped coming, and no one would tell her why.

Anor had come for her though. Him and his creepy little friends. As much as she hated them, she continued to be thankful that at least they only wanted her mind. The constant battering her psyche had taken saw her growing weaker by the day. It was not in her nature to perform like this. The prince's visits, when Estrafin had been on duty, had just about made the rest of it bearable.

More soldiers guarded her now. Melana knew something was wrong, but to her knowledge nothing had changed. When Rae brought her food, she had attempted to question her, but the woman was having none of it. Claiming not to know why Nico had not been to see her, and deflecting every time she inquired about the extra guards. Melana was still sure she knew something. The way Rae behaved towards her had changed too. She was still kind, just seemed warier now. The food, however, had improved dramatically, which was saying something, as it had not been bad to start with. Most recently, Melana had been delivered a hearty stew. The mix of flavours in the simple dish had tasted divine after so long without them. Rae had even served her mashed potatoes and bread for dipping. It made her think of when her and Wren were younger, and they would help their mother to dish up the dinner at home. There was not much more she could have asked for, given the circumstances. One way or another, Nico had ensured she was well fed, kept comfortable and was well guarded. It was not his fault one of those guards was a despicable excuse for a human.

The last time Anor had come for her, he had brought the king with him again. Having to perform for him once more, the lies rolled so easily from her tongue, Melana worried that it would turn silver. Fluffing the truth, she invented scenarios and buttered their egos, but still, it did not seem to be enough. So much so that Melana found she was developing an extensive collection of bruises.

Melana wished that Nico would appear; she would willingly present the man his future. The prince was different with her now. Gone was the coldness and cruelty he was renowned for, instead a certain kindness had been uncovered, lurking underneath his impenetrable exterior. One that she knew had existed there all along. They had built a friendship, an alliance of sorts during his visits. It kept her going. Panic seized her gut, in a way that was becoming increasingly and alarmingly regular. Nico could not die. How could the person she had seen in her visions exist if he was doomed to die. Breathing shallow, the memories wandered freely in her mind. Nico had held her tenderly, stroked her skin with his fingertips. They had laughed and joked together. She had felt safe. This was the reality she longed for. One where they would be united. It was why Melana had sacrificed her freedom: because she had seen a better world. One where they existed in harmony, where their kinds could be together, a step closer to peace. The united kingdoms that Bastian had wanted. It would come to pass. It would. It had to.

Looking through the bars, Melana watched the comings and goings of the world outside her little window. Trying to keep her powers fresh, she held out her hands, closing her eyes, pleased when little gusts of air rolled from her skin, pulsing outward from her fingertips. It was not much, but it was something. Fleetingly, her thoughts turned to their trip in the royal coach, when Astraea had tried to make flowers grow in her palm. It seemed like a lifetime ago now. Her most pressing wish was to know her dearest friend and her brother were safe.

The silence was shattered by several loud voices. Melana jumped, realising it was already the changing of the guard. Her heart felt like it had stopped beating, her eyes growing wide. She could clearly make out the dulcet tones of Anor, and the others who tormented her. They were coming.

When the door scraped open, Melana lay on her blankets, facing the wall as she attempted to feign sleep. But they did not care. Anor slammed the main door closed.

"Rise and shine, sweetheart, you have company."

Rolling over, Melana watched the door to her cell open. There were four of them this time, the most that had visited her in one go. Anor went first; he always did. Begrudgingly she pulled the bucket towards her. As usual with Anor there was not much of a future to see. All eyes were on Melana expectantly when her consciousness re-joined them. Wishing Anor would hurry up and die, Melana suddenly felt terrible. Thoughts like that, were not normally in her nature. She had to be careful that she did not become the monster they all thought she was, the one they detested so strongly. When she did not start speaking straight away, he grew inpatient.

"Well, girl? What did you see?"

Melana debated lying again, but she was tired of this charade. What more could this man think there was to see? He had already spent hours in her company.

"They were all things I have seen before, Anor. I'm sorry."

Pitching forward he shouted, "Then try again!"

"That is not how it works! I can't make myself see new things. I just get what I am given."

"Then try harder."

Kicking her in temper, Anor's boot collided with Melana's gut, forcing all the air from her lungs. Curled in a ball, she tried desperately to drag in much needed breaths. Finally, she vomited onto the flagstones. Grabbing a handful of Melana's hair, he dragged her up to face him. His ivory teeth grinning at her in an accusing snarl.

"Now look what you made me do. Who's going to clean up that mess, eh? You are a fucking embarrassment."

Turning to the other men, Anor's snarl changed into a sadistic grin.

"Shall we teach the little lady a lesson? What do you say boys, want to get your dicks wet?"

Struggling in his grasp, Melana cried out, "I thought you despised me? You said my kind haunts your own." Struggling in his grasp, her voice pitched higher. "You told me you couldn't stand the fact we have to breathe the same air. And now you want my body. Was that all a lie, Anor?"

The man lashed out, his face a mask of fury. Melana screamed as he punched her, his closed fist meant his knuckles connected with her cheekbone. A metallic taste flooded in as blood invaded her mouth, a sharp stinging pain radiating outward from the impact. The sheer force of the blow ripped chunks of her hair from the root; the rest he still held tightly in his fist.

Panic heightening as blood filled her mouth, Melana realised she had bitten her tongue. Gagging as her vision swam, with all her might she spat in Anor's face. Blood sprayed over the man's pale flesh. Melana flinched in his grasp, before fighting back with everything she could muster, but it was not enough. Anor stood there silently for a moment, her blood dripping from his skin as his fury simmered. Then in one swift motion he was dragging her down to the floor. Sitting astride her he spat,

"A hole's still a hole. You might as well be of some use to us. Hold her down, boys."

They did not object. One grabbed at her arms as Anor wrestled with his belt. A second grabbed her head from behind, forcing it back against the floor hard, an arm coming to rest across her throat as it held her there.

Melana's eye was starting to close from the swelling, and everything hurt. It was the most terrified she had ever been. Realising she was pinned, unable to move, Melana felt all the fight leave her. As Anor let his trousers fall to his knees, she stared at the ceiling, a tear rolling down her cheek. She would not look at him. She refused.

Chapter Sixty-Three

Peace, Pain & Purpose

It had been a most peaceful day. The last few had been too manic for Nico's liking. Having attended multiple war rooms and council meetings, he had decided that, if he was to die, then he should make the most of the time left to him, choosing today to take a walk around the city. Strolling through the streets, it was refreshing to roam as if he was one of the common folk. No one was prepared for his visit, no one knew he had left the confines of the castle. It was actually rather liberating. The quaint cobbled pathways with their winding roads were enchanting. Nico could not remember the last time he had been allowed to venture down here. He had found himself particularly taken with the little buildings tucked into the city walls. For the most part they had sold food and clothing, but a few had trinkets of varying sorts on offer. With vague recollections of walking these streets with his mother and Bastian as a child, Nico had then ventured to the gardens near the centre of town, pleased that he remembered the way. They had been well tended and were one of the only places to sprout any real kinds of flowers nearby. It was somewhat of an attraction. Nico had spent hours there, walking amongst the red carnations, gazani's and bougainvillea to name a few. Stopping when he reached the pomegranate flowers, admiring the way the red bled out into the white. Almost like blood spreading across a white garment, in a twisted but beautiful way. Picking one for Rae, and one for Melana, he had ventured back to the castle, only to be accosted by Rae as he returned to their chambers. The pint-sized redhead looked furious as she jumped to her feet, striding towards him and jabbing a finger at his chest.

"Where in the gods' names have you been? I have looked everywhere for you. You could have at least left me a note, Nico."

Reaching into the breast pocket of his jacket, Nico produced the pomegranate flower. It felt like a pitiful gesture now.

Rae glared at the flower as if it had wronged her.

"Honestly, after everything that's happened, how could you just take off like that? I've been so worried about you, you big idiot."

Nico watched the flower tumble to the floor as she smacked at his hand. Bending to retrieve it, he presented it to Rae once more.

"I just wanted a few moments' peace. Is that really so much to ask?"

"Hours, Nico. You have been gone for hours."

Holding the flower out to her, Nico bit his lip, pleased when she finally took the delicate item, twirling it between her fingers before tucking it into the top of her plait.

"I'm sorry. If I feel the need to slip away again, I will let you know where I am going, I promise. I did not realise you would fret so much on my account."

Rolling her eyes, Rae grumbled.

"You are such an idiot sometimes."

He merely laughed, tutting.

"And that is no way to speak to your future king."

Smirking, Nico walked over to his desk, reaching for the decanter that lived there, pleased to find Rae had refilled it. As he lifted the stopper, Rae's hand found his arm.

"Don't you dare. I've got a job for you."

Placing the stopper back, Nico laughed.

"Look at you giving out orders."

Rae scowled at him.

"It's not funny, Nico. Melana's been asking questions. She wants to know where you have been, and why she has additional guards."

Raising his eyebrows, Nico rolled his hand to indicate she should continue, but when she didn't, he responded.

"And you said…?"

"I said I did not know. She is your prisoner, it is for you to tell her. Besides it's been days. I think you owe the girl a visit."

Nico snorted.

"Rae, I am the crown prince; I do not owe anyone anything. But yes, I was going to go and see her today anyway."

"Do you want me to come with you?"

Nico frowned. Perhaps it would be nice to have the company.

"As you prefer. I do not mind."

* * * * *

It really had been nice to have the company; too often Nico had walked these halls alone. Having left the jacket behind, the other flower was now safely nestled in his shirt pocket. But as they approached the gaol, he realised it was quiet – too quiet. Nico hushed Rae, drawing his sword. There were no guards outside the gaol. Their voices could be heard within. Feeling around in the brickwork for the spare key, Nico quietly extracted it from its hiding place. Placing a finger over his lips to be sure Rae knew he wanted her to stay silent, he was relieved when she nodded, fear in her eyes. Sword drawn, he unlocked the heavy old door. Nico was as quiet as he could be; he wanted to see what had been going on. Both he and Rae had been suspicious of Anor since the last incident, when Melana had supposedly tripped in her cell. They had not been able to prove anything yet, but none of that mattered now.

An acrid smell filled the air, a mixture of vomit, sweat and blood. Nothing could have prepared them for what they saw. Rae gasped loudly, unable to hide her horror, clasping her hands to her mouth, covering her silent scream at the scene before them. Seeing red, Nico could not control his rage as he strode straight up to Anor's still-thrusting body, plunging his sword straight through the man's neck without a second thought. Blood sprayed across Melana's face as the shocked man choked on his own blood. It bubbled from his mouth, dripping down onto her, before his body slumped motionless on top of her. Melana did not scream; she did not react at all as Nico hauled the man off of her, casting him aside. The remaining guards shuffled backwards like cowards, away from him, pinning themselves to the wall. They had sealed their fates, but they could wait. Nico was unsure what was worse, the hideous scene he had just witnessed, or the fact that Melana continued to stare at the ceiling as if in a trance. Pulling her into his arms, he sat on the floor, cradling her. Taking in her face, he blanched. One eye was swollen shut, the skin around it a dark purple. The other still bore the traces of the bruising from the last incident, the one she had refused to talk about. Her lip was split, and there was so much blood splattered all over her that there was no way to tell what was hers, and what had belonged to Anor. Carefully stroking around her face with his fingertips he whispered, his voice threatening to break.

"My little doe. What have they done to you?"

Melana's eyes flickered towards him. Straining, she attempted to manoeuvre her head in his hands. Her words were strangled, but Nico was sure he heard them correctly.

"You came."

The other eye closed slowly as Melana let the darkness claim her. Watching her chest rise and fall, Nico held her limp in his arms. Bile rose in his throat. During her darkest moment, Melana had been hoping it would be him who saved her. This was all his fault.

A loud bang had Nico's head swivelling towards the door. Estrafin and Rae had thrown it open with a vigour that left it swinging on its hinges. In the aftermath, Nico had not realised that Rae had gone to fetch help. What a sight they must have been. There, on the floor, in all that blood. The three guards cowered; Estrafin now held his sword out in front of him, blocking their path. Not that they were going anywhere; they already knew that they would not leave the cell alive. Anor's body lay slumped near Nico's feet, his bloody sword on the floor next to them. Soaked in blood, Nico was not sure where it ended or began anymore, only that none of it was his own. Leaning into Melana, he whispered, "You are mine Melana. I will never allow anyone to lay a hand on you again."

But of course, she did not hear him. Relinquishing her care to Rae, Nico stood in front of the terrified men. His voice low and menacing, he addressed them.

"Tell me what happened here."

None of them responded, all refusing to meet his gaze. Allowing himself a good look at each of the men, Nico saw that the one in the middle had pissed himself. His nostrils flared. Pacing in front of them, the prince pointed his sword at each in turn.

"Is this the first time?"

Nothing. He took a deep calming breath and, evening out his tone, gestured around him.

"I may spare the life of the one who tells me how all of this came to be."

As Nico suspected, the middle guard jumped at the chance.

"Please sire, it was not us. Anor made us. He's been using her powers, and today she couldn't do it properly. He got angry. He made us hold her down."

"Made you?"

The guard nodded eagerly. The other two continued to stare at the floor. They were not stupid.

"*Made* you, did he? Now tell me, how did he make you?"

The man's face crumpled as the realisation dawned on him.

"Did he beat you? Threaten you? Or your wives and children? Tell me how he made you."

There was a near hysterical edge creeping into Nico's voice. The man swallowed, his Adam's apple bobbing in his throat.

"He told us to. He issued the command, and we followed it. He was our superior officer."

A growl escaped Nico's throat as he pinned the man's neck to the wall, crushing it with his bare hands.

"Orders are for the battlefields. They are not for torturing a young woman. She is a prisoner of war, for fuck's sake."

One of the others piped up, getting to his feet in a final display of defiance.

"Exactly. She is the enemy."

Nico let go, the man dropped, grabbing at his throat, gasping. Turning towards the other guard, Nico spat, "It would have been bad enough if you had stood by while Anor acted alone, if you had merely looked the other way, but you were complicit in this. You all chose to follow those orders. You pinned her down, you helped him. You took away any chance the girl had of fighting him off. What kind of men are you?"

Nico did not wait for an answer, raising his sword he took the man's head. The snivelling coward at his feet, on seeing the head fall to the floor, screamed like a pig in a slaughterhouse, until Nico brought the sword down again, striking his head clean from his neck. The third man had not moved, and still sat staring at the floor.

"Any last words?"

Nico raised his sword, chest heaving from the exertion.

"I'm sorry. I was too scared of Anor to disobey him."

As Nico swung the blade he shouted, the fury in his voice terrifying, "Well how do you think *she* felt?"

Watching as the guard's head rolled away, the prince sheathed his weapon. Turning, he dropped to his knees, the ramifications of what he had done hitting him, but Nico found he no longer cared. Carefully, he scooped Melana into his arms before carrying the unconscious girl through the castle, all the way back to his chambers, leaving a trail of astonished servants in their wake. Rae followed, leaving Estrafin alone to deal with the mess in the gaol.

Laying Melana down on his bed, Nico had Rae help him treat the woman's injuries. She had just gone to draw another bowl of fresh water when Estrafin ran into the room, out of breath.

"Your father demands you join him at once. Tongues are wagging all over the castle. Nico, he is furious."

Pupils narrowing to slits, Nico seethed. If his father was furious that he had carried the injured fae through the castle, he could only imagine what he would say when he found out his son and heir had murdered four of his more favoured guards.

"Tell him he can fucking wait. I will come when I am ready, and not a moment before."

Chapter Sixty-Four

The Dragon's Wrath

Estrafin returned eventually, his pallor white as a sheet.

"When you are ready, I am to escort you to the king's chambers. Dracul wishes to speak with you, alone."

Bobbing his head in acknowledgment, Nico turned to Rae. Between them they had sponged away the blood from Melana's skin. Carefully washing her, Nico was appalled to find the bruises her clothing hid. Running the length of her abdomen were angry welts in varying shades, all at different stages of healing. They had managed to get her into a clean nightgown, so at least when she awoke, she would not be shrouded in a reminder of what had occurred. Sucking in a sharp breath, Nico murmured, "She looks so fragile, just lying there like that." Ghosting his fingers across her forehead he continued. "What have we become, when our kind thinks that kind of behaviour is acceptable, just because of what she happened to be born? Are we really all that different? After all, we all bleed the same."

Placing her hand on Nico's arm, Rae attempted to console him as his words stuttered to a halt, his voice breaking.

"Are you going to be alright, going alone?"

"I don't want her left alone for a second, Rae. Es will be with me. Please, you are the only one I trust completely."

Eyeing him sadly, she replied, "As you wish."

Nodding as he turned to leave, Nico faltered, adding an afterthought.

"And Rae, can you get more bedding brought up, please? Melana stays with us."

Nico knew his father must be beyond angry. Watching Estrafin as he escorted him towards the king's chambers, the man trembled the whole way. Their footsteps were glacial as they moved through the empty corridors that led to the king's private rooms. When he knocked, it felt as if his father deliberately took forever to respond. The tension in his limbs amplified on entering, when Nico saw Dracul sat indulging in a glass of wine. It would have been lovely to think the king was waiting patiently, but Nico knew his father had no time for defiance, even from his son. The king did not speak as he entered, merely waving Estrafin away without a word. The guard's eyes flitted to Nico for a brief second, unsure, before he mumbled, so that only Nico could hear, "I'll be outside should you need me."

Patting his shoulder, Nico walked over to take his seat in front of his father. The king did not say anything for a long time. His stare felt like it was trying to pierce Nico's soul. He slowly looked him up and down, taking in the blood that marred his clothing. Dracul's eyes were cold, they looked dead, like he was merely a vessel. A chill rolled over Nico. The hairs on his arms stood on end as he shuddered. Finally, the king spoke.

"I trust what I have heard is not true?"

Swallowing, Nico answered, his mouth dry.

"It depends. What have you heard, Father?"

Dracul's top lip curled, exposing his teeth. The man clenched his fists so hard the veins on his arms stood to attention.

"The maids are scurrying about the castle, telling one another how you carried a broken, bloodied girl through the corridors. They say it was the prisoner, the fae. They say you took her to your chambers."

His nostrils flared wide, his breaths heavy as Dracul waited for his son to answer.

"Don't worry, Father. I have no plans to keep her there."

The king's fist slammed into the side table.

"What the fuck is wrong with you? Are you trying to force me into an early grave?"

Trying to remain calm, Nico thrummed his fingers on the arm of the chair.

"Do you know why I was forced to take such action, or do you simply not care?"

Dracul got to his feet, scraping the chair back loudly, shouting, "What possible reason could there be for you to bring that creature into my castle? To your chambers!"

"Your men did this. They beat her and defiled her. Animals are treated better than that." Nico rose slowly as he eyed his father like prey. "YOU placed her into MY care, no one else's. YOU told me to do with her as I saw fit. If you thought it had been me that had done this, I imagine you would be quite proud, Father. So, I ask you: were you a part of this? Did you hurt her too?"

The king did not hesitate, he slapped Nico across the face with his open palm.

"How dare you! Of course I know it was not you. The tender way you looked at that thing is all the foolish women in this castle are speaking of."

Nico's response was spluttered; he had been caught off guard,

"I—I have no feelings for her, Father. I was just trying to do the right thing."

Dracul roared, unbridled rage seeping from within.

"The right thing?" He bellowed. "This is the kind of behaviour I would expect from Bastian, not you!"

Running his fingers along his cheek, Nico snarled back at his father.

"What went so wrong for you? What was it that made you this way? How have we begun to justify treating others like this, just because of what they happened to be born? You were not always like this."

Dracul hit him again, the gold rings that adorned his fingers making contact with Nico's flesh. This time he backhanded Nico so hard the prince pitched backwards, sending the chair flying. Nico knew he was bleeding the instant the king's hand made contact with the delicate flesh at his face. Rolling onto his side, there was no respite as Dracul dragged him onto his back using his collar. Balled fists punched his body repeatedly, gold rings cutting at his flesh as the king screamed and spat at him. When his rage was spent, Nico's eye was swollen shut, and he was pretty sure some of his ribs were broken. His father stood above him, chest heaving with the effort of what he had just done.

"Why are you both so determined to end me? You just couldn't be the sons I wished for, could you? Get out of my sight, and be thankful I still need you."

Using the fallen chair for support, Nico dragged himself to his feet. Blood streaked its way down his face, dripping onto his clothes, mingling with Melana's as it soaked into his shirt. The crushed flower in Nico's pocket, that he had picked for her that morning, was now bathed in a visceral homage to their ordeals. Some droplets reached the flagstones, leaving a trail as Nico shuffled painfully, his feet dragging as he inched towards his freedom. The king stood watching him like a statue, glaring murderously in his direction.

Nico just couldn't help himself. Pulling the door open to leave, he used the last of his courage, turning to face his father – safe in the knowledge that Estrafin was stood just the other side of the door, sword drawn, should he need to make a hasty retreat. Nico allowed a dark troubling laugh to fall from his lips.

"We are really not that different from them after all, as it turns out." Pausing, he watched the king's eyes narrow to slits. "We all bleed the same."

Ducking through the doorway just in time, Nico heard the jug of red wine his father had been working his way through smash against the door, hitting the spot where his head had been moments before. Barely managing a half smirk, Nico leant on Estrafin, wrapping an arm around his shoulders. The man had been stood open mouthed at the state of him, but quickly sheathed his sword, wrapping his arm around Nico's waist to support him. The prince wondered if his father might actually finish what he had started, once he found out that Nico had slain Anor and the others. With a sigh he managed, "Take me back to my chambers please, Es."

The pain bordered on unbearable by the time Estrafin helped the prince settle down onto the bed next to Melana. After her initial shock at Nico's injuries, Rae sat at his side, sobbing, head in her hands.

"What are we going to do, Nico? This can't carry on; he will kill you."

Cracking his mouth into some semblance of a smile, he managed, "I believe that is Gerritsen's job."

His attempt at humour fell flat. Rae was so frightened, she had insisted Estrafin stay on guard outside their door in case any unwelcome visitors came calling.

"It's not funny, Nico. I'm frightened."

"I know. I'm sorry."

Nico squeezed her hand with all the strength he could muster.

"No one else can know Melana is here. You are to take her under your wing once she is well enough. Hide her ears, do you understand? You both serve me now; it is the best way to keep her safe."

"What if the king sees her? What if he recognises her?"

"Then we cross that bridge when we come to it. Dracul won't look for her here. Even he doesn't think I am that stupid."

Rae regarded him sadly, tears still wetting her eyes.

"And what if he does? Is she really worth dying for?"

Rolling his head to the side, Nico looked at the broken woman lying next to him. She had been so fierce, but now, even in sleep, she seemed so fragile. He could no longer deny that something stirred within him when he was around her. Nico had thought it was that he admired her determination, and her defiance. The way she had searched for the goodness within him, even when he had been adamant that there was none. And he supposed it was – but there was also something else. Turning back to Rae, he spoke softly.

"If that is what it takes. I will not back down. I will not fight for a cause I do not believe in. This hatred dies with Dracul. If I am to be his heir, then I will bring peace to these lands."

"Well then, let's hope you live long enough to claim the throne."

Chapter Sixty-Five

With Hope Anything Is Possible

Melana stirred, wincing as she tried to move, realising every muscle hurt. For a moment she wondered why she could not open her eye, but then the attack came flooding back. She had survived. That fact left her reeling, having resigned herself to the thought that they would kill her when they were done using her body. If only she had fought him harder, if she had not allowed the others to grab her limbs and pin her down, then maybe she could have prevented this. Anor had robbed her of her innocence. Once was enough. She had no intention of ever letting another touch her there. Any magic the act could have held for her was destroyed. It hurt. The pain still radiated through her core. Melana could not understand why people would want to engage in sexual acts if it felt like *that*. How could anyone possibly enjoy it? The most frustrating thing was, Melana did not know how she felt, not really. Surely, she should be angry and sad, but she was surprised to find that all she felt was a strange numbness that made her whole body feel empty.

Attempting to roll onto her side, she felt the wonderfully soft mattress beneath her. Melana could not remember the last time she had laid on something so luxurious. Where on earth was she? Crying out as her movements jarred her aching body, Melana jumped when another's hand slid over her own. She was not alone. The prince watched her with his good eye, from the other side of the mattress. Nico. He came – she remembered now. He had saved her. But gods, she was shocked at the state of him. His injuries looked awful. There was so much blood coating him; she wondered how much of it was his. The prince looked about as good as she felt, if not worse.

"You came for me."

Confusion clouded her mind. She was, after all, still his prisoner. Yes, she had prayed for him to save her, but Melana never thought that he actually would.

Wincing, Nico whispered, "I'm sorry, I was too late to save you."

Every word was an effort. It was clear that every breath pained him. Groaning, he reached inside his shirt pocket, retrieving the crushed pomegranate flower, holding it in his palm.

"It's not quite so pretty now."

Squeezing at his hand, Melana's throat bobbed, tears threatening to spill once more. Such a simple gesture seemed to hold so much weight between them. Melana reached for his hand, stroking the petals.

"Is that blood?"

Nico blinked, his earlier thoughts on how he liked the way the colours ran coming back to him. It did not seem quite so appealing, now that they were both laid here, like this.

"Yes," he murmured to her, "it is our blood. It has been in my pocket all day."

Offering the prince a tender smile, her eyes roaming over him, Melana asked, "Did Anor do that to you? Does it hurt a lot?"

"Who remembers pain, once it's over?" Nico echoed her past sentiment back to her. His dark husky laugh was back, even if he stopped to cough, clutching at his ribs. "No, that son of a bitch will never hurt anyone ever again."

If Melana had any tears left to cry, she would have. The amount of pain they both seemed to be in was something she wouldn't wish on her worst enemy. The irony of her thoughts, not lost on her.

"It was my father. He heard I had brought you into the castle."

"Nico, I—"

He cut her off.

"Don't you dare apologise to me. None of this would ever have happened if I had not taken you prisoner in the first place. I could have let you go with Cyrus and my brother. I *should* have let you go. It's all my fault; now I have to live with it."

Melana stopped him, her fingers wrapping around his wrist.

"I survived because of you. I am still here because of you. You saved me."

Tears stung at his open eye.

"You should not have needed saving from my people. It is all so wrong. If I had not felt like I needed to prove myself to my father, this never would have happened to you. But I will make it right. You are going to stay here from now on, with me and Rae. I will not let anyone hurt you again. Not now, not ever. You have my word."

Melana said nothing, unable to help herself thinking that he should not make promises that he might not be able to keep. Rolling onto his back, Nico closed his eye to focus on his laboured breathing, never letting go of her hand. They remained there, fingers clasped between them, while the pair continued to rest.

* * * * *

When she woke again, Melana could hear Rae's voice at the other side of the bed. Flexing her fingers, she found her palm empty. Nico's laboured words filled the void.

"Let her rest, there is no sense in moving her until she is ready."

Rae's words grew hushed, the fear in her voice evident.

"What if your father comes here? What if he sees you both?"

"Fuck my father."

"Nico, don't—"

Speaking over her, which Melana thought was a feat in itself, Nico rasped out every word.

"What is there to see? Us both lying half dead together? Let's face it, he beat me half to death just for bringing her into the castle. If he finds her still here, I do not think it is going to matter whose bed she is in. Please just get her a bed ready for when she is strong enough to move. Until then, leave her as she is."

Melana wondered when he had started to care so much for her wellbeing. She thought perhaps there was something wrong with her. Melana had felt so frightened, so alone. And yet in her darkest moments, she had just wanted Nico to come for her. Melana was not sure exactly how she knew Nico would keep her safe. It was a strange feeling, more than just her visions now; she had begun to see the person he kept hidden from the rest of the world, and gods help her, she liked it. She liked him. It pained her that he had been hurt on her account. His face, once so striking, was little more than pulp on one side. Still, time would heal the physical wounds eventually; the trauma she had endured, on the other hand, was something Melana thought she might never recover from. If only she could just *feel* something...

The redhead tutted as Nico nonchalantly fiddled with a flower. It was crushed, red where blood had soaked into the whites of the petals. Melana's heart leapt as he twirled the stem between his fingers, realising it was the one he had shown her. She dare not move and risk them discovering she was awake and listening.

Grumbling, Rae scolded him.

"You are playing a very dangerous game, Nico Castillo. Just be sure you know that."

There it was again, that laugh.

"I have no idea what you are talking about."

* * * * *

Days bled into one another, a week had passed or perhaps it was two, Melana was not sure anymore. When she had been well enough to stand, Rae had helped Melana to her bed. It had been placed next to her own, in their part of the prince's rooms. She had not seen Nico since.

Thankfully, they only had one close call, when Estrafin had rushed to tell them that Nico's chambers were to be searched. Between Es and Rae, they had only just managed to shift the spare beds back into the room along the corridor, concealing Melana there too, until Nico was satisfied that his father's guards would not return. Other than that, Rae had refused to let Melana leave her bed, unless it was to use the bathroom. From what the fiery redhead had told her, Nico was being treated in exactly the same way, much to his displeasure. Although Rae did report that his chest and face had improved considerably. Unlike her, he would have to rest for a few more weeks yet. Although Melana had been covered in some extensive bruising, all in different stages of their existence, she had sustained no broken bones. It was little consolation.

Now the numbness had begun to wear off, Melana felt like she was spiralling. Everything was out of her control. It may have seemed silly to anyone else, but she did not even have a say in what she was fed. Melana longed to leave the room, but was equally terrified at the thought. When she thought Rae was not around to hear, Melana let everything out, screaming and crying into her pillow, as anger and sadness crept in, taking over her thoughts, and consuming her mind. It was a struggle to feel this way. It was so unlike her, she hated it. Hated feeling so out of control, so frightened and so very alone.

Night-time was the worst; she had woken Rae several times now, screaming as the nightmares took her. Anor was there. She could hear his grunts, smell the staleness of his breath as he thrust into her. The pain felt real again; she was dry, bleeding beneath him. Until she woke, spending the following hours shaking uncontrollably, crying in Rae's arms as the poor girl tried to soothe her. Worse, the whole time she wished it was Nico that held her. Melana longed to smell the spices that clung to him, to feel the warmth of his touch. The guilt consumed her. How could she feel like this after everything that had happened? Surely the mere thought of a man anywhere near her should send her running for the hills – and with most men, it would have. But not him. Melana found she missed his presence deeply. His company had been stimulating, and in the end, she had looked forward to it. It did not help that having these feelings for him felt like she was betraying her people. She still had yet to find out what had become of their queen, and of course then there was their fallen king. Astraea's father. Her best friend; how her heart ached to see her again, and Wren. Good, kind, reliable Wren. How she missed them both. In the endless lonely hours, Melana often thought of her parents too. She hoped that they were somewhere out there, unscathed. Because hope was all she had now.

Chapter Fifty-Six

Perfect Imperfections

The Brigantine was visible on the horizon long before they reached the dock, her two masts towering over the vessel. Wren could feel an anxious energy crawling around his insides. It brought a certain kind of nausea with it. The closer they got, the more he found his tongue tingling, his mouth dry, as he tried his best to remain indifferent to their surroundings. The last time he had been at sea, it had ended in disaster. Wren had scarcely survived, losing his leg in the aftermath. The last time he had been on a vessel, far from land, he had lost everything he held dear. Haunted by never having the closure of knowing whether his family had lived or died, but always assuming the worst, Wren had drifted through the latter part of his life. Happy with those he called his family now, he had never been fully able to let the memory of his birth family rest peacefully. His father had never surfaced after the shipwreck, and Wren's last memory of his mother and sister was watching their fading outline, until he could no longer make them out in the distance.

When they stood beneath the magnificent vessel, Wren stared up at the ship, shaky as adrenaline coursed through him, fight or flight kicking in. In an instant, Cyrus was beside him, his arm wrapped around his shoulders, pulling Wren into the heat of his body while the fae trembled at his side. Cyrus leant in, his lips brushing the sensitive flesh at Wren's ear in a gentle kiss, as he whispered, "I've got you."

Sliding his own arm around Cyrus's waist, Wren allowed his head to rest on the man's shoulder. Enjoying the warmth of the moment, it distracted him enough that, when Bastian called their names, Wren realised that his body had ceased to shudder. Wren smiled; he felt safe with Cyrus. There was no part of him that cared anymore whether it was wrong to feel like this for a dragon, for his mate. Knowing innately that, with Cyrus around, no harm would be allowed to come to him.

Beckoning them towards the gangway, Bastian called for them to hurry. Aiko had already boarded ahead of them, and was stood conversing in an animated fashion with what Wren assumed was the ship's captain. They stood with their back to the dock as the pair boarded, making their way up the narrow ramp and onto the ship's wooden deck. The captain wore brown boots, over brown trousers, with an elaborate blue jacket that matched the band they wore around their head. Elven ears peeked through long mousy brown hair, that billowed in the breeze. Gesturing to them, Aiko made the initial introductions, naming the ship's owner as Captain Ember Delphine.

The captain bowed with a flare and enthusiasm that Wren could only dream of.

"Welcome aboard the *Mary Anne*, it's a pleasure to make your acquaintance. I hear you require safe passage to Oldir."

Watching Bastian swoop in to be his usual charming self, Wren and Cyrus hung back, curiously wondering if Ember was a very feminine man, a woman, or something somewhere in between. Wren's mind wandered until a fluffy ginger tail wafted at his knees. Tormund rubbed himself along his leg in a polite attempt to remind him that it was almost time for his dinner. Ember spotted the animal, suddenly waggling a finger in their general direction.

"Oh no, no pets on this ship."

Horrified at the thought of leaving the cat behind, Wren bundled Tormund into his arms, the outraged cat crying out, "Who do you think you are, calling me a pet?"

The captain's face morphed into a mask of shock when the animal spoke, their voice full of awe as they asked, "It's elven?"

Tormund's eyes boggled, his chin bobbing dramatically as he mewled angrily, "Of course I am. Look at me."

Stroking his head, Wren attempted to calm the hissing ball of fur trying to fight his way out of his arms.

"Tormund has to come. Please, he is family. I will keep him in our cabin, you won't even know he is there."

The captain looked between him and the cat before rolling their eyes.

"Fine – but any mess and he is going overboard."

Wren overheard the captain moan to Aiko that she had not mentioned the animal, elven or otherwise, catching her eye as the irritated elf glared at him for earning her a scolding. Ember followed her angry gaze, motioning to one of their crew.

"Baldwyn."

Another elf swung down from the rigging. Scruffy blond hair framed his face, bouncing as he landed on the deck in front of them. A lute hung strapped across his back. A bard. Wren thought he could be entertaining, something to pass the time, at least. He had really missed music.

"Can you show Aiko's friends to their cabins, please?" After a beat they reluctantly added, "And the cat."

As Aiko scoffed at the implication they were friends, Dimitri chuckled under his breath. Earning another death-stare from the small but scary woman. If he noticed the scowl Aiko gave him, he did not let on, chuckling away to himself as they all headed below, leaving Aiko to speak to the captain alone.

It was fairly dark and somewhat cramped below deck, as they made their way down the rickety wooden steps using only the light of a candle. When they reached the bottom, the scruffy bard told the group, "When you're settled in, get yourselves back up on deck. Captain always appreciates those willing to muck in."

Winking at Wren he continued, "Especially you two. It will make up for that."

The man gestured towards Tormund, who hissed at him, darting behind Cyrus for safety.

The first cabin, he offered to Dimitri, who went inside briefly before dropping his bag onto the bed and closing the door behind him. Next, Baldwyn assigned a cabin that only had one large bed, to Astraea and Bastian. Wren looked on amused as his friend's face turned bright red, the dragon prince looking at the floor bashfully as they both muttered about how they were just friends, and asking if there were any cabins with separate beds. Allowing a few awkward moments to pass, Wren eventually volunteered him and Cyrus for the room. There was more than enough space in there for them both, and Tormund. Moving next door, Wren heard Baldwyn allocate the prince and princess a smaller cabin, apologising, but from what he could hear, it had two beds. Which by the sound of their repeated thanks, they were obviously more than grateful for. Wren wondered if Astraea would ever give in to her desire that clearly burned for the young prince.

Cyrus closed their door, watching Wren over his shoulder. Turning to face him, he grinned as he stalked towards the bed, cornering Wren until he tripped backwards onto the dark blankets. Wren could have sworn he felt his heart sing as Cyrus came to rest, kneeling astride his lap. The dragon, with his jet-black hair and alluring honey eyes, leaned in, planting soft kisses on his neck, his cheek and then his nose. They were interrupted by a small furry face, peering up over the side of the bed. Speaking with the barest hint of disgust, the cat asked, "Do you have to do that?" His little amber eyes were wide with concern.

Turning to face their furry companion, sulking, Cyrus pointed out that they were just kissing.

Tormund bawled loudly, "I know, it's what it leads to that I'm worried about. I don't want to be scarred for the remainder of my lives."

Laughing, Cyrus rolled off, laying himself down next to Wren. The gravelly noise went straight to Wren's groin, but he ignored it, instead pulling himself up and into Cyrus's waiting arms. He rested his head on the dragon's chest, while Cyrus patted his abdomen. Tormund accepted the invite, hopping up onto the bed before strolling across the blankets to settle there, in the middle of their embrace. Tilting his head up, Wren kissed Cyrus's jawline, before snuggling back down. This was perfection, he wished they could stay like this forever.

The next thing Wren knew, Cyrus was rocking him gently by his shoulder. As the fae's eyes flickered open, he did not need anyone to tell him they were at sea. The ships rolling movement told him that. The boat had left the harbour, their journey had begun.

"Was I asleep for very long? We should probably go and help out on deck."

Stroking the length of his arm, Cyrus replied. His voice had its usual low rasp, but his words seemed silky, as if they held a million unspoken promises.

"No pet, barely an hour."

Their lips found one another's again as the cat dove from the bed, hiding in the darkness beneath it. Climbing on top of Cyrus, Wren quickly devoured the taste of the man's tongue. It was only when he felt himself growing hard that he stopped, breaking their contact, as they both sucked in much needed air. Sliding from the bed, Wren could see the outline of Cyrus's cock straining against his trousers. Gods, he wished they did not have to leave the cabin. Rising from the bed, Cyrus placed a tender kiss on Wren's forehead, rearranging himself before they opened the door to join the others. When the door closed firmly behind them, Tormund peeked out to see if it was safe, before returning to the warm spot where the pair had lain in the middle of the bed.

Chapter Sixty-Seven

A Heart Full of Love

He loved Wren. The emotion swelled in Cyrus's chest until he thought his heart would burst. It was unsettling, he had never felt anything like this before. Though he had liked Nico well enough, and others before him, this was different. Whenever they were alone together, Cyrus felt like all the oxygen had been sucked from the room. When they kissed, his lungs burned with a need he had not thought possible, and he found his mouth longed to find any part of Wren that it could. Just looking at the fae made his insides ache with a wanton need. Every time their lips met, Cyrus had to restrain himself. He wanted each and every interaction between them to burn brighter than the one before it, but he knew if he allowed it, like a blazing fire, Wren would consume him. They had the potential to destroy each other. And part of him worried that the brighter they burned, the faster the fae's affection for him would fade away. Their pairing would prove to be either beautiful, or tragic; perhaps it would be both. For better or worse, this was it now: Cyrus loved Wren. His lust for wealth and power paled in insignificance to what he felt for the other man. Cyrus knew deep inside his soul, death would be the only escape for him now – if Wren ever left, or anything were to happen to him. Now that he had been given a taste of him, without his mate, Cyrus would never survive alone again.

Following behind him as they navigated the narrow stairway once more, he couldn't help but admire Wren's perked bottom. The fae really was a perfect specimen. How he longed to just reach out and grab him. But then, he knew, they would end up back in the cabin, traumatising Tormund – and besides, they really needed to get the captain and their crew on side. If they were to succeed in retrieving the relic from the pantheon, they were going to need a way back home. Gods, he hoped they made it home. This was the first time he had had something more than himself to fight for. Fragments of his old life flashed before him, and for the first time in his adult life, Cyrus realised he did not know where home was. The thought lingered – but come what may, at least he had Wren.

Making their way out onto the deck, Cyrus watched as Wren stopped for a moment, before heading over to the railings, gripping them tightly until his knuckles turned white. Pressing his body flush against Wren's back, Cyrus wrapped his arms around his mate. And together they stood, until he was comfortable enough to let go of the rail. Watching as the land that was Carpathia disappeared into a tiny dot on the horizon. He had felt eternally grateful to Astraea, who had hushed Aiko. The elf had been about to bark orders at them when they had emerged. But the princess knew as well as he did how monumental it was that Wren had gotten back on a boat. Relinquishing his control to the sea had been a huge obstacle for him. One that Wren had managed to overcome with Cyrus's support. It left the dragon feeling heady.

Eventually Wren let go. Standing without the aid of the rail, he slowly turned to Cyrus, the ghost of a smile playing at his lips.

"Let's get to work."

Looking up, Cyrus spied Baldwyn stood atop the yard. The elf had one arm wrapped about the mast, staring into the distance, his other hand shielding his eyes from the sun. Astraea was at the helm with Ember, the petite fae steering the *Mary Anne* under the captain's watchful eye. Aiko was quick to send Wren to the ship's kitchen, back below deck where he clearly felt more comfortable, so that he could join Dimitri in preparing their evening meal. Cyrus watched him go, reluctantly letting Wren's fingers slip from his palm as the fae walked away. A harsh voice brought his thoughts swiftly back to the present.

"Cyrus, I need you to go and help the boatswain."

There were a lot of things that Cyrus knew like the back of his hand, after years of study, but the terminology for the running of a ship was not something he currently held in his repertoire. When Cyrus looked blankly at her, Aiko finally snapped, throwing her arms up in exasperation.

"Baldwyn, I need you to go and help Baldwyn."

Looking up at the mast, Cyrus replied, "How on earth am I meant to get up there?"

But Aiko was already walking away to oversee the others. With a brief glance back over her shoulder, she shot back at him with false cheer, "I am sure you will figure it out."

That stumped him. There were many, many things Cyrus knew how to do, but flying was not one of them. Unless he sought out the aid of his dragon – but somehow, he did not think anyone else would appreciate it. Especially because, given his size, he would likely destroy the ship. Looking the mast up and down, he was debating an attempt at shimmying up, when Baldwyn slid down the rigging, landing beside him. The sudden displacement of air against his face caught Cyrus off guard, and he jumped as the man spoke.

"Captain says you have a compass and a spyglass?"

Righting his footing, Cyrus responded bemused, "I do indeed, although they are back in my cabin."

The elf nodded, pointing skyward.

"Smashing, go fetch them, then I'll show you how to get up there."

* * * * *

Opening the little wooden cabin door below deck, Cyrus was accosted by a ball of ginger fur, squealing at him in a high-pitched voice.

"Where do I go to the toilet? There is no soil anywhere!"

Tormund wailed loudly, while Cyrus sighed.

"Can you use the bed pan? I'll empty it when you're done."

The cat stopped dead, horrified.

"But there is nothing to dig in. Besides, what will you use?"

"Tormund, pal, calm down. I will empty it; we aren't going to leave it in here."

Tormund's eyes were like saucers as he danced on the spot, all four paws fidgeting in desperation.

"Can't I just go on deck?"

Cyrus's hands found his hips, exasperated, he leaned back against the door frame.

"You heard what the captain said. Besides, there is nothing up there but sea and sky surrounding us. You will have to get used to it, pal. It is only while we sail."

The cat reluctantly disappeared under the bed grumbling, while Cyrus dug around in his bag for the compass and telescope.

"You get to use a toilet."

Rolling his eyes Cyrus replied, "We are people Tormund. Besides, its pretty grim. You are probably better off with the pan."

* * * * *

After a slight detour to empty the bed pan and return it to the ungrateful animal, who was still sulking where he lay, Cyrus stood on the deck with Baldwyn, awaiting instruction.

"So, how do we get up there?"

Baldwyn smirked at him. Struggling to hide his irritation, Cyrus looked up at the huge sails. Raising an eyebrow, the elf simply said, "You climb."

"Climb?" Cyrus parroted back. Baldwyn continued.

"By holding on to the shrouds. They aren't actually vertical. It is much easier than it looks. You tread on the ratlines like you would climb ladder rungs."

The elf looked at him encouragingly, but Cyrus's face must have been a picture of confusion, because Baldwyn laughed. Pressing his palms to his knees he bent over, having a good chuckle at Cyrus's expense, before straightening up, saying, "Here, let me show you."

Cyrus watched in awe as the elf skittered up the rigging, the way a squirrel would climb a tree. Throwing caution to the wind, he thought, How hard could it be? It turned out that he was nowhere near as graceful as the boatswain, but eventually Cyrus made it to where the elf waited patiently for him. Baldwyn sat on the yard, legs swinging. Like it was the most natural thing in the world to be this high up and not hold on to anything. Clutching the mast with both arms as far about it as he could manage, Cyrus let several curses slip, before relaxing enough to stand, one arm steadying him on the mast as he stood on the yard, taking in the horizon. There was nothing surrounding them. Only the sea and sky.

"You call yourself a dragon? How can a dragon be afraid of heights?"

Scoffing, Cyrus looked down his nose at the other man.

"It's not the height I am afraid of. I'm scared of falling to my death. The two are very different things, Baldwyn."

The elf laughed. It was a soft sound, a million miles from the gravelly depth of his own voice. Pulling a spyglass from his breast pocket, Baldwyn extended it, observing their surroundings until he was satisfied, folding it down again before returning it to his pocket.

"Would you not just use your power if you fell?"

"If I did, it would save my life, but destroy your ship. I am far from small in my dragon form."

Distracted by the thought, Cyrus contemplated what he would do in that situation. Before, he would have shifted, and called the loss of the *Mary Anne* collateral damage. But now, Wren's face swam in his mind, and he knew that he would fall to whatever fate awaited him on the deck below. If that was to be his end, then his final thoughts would be of his mate.

"Gods, you have got it bad, haven't you?"

"Hmm…" Cyrus head snapped up to find Baldwyn staring at him, a smirk spread across his lips. "Sorry, I was miles away."

"You don't say. You were thinking of the fae you're bunking with, weren't you? Are you two a thing?"

Cyrus's heart felt full, his chest fuzzy, as he replied with absolute certainty, "Yes, we haven't been together long, but I love him very much."

Baldwyn smiled, it was genuine and warm this time. Not one of the sarcastic ones he had offered out to Cyrus until now.

"You can tell. I loved someone like that once, but it was a long time ago now."

The elf looked away, and Cyrus could see his eyes glistening in the sunlight.

"What happened to them?" After a moment he added, "Sorry, that was rude of me, you don't have to answer that."

Baldwyn smiled wistfully, a stray tear escaping down his cheek.

"It's alright." Turning back to look at Cyrus, he explained. "I know how you feel, because that is how I used to look at Arlo. He was my everything. When he died, I joined Ember's crew. If I hadn't, I think I would have gone mad. At any rate, I think the pain would have killed me. The crew became my family. They gave me another reason to carry on. This lot make the worst days seem… not quite so bad."

Carefully, Cyrus lowered himself to sit beside the elf, still keeping an arm against the mast to steady himself.

"You are very brave."

Baldwyn turned to him, tears in his eyes. "You think so?"

Eyeing the other man sadly, Cyrus exposed his own truth.

"I don't have to know you, to know that you are. I have already decided that if Wren dies, then I will follow him. I could not continue to walk through this world without him. His loss would destroy me. Even if I could live without him, my dragon would never survive it. We are tied together by a fated bond. He is my mate."

That revelation clearly shocked Baldwyn. He sat up rigid in an instant, his interest piqued.

"But you are not the same."

"I know."

Baldwyn sat there for a moment, looking as if he were trying to work out a terrifically hard equation in his head, before muttering, "How strange."

"Oh, believe me, I know. I thought so too, but my feelings for him are so strong, I can't question them anymore. It just is what it is."

Baldwin raised a hand, scratching his chin thoughtfully, his back relaxing slightly as he had an epiphany.

"He couldn't be a hybrid, could he?"

Cyrus had contemplated it already, but it just seemed so impossible. Wren was so fae. While he was fierce, he was also feminine, delicate – and those ears. Gods, those ears. They made him want to do things to Wren that he was pretty sure would be highly frowned upon. If anyone ever got a glimpse of his darkest thoughts, he would be in trouble for sure. No, if he was part-dragon, Cyrus was certain Wren had no idea. The fae had been so angry at the thought of what he had almost done with him, the enemy, when he found out what Cyrus was. Or perhaps that was just because he had failed Melana. He truly hoped that the girl would still be in one piece, if they ever saw her again. Otherwise, Wren might actually kill him. But despite everything, he still believed in Nico. Cyrus knew he was no monster, but if Dracul had claimed the fae as his prize... well, then anything could have happened to her. If that were the case, there was every chance she was no longer alive. Finally, Cyrus answered him.

"It's possible. If he is, he does not know it."

A gong sounded from the deck. Cyrus risked a glance down, seeing Dimitri stood there with the large disk in his hand as the sound echoed around them.

"Come on, that's dinner."

Cocking his head Cyrus asked, "Does no one stay up here?"

Motioning to a female up in the crow's nest, Baldwyn grabbed a piece of the rigging, having wrapped a lump of fabric about both hands.

"Fearne does. She will have hers later. We take turns staying up here, but she reads the maps. It is a skill not many possess. She has been teaching me, but it takes time." Nodding, he added, "I suggest you climb back down."

His parting words had Cyrus closing his eyes, with a devilish smile on his face. And then Baldwyn was gone, sliding himself down the full height of the mast. Cyrus whistled through his teeth, impressed, watching as the elf stuffed the fabric back into his pocket, he shimmied across to the rigging. Map reading was much more like it; he would ask if he could join this Fearne in the safety of the crow's nest tomorrow. With his pondering safely shelved for later, Cyrus began his own descent.

Chapter Sixty-Eight

Calm Before the Storm

Having been eased into his job in the kitchen, Wren found their meal for the evening had been quick and simple to prepare. Tonight, they would be dining on vanilla pumpkin pie with a sugar topping. It was a simple meal, but it smelled delicious, warming their insides as they ate. Wren was pleased, watching eagerly as everyone around them quickly cleared their plates.

Now back in their cabin, Wren lay in Cyrus's arms. Tormund, thankfully, was asleep under the bed, snoring soundly. Deciding to claim the moment while they could, Wren ran his fingers across the man's bare chest. Rolling to face him, he was pleased when Cyrus's lips met his halfway. Moaning against them, he murmured, "You taste nice."

Cyrus pushed him onto his back, tugging Wren's tunic off over his head, he climbed on top of him to claim his mouth, moaning obscenely in a way that had Wren instantly hard beneath him.

"Honestly, you taste so good right now."

Wren could see the outline of Cyrus's arousal as he straddled him. It had him grinding himself against it, desperate for the contact. The dragon leant in, biting Wren's lip hard, sending his pulse skipping under his skin.

"Gods, Cyrus, please, please…" he begged.

His lip was released, and Cyrus moved to his neck, nibbling his way up, before kissing all the way along to Wren's ear. When he reached the tip, Cyrus whispered into it, "What is it you want from me, my love?"

Voice breathless, Wren replied with a frustrated whimper.

"You. I want you, Cyrus. All of you."

Cyrus stopped. Honey-coloured eyes searched his.

"You're sure?"

Wren pulled his mate down to meet him, kissing him passionately, their teeth colliding. When he was satisfied, Wren returned the bite. Probably far too hard, but he did not care, panting.

"I have never been surer of anything in my life."

Making a near feral noise, Cyrus tugged at his breeches, helping the fae shuffle out of them. Reaching over to his bag, he rummaged until he found a small vial of oil. Popping the lid off, he coated three fingers. Wren watched him, pupils blown wide.

"Where did you get that?"

"Oh, er, it's from one of the oil lamps back at the log cabin. I had the container, and I thought it would be a shame not to, um, you know, be prepared."

Sensing the fae's sudden hesitation, Cyrus fell silent for a moment, stroking Wren's jaw with his other hand.

"I can stop at any time, Wren, you only have to say the word."

It was tempting to object. Wren was offended that Cyrus had obviously decided that they were a foregone conclusion. But he had to admit, the man had been right; they always had been. And the thought of telling Cyrus to stop right now… it felt like it would be the furthest thing that could possibly fall from his lips. Instead, he simply nodded, leaning up to claim Cyrus's mouth as the dragon rubbed an oily finger over the tight ring of muscle at his entrance. Slowly, Cyrus slipped the finger inside him, first to the knuckle, then pushing in further before adding a second. Wren manoeuvred his legs, resting them over Cyrus's shoulders now, as his lover slowly worked him open. Moving his fingers at a maddening pace, which held no sense of urgency, Cyrus lazily grazed the bundle of nerves inside him. All the while letting his tongue explore the planes of Wren's chest. When he couldn't take the mounting pressure anymore, he cried out, "Please Cyrus, I need you inside me."

Wren felt empty when Cyrus's fingers slid from him. But a moment later, the feeling was replaced by a blunt pressure, the head of Cyrus's cock resting snugly against his hole.

"You're sure this is what you want?"

"Gods, yes, please Cyrus. I'm sure, so sure."

Cyrus did not ask again. Instead he thrust into him, gently working him open an inch at a time. An interesting array of noises tumbled from Wren's lips. Both pain and pleasure, as the burn quickly faded, and his innards rearranged themselves to accommodate the other man's length. When he was completely seated inside Wren, Cyrus was bent over him, so close their noses almost touched. Worried honey eyes met his once more.

"Are you alright?"

Wren could feel Cyrus's breath warm against his lips. The smell of sweet vanilla and cinnamon lingering there. So different from the usual scent of whiskey or wine that he'd become accustomed to. This time his resolve crumbled, losing his temper he cried out with abandon, "Move, please just fucking move, Cyrus, you aren't going to break me!"

As Cyrus canted his hips, quickly thrusting back into him, Wren cried out again. A sleepy voice from under the bed grumbled out of the darkness.

"What on earth is going on up there?"

"Tormund, if you know what's good for you, you'll stay under there until we tell you it is safe to come out."

Shouting back at the cat, Cyrus pulled back once more. Diving back into Wren in long lazy strokes that had the fae writhing beneath him. The feeling of his head grazing the sensitive nerves inside him had Wren begging around moans, "More, please, harder, please Cyrus."

Picking up the pace, Cyrus rolled his hips hard. Pounding into Wren relentlessly, until the fae was a babbling mess beneath him. Only allowing himself release when he felt the slippery heat of Wren's between them. Collapsing on top of him, he buried his face against Wren's neck, leaving a trail of kisses as he inhaled his scent.

In the afterglow, Wren giggled when Cyrus theatrically draped a blanket over his bare behind, pulling it across so it covered them both. Lying next to him, Cyrus continued to embrace Wren, as he lazily told the darkness under the bed, "There you go, we're decent."

Tormund's face popped up, scowling.

"I hate you both."

Wren grinned, unable to help himself, as Cyrus rested his head on his shoulder.

"No, you don't."

Mumbling, exhausted, Cyrus tried to appease the cat, "Just pretend it was a bad dream."

"A bad dream!" Tormund wailed, "I will be having nightmares for weeks."

Once the cat had finished giving them a piece of his mind, Tormund returned to his spot under the bed. It was not long until little snores worked their way up to their ears.

Tucked safe and warm in Cyrus's arms, Wren mused aloud, "Do you think he will ever forgive us for that?"

Snorting, Cyrus responded, "I'm sure he will use it as leverage for as long as he can first."

Blushing to the tips of his ears, Wren buried his face against the other man's chest.

"Sorry I was loud, you just… it just… What I'm trying to say, is it felt so good to finally have you inside me."

A chuckle reverberated through Cyrus's chest, his cock attempting to rally from where it lay pressed against the dragon's thigh.

"As much as I would love to go again, I don't think Tormund would survive the trauma. Once we are back on land, I will take you as many times as you wish, in whatever way you wish."

Wren's face flushed a deeper shade of red at Cyrus's words. Finding himself adding as an embarrassed murmur, "Preferably somewhere with no audience."

Cyrus planted a kiss firmly on the top of his head, agreeing, "Just us."

"Always?" Wren asked, hopeful.

Nodding, Cyrus's lids were heavy as he looked down at Wren through his lashes. "Always."

His heart felt like it was beating double time, a fuzzy feeling crawling through his insides as Cyrus held him. Was this what love felt like? Wren was not sure, but he knew he wanted more of it, more of Cyrus.

Chapter Sixty-Nine

To War

Waking with a start, the screams made Nico's heart ache. It was still dark out, the middle of the night. Melana was having another nightmare. Placing his hands over his ears, Nico tried to drown out the sound as it reverberated around his head, tormenting him. When his efforts failed miserably, he raked his nails across his scalp. Pressing his palms to his eyes in anguish. His face still hurt him a little – especially when he did that – but it helped. All he wanted was to go to her, to try and ease her suffering, but Rae had forbidden him. His friend did not think it would do her any good to have him appear after one of her nightmares, and he supposed she was right, but it did not make it any easier. As her screams turned into sobs, and inaudible words, Nico scrunched his eyes shut tightly. In his mind, he saw that pathetic excuse of a man thrusting on top of her, right before he met his end. The fact that Anor had met a grizzly end at his hand had been the only comfort Nico could take from the situation. It had been perfect for the depraved nature of the man's soul. Nico's only regret was that he had not drawn it out. He should have made Anor suffer in the manner he had deserved. Perhaps he should have cut off his cock and let him bleed out that way, but in that moment, all Nico could see was Melana being defiled. That had been the quickest way to end it, for her. Gods, he wanted to resurrect the man just so he could kill him again, and he did not care how twisted that made him.

How had he ended up caring so much for this woman? How had she come to haunt him, even in his dreams? On some subconscious level, Nico felt like there had always been a spark. Even from that very first day, when she had so openly defied him. That was why, when his father had told him he could do with her as he wished, he had been reluctant to take her as one of his servants straight away. Without even realising it, Nico had known it would be safer for him to keep his distance from her. But having Melana in his life, even briefly, had made him understand what he wanted – no, needed. Now he knew that, while he had been infatuated with Cyrus, he could never have had him stand at his side, ruling as an equal. It never would have worked. The other man was too hungry for power. But with someone like her, it could. Melana was, in fact, his equal in every way that it mattered. She was kind, caring, and witty; they sparred intellectually; and gods forgive him, when she was happy, she was possibly the most radiant woman he had ever seen. When she laughed it ignited his heart, spreading a warmth through him that he had not been sure existed. That was why her torment destroyed him. Laying there, his eyes scrunched shut, Nico searched for her face in the darkness. Her soft brown skin floated into his mind's eye, her wild dark hair bouncing around her face, framing it perfectly. The warmth of her eyes melted his core, and Nico wanted so badly to kiss her full, perfect lips. And now he was stuck, never being able to admit it to another living soul. It was torture.

When the first cracks of morning light shone through the window, Nico opened his eyes. At some point sleep must have taken him. Already deciding that he needed a drink to get through this awful day, Nico hauled himself out of bed. Today he had to sit in on a meeting of the council with his father and Gerritsen. The topic would be the war, or the lack thereof. Today they would decide on how it would progress further. Nico felt certain that sticking pins in his eyes would be more fun. Venturing from his bed chamber, he looked around, overwhelmed by the silence. He had grown fond of hearing Melana and Rae's chatter in the mornings, but it would seem they had already left. They were probably in the kitchens; it was one of the only places in the castle that they were sure both Dracul and Gerritsen never bothered to enter. There had never been a need for them to venture down there. That, as his father loved to remind him, was what servants were for. Rae had gone to great lengths styling Melana's hair since she had been staying in the castle with them. Making sure it sat just right, covering her long ears, but it was still not enough. They dare not risk her being seen in the main parts of the castle.

His father had taken the guards deaths about as well as one could expect, only he couldn't beat Nico again. Even when he demanded to know where the prisoner was being held. Outraged when Nico refused to tell him, he had flown into a violent rage once more, but Dracul was not stupid; he knew that Nico was still injured. To beat him again was to risk killing him. Nico had known it too. It was a gamble he had taken, knowing how Dracul put the continuation of their bloodline above all else, and thankfully it had paid off. Granted, it had helped when he pointed out that Anor had defied his father's law. Laying with the fae, he had committed treason, so by Dracul's own decree, he would have been bound to die anyway. Nico had simply, as he put it, cut out the middleman. Still, he knew his father had seethed at his actions; he too was not stupid. Now Nico had guards he trusted stationed on the door to his chambers at all times. If nothing else, it would buy them precious time to hide Melana, should they need to. There was no way he would let his father own him. He refused to be Dracul's echo. Not anymore.

When Nico made it to the war room, his father and Gerritsen sat at the head of a large table with a map of the realm pinned upon it. Around it sat several of the king's advisers and some of the elite soldiers that served under Gerritsen in the royal guard. When they convened, it was quickly decided that they would go to war. From Viriador, they would march on Carpathia. That much he heard, but for the most part Nico had managed to get through the meeting by thinking about the decanter of whiskey waiting for him back in his chambers. Rae had managed to source a good one; it had a certain spicy kick to it, for a change. It was only when he heard his name that his attention was drawn back.

"Nico will go with you. He will lead our army into battle."

His jaw fell slack, as his father continued, looking right at him.

"You will prove to me that you are worthy to bear the name of our house, you will ride into battle under our banner."

Gerritsen interjected, "But sire, do you not need an heir? What if he does not return?"

Dracul laughed, cold and cruel.

"There is still life in me yet. I have time. I am sure I could provide a new heir if it came to it, but I am confident Nico will be just fine."

The king's sneer was savage, teeth on display as he leered at Nico. Here it was: his ultimate punishment. Worse was to come as his father went on, detailing how he wanted Bastian and Cyrus tried for treason and executed if they were found. Murmurs of agreement rumbled along the table. What was wrong with these people? How were they so readily swayed to kill their own prince? How could Dracul take so much pleasure in the thought of murdering his own son? And now, Nico thought, there was every chance he would most likely die too. While he was proficient in the field of combat in theory, he had never had to fight in a real battle.

The pinnacle of the meeting was when they decided that those who could fly as far as the Glowing Isle would leave two weeks from today. The rest would leave in one week, by boat. Nico knew he still was not fully healed; this was his father's idea of a cruel joke. A way of teaching him a lesson, or sending him to his death, and evidently the king did not seem much bothered by either outcome.

With no way that the day could get any worse, all Nico wanted to do now was get back to his chambers and free his mind. Every cloud had a silver lining though: at least he no longer had to worry about Gerritsen killing him. The elves could do that for him instead. Imagine, the crown prince being taken out by elves; he would laugh if the threat was not entirely real. When the council dissolved, Nico staggered back to his chambers. The shock made his limbs feel heavy. Dragging his feet as he tried to coordinate them, he felt sick. Nico had effectively as good as received his death sentence.

There were still no signs of life, when he cautiously opened the door to his chamber. Only Estrafin, who gave him a strange look as Nico passed by, but said nothing. Pleased that he was alone, Nico collapsed into the chair. He would not let them see his fear. Downing the first glass of whiskey, he wondered if he would feel any braver if he could take the fiery liquid with him to war. Making quick work of a second glass, Nico poured a third. He could feel the edge lifting from his panic-induced state. By the fifth glass his body felt warm, his limbs heavy, but in a nice way. Nico eventually slowed his pace, now enjoying the way the liquid burned the back of his throat as he swallowed.

Voices. The ladies were coming back. This should be pleasant. An alcohol-induced grin was plastered across his face when the pair entered his chamber. Melana stilled. She eyed him nervously. It was probably the way he stared at them both, eyes wild and hair a mess where he kept raking his fingers through it. Rae approached him in her usual manner, that she saved for when he had been drinking, as if talking to a child.

"Nico, what happened?"

Kneeling down next to him, she peered up at his face. Both women were alarmed when Nico barked out a dark laugh, tilting his head back, till he stared up at the ceiling.

"Guess where I am being sent."

"Where?" Rae asked, coaxing him softly.

"Going to war. Carpathia."

He drawled slowly, his words slurring together.

"Shit."

She grabbed his hand, and he watched as Melana's mouth fell open in disbelief. Nico let a final word fall from his lips before he knocked back the rest of his glass.

"Indeed."

Chapter Seventy

Remember Me Fondly

Melana could feel her heart sinking to the pit of her stomach. Nico was being sent away. They were at war. There would be no one left here to protect her, no one but Rae, and she could not rely on the woman to hide her any longer. She had been kind to her, helped her when she need not have. But Melana knew she had done it for Nico, not her. Melana had never been truly safe here, but now her life was most definitely in danger. If Nico left, she was as good as dead.

The man sat in front of her was a far cry from the one she knew. Listening as Rae began to scold him, telling him that drinking himself to death would not help. Her heart filled with pity for Nico when he responded that it would save his father a job. Unsure what she hoped to achieve, Melana found herself moving towards him, startled when he got to his feet to meet her. She had not been privy to this side of Nico before, and she found the unpredictability of his alcohol-induced state a little frightening. Though she had seen him drunk many times before, this, this was something else. This was pain and sorrow, anger and regret, all bubbling under the surface.

"You can't leave."

Her words were nothing more than a stuttered, broken sentiment.

Meeting her halfway, Melana's breaths turned shallow when Nico brought a hand up, skimming her waist, his fingers coming to rest on her lower back.

"In the dead of night my mind wanders. It is always you it desires. I am plagued by thoughts of you, things I should not think, dreams I should not dream."

Nico pressed a kiss to the top of her head, making Melana stiffen in his arms, as she tried to process his declaration. The prince sniffed her hair, inhaling deeply, before he continued.

"I do not know what is worse: that I have wanted you, so much, for so long; or to know that, now, I will never be able to have you."

Then Nico was leaning in, tilting her chin up to him, his mouth claiming hers in a kiss that was near feral. To her own astonishment, Melana kissed him back, her arms slid up around his neck as he grabbed at her waist, pressing her body against his own. Rae was the one to bring them back down to earth. She was on her feet, horrified, pushing them apart as she shouted his name, asking Nico what on earth he was thinking.

Melana recoiled as her brain caught up with the moment, turning away from Nico, from what they had just done. He and Rae argued, shouting at each other, but she couldn't hear their words. Sliding down the wall, Melana simply tried to breathe. With each breath she found it more and more difficult. She had kissed the crown prince, the man who had stolen her away from her home, her family, and Astraea. His people had killed her king. What was she doing? Their voices were getting louder, her breaths got faster, growing more and more shallow until the edges of her vision blurred. Finally, Nico pushed past Rae, who stood watching them, hands on her hips. The shouting continued. Sliding down the wall next to Melana, Nico offered out his arms, waiting to see what she would do. Melana hesitated for the slightest moment, but she already knew it was futile. Nico was not his father, and he was under her skin like a splinter. If she put aside that it was him that had been sent to capture them, then really, all this time he had been nothing but kind to her. He had been the one to act, saving her when she had needed it the most. She had seen the way he would be with her, tender and loving. He had to survive, he just had to. In a way, Nico had saved her in every way that mattered, and she knew that, given the chance, he would continue to. There was no decision to make; she crawled into his arms, curling herself around him. Pressed against the heart of him, in the place she felt the safest, she wept. Head resting at his neck, Melana murmured into his skin.

"You can't go, you can't leave me here."

That was when she realised he was crying too. Born of frustration and fury, hot, salty tears hit the side of her face. Colliding with her own as they ran down to her chin, then the length of her neck, until they found the fabric of her dress, dying there as they soaked in over her heart.

Melana wasn't sure how long they stayed curled in on one another, but it had been a while. Long enough for the tears to dry completely. Neither of them had attempted to move. At some point, Rae had given up shouting at them. Now Melana could hear her helping herself to Nico's liquor. He evidently did not care, content to rest his chin on top of Melana's head. A couple of times she had felt him lean in, inhaling the scent of her hair again, like he was committing it to memory. After a lot of pacing, Rae finally slumped down next to them, resting her head on Nico's shoulder in defeat.

"Now what do we do?"

"There is no 'we'. Not anymore. You have each other now, that will have to be enough."

Rae's voice was strained,

"But what if it's not, Nico?"

Slowly he turned to face her.

"Rae, I'm tired. I'm tired of having to pretend all the time. Of having to fight my father at every turn. I am always having to second guess myself. Who I am, and what I stand for. I have been fighting my whole life for a throne I have never truly cared for. I just wanted to make things better for our people. To keep Bastian from harm. And I have failed. None of it matters anymore."

Melana's heart ached at his words. She had never heard someone sound so defeated, so well and truly done. Risking a glimpse at him, Melana saw that even his eyes seemed devoid of life. They were dull, covered by the glassy sheen of fallen tears. The light in them had gone out. Perhaps it was the drink, or perhaps he really had given up.

"If I only have a few days left in this world then I just want to exist, on my own terms. Surely you can give me that much. It might be entirely selfish, but I just want to be happy for one godforsaken moment of my time here. If that is all I can have in this life, then I want to make it count for something. I want to be remembered fondly. Not as a prince that was fierce and cruel, heir to a throne he would never claim. At least you will know the truth of what I was. I suppose that is all that matters in the end, that someone truly knew me."

Snapping her head back until it collided with the wall with a thud, Rae growled angrily.

"No, there must be another way. We could get you out of here. We could run." Her words too became sobs of frustration. "If you go, you have to fight, you have to come back. You have to at least try, Nico."

Melana watched the two unlikely friends as they struggled to come to terms with the situation. If someone had told her back at the start that she would feel this strongly, Melana would have told them they were mad. She longed to feel something, but her body had been stripped of emotion once again. Nuzzling her face closer to Nico's throat, Melana let her lips rest where his pulse fluttered under his skin. The thought of Nico not returning had rendered her numb. The only feeling to remain was a subtle nausea that rolled in her gut, dancing on the fringes of her being.

"In the end we are all little more than stories. Memories passed down with warm sentiments. When you tell tales of me, just make sure you remember me fondly."

Nico looked between them. His face now relaxed. A soft, gentle smile played at his lips. The expression he wore was one of acceptance. He was at peace.

Chapter Seventy-One

Please Don't Break It

It had been another long day, assisting the crew with the running of the ship. But now, as the night wore on, the sea grew choppy. Holding Wren tightly in his arms, Cyrus attempted to sooth his anxiety at the *Mary Anne*'s exaggerated motion. Gradually the sea grew choppier, until by first light the ship rolled violently with every wave. A storm was brewing. Low clouds hung on the skyline. Unlike the day before, so silent and still, the waters now danced with the full force of nature's wrath. By the time most had made it onto the deck, the brigantine, battered by the waves pushing her to and fro, had no choice but to receive every furious attack thrown at her. The wood creaked as merciless waves struck loudly, lashing against the hull. Tormund clung to the blankets, swearing he would never board a boat again, while Wren lay trembling in Cyrus's arms. This was exactly the kind of storm that had cost him so dearly the last time he had ventured from dry land. The ship's bell sounded; they were needed to help the crew, to try and help them survive this lethal spar with nature. When they made it onto the deck, Wren was pale, fearfully staring out into the abyss. Terrified that they were stuck out here on an amalgamation of brittle wood. Lightning darted across the empty granite sky, thunder sounding overhead as the ship was thrown about in the inky void of the ocean. Wren became aware of Aiko shrieking at them to release the sails, but he was frozen to the spot. Cyrus was no longer at his side and Wren watched in horror as the man began to climb the rigging. Astraea was up there too, so was Baldwyn. The captain was at the helm, struggling to maintain control of the vessel in the wake of the vicious storm. They refused to back down, manoeuvring the defenceless ship with determination.

In the hours that followed, Wren was fearful that his friends would succumb to exhaustion. He had just about managed to pull himself together enough to help the captain keep control of the wheel. The others continued to scale the rigging, or scramble around the deck following orders. Finally, after what seemed like an eternity of feeling out of control, a glimpse of sunlight broke through the clouds. The waves began to subside as the sky started to glisten. The thunder had stopped a little while ago now, and the boat became more settled in the still-relatively-volatile water. Cyrus descended the rigging, carefully making his way back towards the deck, and Wren's nerves felt substantially less frayed than they had when the storm began. They had survived the worst of it.

A shriek pierced the air. A body tumbled, rushing past them as it plummeted into the dark waters. Those on deck ran to the starboard side, pressing up against the railings. Before he could let fear win, Wren found himself joining them. Bastian was already irate, shouting that he could not swim. Watching the water intently, Wren waited for the surface to break, for a being to rise desperate for air. But they did not. Looking around him at the gathering crowd Wren blanched when he realised who was missing. It was Astraea. Everyone was shouting around him, movements rapid, but the world felt like it had ground into slow motion. Mouths moved, but no sound reached his ears. Turning to where Cyrus had been standing beside him just a moment before, Wren found nothing but an empty space. A scream tore from his lungs as a splash sounded and Cyrus hit the murky water below. When he too did not surface, Wren screamed his name.

"Cyrus!"

The dragon's name burst from his mouth again and again until his lungs burned, and his legs gave way. Wren's vision glazed as he sunk to the floor, too stunned to do anything more than stare at Bastian, who still clung to the railing, searching desperately for any signs of life. Around them, the rest of the crew fell quiet one by one until they were surrounded by the sound of silence. What had just happened slowly dawning on them all. Suddenly Bastian was animated, pointing over the rail, shouting as he climbed the wooden slats.

"There! There, I see them! I see them!"

Wren was on his feet in an instant. Bastian was right: he could see them, Cyrus holding Astraea's head just above the water as they were thrown around in the unforgiving sea. Adrenaline coursed through Wren's veins as he watched them struggle against the waves. Should he risk jumping in? Would he be able to help them? Wren was not even sure he could still swim; he had never tried again after that fateful night when he was still just a child. Only, he was sure it was one of those things that, once you learned how to do it, the muscle memory persisted. Panic sent thoughts flying through his mind at lightning speed. Nervous energy coursed through him as he contemplated jumping in, just as a length of rope was thrown past him, flying over the side, Baldwyn at the other end as he shouted for Cyrus to take hold.

Both himself and Bastian strained against the ship's side, desperate to be closer to the ones they cared for. Wren held his breath, watching as Baldwyn and the crew hauled his mate up the side of the *Mary Anne*, Astraea wrapped around him as they held on tightly to the rope. Wren felt awful. While he was frightened of the open water, he assumed that he could still, in fact, swim; only fear had prevented him carrying out the act that Cyrus had just so bravely and selflessly committed. As the rest of the crew dragged the pair back into the safety of the ship's confines, Wren threw himself on Cyrus in an instant, just as Bastian was at Astraea's side. She was slightly more worse for wear than the dragon was, having swallowed quite a bit of water. Laid on the deck, she was supported by Bastian, who held her with tender concern as Astraea coughed and spluttered, her lungs ridding themselves of the salty water. Cyrus pushed himself up into a seated position, leaning back on his hands as Wren beat the man's chest with his fists.

"You idiot, you absolute idiot! I thought I had lost you. I really thought—"

Sobbing, he broke down on Cyrus, falling forward. Strong arms wrapped around Wren, comforting him as he shook with the force of his tears.

"Hey, hey, I'm sorry I scared you."

Wren sobbed harder as Cyrus pressed his lips to his forehead.

"You are such an arsehole, Cyrus. How could you do that to me?"

"Well, no one else was rushing to save her."

Placing a hand on Wren's shoulder, Aiko offered Cyrus her thanks, a silent acknowledgment that he had saved the princess and earned her respect.

A flurry of emotion caught up in Wren's brain as relief flooded every inch of his fraught body. Glancing over, he could see Astraea wrapped in the safety of Bastian's arms.

"Thank you for saving her. I am sorry. Thank you, so much."

Cyrus wrapped the fae in his arms tightly as he sobbed harder, both their clothing now dripping wet.

"You do not need to apologise to me."

Before carrying Astraea below deck, lips pressed together in a tight line, Bastian nodded his thanks to Cyrus. The man dipped his head in acknowledgement. Getting to his feet, he dragged Wren up with him. Speaking to the rest of the crew, who had for the most part observed the scene in stunned silence, Cyrus told them, "I trust you can manage for now. We need some time alone." Before half carrying Wren, who still had tears trailing down his cheeks, back to their cabin.

Approaching the door Wren stopped Cyrus in his tracks, pulling himself around to face the man, Wren gazed up into Cyrus's eyes.

"Cyrus, I need to say this, I need to make you understand. When I met you, I thought you arrogant, another pretty rich man. I felt the pull, I knew there was something there between us, but I mistook it for physical attraction. I never thought you would break down my walls the way you have. There were times I could have wrung your neck, you made me so angry. I never, ever thought I would find you funny and endearing. I never thought that you would love me. Because of you, I will never have to question who my heart belongs to again. It is yours, Cyrus, yours to treasure, yours to destroy if you must. But it is yours, Cyrus. For as long as you want it."

Warm pools of honey gazed back at him, but Cyrus did not speak. His breaths became a little short, a little shaky, as he soaked in Wren's words.

"Are you— are you saying you love me too?"

Wren swallowed, "When I thought I had lost you, I had never felt an emotion so terrifying. That was when I knew that my heart belongs to you. I no longer have control over it. If that is what it feels like to lose you, then please, don't break it. I think I would rather die."

Squealing as cold wet arms lifted him, Wren wrapped his legs around Cyrus's waist. His prosthetic slid awkwardly back down till it dangled, but neither of them cared as Cyrus held him in place kissing him deeply. When he was put back down, Wren was suddenly very aware of the way Cyrus's wet clothes clung to his body. Looking up at him he was confused to find Cyrus's brow pinched, he looked worried, his eyes still searching Wren's face as he asked again, "You love me?"

"I do. I love you, Cyrus."

Wren watched his brow relax, creases fading as their mouths collided once more. Carrying his fae, Cyrus opened the little wooden door. Tormund looked up in alarm, tangled in a pile of blankets looking most dishevelled, as Cyrus manoeuvred Wren towards the bed. The animal got himself free just in time to skedaddle out of the way, taking up his position under the wooden structure. Cyrus carefully placed Wren down, but he did not let him go.

"Just so you know, I would claim your heart and soul in every lifetime, Wren."

Straddling his lap, Cyrus pressed a chaste kiss to Wren's forehead, before trailing kisses along his sensitive ears. Removing each other's clothes, they threw the sodden items to the floor. A small voice under the bed could just be heard sighing in the darkness as Wren began to moan.

"Oh no, not again."

Chapter Seventy-Two

A Perfect Storm

Gingerly, Bastian lowered the princess to her feet, once they'd reached the confines of their cabin. Holding one of the many blankets out in front of him, Bastian turned his face so that Astraea could strip off her wet things while still maintaining her dignity. Once she had dressed again, he lowered the fabric between them, watching her shiver. Her blonde hair, usually so vibrant, hung in dull bedraggled clumps that reached her breasts.

"May I?"

Bastian reached out a hand, while Astraea chewed nervously on her bottom lip. Carefully he wrapped her hair, coiling it around his wrist, his forearm pressed against her face. Wide eyes studied him, unsure, until she felt the heat. Quickly the princess found herself unconsciously leaning into the warmth Bastian created. When the first chunk of hair fell in a perfect wave, Astraea watched in awe, as the prince repeated the movement. Shifting so that he stood behind her, Bastian began the process again on the back of her hair. It was a simple gesture on his part, something that she needed that he could provide, but Bastian forgot himself. Allowing his arms to weave around her waist, Astraea's gasp was loud enough to bring him back to his senses. When she spun in his arms, the prince was so taken aback that, for a moment, he forgot how to breathe. Their chests pressed together, Bastian could feel hers heaving with every breath, unsure if it was the effect he had on her, or the lingering aftermath of her ordeal. Dainty fingers brushed his cheek and Bastian leant in, closing his eyes, his own heart hammering as her soft lips brushed over his. Allowing their foreheads to rest against one another, he could have sworn she seemed content, but then Astraea pushed herself away from him.

"I'm sorry, I can't."

Reaching for her hand, Bastian's eyes searched hers, pleading.

"But you just did."

Astraea refused it, instead stepping further from his reach.

"When my mind wanders," she said, "it is you I think of. Every time

I close my eyes, it is you that I see. I desire you, even though I know it is forbidden. Even though I know the penalty, where you are from, would be death."

A pathetic sniffle escaped her, Bastian's own eyes brimming with tears as she continued.

"I am consumed by thoughts of us, Bastian, of what we could be, if it were not for our positions. If it were not for your father. But it is too late for what-ifs now. I do not think we can dwell on dreams any longer; it will not make them a reality."

Turning away sadly, Astraea picked up her blankets, gathering them to her chest. Casting Bastian one more tepid glance over her shoulder, she climbed into bed and lay facing the wall, leaving Bastian dumbfounded. Watching as the princess curled up in her blankets, pulling them over her face, Bastian listened in silence as she began to sob, quickly deciding it was best if he left, for a while at least.

Slipping from the room, he closed the door behind him with a dull thud. Reeling, he made his way along the narrow corridor to the dining room, where he found Aiko and some of the others sat at one of the long tables. He had hoped that the rest of the crew would still be up on deck, but no matter. There was no way he was going back to the confines of the shared cabin now, after what had just played out.

"How is she?" Baldwyn asked.

Dropping down onto the bench next to Dimitri, Bastian replied, "Fine." The lie came almost too quickly. "She will be fine, I mean."

"The princess is incredibly lucky that Cyrus acted as he did. Otherwise, it could have been a very different story."

Cyrus. Yes, he would have to seek the man out and thank him properly. Bastian found it strange that after years of dislike and distrust, when it counted, Cyrus had not hesitated in risking his own life to save another. It just showed that he never should have judged him based on shallow misconceptions. Now that Bastian knew his story, he understood a little better why Cyrus was the way that he was. Not that it made his moral compass right, exactly, it just made his actions a lot more understandable. It pained Bastian to have been so wrong about the man. Now that Wren had accepted him as his mate, the young prince watched day by day as Cyrus morphed into a better version of himself. A version that Bastian found he rather liked.

Nodding his agreement, Bastian settled in, letting the conversation flow as he sat observing from the sidelines. When Captain Delphine joined them, Aiko took on a new lease of life, her smile wide and her voice loud. She spoke with vigour, gesticulating wildly as they conversed. Food was already being passed around when Bastian saw Cyrus making his way over to join them, but there was no Wren.

"Has Wren recovered?" Bastian asked.

Cyrus sat down next to him, a wry smile creeping across his face.

"Asleep. He is alright, just exhausted. How is Astraea?"

"She will be fine," Bastian answered, a small sigh escaping him.

Brow quirked, Cyrus gave the prince a strange look. It was like he could see straight through him, but he continued regardless. "That was quite some storm."

"Quite." Reaching for some bread, Bastian remarked, "You know, it was a lot easier to hate you when you were an insufferable arse."

Cyrus laughed, his voice gruff.

"I am flattered to know I affected you so. If it makes you feel any better, I like you a lot more now I know you are not completely incompetent."

Bastian's grin was infectious.

"I take it all back, you are still a cocky son of a bitch."

"And you, my friend, are still soft."

The world seemed to stop for a moment as Cyrus ruffled his hair affectionately, leaving Bastian wondering if he had slipped into a parallel universe. It was not long before Cyrus filled a plate and, taking his leave, headed back to feed Wren and Tormund. Bastian supposed he should probably take some food back for Astraea. This was going to be one hell of an awkward evening.

Climbing from the bench, Ember offered up their apologies for an abrupt departure, before heading back up on deck to work the crew. As others swapped in to eat, it was just him and Aiko left at the table now. The elf sat quietly finishing her food a few seats away.

"You know, you are very confident and surprisingly loud, given your size," Bastian ventured, in an attempt at conversation with the elf.

"Apart from when I am ignoring the company."

"Well, yes. Obviously not then."

Raising her eyebrows at him in a sarcastic manner, Bastian responded, placing his palms flat on the table.

"Right, well. I will take that as a hint then."

Quickly piling some food on a plate for Astraea, Bastian made his way back to their shared room. Knocking gently, when he got no response, he entered. The princess still lay where he had left her, although she had stopped crying now, so that was something.

"I brought you something to eat," Bastian offered, keeping his voice purposefully soft.

Bastian placed the plate next to the pile of blankets, before sitting back on his own bed. And after a few moments, the pile moved, Astraea rolling over, indeed confirming she was still in the land of the living. Silence stretched between them as the princess sat up facing him. From the state of her face, Bastian could tell she had cried for a long while after he had left. Her eyes were red and puffy, her cheeks a little swollen. A pang of guilt swept through his chest at the thought of her here, crying alone, while he had gone for dinner. But then he remembered the kiss, remembered her pushing him away. Telling him how much she wanted him, but why they could never be. The feeling quickly fizzled out.

"How did you fall anyway?"

"I slipped as the ship rolled. I couldn't grab hold of the rope again."

Astraea's voice seemed distant to him. Her thoughts somewhere far away.

"Well, I am glad you are alright. Would have been really rubbish if you hadn't made it. You know, feelings and all." Motioning between them he continued. "I said thank you to Cyrus on your behalf, by the way."

"I still can't believe he jumped in after me."

Bastian blushed,

"About that, I would have, erm, tried to save you, but I, erm, can't swim."

Astraea laughed at his discomfort, a light chortle.

"Probably best you didn't. Wouldn't want to make things between us any more awkward than they already are."

The princess sniffled as her words trailed off, and Bastian was sure she was seconds away from crying again. Offering Astraea a genuine smile, he tried to reassure her.

"Honestly, don't worry about it. I am just glad you made it."

And he meant it, continuing to smile warmly as she gingerly tried the food he had brought her. When she had finished, Bastian gave her a quick embrace, saying as much for his benefit as her own, "Get some rest, tomorrow is a new day."

Chapter Seventy-Three
Whatever Possessed Him

The darkness had closed in, hours bleeding into one another. Still unable to sleep, Bastian wondered what had possessed him. He had allowed his newfound confidence, and the princess's gratitude, to cloud his judgment. Of course he did not deserve her. Awash with an all-too-familiar anxiety, Bastian stared at the ceiling. While it was true that Dracul was the worst of them, it dawned on Bastian that he could never be worthy of Astraea. Even if he were the best of his kind, and she were not a fae princess. As a dragon, he would always have the potential to be every inch the monster she feared his kind to be. Tiredness creeping in, his thoughts became hazy. And just before he succumbed, his last was that he did not want the woman he loved to have to live the rest of her life in fear.

Chapter Seventy-Four

To Dance With a Dragon

The hours seemed to pass painfully slowly over the coming days. The morning after, Nico had acted like nothing had happened between them at all. Melana was not sure if he did not remember, or was choosing not to acknowledge it. Either way, it was for the best. Since that night, they had skirted around each other, always awkwardly on the fringes of an encounter in the confined space that was Nico's chambers. In fact, where possible, Rae had kept the pair of them out of the way, working in the kitchens, so that time spent together in a confined space was minimal.

On the outside, the crown prince was back to his usual demeanour. Upholding the pretence that he was fierce and passively withdrawn. Melana could not help but wonder what was going through his head as he continued to brush her and Rae aside. Engaging with them less and less every passing day. It was like he had switched off his emotions. Melana had not caught him stealing glances at her since that night, like he had so many times before. Their eyes catching one another's for the briefest of moments, before quickly looking away again.

Since that night, Melana had tried repeatedly to see what the future held for Nico. She had searched time and time again, staring into a bucket's abyss, until she thought blood might pour from her eyes. But it had been fruitless. All Melana had managed to see were battlefields and blood. Then there was his fight with the black dragon. She was no closer to discovering why she saw that particular event replay so often when she searched his future. Still, it did not matter: Melana's search always ended in the same way. The black dragon would bring him down. There was nothing else. No more snippets of a future where they were together, and it caused her heart to grieve a loss that was still yet to come.

From where Melana sat on the edge of her bed, she watched Nico. He looked so stern sat at his desk, working his way through a small pile of parchments. Rae was still working in the laundry room and had told Melana to return to their chambers, with explicit instructions to stay out of Nico's way. She contemplated it for a time, but finally with a sigh, Melana stood, quietly making her way over to him. Coming to rest silently a step behind his chair. To her, he had become someone to lean on, the unlikely friendship they had forged unwavering. Now it seemed Nico was loyal to her and Rae, and perhaps Estrafin; but it was to them, and them alone. Eventually Melana placed a hand on his shoulder. She needed to clear the air. Nico would be gone in a few short days, and she knew that she could not leave things like this between them. When he did not flinch at the contact, Melana knew that Nico had sensed her standing behind him. For a moment she wondered why he had not said something sooner, but then his left hand reached across, resting on top of hers before Nico gently squeezed Melana's fingers.

Slowly he turned in the chair to face her, before rising, pushing it out of the way until they were stood face to face. Neither of them spoke for an age. They simply gazed at each other, their eyes searching, for a sign, a glimpse of something, anything that would indicate what the other was thinking. It was Nico that broke the silence.

"You know, sometimes, Melana, when you look at me, I feel like you see right into the very depths of my soul. You see my pain, how broken life has made me. Yet you have never let it drive you away. If anything, you seem more eager to indulge me. You see all the hidden parts of me, parts I do not even fully understand myself. I have never met another soul that makes me feel as you do. I think perhaps we knew each other in another life. In a world where things were pure, and simple."

Raising his hand, Nico gently tucked a whisp of hair behind her ear. Melana froze, her eyes wet as she gazed up at him. He really was striking, all cheekbones and ice-blue eyes. Nico's lips parted as he stared at her mouth, and Melana wondered for a moment if he would kiss her again. His gaze flickered back up, searching hers once more, and finally, Nico made his decision. Bowing his head, his lips pressed to hers, barely brushing Melana's flesh in a testing kiss. Pulling back a little, for just a second, Nico stilled; but Melana moved up to meet him, pressing her lips firmly against his. This kiss was soft and warm, and lasted for a long while.

When Melana eventually pulled away, she rested her head to his chest. Inhaling deeply, she let his scent fill her nostrils. The warm spices that lingered on him helped to calm her racing heart. Wrapping his arms around her, Nico held Melana tightly against him. That laugh rumbled through him, his chest vibrating against her cheek.

"I'm sorry, I should have done that days ago. I told myself I would not burden you with my weakness, but I can never seem to keep my word when it comes to you. I think it only fair we should both get to keep these moments, these memories, if that is all that they will ever be. There is not much time that remains for us now."

Nico paused, swallowing hard. His tone had changed, it was softer now. He pulled back so he could look at her, really look at her. Melana watched, transfixed as his gaze roamed over her. Taking in every detail, committing it all to memory. Using two fingers, Nico tilted her chin up so that he could look right into her eyes.

"I think I am in love with you, Melana."

His words were scarcely a whisper. The icy pools she looked into pleading, beckoning her to say something. Taken aback, Melana noticed how much younger the crown prince seemed suddenly. She could tell he was terrified. More unnerved than she had ever seen him before. Nico's face was pale, and she could have sworn his hands trembled slightly.

"I think… I think I am falling in love with you, too."

The words were out before she could rein them back in. Nico wasted no time; his hands were on her in an instant. Pulling Melana close, he kissed her fiercely, moaning into her mouth as his hands gently roamed her back. At last, he pulled away, rasping, "Come to bed with me."

Melana inhaled sharply, her entire demeanour stiffening, her mind stalling. Nico sensed it; taking her gently in his arms, he whispered in her ear.

"Not like that. I just want to spend my last hours close to you. We do not have to do anything that you do not wish to."

Breathing slowly in through her nose, and out through her mouth, just as she had practiced with Rae, Melana eventually nodded. *It is Nico, he will not harm you.* Repeating the mantra to herself, she went with him.

Shoes abandoned on the floor, they climbed into his huge four-poster bed. Nico reached over, pulling Melana into his arms, kissing her passionately as he did. But, true to his word, he did not pressure her further. It was only as they lay there, hands slowly exploring one another through their clothes, that Melana could feel a warmth building in her core.

Hands shaking and breathing shallow, she found her fingers tracing the length of his jaw, gasping loudly when Nico took one of them in his mouth, sucking on it, grazing her skin gently with his teeth. Melana felt a rush of heat pool in her groin. Alarmed at the sensation, she let herself sink further into the mattress as she watched Nico, his breathing as erratic as her own. She could feel him, his hard length pressed against her thigh. Nico wanted her, but he was showing such restraint, for her. It made the warmth spread inside her. Nico brought his mouth back to hers softly, before trailing kisses the length of her jaw, and down her neck, his fingers digging into the flesh at her waist as he held her. Melana wanted more of him. Needed more of him. Reaching out she began to unfasten his black shirt. Nico let it fall away as he dragged her further into him, undoing her bodice. As it fell on to the cream sheets he pulled back, whispering.

"Are you sure?"

Panicked thoughts began to race through Melana's head, leaving her mind reeling like a ball of yarn unravelling across the floor. But her treacherous body betrayed her, and Melana found herself murmuring her consent. Looking up at him through her lashes, Melana's big brown eyes bored into him longingly.

"Oh, my little doe, I will be so gentle with you. I promise you, by the end I will have my name falling from those perfect lips of yours, my love."

Their kisses became frantic, feral, as each of them rid the other of their clothes, Nico's pale hands slowly exploring every inch of her brown skin. Finally, his fingers found that sweet spot between her legs. He moved slowly, gently, circling Melana's sensitive flesh. Moaning her name as he slipped a lone finger inside her, Nico found her wet, her body willing. Something primal in her stirred. She wanted Nico, all of him, she needed him. Melana thought she would drown in her longing. Feeling herself blush at the overwhelming sensations flooding her, she reached up stroking his jaw once more, whispering, "I am yours, Nico Castillo."

Melana felt him growl more than she heard it, a gravelly sound that reverberated through the very core of him. Nico's mouth claimed hers, and Melana found herself wrapping her legs around him as he rolled them so that he was on top of her. Wincing, his ribs still sore, he stopped only to ask her, "You are sure Melana?"

"Yes," she moaned, breathless.

Nico kissed her again, slowly pressing himself inside her an inch at a time, waiting for her to relax when she inhaled sharply at the invasion.

Once he was fully seated, Melana brought her mouth to his, kissing him deeply as he began to move, gently pulling out, before slowly thrusting back into her. Melana revelled in the feeling as warmth pooled inside her; she hadn't realised that it could be like this. That she could want it. The relief flooded her until tears started to flow down her cheeks. Nico stilled when he noticed.

"Have I hurt you? Do you want me to stop? You only have to say the word."

"No, no, Nico, don't stop, I'm just happy. I never thought I would be able to enjoy it, and I am just so pleased that it is you who can make me feel this way."

Pulling him down to meet her, their kisses turned frantic once more, his fingers working their way between them, so that when his thrusts began to falter, Melana was right there with him, her breathless moans giving away how close she was. When Nico went over the edge, he took her with him, crying out his name as she came. Collapsing down on top of Melana, he kissed her deeply, and she kissed him back with equal ferocity as they drank in the afterglow of their lovemaking.

Neither of them had heard Rae enter as she slipped into the chamber. Sneaking to her own bed, she had heard most of their liaison. Staring at the ceiling she wondered what, if anything, she should do about it. Between their moans, one thought stuck in Rae's mind. No good would come of this for any of them.

Chapter Seventy-Five
Daisies & Dalliance

Stirring, Nico embraced the feeling of waking to the warmth of another in his arms. The first rays of morning light slipped in through the heavy gold curtains. Melana's soft skin caressed his own as their naked bodies lay entwined between the sheets. Looking down at her, Nico ran his fingers through her hair, not able to remember a time that either of them had slept so soundly. Heat spread through his groin, simply from where their bare skin touched. Melana was exactly as he had dreamed; and as she lay nestled in his arms, Nico found he could not help the tingling feelings of pleasure that were taking him over as he felt himself grow hard.

Seeing that one of Melana's long pointed ears now poked through her curls, leaning in, Nico softly kissed the tip. What a cruel trick the gods had played in letting their paths cross. Nico was the crown prince, heir to the throne, Melana a humble serving girl. Dragon and fae, a union that could never truly be. But that was the problem: now Nico had been given a taste of her, he knew that Melana was the only one he wanted. He would have her rule Predoran at his side. There would be no lengths that he would not go to in protecting what was his. Last night Melana had said that she was Nico's, but he knew now that a part of his soul belonged to her too. He was hers for as long as Melana would have him.

Nico wanted to live now; he wanted it so badly. If nothing else, he wanted to live for the time he could have with her. So that he could worship Melana, mind, body, and soul. And for the first time, Nico contemplated, as he lay there in his luxurious bed, whether he should run away with her. Away from his father, and from all that was expected of him. He thought he would prefer a life running with Melana, to no life at all. All the riches in the world were of no comfort to him, if Nico could not share all that he had with her. They might end up with nothing, but they would have each other, and that would be enough. But Nico knew his father would never let them go. Dracul would hunt them to the ends of the earth if he knew what Melana was to him. Knowing full well the kind of man his father was, Nico knew he would torture her slowly and make him watch as she suffered. The thought terrified him. It made him pull Melana in closer, till she was laid flush to his chest.

Through fluttering lashes, warm brown eyes peeked up at him as Melana woke. Writhing against him, she snuggled sleepily until her head rested in the gap at his collar bone. Pressing a kiss to the top of her head, Nico's hand roamed her flesh. Cupping her breast in his palm, Nico teased her nipple between his fingers, causing her to moan his name into his skin. As she ground herself against his thigh, he could already feel the heat of her arousal. Their mouths met, their lazy kisses were lingering, slow and gentle, until Nico bit her lip between his teeth, making her squeal. He found her wholesome laughter the most glorious sound. Their kisses quickly deepened, and Nico found his hand wandering south with intent. His fingers found her wet already, as he slipped two inside her. Melana moaned, grinding herself against his thumb, as Nico teased the little bundle of nerves at the apex of her. When he positioned himself between her thighs, claiming her with his mouth, Melana clasped the sheets, bunching them in her hands as her back arched from the bed. Nico could not help but feel a certain sense of satisfaction at how receptive she was to him. After everything that had happened to her, he had not been sure how Melana would react. But, as with everything about her, Nico found himself pleasantly surprised. Not only by how open she was to try, but how trusting of him she had been. And now, as she squirmed beneath him, golden light radiated at her fingertips. Daisies began to wind their way around her wrists, creeping up her arms until they reached her elbows as her magic spilled over. Nico found himself overwhelmed in the best possible way. Looking up at her, he thought Melana so beautiful. Biting the inside of her thigh, it was all he could do to keep himself from spilling his seed on to the sheets untouched. Her fingers wound through his short hair, tugging gently until Nico looked back at her. Melana beckoned him back up the bed, only satisfied when his mouth was on hers once more. Feeling the vibrations as she moaned into his mouth, Nico knew she could taste herself on his tongue. The thought aroused him more than he already was. Shifting so that he was on top of her, he smiled at the sight of her sprawled beneath him. Nico's name falling from her lips like silk as he slid himself inside her. Taking his time, he made sure Melana was comfortable before he moved. Once she was thrusting her hips in time to meet him,

Nico's movements became fast and frantic, until he spilled inside her. Using his fingers, he brought Melana to her second climax that morning. And when they were both spent, the pair lay panting in each other's arms. Nico, dropping little kisses to her forehead, had Melana sighing, content as she rested her head on his chest. He did not want this moment to end, and it pained him that it had to.

Chapter Seventy-Six

The Greater Good

Balling her fists, Rae sat on her own bed, quietly listening to the pair of them frolicking behind the curtain that divided Nico's bed chamber from the rest of their living space. How quick they had been to forget all about her. Or perhaps they simply did not care if she heard. Rae was furious with both of them, but Nico more so. How could he risk everything for a woman? It was bad enough that he was already riding a thin line with his father, who was apparently more than happy to gamble with his life to prove a point.

How could Nico go to war if he were preoccupied, worrying about her wellbeing? And how would Melana survive, left behind without his protection, having to navigate a world full of dragons, most of whom would happily see her kind extinct? The predicament she found them in was madness. If Dracul caught them, they would both be damned; Rae too, for knowing what had taken place and not going to the king with the information. Unable to believe how utterly selfish Nico had been in allowing this to happen, knowing he would be gone in a day's time, Rae had to fight to keep her dragon contained. The palms of her hands heated as the creature within threatened to break free.

Their voices grounded Rae, returning her to the moment. Peeking from behind her own fabric partition, she saw them stood there, gazing into each other's eyes. Nico ran his fingers down the sides of Melana's face as if it physically pained him to leave her. Perhaps it did.

"Will you stay with me again tonight? I want to savour every moment we have left."

His voice was breathless. Nodding, Melana replied, her words filled with sadness. "Of course I will."

Rae continued to spy on them, vexed when Nico bowed his head to kiss Melana tenderly before he slipped from the room to attend his training session with the royal guard.

Once she was sure that Nico was far enough out of earshot, Rae stepped from behind the curtain. Melana froze when she shouted at her.

"Are you mad, or just stupid?"

Flinching at the woman's tone, Melana stuttered.

"I—I'm sorry?"

"How do you think you will survive here once he leaves? What do you think it will do to Nico if anything were to happen to you now? How do you think he will feel going off to fight, going onto the battlefields, wondering if you are safe?"

"You heard us, then."

Rae's brows raised; her head tilting she looked down her nose at Melana, scoffing.

"It was hard not to."

Melana's face turned red as she continued to stare at Rae blankly. In the end, the other woman screamed in frustration.

"You are as bad as he is, and you are going to get us all killed."

Melana reached for Rae's hand, but she pulled away.

"Don't. Just don't. How did you manage it anyway? I'm surprised you let him touch you after all those nights I've sat with you while you cried."

The colour drained from Melana's face. Walking past Rae, she leant against Nico's desk, arms crossed across her bodice, hugging herself as she spoke.

"That is not fair, Rae. That day will haunt me for the rest of my life. No matter how many times I have tried to erase it from my mind, it never truly leaves. The way he…" Melana gagged. Bringing a hand up to rest on her breastbone, she continued, "The sounds, the smell; it never goes away. It's like a noose around my neck, slowly starving me of oxygen. The only place I feel safe is at Nico's side. I know he will protect me; I know he would kill for me. So no, I did not like being touched. I craved it, craved Nico. I enjoyed every moment that we were together, because it was him, and I will not apologise for it."

Melana was walking towards Rae now, her tone imploring her to listen, but the other woman still stared at her, face filled with scorn.

"That is the problem. Nico might kill for you, but he would die for you, too. You are more of an idiot than I thought if you cannot see that."

"I would not want him to. I'd never expect that of him."

Melana floundered, drowning in her own words as it slowly dawned on her that maybe Rae was right.

"If it came to it, it would not matter what you wanted. For all our sakes, you need to let him go. You have the perfect guise; he will need to know you are away from here, somewhere safe, so give him that. Nico is a liability, a loose canon where you are concerned. He killed Anor without hesitation, without a moment's thought of what that would mean for him, or anyone else, for that matter. Look at what Dracul did to him just for bringing you into the castle."

Melana cut her off, imploring.

"And where would you have me go? Where would you send me, that you could guarantee my safety?"

Balling her fists at her sides until she thought the flesh of her palm would bleed, Rae stood rooted to the spot, staring down the fae that now stood a few feet away. There was nowhere that Melana would be truly safe. Even if she made it back to Viriador, the enemy occupied her former home, most of the land now under the banner of the dragon. Melana's voice cracked as she spoke again, tears threatening to fall.

"There is nowhere, is there? You just hope by then he will be home safely, and he can mourn me then."

Now all that Rae felt was a crushing hopelessness. For Melana. For Nico. For herself. For what she had already decided she was about to do. Unclenching her hands, Rae let her features melt into something close to sympathy, but in reality, she felt it was closer to despair. Opening her arms to Melana, she beckoned her into them. When the fae moved into her embrace, Rae squeezed her tightly. Kissing her cheek as Melana pulled away, she whispered, "I am sorry."

While she ran her fingers through Melana's hair, affectionately tucking some loose curls behind her ear, Rae made sure that the tip was visible before she held Melana at arm's length, smiling at her warmly.

"Forgive me, I just worry for you both – for all of us. I care, that is all. I'm working in the laundry again today. Will you be alright in the kitchens without me?"

Her smile wavered, but only for a moment. She could do this. Rae was not about to see Nico throw away everything he had worked for his entire life. Even though her and Melana had somehow forged an unlikely friendship, no one was worth his life. He was the future king, and Predoran needed him. Nico had to live.

"Of course."

As Melana turned to leave, one hand already on the door handle Rae called out.

"I really am truly sorry, Melana."

The fae smiled at her.

"I know you care for him too, Rae. There is nothing to forgive."

When the door closed, Rae slumped into the chair. Resting her head on her arms she cried until the tears dripped through onto the solid wood of the desk. There was no where she had to be today, and she knew Nico would have had her go with Melana, to make sure she was safe, as she always did. Rae had been the perfect little shadow, until now. But she'd had to do it. She'd had to. They had crossed a line, and neither of them would listen to her. Nico was the future of their kingdom, the future of their race; she could not let him throw everything away. Not while such a brutal king sat on the throne. Rae knew Nico, sometimes she thought better than he knew himself. It would only be a matter of time until his loyalty to those he cared for got him killed. With Melana around, she could almost guarantee it would be sooner rather than later. That was why she had done it, Rae told herself: for the good of Predoran. After all, she thought, forbidden love was merely a type of addiction. Nico would get over it in time. It was for the survival of their race. It was for the greater good.

CHAPTER SEVENTY-SEVEN

Not All That Glitters Is Gold

The rest of their journey had been rather unremarkable. Astraea had watched Cyrus blossom as he learned the art of cartography, taught by Fearne. The young lady did not talk much to the rest of them, but she seemed to have taken a liking to Cyrus. The man had gained a newfound respect from most after his feat of bravery, for which Astraea remained eternally grateful. Whenever she ran into her friend Wren, Astraea's heart felt full. It was lovely to see him so blissfully content with his newfound mate. Unlike when she saw Bastian, who to his credit, tried his best to act normally around her. But it only made Astraea feel like all the oxygen had been punched from her lungs. Alone in their room, the air seemed to sizzle, tensions remaining fraught between them. Despite their best efforts, there was no way that, when all this was over, they could continue to be friends. She did not need him to tell her, to know that it would be far too painful, for both of them.

Making her way back towards the cabin they shared, a fluffy tail brushed against Astraea's leg. Smiling, she remembered how she had begged the captain to allow Tormund to roam, emphasizing how much safer she would feel if he was allowed to stay with her. The cat had been delighted. Eager to venture from the boys' cabin and explore the rest of the ship. Thankfully, Astraea's duties had been kept light after her ordeal, giving her and Tormund plenty of time to catch up. It was only in the dead of night, when she slept soundly, that he would creep back into the boys' cabin; so that he could sleep curled at their feet. But in the daytime, and for much of the evening, Tormund followed Astraea around. That way she had someone to keep her company, and his humour helped to buffer any awkwardness between her and Bastian.

Tonight would no doubt be particularly awkward. They were nearing the end of their voyage, edging ever closer to Oldir as the days passed. To celebrate, Captain Ember had announced they would have a night of frivolity. They had all been lured into the idea with the promise of music and dancing, and told there would be plenty of food, ale and wines to suit every taste. When Astraea reached her cabin, Bastian was waiting there for her as she had predicted he would be. Sat on his bed, he fidgeted, nervously rolling a small package in his hands. Startled from his thoughts as the princess entered the small space, Bastian jumped. Staring at Astraea, eyes wide, he quickly addressed her.

"Princess, I need to tell you something."

Sighing, Astraea slumped down on to her own bed. Now sat facing him she responded.

"Bastian, we've been through this, I can't—"

"No."

Cutting her off bluntly, Bastian reached for her hand.

"No, Astraea. I need to say this. I respect that you do not wish us to be together. I know that we can't all get what we want. Someone always has to be unhappy; it is the balance of the world. But if all I can have of you is as my friend, then I would jump at the chance every time."

Bastian's words came out as an avalanche, an adrenaline-fueled tirade. One hand still gripping hers tightly, on the other, his fingers still played nervously with the little bundle now in his lap.

"I got you something. Back when we hadn't even met yet, and I was certain I would make you mine. I was going to give it to you that night at the ball, and I have been carrying it with me ever since."

Astraea's stomach was somersaulting. She hated that all she wanted to do was to fall into his arms. To tell him that she felt the same. Why on earth did he have to be so kind? And awkward in an adorably endearing kind of way.

"Bastian—"

"Wait, just let me finish, Astraea. What I'm trying to say is, I care about you, more than you will ever know. But, if your friend is all you ever wish me to be, then I want you to have this as a token of my loyalty."

Letting go of her hand, Bastian placed the item in her palm, staring at the princess intently as he waited for her to open it. Feeling a little sick, Astraea peeled back the cloth, revealing a bangle. It was silver with little leaves that trailed the length of it, and winding around the arm at either end was one big leaf. And Astraea realised where she had seen it before. Scrunching her brow, the princess's eyes searched his, confused.

"You wore this. It was on your arm the night we met."

"I intended to wear it until I gave it to you, you know, so I was giving you something of mine. I thought that way it would mean more, but then everything went so sideways… it's been in my bag ever since."

Astraea could feel the tears welling behind her eyes.

"Oh Bastian, it's beautiful, but I can't accept it. It's too much."

"Please," reaching for the bangle Bastian slid it over her hand, gently pushing it up the length of her arm, "it would be such a shame to see it go to waste. Just enjoy it. For me."

As the bangle came to rest at her bicep, Bastian's hand fell away, leaving only the cool metal touching her skin. The loss of contact made her heart skip. She wanted him to touch her again. Pulling back, he smiled at the princess, his grin lopsided, half happy, half sad.

Smiling back, all Astraea could manage was, "Thank you."

Chapter Seventy-Eight

Sea Shanty

Tormund excitedly scampered through the passageway. It was one thing to be allowed to roam, but it was another thing entirely to be invited to a party. Tonight, there would be music and merriment. And having now groomed himself several times in preparation, the cat could barely contain his growing enthusiasm for the evening ahead. Cyrus and Wren walked ahead of him, hand in hand as they approached the dining hall.

"Wren, Wren," Tormund squealed as he bounced along behind his master, his furry hips swaying as he went.

"Yes pal?"

"Do I look alright?"

Stopping dead, Wren turned, scooping the fur ball up into his arms. Cyrus leant in, tickling under his chin, and for a moment Tormund let him. Purring happily, until he realised the enormity of the situation.

"Don't mess up my fur. I want to look perfect."

"Buddy, it's only dinner with us lot, and a bit of music. The queen won't be there." Flinching at his choice of words, Wren added with a spark of irritation, "You need to relax pal."

Wren spoke to the cat, voice passive, while Cyrus ruffled his furry head.

Bastian, who had arrived behind them in the corridor chimed in, "You do seem a little intense today, Tormund."

Astraea's gentle laughter filled the space around them as the cat flopped from Wren's arms, outraged. Strutting ahead of them, head high, and tail in the air, he grumbled, "Heathens, the lot of you."

When they entered, Tormund sniffed the air, beads of dribble accumulating at the edges of his mouth. Meat was definitely on the menu tonight. The smell was divine to his delicate little nose. Watching as the others claimed their places at the long tables, Tormund used his full weight to launch himself on to the end of theirs, so that he snuck himself between Bastian and Cyrus, who were sat facing each other. Looking around eagerly, Tormund spotted the tall bottles of different-coloured liquids that decorated the table, along with a collection of fancy goblets and tankards, before he spied the captain, who was getting to their feet now that the last of the crew had settled in their places. Ducking, Tormund hopped down into Wren's lap. The last thing he wanted was to be chastised by the captain this early in the evening. Raising their voice, Ember began, "I'm sure that you've all noticed by now that we have dropped anchor, so that everyone can enjoy the evening. Don't worry though, we are still on course and set to arrive at Oldir in the next couple of days. For tonight, I want you all to enjoy yourselves." With a wry grin, and a nod towards their table, they added, "I feel we have all earned it."

With that, Aiko and Dimitri emerged from the kitchens to distribute plates, fresh and steaming along the middle of the tables. Fearne rose to join them, helping to ferry food from the kitchen. The aromas were overwhelming, fish, pork, rice, noodles and vegetables filling the dishes. Undertones of ginger, garlic, and lime swirling through the room. Dimitri had even brought Tormund his own little plate of cooked meats, minus all the vegetables. Thrilled, the cat set about clearing his plate as his companions began to pile theirs with scoops from the variety of dishes.

After a few minutes Baldywn rose, one hand pushing his long fringe out of his eyes. Sliding the lute that never left his side around to his front, the elf positioned himself sitting on the edge of the table next to them. Feet up on the bench, he began to play.

Too long too far from home we wander,
never reaching our destination nor getting any younger.
Together we have found purpose,
as the evening stars shine above us.
We find direction in our journey's end,
along this trail where we have found our friends.
Danger and darkness we must face,
for those around us cannot be replaced…

Sneaking back up to sit on the tabletop, Tormund complained loudly, "It's not very cheery, is it? I thought there was going to be dancing."

Leaning across Bastian, oblivious to the way his skin flushed red at her touch, Astraea hushed him. Scratching under his chin until he purred content, murmuring, "Not fair."

When the bard had finished his painful rendition, Astraea was on her feet telling Baldwyn how wonderful the song had been. How profound, deep and touching. Both the cat and Cyrus noticed the way Bastian's jaw tightened, fingers flexing as the princess gushed over the bard. Tormund watched with interest as Cyrus leaned in, tapping Bastian's arm. Swivelling his head back around the prince snapped, "What?"

Smirking at Bastian's displeasure, Cyrus replied, "He's gay."

"Sorry?"

Cyrus grin was enigmatic now.

"We aren't blind Bastian. You are physically twitching, watching her swoon over his music."

"I was not—"

Cyrus cut him off.

"You're fine. He likes men. Enjoy your ale."

Bastian's features visibly relaxed. Getting comfortable in his seat again, he lifted his tankard to his mouth before stopping mid-air. Enquiring, eyes narrow as he peered over the top of it, "How do you know he likes men? What have you done now, Cyrus?"

Swatting the air, Cyrus reassured him, one hand squeezing Wren's knee in a comforting gesture.

"When I was helping Baldwyn, he and I spoke about Wren, and he told me about the love of his life, Arlo. He died, you see, and I think he took a part of Baldwyn with him."

"No wonder he is sad," Tormund chimed in, and Wren nodded.

"I agree pal."

As the evening wore on, the cat watched as those around him became steadily more inebriated. The music had picked up the pace after the bard's initial sad start. As it turned out, Astraea informed them on her return to the table, that Baldwyn had written it about all of them. It was an ode to their journey, their story. He'd also told her that several of the crew were debating joining them on their search for the relic, himself included. The way he had described it made their quest sound like a suicide mission. Tormund was horrified as he listened to Astraea recount the elf's description of their quest as 'a last hurrah', and his use of the phrase, 'But what a way to go out, saving the world.' He made it sound dreamy, and the thought of their deaths being trivialised made Tormund furious.

Puffed up and spitting, it had taken the whole group to calm him, and assure the livid animal that the bard was being over-dramatic. They told him that as long as they all stuck together, then everyone would be just fine. But the enraged creature did not miss the little looks they gave each other. Brief glances to one another, stolen at every opportunity. Liars, the lot of them. Still, he had eventually calmed down, and now watched as Aiko sat draped across Ember's lap, her tongue down the captain's throat.

"Well, that escalated quickly," The cat muttered aloud to himself. As others agreed heartedly that they had not seen it coming either, a few seats away Dimitri's face lit up in a winsome smile.

"Actually," he said, interrupting their whispers, "they have been together for a number of years now. They just hadn't shared their relationship with you yet."

At that, Wren blurted, "I thought Ember was a woman."

At the same time Astraea responded far more emphatically, "Why would they have felt the need to, we are practically strangers after all."

Tormund, on reflection said, "I suppose Aiko does seem a little fruity."

Astraea immediately scolded Tormund for being rude, the cat quickly responding like a sulky child, "I don't hear my dads complaining."

Bastian chuckled at the cat, seemingly not fussed by the new information either way. Only Cyrus sat quietly with a triumphant smile glued to his face as Dimitri attempted to answer their questions.

"Well, no, Ember's not a man or a woman actually. They are more… androgynous."

Wren looked stumped now, "Andro what?"

Tormund thought Cyrus looked smugger by the second as Dimitri floundered, trying to explain to the rest of the group.

"Ember's identity changes, sometimes daily, or it can even depend on their mood."

"Oh, right."

Wren's face was blank. Astraea's expression was one of confusion. Only Tormund looked appeased by the knowledge. Tucking his legs under himself like a chicken, the cat settled back onto the table.

"Bit like a cat, then. We don't worry about what we are; we just are."

"I somehow doubt Captain licks their own arsehole."

"Wren! Don't be so crude, for goodness' sake."

Astraea smacked his leg under the table in the same way Melana used to, causing him to jump. Tormund missed her. Melana had always been the voice of reason among them... well, until Cyrus came along. As if he had read Tormund's mind, Cyrus spoke.

"Basically, it refers to an individual's choice of style. Somebody who is androgynous presents to the world in a way that isn't defined by looking feminine or looking masculine."

"Yes, thank you, Cyrus. How Captain acts and identifies just depends on how they are feeling at the time. Ember knows that not everyone will understand it. It's why they don't really go into detail unless someone asks, but depending on where we are in the world, it is not always met well. They obviously feel comfortable around you all, Aiko too."

"It's not a new concept. It has been around for centuries," Bastian chimed in, sipping at his drink. Gazing over at the pair, who were still in the same position, mouths locked and hands roaming. Blissfully unaware of the conversation unfolding a few feet away. Gesturing towards Cyrus and Wren, brow raised, Bastian revealed, "For years, men and women wore garments that are more akin to dresses today. Hell, our own army did for over a century. The lines between genders used to be far more blurred. These days it's still far less scandalous in Predoran than, say, a dragon mated to a fae."

"Touché," was all that Wren could manage, as Astraea held up her hands.

"No judgment here. I simply had not heard of such a thing before. If Captain wishes to go by they, it does not affect me. If that simple act brings them comfort, then I am happy to honour it."

Wren nodded his agreement bashfully, still rubbing his thigh.

Baldwyn gestured to the group, calling them over, and not a moment too soon. When the others did not rush to move, all suddenly preoccupied with their drinks, Tormund stretched, snarking, "I'll go, shall I?"

Hopping up next to Baldwyn, Tormund was thrilled when the elf suggested, "As I appear to have lost most of my audience to frivolous pursuits, did you want to sing a sea shanty with me?"

Gleeful, the cat's eyes widened as he purred loudly, "I would love to, but I don't know the words."

"Ah, that's half the fun with this kind of thing. I'll play a verse on a loop, and you can just make the words up as you go. I think most people are too drunk to care what I'm playing anymore, to be honest."

"You're telling me. You just missed the most awkward… Do you know what? Never mind. Yes, I would love to sing with you."

Grinning, Baldwyn strung together some chords. The unlikely group all looked his way, affectionate smiles on their faces, clapping in time with the song as it began. Tormund let the verse play out twice, bobbing along to the tune, before joining in.

There once was a cat
And that cat was me
I got on a boat
And I went to sea
My tail fluffed up
And my ears flattened down
But I am a pretty cat meow
Soon may my masters come
They'll bring me food
To fill my tum
And if they scratch my bum
I'll give them my loudest yowl.

When his friends clapped, Tormund looked around the room, excited and so incredibly pleased with himself to have managed two full verses. A shiny goblet caught his line of sight, and in his elation, Tormund's feline inclination towards unexplainable chaos seemed to kick in. Before he could think to control himself, Tormund found his front paw was in the air, batting the offending article from the table, to a resounding chorus of, "Tormund!"

Chapter Seventy-Nine

Darkness in Daylight

Back in their cabin, Tormund sulked on the end of the bed, grumbling as first Wren and then Cyrus got on.

"I still can't believe Captain threw me out."

Cyrus chuckled darkly.

"Count yourself lucky they did not have you thrown overboard."

As Wren laid back in his arms, Cyrus dropped a kiss onto the top of his head. The cat asked, "So how did you know what Captain was?"

Scoffing, Cyrus replied, "That is easy. The crew only refer to Captain as they or them. And, in our culture, as Bastian rightly pointed out, it has been normal for centuries. Not so much these days, but it is still something that would not normally bother our kind."

"Fair enough."

Tormund mused, making puddings in the blankets, circling as he attempted to get himself comfortable.

"Do we know anything of Aiko's history?" Wren asked curiously. "She does not seem to tell anyone an awful lot of anything."

Cyrus shrugged. "Only that she is elven. I do not know much else." Stroking his chin, he added, "Dimitri probably does though."

"Hmm…"

Shifting in his arms Wren made himself comfortable.

"I think something must have happened to make her so volatile."

Snorting, Cyrus replied, "Oh, I would wager there is definitely a story there. I am sure Aiko will share it with us when she is ready."

Soft snores wafted from the end of the bed. Wren looked at the sleeping cat, smiling for a moment before his face fell. Shifting in Cyrus's arms, Wren peered up at him through his lashes.

"Do you think we will all make it?"

"Why wouldn't we?"

"It is just… never mind. You know I worry."

Wriggling, Wren grumbled as he snuggled further into Cyrus's chest.

"Hey, do not stress, sweetheart. It will all be fine, you will see. You get some sleep."

Chuckling, Cyrus kissed Wren's temple, holding him close. But despite his cavalier attitude, Wren could not shake the thought that, somehow, he did not believe his own words.

Chapter Eighty

Too Familiar Pain

The icy water hit Astraea's skin, leaving it feeling as if it were pierced by thousands of needles. Darkness surrounded her, her sodden clothes pulling her under. Lungs burning as she fought her way to the surface. She needed air.

Sitting bolt upright in her bed, Astraea gulped down hurried gasps of air. Bastian, too, shot upright in the bed opposite, looking her way, concerned.

"Princess?"

As her thundering heart began to return to its normal rhythm, Astraea got up, tucking her hair behind her ears.

"It was a bad dream. I just need to get some fresh air."

Despite Bastian's protest that he should join her, Astraea wrapped herself in her cloak, hushing him, before making her way up on deck.

Chapter Eighty-One

Feline Intuition

Self-loathing kept Wren awake into the early hours. He felt utterly helpless to stop the avalanche of worries pulling him under. When he could not stand the thoughts swirling in his mind any longer, he shimmied his way from Cyrus's grasp and slipped from the bed, his movements waking Tormund in the process. The cat stretched, sauntering to join the fae in the passage outside.

"It's OK, Tormund, go back to bed. I just need to clear my head."

Sighing, Wren bent to pet him before turning and heading in the direction of the stairs.

Tormund yawned, wondering if the cabin next door would fare any better for a peaceful slumber.

The short answer was no. The sleepy feline nudged the door open, strolling in, to find Bastian alone in the darkness. Sat on the edge of the bed, he stared straight ahead at nothing in particular. Stretching once more, Tormund jumped up into the space next to him. Nuzzling Bastian, he asked with a purr, "Urm, where is the princess?"

Bastian looked down at him in acknowledgment, offering the animal a half smile. His eyes so watery, the feline felt the prince's mind had been wandering, somewhere far away.

"Astraea wanted some air; she had a nightmare."

Furry brows raised at his response.

"Don't give me that look, I offered to go with her."

"Hmmm…"

The cat sat back on his haunches, staring Bastian straight in the eye.

"So, tell me, when do you plan on professing your undying love for her?"

Allowing a humourless laugh to punch from his chest, the prince responded, "That ship has sailed, my furry friend."

"I'm sorry? I thought you just implied that you let her go."

Letting out a nervous laugh, the cat's eyes widened.

"I did. I let her go, Tormund. I cannot keep pursuing her. It is not fair on either of us."

Now Tormund's eyes boggled so hard he thought they might pop from his head.

"Why? Bastian, why?"

"I had to."

Jumping up, Tormund paced manically.

"Why? Why would you do that? You were so close." A rumbling growl shot through him as his furry brows pinched, ears flaring to the sides. "This doesn't make sense. Any fool can see how you feel about each other."

Offering the cat a melancholy smile, Bastian reached out to stroke his head, earning a hiss from the offended animal.

"Tormund, pal, if you truly love someone, sometimes the best thing you can do for them is to let them go."

The ginger fluff ball arched his back hissing.

"But what about your feelings? And more to the point, what about hers? I'm pretty sure she is madly in love with you, you big idiot. Honestly, for someone educated, you have really poor judgment."

This time it was the prince's eyebrows that reached his hairline. His lips drawn thin as his expression became grim. All the while Tormund marched about the bed in an outraged fashion.

"Says you."

"Yes, says me. I probably know her better than the rest of you. Do not forget, at one point, she thought I was just a regular cat. I know all of her secrets, Bastian. ALL OF THEM. And I know her. I am telling you, she loves you. You should go to her."

Standing abruptly, Bastian cut him off.

"Fine. Fine, I will. But when she rejects me again, Tormund, can we just agree to leave this madness?"

Ears flat to his head, the cat's sides sucked in with every furious breath as he contemplated his response. After a moment, when they had returned to their usual height and he no longer felt the need to breathe through his mouth, Tormund nodded slowly. Left alone in the darkness, the cat watched anxiously, as Bastian left to find his princess.

Chapter Eighty-Two

Leave Me Slowly

A familiar figure stood in the darkness, his arms resting on the railing as Wren gazed out at the inky abyss. Approaching him, Astraea felt a sense of familiar calm wash over her. Wren was the embodiment of everything that meant home. He had been her safety, long before she had ever chosen this band of misfits as her family. Turning just enough to acknowledge her presence, he simply said, "Hey."

"Hey yourself," she retorted playfully, coming to rest at his side, their shoulders touching. Wren smiled at her reassuringly, checking that she was alright with just a look.

"Couldn't sleep?"

"No, I had a bad dream. You?"

"Just needed space. My mind was racing, and I was restless. Cyrus was asleep. I did not want to wake him." Pausing he added, "No Bastian?"

A sly smile tugged at Astraea's lips.

"He did try to come with me, but I told him I wanted to be alone for a while."

Wren nodded noncommittally, before gazing back out at the water. The glassy sea was eerily calm, a sky full of tiny stars reflected in its obsidian surface. After a beat, still staring out to sea, he spoke again.

"The king would have liked him, you know. He cannot help who his father is, Astraea."

Wren turned his face to hers, an encouraging smile lingering. He placed his hand over her fingers where they gripped the rail, giving them a gentle squeeze. At that, a small cry broke free from Astraea's throat.

"But how can I allow myself to love him after everything his people have done to us? His father had mine killed, Wren. What am I supposed to do? Pretend it never happened?"

Wren offered her a sympathetic glance.

"If it helps, I do not hold Cyrus accountable for the actions of his people. And regardless, I do not think you can choose who you fall in love with."

"That's different."

"Why?" Wren countered curiously.

"It just is."

"What, because you think the two of us are drawn together, that made me feel any better?" Astraea looked at him blankly. "Of course it didn't. Why do you think I tried to push him away? I felt so guilty. I still do." The princess stared at him, expression unreadable, as Wren continued. "Because of you, because of Emil, because of what his people did to ours. But then I realised that none of it mattered, Astraea, because Cyrus is his own man. He has not done any of those things to us, or our kind. The only thing he is guilty of is being born as one of them, as opposed to one of us. The way I see it, life is nothing more than a series of incidents, barrelling their way towards the end. Sometimes they are a triumph, sometimes a tragedy. But ultimately, life is what you make of it. The two of you could be perfect for each other, consolidating our kingdoms. Or, you could be a beautiful disaster, and tear our lands further apart. But you will never know if you do not take the risk."

Her mind reeled with snippets of all the times Astraea had been scolded in her youth. *Glide, a princess does not walk, she glides. Do it again, back straighter, head up. Do not whistle. Do not shout. Do not run. A lady does not say such things, nor should she think them. One's actions should be carried out with grace and precision. You will marry a high-born man; we must make sure you are worthy of him.* But as Astraea's thoughts slowed, a final one struck her. Had her parents, her tutors, anyone that had been involved in her upbringing, ever wondered if the nobleman chosen would be worthy of her hand?

Behind him, Wren's sensitive ears had picked up Bastian's footsteps as he crept up on them. Glancing over his shoulder with a wry grin, he half whispered to Astraea, "Speaking of which, I am going to retire for the evening. Remember princess, follow your heart, you have to do what will make you happy. We are not here long enough to have regrets."

As the men passed by, they both nodded their acknowledgment to each other, before Wren disappeared below deck once more.

Stopping as he reached her, Bastian pried, "Astraea? I just wanted to make sure you were alright. You were gone for a while…"

Worried eyes searched hers. Then without hesitation, she leaned up, pressing her lips to his. For a moment Bastian kissed her back. Stepping into her space, his fingers gripped at her shoulders, but then he pushed her away. Astraea's brow furrowed; she had thought this was what he wanted. Instead, he stood in front of her, a deep scowl etched on his face, staring at her like she was a complex problem that he could not quite solve. Astraea knew this was it. It was now or never for them. Her voice wavering, the princess demanded, "Look me in the eye and tell me that you do not want this, Bastian."

The prince of dragons flushed scarlet as he tripped over his words, his icy façade melting away instantly.

"I am a dragon. You have made it abundantly clear on multiple occasions why we can never be. It is too dangerous; my kind are monsters."

Taking a step towards him, Astraea's chest was heaving, adrenaline coursing through her veins.

"That is not what I asked." She took another step. "Would you see our kingdoms united under one banner?"

Swallowing hard, Bastian nodded, his gaze never leaving hers, watching as she took another step towards him.

"Would you rule at my side?"

"Yes."

The word escaped him, a breathless whisper, as Astraea closed the space between them.

"Do you love me, Bastian?"

"When I look at you, my world makes sense. All the broken pieces in my life fit back together. There is nothing I would not do for you. I would sail to the ends of the earth if it meant keeping you safe. Your smile, your laugh, they light up my world. Of course I love you, Astraea. I have loved you from the moment I saw you walk down the staircase back in Viriador, and I would love you my whole life, if you will let me?"

All Astraea could do was nod fiercely as Bastian brushed a stray piece of hair behind her pointed ear, before leaning in and pressing his lips to hers once more. This kiss was different, it was long and lazy, drawn out over minutes as Bastian held her firm in his arms. It was every bit as good as she had dreamed it would be. His fingers tenderly stroked the backs of her arms for a while, before his hands slid lower, coming to rest on her back. When they finally broke apart, the pair both wore broad grins, their faces flushed as Bastian offered his hand to Astraea.

"Come on, you need your beauty sleep."

Scooping her into his arms, Bastian carried Astraea below deck. When they reached the cabin, he allowed Astraea's feet to find the ground, before kissing the princess once more. Slowly pulling her down into his bed, their exchange was gentle. Soft kisses endured for a while. But, in the end, Bastian simply held Astraea, his arms wrapped around her. And the princess, processing all that had happened that night, was beyond pleased that she had taken her friend's advice. With her father gone and her mother's future uncertain, her path was her own to forge; and for once, Astraea had put her own happiness before everybody else's. She would deal with any fallout as and when it came about. For now, all that mattered to her were the words that Bastian breathed against her skin.

"I promise I will look after you."

"And keep me safe?" Astraea whispered into the darkness.

"Always."

His lips found hers once more.

"Forever?"

The princess whispered questioningly, when they broke apart. Pressing his lips into the column of her neck, Bastian murmured into her skin, "Forever and Always, Princess."

"I love you, Bastian."

Her voice came out a whisper, a shudder rolling through her, as Bastian slowly, sensually began to kiss his way down her throat, all the way to her sternum, before coming up to claim her mouth once more.

"I love you, too."

Underneath the bed, a relieved pair of amber eyes gleamed in the darkness, accompanied by a tiny tooth-filled grin. The cat, now merrily purring, curled himself into a tight bagel before he let the world fade away.

Chapter Eighty-Three

The Pretender

The door closed just a little too loudly for the late hour, causing Cyrus to shoot up in bed, his heart tripping in his chest.

"Wren? Where did you go?"

"I just went for a walk. I needed to clear my head. That's all."

Unbuttoning his shirt, Wren left it hanging open as he crawled onto the bed, sitting cross legged in front of Cyrus.

"Are you alright?" The dragon tilted his head inquisitively, clearly unsure how to approach Wren's unrest. "Please tell me what's wrong. What is worrying you?"

Wren let his shoulders fall as he released a heavy sigh, dropping his head so that he stared into his lap.

"Everything."

Looking up into Cyrus's concerned gaze, he let it all out.

"I'm a fraud. I am meant to be a soldier, a guard, I am meant to keep the princess safe. And I could not act when it mattered. I failed Melana. Gods only knows what is happening to her right now. I am just a cripple, plagued by nightmares from another life. Everything is such a mess. I am running from the guilt of my own happiness. I cannot keep the mask in place, Cyrus. I feel like I don't even know who I am anymore."

Out of nowhere, Cyrus gripped his wrist.

"Wren, I promise you that none of that is true. I jumped in after Astraea because I am a strong swimmer, nothing more, nothing less. If I hadn't, who is to say what you would have done? As for Melana, she knew what she was doing; she made her own choices. But if anyone should feel guilty that she was captured, then it is me."

Running his fingers along Wren's cheek, Cyrus wiped away a rogue tear, smiling warmly at his mate.

"Do not ever think that this," leaning down he kissed the flesh at the seem of Wren's prosthetic, before bringing his burning gaze back to his lover's once more, "makes you any less. If anything, it makes you more.

You have had to work so hard to master swordsmanship, to be the soldier you are today. You are the personal guard to Princess Astraea Thandal, for goodness' sake. How can you doubt yourself like this?"

Swallowing hard, Wren laughed, fighting back the tears.

"It's just... I have never felt good enough, my whole life. Even when I achieve what I set out to do, I always feel like... I do not know... it's lacking, I suppose. And now, I finally thought I had a prosthetic that would not cause me issues, and yet I ended up with an infection. How am I meant to go on a quest, trekking through the wilderness, if I am nothing but a liability?"

"Wren, no. You got stabbed and the wound got infected. That has nothing to do with your disability, it could have happened to any of us."

"But it didn't, did it? It happened to me. I fell because I lost my footing and..."

"Wren. Wren, stop. You fell because there was a bloody great hole in the ground that had been covered over. Anyone could have fallen in it." Sighing, Cyrus ground out, "I'm going to murder that cat."

Sniffling Wren levelled his glare.

"No, you won't."

That made Cyrus chuckle,

"No, you are right, I won't. I love the furry little git. But you need to stop blaming yourself, Wren. You have to stop. Otherwise, you are going to make yourself ill. And you should never have to feel guilty for falling in love." Taking Wren's hands in his own, the dragon leant in, "Do you trust me?"

Blinking, he nodded, his green eyes wide as dark tendrils wove their way from between their entwined fingers, dancing in the space between them. Carefully, Wren loosened his grip, as if he were afraid breaking the contact would make the magic disappear. Watching as the dragon sat back, turning his palms skyward, the wisps of black smoke climbed above them, until with a flick of his wrists, they ignited briefly, exploding into hundreds of blood-orange chrysanthemum petals. The silence that followed was deafening. The tips of Wren's ears twitched visibly; his eyes so wide they looked like they might fall from the sockets.

"What *are* you, Cyrus?"

A small smirk quirked the other man's lips as he reached for Wren's hands once more.

"That's the thing. I do not know."

"Wow. So how did you…"

Confused, Wren gestured between them.

"All my life, I've always let slip little bits of magic without really trying. The older I got, the more I managed to control it, but now… I can manifest what I read. All the historical texts, and the dark arts. Some of it is easier than others, but if it contains some form of magic, I seem to be able to master it."

"So that is why you have been reading all those old fusty books."

Laughing, Cyrus responded, "No, actually, I have always read a lot. Especially ancient texts. Now it is just a little more about practical application."

Drying the last of his tears, Wren whistled through his teeth and Cyrus relaxed. At least he had not run. He watched as the fae undid his prosthetic, propping it against the other side of the bed, vulnerable only for him. Sliding back into Cyrus's arms, the other man welcomed him back between the sheets, holding him tightly as they lay in the covers, the air still heavy around them. There was one more thing that Wren needed to get off his chest. He had to ask, he had to know for sure.

"Do you really believe that we will all make it back home?"

The chest beneath him ceased to move for a moment, until Cyrus exhaled heavily.

"Honestly?"

Wren held his breath now, waiting on the words he knew were coming, but dreaded all the same.

"No. No, I do not. But I give you my word that as long as I draw breath, I will do everything in my power to protect you, Wren."

Voice threatening to break again, Wren cried out, "What is the point of any of it if you don't think we can do it?"

Heaving a sigh once more, Cyrus shuffled down the bed, taking Wren's face in his hands.

"Why do you think I am trying to harness my powers? The more skill we have in our arsenal, the better chance we all have of making it home. The more in tune with my power I am, the more I can protect you all. There is always hope, Wren. The world has a checkered history. Nothing has ever been black and white, more well-defined shades of grey. If we succeed, it does not have to be that way. Not anymore. We owe it to ourselves to at least try. For the future of all in Meohithra."

Planting a soft kiss on Wren's lips, he was relieved when his mate kissed him back. Running his fingers the length of his face, Cyrus offered, "You know, you don't have to come with us, Wren. You could stay here with Tormund."

Pulling back, the fae looked at him, horrified.

"No, no. Absolutely not. If we go, we go together. Always, remember?"

Biting his lip, Cyrus nodded. He knew the bond that tied them, and as much as it pained him, if something were to happen to either of them— Cyrus stopped, blocking out that painful thought, increasing his grip on Wren's hand. The pair clung to one another, embracing the warmth their tangled bodies provided. Eventually, when Wren slept soundly in his arms, Cyrus allowed himself to come to terms with the fact that Wren was right: one could no longer survive without the other. Somewhere along the way, their souls had become one.

Chapter Eighty-Four

Ifs, Buts & Maybes

Making her way down the dimly lit stairwell, Rae's words played on Melana's mind. What if Nico did do something stupid because of her, how would she live with herself? But it was all ifs, buts and maybes. Melana was not about to leave because of what *might* happen. Not now, not after everything she had been through. They might not get their happily ever after, but Melana thought that she would settle for every second she got to spend with Nico. If that meant taking the risk, carrying on as she had been, remaining undiscovered until Nico's return, then so be it. Melana would speak to him later.

The dress she had chosen today had a little more give than her usual attire. The golden-brown skirt bounced as she descended into the castle's depths, her black and gold bodice holding her breasts firmly in place. Melana had chosen it because it made her feel pretty, and she knew Nico would like the golden flowers that adorned it. The mental image of him undressing her later that evening had been the deciding factor. With a smile, she made her way dreamily into the kitchen. Melana was not about to let anyone ruin the last hours she might ever get to spend with Nico. Everything else could wait.

Busying herself, Melana swept the floors and peeled the potatoes alone. Humming aloud, she wondered if anyone else would come down to work with her today. Filling a cauldron with water, Melana set it over the fire to boil. Adding the potatoes, she had moved on to chopping carrots when she heard voices, as two more servants descended the stone stairs. Finally, she thought, some help would be most welcome. But when they entered, they did not say hello to her. Instead, a pile of pans crashed to the flagstones and one of the women screamed. Jumping in alarm, Melana dropped the knife, whirling around to find the cause of the woman's distress – only to find an older woman, wrinkled, with greying hair, pointing straight at her. One hand clasped over her mouth, her eyes wide with horror. Spinning back around, Melana's heart sank. There was nothing there. The woman was pointing at her.

"You. You're the creature they have been hunting."

The other woman stood open mouthed. Melana knew her well. They had worked together many times before now.

Her hands flew to her ears, confirming that one was indeed exposed. Melana's heart plummeted as she watched the older woman flee from the room, shouting to her friend that she was going to get help.

"It's you. You're the fae the prince brought into the castle."

Melana's mouth gaped open. Her blood felt like it had turned to ice as the woman strode up to her. Gripping her shoulders, she gave Melana a gentle shake.

"Melana, you need to get out of the castle. Now. Run, don't look back."

Panic seized her, there was nowhere for her to go. Heart pounding as the woman shook her again, she could hear her voice, distant, telling her to run. When her feet finally started to move, her heartbeat was rapid, she could feel it in her chest, hear it thundering in her ears. Melana was drowning in her own fear.

All these weeks, no, months, of Rae protecting her, watching out for her, making sure she was not discovered, only to betray her now. Feeling her heart break, Melana wondered if she had ever meant anything to her at all. The betrayal hurt, and she wondered if it was possible that anyone had heard her heart violently cracking open. Skirt billowing around her as Melana ran, she took the stone steps back up to ground level two at a time. Dragging her hair back over her ears as she reached the courtyard, she slowed her pace just a little, enough that it was not so obvious that she was attempting to flee.

It was eerily quiet, only a few people were roaming about outside, and as she neared the gates, Melana thought she had not heard anyone raise the alarm yet. Perhaps she would get away with it. Perhaps she would gain her freedom. But then she thought of the cost. Suddenly, she longed for Nico to be there, running with her. Her heart hurt. He would think she had abandoned him. But Melana did not stop as she reached the golden gates, slipping out of the castle grounds, picking up her pace once more.

Everything she passed bled into flashes of colour, and it was not long until Melana realised she hadn't a clue where she was going or where she had been, as she weaved her way through the city streets. Melana was lost.

The walls felt like they were closing in as she made her way through the rows of tightly packed houses along the narrow cobbled streets. All of them were beige, winding rows of buildings three storeys high. They all had little arched doorways, and the same lanterns hung by their doors. There was no way to tell any of them apart, until Melana turned a corner. This road had steps leading uphill, away from the claustrophobic, tightly packed rows of buildings that had been suffocating her. Turning the blood in her veins to fire, her muscles burning as she ran. Taking her chance, Melana followed the path up, panting now as she sprinted. Knowing she had to put as much distance between herself and the castle as was physically possible, Melana cried out in frustration when she reached the top of the hill. All that lay before her now were trees. The path out of the city had led her straight to the landscape she had most wanted to avoid. Arbutus and Carballo oak filled the plane in front of her. But it was too late to worry about that now. Melana shuddered as a dragon's roar filled the sky. They were coming for her.

Chapter Eighty-Five

One Light in a Sea of Stars

Stalking through the corridors after training with the guard, Nico's tunic was slick with sweat. A hazy smile painted on his face as he thought of what this evening would hold. He planned to indulge in a nice hot bath, and have food brought up to his chambers for them once Melana returned. Biting his lip, Nico imagined how he would spend the rest of the evening making her cry out his name. If he was going to be forced to fight in a war that he did not even believe in, a war he did not want, then Nico wanted this last night of freedom to be filled with the sweetest memories. Something that both himself and Melana could hold on to until he returned. And he would make sure that he did return. For her.

Pushing wide the door to his chambers, Nico stopped when he saw Rae sat there alone. Eyes red rimmed, puffy from the tears she had shed. Moving towards her, brows furrowed, Nico felt his chest tighten.

"Are you alright?"

Sniffling, she replied, "Melana and I had a bit of a run-in, that's all. I wanted to talk to you actually, before she comes back from the kitchens."

"You let her go alone?"

Nico cut in, as Rae waved his concern away.

"She will be fine, Nico. Melana has been down there enough times by now."

His lips pressed into a thin line as Rae continued, losing their colour as he crushed them between his teeth.

"What do you want, Rae?" Nico ground out.

"Whatever there is going on between you, it is not safe. One way or another, one of you is bound to get hurt. I do not want to see either of you get yourselves killed. It just seems such a waste when you have no time anyway. Why start something now that will bring you both nothing but pain in the end. You cannot afford to be distracted, Nico, you have a country that will need their king."

Scoffing, he reached past her for his decanter. Grabbing a glass, he quickly filled it, swilling the liquid about before he took a mouthful. Nico's voice was cold now, brutally detached, void of emotion.

"We all run out of time eventually, Rae. Mine is just one light in a sea of stars. Why should my life be worth any more just because I am the crown prince? My whole life, there has been no one who would truly care if my light was extinguished before its time. Well, maybe Bastian, but I doubt he would care now, not anymore. No one would truly mourn my passing, apart from her."

Rae could feel her self-control spiralling as she yelled at the prince.

"I would mourn your passing, Nico! I would care. My loyalty is to you, it always has been. You are my friend."

Her screams were filled with pent-up rage as she told Nico all the ways in which she would care if he were no longer there, but he just stared at her blankly.

"When Melana could cost you everything, why can you not consider settling for someone less risky? Why does it have to be her?"

Nico's smile reemerged, but it seemed somehow sinister now.

"Why would I entertain anyone else when she exists, Rae? If I had to choose again, I would still choose her. In any lifetime, it would always be her. We understand each other, we both have demons from our pasts. We are both fighting battles no one else knows about. I could not possibly expect you to understand."

Sobbing now, Rae grabbed at his tunic.

"Please listen to me. You are just two broken souls playing a dangerous game. Two damaged people trying to heal each other. It's not love, Nico."

"Then what is love?" he bellowed. "Who gets to say what love is? Yes, my actions might be selfish, but I feel like I can no longer breathe without her. What was I meant to do? Leave with the possibility that I may be going to my death, without ever telling her I love her? Tell me, what would you have done in my position?"

"I—I don't know."

On her knees before him now, Rae's chest heaved as she sobbed, clinging to the hem of his tunic. Nico was far too angry with his friend to question why she was quite so bereft. He continued to rant.

"Meeting her, having her in my life, it has made me realise – *she* has made me realise – that I wanted things I did not even know existed. To me, she is perfection. And now I need her, like I need oxygen, Rae. Do you understand now? If I lost her now, you might as well deprive me of the very air I need to breathe."

Without warning, the door to their chamber swung wide open. Estrafin staggered into the room, clutching a dagger lodged deep in his gut. Nico was at his side in an instant, catching the man as he fell, easing him to the floor. Rae was silent, deathly pale when she joined him at Es's side.

"I tried to stop him."

Rae supported his head in her lap as Estrafin's body started to twitch, shock setting in. Her eyes met Nico's, only for a moment; they were wide, filled with fury as he spoke.

"Es, who did this?"

"Gerritsen. I tried to stop him. He has gone after Melana. They know who she is, Nico."

Closing her eyes, Rae sucked in a shaky breath, murmuring, "What have I done."

Nico's gaze turned savage as he eyed his friend like prey. Seething, his voice dripping with anger, Nico shouted at her with such force that, for the first time ever, she found herself genuinely afraid of him.

"What do you mean, what have you done? What *did* you do, Rae?"

"I thought if she left, it would make it better somehow. But she would not leave you, she would not go."

Wailing her words, Rae cradled Estrafin's head against her chest, watching horrified as he tried to prize the dagger free.

"No Es, don't. We will get you help. Leave it there, otherwise you will bleed out."

Estrafin looked up at her, eyes filled with sadness.

"I am no fool, Rae. I am dead either way. Leaving that there is only prolonging the inevitable."

"What have you done, Rae, you foolish, foolish woman?" the prince spat, his words filled with venom. Cowering from Nico's wrath, Rae focused on Estrafin, but he merely looked past her to Nico.

"Don't let my sacrifice be in vain. Melana was last seen heading out of the city. Go to her."

Nico nodded. Before bolting for the door, he rested a hand on Estrafin's shoulder.

"Thank you for your loyalty, and your service. Rest easy, my friend."

"Nico." His wavering voice called out after him. "For what it's worth, I think you will make a fine king, Your Highness."

Bowing his head respectfully, Nico turned to leave, but Rae cried out after him.

"Nico, you cannot go. Remember the black dragon? You cannot abandon your people. You cannot. You cannot do this. I will not let you."

The prince strode back through the doorway in an instant.

"I'm a selfish prick, remember, Rae? I do what I want, when I want, consequences be damned."

His tone left no room for argument.

"I will choose her life over mine every damn time."

And then he was gone, leaving Rae to comfort Es, as he lay dying slowly in her arms. When he lost consciousness, Rae begged his forgiveness, unsure if he could hear her words. Again and again she asked for it, well aware the man would never respond. When Estrafin's chest rose and fell for a final time, his eyes turning glassy, Rae cried until she had no tears left. Screaming into the abyss until her lungs were raw. The walls threated to close in as she collapsed back against the wall. Finally, Rae sat, her own eyes glazed as she stared into space. Guilt eating at her, hopelessness flooding through her, as Es's lifeless eyes bored into her. All she had wanted to do was help. But, in the end, her worst fears had been confirmed in the final words that Nico had spoken to her before he followed Melana to his death.

Chapter Eighty-Six

How Dangerous to Finally Have Something to Lose

Nico did not walk, he ran, his feet pounding through the castle corridors with a speed he had not known he possessed. Catching his hand against the jagged stone wall as he went, Nico did not even flinch as blood crept to the surface of the cuts. Fear churned its way through his insides. What if he was too late? What if that bastard hurt her? Nico thought of all the times Rae had asked him if Melana was worth dying for. This was what it came down to: he was likely about to give his life for hers, and the prince realised that he would do so gladly, if it meant keeping her safe. No thoughts for the longevity of his own life remained, only Melana's, as Nico tore outside.

His feet barely made contact with the gravel surface of the courtyard before they morphed into talons, scales bursting from his clothing, rippling across Nico's skin as his form changed into that of his dragon. Hearing Gerritsen roar in the distance as he searched from the skies, Nico was barely in the air before he let out an ear-splitting shriek of his own. Far too close to the castle, he caught his almighty wing on one of the turrets as he took to the sky, tearing through the roof, sending rubble flying. Not once did Nico avert his attention from the black dragon in the distance. Not even for a second, as blood and debris rained down on the screaming crowd of servants that had started to gather below. Each fighting to see what all the commotion was in aid of. How dangerous it was, evidently for everyone, for him to finally have something worth losing.

* * * * *

Running through the barren landscape, the air was hot. Sweat coated her brow as Melana tried desperately to outrun the dragon that was fast approaching in his search for her, but it was to no avail. The shadow of the colossal beast dwarfed her. What was the point? There was no way she could out-pace a dragon. Doubling over, Melana sucked in much needed lungful's of air, her hands pressed to her knees. Risking a glance at the sky, she screamed as the huge obsidian dragon caught sight of a red dragon's approach, turning mid-air to face him. Nico. Melana's heart hammered in her chest. Blood dripped from gashes that gaped in the membrane on one side of Nico's wing. He was already hurt. Feeling the blood drain away from her face, Melana's stomach churned when the two dragons collided forcefully in the air. She knew she should use the time Nico was giving her to get away, to hide, but she could not bring herself to move. Instead, Melana stood rooted to the spot, ice clawing its way up her spine as every hair on her arms rose, her skin erupting in goosebumps.

Talons tore at flesh as the dragons dug their claws into one another. Gerritsen lost part of his wing before Nico had several large chunks gouged from his chest. Blood fell from the sky, droplets raining down, splashing as they landed on her. In her hair, covering her skin, and soaking into her clothes. Melana tried to shield her face with her hands, but it was useless. It was not long until she was drenched. The harder they fought, the more she screamed. His name falling from her lips again and again as she looked on, helpless.

There was a moment when the bundle of red and black scales tumbled towards the earth, before they pulled apart, recovering enough to take to the skies for another round. Melana fell to her knees, continuing to scream Nico's name until her throat became raw. There was nothing she could do now but wait. This was how she had seen him die.

That was when Gerritsen went for Nico's neck, sinking his teeth in, biting at Nico's face and throat with his huge jaws. Then, Gerritsen let him go.

Nico began to fall. First as his dragon, but then he must have lost consciousness, his body morphing back into his human form as he plummeted towards the earth below. Reacting impulsively, before her brain had a chance to catch up, Melana threw everything she had into her outstretched palms. All of the grief and rage, everything that had been bubbling within her, using it all to blast a wave of air. Shrouding Nico with one hand, Melana used the other to knock Gerritsen from the sky, sending him cascading backwards, before he tumbled out of sight into the trees. Managing to hone the last of the magic left within her, Melana cushioned Nico's fall enough that maybe, just maybe, he could have survived it.

When Nico hit the ground, Melana was so completely and utterly drained that as she tried to run to him, she faltered. Falling to her knees, she crawled across the dry grass to Nico's lifeless form. She had never used magic on that scale before. Vision wavering, blurring at the edges, Melana dragged herself slowly towards him, an inch at a time. Wailing, she watched blood pool from Nico's wounds. No, was the only word to fall from her lips. Repeated again and again, agonisingly drawn out between sobs until she was at his side. Dragging Nico into her arms, Melana cradled him to her chest. Deep wounds raked down the length of his neck, four large gouges stretched diagonally across his torso. The flesh of his right arm was shredded; she was sure that if he survived, he would lose it. But it was his eye that panicked Melana the most as he lay unconscious in her arms. It was a mess. All that seemed to remain was a bloodied gash from his forehead to his cheek.

There would never be a world in which Melana would not be eternally thankful that Nico had survived the fall, but as the adrenaline started to ebb, she began to shake, the reality of his injuries setting in. When Nico failed to wake after a few minutes, everything caught up with Melana at once. Leaning away from her prince, who remained motionless in her arms, Melana emptied the contents of her stomach onto the grass, wondering what in the god's names she was going to do now.

Chapter Eighty-Seven

Queen of Nothing

Past weeping, Briana rocked violently, arms clasped about her knees. No one had been to antagonise her. Instead, days had passed since anyone had so much as slid her food or water through the hatch in the door. Even before this isolation, when guards had come, no one had spoken to her. There was no telling anymore where the mixture of dirt, blood, and grime ended or began.

When they had taken her from the tower that the queen had assumed would be her gaol, she had been frightened, trembling as guards had escorted her below ground. But in her most vivid nightmares, she had not expected what the coming weeks had brought. Dracul, who had once professed his undying love for her, had her chained in a dark, dank dungeon in the very bowels of the castle.

At the start she had been deprived of sleep for days on end. When that failed, the torture escalated. Burns marred her once-perfect skin; Briana still flinched every time she thought about it. The pain had been intense, but to their fury she would still not yield. Since then, her hair had been hacked away and she had been left bloodied, alone in the remnants of her own filth, but she would never agree to live among them again. She would never agree to be Dracul's queen. Briana had refused to be his then, and she would not be his now, despite what it had cost her all those years ago.

Now, locked away, utterly alone, Briana had never realised how soul-crushing silence could be. The only relief from it had been when the guards came. Dracul had visited her himself at the start, but when she refused him time after time, he had lost interest. She would not give in. They would have to kill her. She refused to betray her people. Briana's hope for a quick death was a distant memory, as the understanding that she had probably pushed the dragon king too far now dawned on her. Maybe she should have given him a crumb, a morsel, *something*, because now she had been left here to rot.

For days she had wept in the darkness. For herself, for her kingdom, her husband and daughter. For everything that once was, and for everything that would never be again. It should be her that was dead, not her beloved Emil. How had she survived when he had not? It was for their love that she had risked everything. Now, all that enveloped her was a hollowness, slowly consuming her a piece at a time. When she had finished weeping, Briana screamed into the darkness until her throat was raw. When it all became too unbearable for her mind to comprehend and she could no longer function, Briana rocked, the movement soothing her broken soul. She was alone and no one was coming for her. Not now. Not ever.

Acknowledgements

I want to thank my mum (I wouldn't have made it very far without her): thank you for always believing in me. And my husband, who has listened to me wittering on about this world for the past five years.

Onley James, Luna Daye & Noah Hawthorne inspired me to put pen to paper and allow my characters to be themselves. Similarly my colleagues, who have listened to me waffle about writing this since the start of the pandemic. You guys will always hold a special place in my heart.

Mollie: thanks again. Without you this world would still be just an idea, and the book would probably still have no name.

My amazing beta readers, Mollie, Liz, Maria, Chloe and Trish: thank you so much for coming on this journey with me, and for all the help you've given me along the way. My arc team: you have all been a pleasure to work with. And my editor Paul, who saved me from throwing my laptop out the window on many occasions.

Lastly, but by no means least, you, my wonderful reader. Without you I wouldn't have an audience, and for that I am most grateful.

Printed in Great Britain
by Amazon